The Love of my Life

Also by Rosie Walsh

The Man Who Didn't Call

The Love of my Life

Rosie Walsh

MANTLE

First published in paperback 2022 by Mantle

This edition first published 2022 by Mantle
an imprint of Pan Macmillan
The Smithson, 6 Briset Street, London EC1M 5NR
EU representative: Macmillan Publishers Ireland Ltd, 1st Floor,
The Liffey Trust Centre, 117–126 Sheriff Street Upper,
Dublin 1, D01 YC43
Associated companies throughout the world
www.panmacmillan.com

ISBN 978-1-5290-2035-9

1 3 5 7 9 8 6 4 2

A CIP catalogue record for this book is available from the British Library.

Typeset in Sabon by Palimpsest Book Production Ltd, Falkirk, Stirlingshire
Printed and bound by CPI Group (UK) Ltd, Croydon, CR0 4YY

For Sharon

PART I

LEO & EMMA

Prologue

We walked north, separated from the main sweep of the beach by kelp beds and rippling tidepools. The sea was a field of white crests and the few clouds in the sky moved fast, throwing spiral shadows across the sand.

It felt good for the two of us to be here, in this liminal place where the land shelved into the sea. This realm wasn't ours. It belonged to the sea stars and limpets, the anemones and hermit crabs. Nobody noticed our togetherness; nobody cared.

It rained for a while and we sat in a shack hidden in the dunes, eating sandwiches. There were middens of dried sheep droppings in the corners and the rain drummed on the roof like gunfire. It was the perfect sanctuary. A place just for us.

We talked easily, as weather systems tore back and forth across the beach below. In my heart, hope grew.

We spotted the crab skeleton at the far end of the beach, soon after our picnic lunch. Medium-sized, dead, alone on the strandline amid deposits of driftwood and dried spiral wrack. There were razor shell fragments stuck to its abdomen, a bleached twist of trawler net hooked around a lifeless antenna, and peculiar, signal-red spots on its body and claws.

Tired now, I sat down to examine it properly. Four distinct spines crossed its carapace. Its claws were covered in bristles.

I looked into its unseeing eyes, trying to imagine where it might have travelled from. I'd read that crabs rafted long-distance on all sorts of vessels – pieces of plastic, hunks of seaweed, even the barnacled hulls of cargo ships. For all I knew this creature could have travelled from Polynesia, surviving thousands of miles just for the chance to die on a Northumbrian beach.

I should take some photographs. My tutors would know what it was.

But as I reached into my bag for my camera, my vision took a sudden pitch. Light-headedness dropped like marine fog and I had to stay still, hunched over, until it passed.

'Low blood pressure,' I said, when I was able to straighten up. 'Had it since I was a kid.'

We turned back to the crab. I got up onto hands and knees and photographed it from every angle.

The dizziness returned as I put my camera away, although this time it ebbed and flowed, imitating the waves. Pain was beginning to gather in my back, accompanied by a darker, more powerful sensation near my ribs. I knelt down again, tucking my hands in my lap, and the dizziness billowed.

I counted to ten. Murmured words of concern, laced with fear, tumbled around above my head. The wind changed direction.

When I finally opened my eyes, there was blood on my hand.

I looked carefully. It was unmistakably blood. Fresh, wet, across my right palm.

'It's fine,' I heard myself say. 'Nothing to worry about.'

Panic rolled in with the tide.

Chapter One

LEO

Her eyelashes are often wet when she wakes, as if she's been swimming a sea of sad dreams. 'It's just some sleep-related thing,' she's always said. 'I never have nightmares.' After a fathomless yawn she'll wipe her eyes and slip out of bed to check Ruby is alive and breathing. It's a habit she's been unable to break, even though Ruby's three.

'Leo!' she'll say, when she gets back. 'Wake up! Kiss me!'

Moments will pass, as I slide into day from the slow-moving depths. Dawn will spread from the east in amber shadows and we will burrow in close to each other, Emma talking almost non-stop – although from time to time she will pause, mid-stream, to kiss me. At 6.45 we will check Wikideaths for overnight passings, then at 7.00 she will break wind, blaming the sound on a moped out in the road.

I can't remember how far into our relationship it was when she started doing this: not far enough, probably. But she would have known that I was on board, by then, that I was no more likely to swim back to the shore than I was to grow wings and fly there.

If our daughter hasn't climbed into our bed by that time, we climb into hers. Her room is sweet and hot, and our early-morning conversations about Duck are among the happiest moments my heart knows. Duck, whom she clutches tightly to herself all night, is credited with incredible nocturnal adventures.

Normally I'll dress Ruby while Emma 'goes down to make breakfast', although most days she'll get sidetracked by marine data collected overnight in her lab, and it's Ruby and me who'll sort out the food. My wife was forty minutes late for our wedding because she'd stopped to photograph the tidal strandlines at Restronguet Creek in her wedding dress. Nobody, except the registrar, was surprised.

Emma's an intertidal ecologist, which means she studies the places and creatures that are submerged at high tide and exposed at low. The most miraculous and exciting ecosystem on earth, she says: she's been rockpooling since she was a young girl; it's in her blood. Her main research interest is crabs, but I believe most crustaceans are fair game. Right now she's got a bunch of little guys called *Hemigrapsus takanoi* in special sea-water tanks at work. I know they're an invasive species and that she's looking at some specific morphology she's been trying to pin down for years, but that's as much as I'm able to understand. Less than a third of the words biologists use can be understood by the average human; getting trapped in a group of them at a party is a nightmare.

Emma is singing to John Keats when Ruby and I arrive in the kitchen this morning, the sun jagging across the worktops and our cereal hardening in bowls. Her laptop, which displays a page of mind-boggling words and squiggles, plays a track called 'Killermuffin'. When we rescued John Keats from the dog shelter they told us that jungle at a low volume soothed his nerves, and so it has become the soundtrack to our lives. I'm used to it now, but it took a while.

I stand in the doorway with Ruby perched on my hip, watching my wife singing tunelessly to the dog. In spite of a bunch of musicians in Emma's ancestry she is incapable of singing even 'Happy Birthday' in tune, but this has never stopped her. It's one of many things I love about my wife.

She catches sight of us and dances over, still singing appallingly. 'My favourites!' she says, kissing us both and extracting Ruby from my arms. She whirls off with our daughter and the dreadful singing gets louder.

Ruby knows Mummy's been ill; she has seen her lose her hair thanks to the special medicine she gets at hospital, but she thinks Emma's better now. The truth of the matter is, we don't know. Emma had her post-treatment PET scan yesterday and an appointment to discuss the results has been booked for next week. We are hopeful, we are frightened. Neither of us is sleeping well.

After a brief stint dancing with her mother, Duck whirling around their heads, Ruby wriggles off to take care of some urgent business.

'Come back!' Emma cries. 'I want to cuddle you!'

'I'm too busy,' Ruby says, regretfully. Then: 'Hi,' she whispers, to the plant she's looking after for nursery. 'I'm going to give you a drink.'

'Anything?' I ask, nodding at the computer. Emma presented a BBC wildlife series a few years back and continues to receive messages from weird men, even though she hasn't been on telly since. But her series was repeated recently, and as a result the messages have increased. Normally, we laugh at them, but last night she admitted she's had some more disturbing ones of late.

'A couple more. One tame, one less so. But I've blocked him.'

I watch her carefully as she fills our water glasses, but she doesn't seem bothered. I think it's fair to say I mind about these messages a lot more than she does. I've tried to get her to shut down her public Facebook page, but she won't. People apparently still post about wildlife they've been tracking, and she's not willing to close the resource down 'simply because of a few lonely men'.

I hope they are just lonely.

'I love your piece on Kenneth Delwych,' Emma tells me, keeping an eye on Ruby, who's climbing up to the sink with her watering can. My newspaper is on the table with the obituaries page open.

I go over to John Keats and fold one of his flappy silken ears around my finger, waiting for the *but*. The dog smells of biscuits and singed fur after a recent encounter with the iron.

'But?' I prompt.

She stops, caught out. 'No but.'

'Oh, Emma. Come off it.'

After a moment, she laughs. 'Fine. I do love it, but the female priest is the real show-stopper. Hey, Ruby, that's enough water.'

John Keats sighs deeply as I lean over to study my articles. Kenneth Delwych, a peer famed for the legendary orgies he hosted at his Sussex vineyard, is sharing the obituaries page with a Bomber Command navigator and a female priest who had a heart attack during a wedding ceremony last weekend.

'You're at your best when you're completely deadpan,' Emma says. She puts bread in the toaster. 'That actor last week – the Scottish one, what was his name? Ruby, please don't drown the thing . . .'

'David Baillie?'

'David Baillie. Yes. Perfection.'

I reread my Kenneth Delwych piece while Emma deals

with the inevitable overflow of water and soil from Ruby's plant. She's right, of course. The female priest, with her far shorter obit, reads better.

Unfortunately, Emma's often right. My editor, who, I suspect, is in love with my wife, often jokes that he'd sack me and hire her if she ever decided to quit marine biology. I actually find this quite offensive, because unless he's secretly read her scientific articles, he has only one piece she wrote for the *Huffington Post* to go on.

Emma is a research fellow at the Marine Biological Association in Plymouth, which takes up two days of her week, then she comes back to us in London to teach estuarine conservation at UCL. She is an excellent writer, with instincts frequently better than mine, and she really does enjoy cruising Wikideaths, but this has more to do with her love of a good story than any interest in stealing my job.

Ruby and John Keats go out into the garden, where the sun steals through gaps in next door's sycamore, spotting our tiny lawn with gold. Smells of an early city summer roll through the door: still-glossy grass, honeysuckle, heating tarmac.

I try to rehydrate our cereal, while outside the dog runs around our pond, barking. It's alive with baby frogs at the moment, which he seems to find unacceptable. 'John Keats, will you be quiet?' Emma asks, from the doorway. The dog takes no notice. 'We have neighbours.'

'JOHN!' Ruby yells. 'WE HAVE NEIGHBOURS!'

'Shhh, Ruby . . .'

I find some spoons and take our breakfast out to the garden.

'Sorry,' Emma says, holding the door open for me. 'Me and my unsolicited opinions on your work. It must be annoying.'

'It is.' We sit at the garden table, still bobbled with dew. 'But you're mostly polite. The main problem is that you're often right.'

She smiles. 'I think you're a brilliant writer, Leo. I read your obits before I even open my work emails in the morning.'

'Hmmm.' I keep an eye on Ruby, who's just a bit too close to the pond.

'I do! Your writing is one of your sexiest assets.'

'Oh, Emma, seriously, stop it.'

Emma has a spoonful of cereal. 'Actually, I'm not joking. You're the best writer on that desk. Period.'

Embarrassingly, I can't stop myself from beaming. 'Thank you,' I say, eventually, because I know she means it. 'But you're still annoying.'

She sighs. 'Oh, I know.'

'For a whole host of reasons,' I add, and she can't help laughing. 'You have far too many opinions on far too many things.'

She slips her hand across the table and squeezes my thumb, and tells me I am her favourite, and I find myself laughing too – and that is our rhythm. That is us. We have been married seven years; together nearly ten, and I know every part of her.

I think it was Kennedy who said we are tied to the ocean – that when we return to it, for sport or leisure or somesuch, we are returning to the place whence we came. That's how I feel about us. To be near to my wife, to Emma, is to return to source.

So when I learn, in the days following this morning – this innocent, commonplace morning, with dogs and frogs and coffee and dead priests – that I know nothing of this woman, it will break me.

Chapter Two

EMMA

One week later

'I'm going to be fine,' I reiterate, into the darkness of our bedroom. I've lost track of time. The hours have melted and dripped all over each other and, when Leo fails to reply, I realise he isn't even in bed. I must have dozed off.

I check my watch: 3.47 a.m. The day of my hospital appointment is here, at last.

I wait for the sounds of a flushing toilet and our cacophonous floorboards, but nothing comes. Leo is almost certainly downstairs, eating something in the yellow glow of the open fridge. An emergency ration of ham, probably: he said that if my chemo doesn't work he'll go vegan to support me. I went vegan following my diagnosis four years ago, although on more than one occasion since I've eaten cheddar straight from the packet in the Sainsbury's car park in Camden.

I get out of bed. I never enjoyed hugging in bed before Leo, but when he isn't here, my body misses his.

He isn't in the loo, so I go down to the kitchen. I run my hand over the wall as I descend, thickened and lumpy after decades of paint on paint. I sing 'Survivor' under my breath.

I edge past a tall pile of books. On top sits an enamel bowl of things we never use – keys for unknown locks, paperclips, an economy pack of Vilene Wundaweb. Leo keeps moving the pile to the centre of the hallway to make me address it, I keep moving it back. The solution is more shelves, but I am no good at shelves.

The problem with this is that Leo is no good at shelves either, so we're stuck in a holding pattern.

'Leo?' I whisper.

Nothing. Just the near-theatrical creak of the staircase, which babysitters find so unsettling none of them ever comes back.

I inherited this house from my grandmother. As well as being an MP and amateur violinist, she became a medium-grade hoarder and didn't remove anything from the house for the last ten years of her life. Leo thinks I'm showing all the signs of having inherited her problem; my therapist, worryingly, agrees. *When we have experienced more loss than is bearable*, she says, *we hold on to everything*.

The house is part of a tiny Georgian terrace in a lane off the top of Heath Street, where Hampstead Village gives way to the glorious roll of the Heath. It's falling apart and impossibly cramped, and the truth is that we'd probably make a small fortune if we sold it. But these four walls are so much a part of my story, a part of my survival, I couldn't bring myself to leave.

Last week Leo showed me details of a spacious three-bed terrace in Tufnell Park. 'Look at the size of those bedrooms!' he whispered, his face ablaze with hope. 'We'd have a spare room! A downstairs toilet!'

I felt bad. But what can I do? Sell my one safe space for the sake of a downstairs loo?

Leo isn't in the kitchen. He isn't in our tiny little study, either, which is a relief. For a moment I thought he might be in there writing an advance obituary for me, which would be intolerable. Every newspaper in the world has a stock of pre-written celebrity obituaries: obit editors live in fear of being caught out by a significant death. And while I'm no celebrity, I probably would merit an obituary in his newspaper.

I keep on singing 'Survivor' and try the little dining room, even though neither of us ever goes in there. It's virtually unusable, swimming with Granny's vaguely stacked detritus and old violin sheet music, but I've promised Leo I'll sort it once I've got this year's master's dissertations marked.

'Leo?' My voice sounds exactly as it always has. It carries no trace of cancer. I imagine the possibility of malignancy still circulating around my body like cheap wine, but it doesn't ring true.

Then a fear fogs in from nowhere: what if Ruby has gone missing too? I run upstairs, so fast I stumble and land on my hands, but she's there.

Of course she's there. And of course, when I check, she is breathing.

I look for Leo in the airing cupboard, the trapdoor to our unsafe roof terrace. No sign.

Anxiety begins to prickle. What if one of those weird men from the internet has got fed up with me blocking his messages and decided to punish my husband?

Ridiculous, I tell myself, but the idea's taken hold. Leo opening the door, only to be knocked out. Leo letting John Keats out for a late wee and being bludgeoned to death by some lonely maniac who thinks he owns me, because he enjoys me talking to grebes on telly.

It's not *that* bad, of course, but it's been worse than I've let on. Some of them get angry when I don't reply. I block all of them, but a few have simply invented new profiles so they can come back and shout at me a bit more. For a long time I managed to brush it off, but lately I've reached my limit. I'm not frightened as such, just sick of it.

Although I do think someone was waiting for me when I left the lab in Plymouth last week. There was a man sitting on the grassy mound that borders the driveway, which was unusual only in that he had his back to the sea. Who goes to stare at a private driveway on a sunny afternoon, when right behind them is a perfect view of the sparkling Plymouth Sound? I also didn't much like the way he pulled a baseball cap right down over his face as I walked up the drive, turning his face away as I passed.

Probably nothing, but it bothered me.

I sit down on my bed, trying to focus. My priority in this moment is finding my missing husband.

I check my text messages. Very occasionally, if someone of huge importance has died, Leo has to fire up his laptop in the middle of the night. Maybe something huge has happened, like the Queen or Prime Minister dying? Maybe he's actually had to go into work?

There are no messages from him in my phone. Only my Google search for a man I shouldn't have been searching for; the last thing I did before falling asleep earlier on.

The memory of this morning's phone call seeps through again, like flood water under a door. *I just want to talk to you*, he said at the end. *Meet me. Face to face.*

I put the phone down when he said that.

'Leo?' I whisper. Nothing. 'Leo!' I repeat, louder this time. 'I could still have cancer! You can't abandon me now!'

Then, after a pause: 'I love you. Where are you?'

There is no answer. The man has completely disappeared.

I find him in the garden shed, eventually. About five years ago he became so furious about the state of the house that I paid a handyman to empty the shed. We insulated it and ran an all-weather cable outside, so Leo could work there if he wanted to. I put in a sofa and a rug and a bookshelf, and promised I would never transfer any stuff in there 'for sorting'. Leo fell in love with it, then promptly forgot it existed.

Now, though, he's sitting inside, coughing up cigarette smoke.

'Leo.' I stand in the doorway. 'What are you doing?'

He looks sheepish. 'Having an emergency fag.' There's a packet of cigarettes next to him, crudely opened. Nearby, the long plastic device we use for lighting the gas stove.

The dog, who followed me out, looks at Leo, then me, as if to say, *but he doesn't even smoke*. 'But you don't even smoke,' I say.

'I know.' He picks up the stove lighter and presses the ignition button. A blue-orange flame illuminates his face, tired and frightened, and even though this breaks my heart, I find myself laughing. My husband is in his shed having an emergency cigarette, lit by what amounts to a domestic blow torch.

'Don't laugh at me,' he says, laughing a little himself. 'I'm scared.'

I stop laughing. I have thought about this often, during my illness, the possibility of dying on a man whose entire emotional landscape has been shaped by loss. I've been afraid for myself, of course, and the imagined grief for Ruby has been unbearable, but in many ways it's Leo I worry about most. I think most people see in my husband a quietly confident man, a man with a quick wit and a big brain, but that's only the top layer.

Our little family is the first place he's truly felt he belongs.

'Oh, Leo . . .' I say. 'My darling, couldn't you have had a whiskey?'

He shakes his head. 'I promised you I'd give up alcohol. I'm a man of my word.'

I sit next to him on his sofa, from which a small cloud of dust plumes, and hold his hand while he admits to having taken John Keats down to the late shop for cigarettes. He also bought some dairy-free chocolate.

'It was disgusting,' he says, miserably.

I loop an arm through his. His poor body is braced, as if ready for attack. 'You don't have to give up alcohol yet,' I tell him. 'Or meat, or dairy.' His hair has gone quite mad. There are deep creases under his eyes, and he needs a shave, but, God, he's beautiful.

I watch him, wishing I could somehow convey how deeply, how completely I love him. How I want to protect him from what might happen to me.

John Keats settles at Leo's feet, muttering.

'I'm going to be fine,' I say. 'We're going to walk into that appointment and Dr Moru is going to give me the all-clear, and you're going to sit there, silently accusing him of being in love with me –'

'Because he is.'

'He is not. The point is, he's going to tell me the cancer has gone, and that we can get back on with our lives. And we'll go and collect Ruby from nursery and take her to the swings and then come home and get her to bed and then have dinner and wine and maybe sex. There are only good things ahead.'

Silence. 'I might even clear up the house,' I add. 'Although it would be sensible not to get too excited.'

He reignites the stove lighter to look at my face. I stroke a finger down his cheek, and he pulls me in to him.

'I'm sorry,' he says. 'I was feeling quite confident about tomorrow, but then you went off to bed and I just . . .' His voice peels away.

'It would have been wrong to turn to ham, or whiskey,' he says, eventually. 'I made you a promise.'

'Vegan chocolate and nicotine all the way,' I agree. 'Although you promised you'd swear off only if it was bad news tomorrow. Does this mean you know something I don't?'

He smiles briefly. 'No, Emma, it does not. It means I just wanted to . . . I don't know. Honour you.'

He studies me for a while, then kisses me. He has horrible smoker's breath, but here, in this cold shed, our future encrypted in NHS files, I don't mind at all. My husband is a master kisser. Ten years in and I still get tingles.

'I love you,' he says. 'And I'm sorry I panicked. Not helpful.'

I rest my head on his shoulder, noticing only now how tired I am. Deeply, fatally tired; the sort of tiredness I felt when I was eight weeks pregnant and could have slept on a cheese grater.

I make a mental note: *Extreme fatigue*. For the last four years, since an apologetic registrar told me I had a cancer called extranodal MALT lymphoma, I've been studying my body as a marine biologist would a microorganism in the lab. And each time I record something new, or different, the same little gape of fear opens in my pelvis.

The cancer was classed as low-grade at first, so low they said there would be 'no clinical advantage' to treating me. At the time Leo and I were three years into trying to get pregnant, and had just started an IVF cycle. My cancer team were happy for us to carry on with the fertility treatment; they'd review in a year if we still hadn't conceived.

I trusted them when they said there was no reason to treat me yet. That it could be years before chemo became necessary, that quarterly chest X-rays would pick up any changes in plenty of time – but the fear was still like a stun-bolt to the brain. I felt cognitively disjointed, untethered.

Thoughts and desires I'd believed long dormant started to ambush me. I lay awake at night, full of wild imaginings and regrets about my university days; my twenties.

And of course about him.

I started having vivid, photo-real dreams about us meeting, the feel of his skin, the smell of his hair. And so, when the thought came to mind – *I want to call* – I didn't immediately dismiss it.

It kept coming back. *I need him to know I'm ill. I need to see him.*

A few days after the diagnosis, I caved and made the phone call.

The first two meetings were in a hotel, miles from London, the third, a greasy spoon near Oxford Circus. I quivered in a smog of need and the fertility hormones I was injecting myself with every day. Each time, I told myself this was OK; that nobody could get hurt. It was, simply, the continuation of a conversation that had been going on for nineteen years. But of course it wasn't OK. There was no solution that didn't involve the destruction of a family.

In the end, I agreed to break off contact yet again.

Six weeks later, I held a positive pregnancy test in my hand. I showed it to Leo and neither of us knew what to say. The next day I did another test, and then another, and another, until it occurred to me that the tests weren't wrong. It's hard enough to contemplate the circle of life when you have been trying for years to get pregnant without success, but when you're looking through the prism of cancer, it's near-impossible.

That was four years ago. The beginning of Ruby.

The disease remained static through my pregnancy and

the war of early motherhood. My chest X-rays kept coming back clear, and everything else was normal. Leo and I were so busy trying to keep a small child alive, we frequently forgot I had blood cancer.

But it couldn't last forever. Last year, when Ruby was two and a half, I started losing weight and having stomach pains. After a gastric bleed they scanned me, and a few days later I was shown a picture of a malignant ulcer lurking in my stomach.

'It's progressed, I'm afraid,' Dr Moru, my haematologist, told me, his usual smile absent. Apparently I now had an aggressive kind of non-Hodgkin lymphoma and was to begin treatment without any delay.

'We've been trying for a second child,' I began, but he held up a hand.

'You can think about that when you're not staring death in the face.'

He's not normally a stern man.

Now, several months later, treatment finally completed and remission prayed for, it's the fatigue that frightens me most. The deep pull of it, the still darkness below.

Perhaps I'm not a survivor.

Leo locks up the shed and we walk slowly to the back door. The grass is sodden underfoot, even though it hasn't rained for days. Daybreak must be close.

Once in our kitchen we close the door against the perfume of our night garden, and Leo throws his emergency cigarettes in the bin.

'Can you promise me one thing?' I ask. He's standing in front of the fridge, appraising its contents with apparent curiosity, even though we both know what he's there for. My husband wouldn't survive a week vegan.

'Anything.'

'Oh Leo, just eat the bloody ham.'

He frowns, and opens the vegetable drawer. 'What do you want me to promise?' he asks, obstinately leafing through wilting herbs.

'That if there is bad news, you won't pre-write my obituary.'

He straightens and snatches the ham off the top shelf. 'Of course I won't.' He rolls a slice into a baggy cigar and crams it into his mouth.

'You might feel like you have to. I don't know – professionally, personally; both. But I don't want anyone writing about my death while I'm still alive. Least of all you.'

'It hadn't even crossed my mind.'

I watch him for a while. 'Are you sure?'

'Yes!' He looks quite upset.

'Sorry, darling.' I sit down, suddenly. 'Sorry. I just can't stand the thought of you imagining me already gone. I . . . I can't cope with that.'

Leo shuts the fridge. 'I get it,' he says. He kneels down in front of me. 'I get it.'

John Keats watches us uncertainly. Leo strokes my hair. He knows not to say anything.

I find myself wondering, as I have done so many times in the last few years, what the moment of death feels like. How much we know; whether there's any sense of letting go. I don't believe in tunnels or white lights, but I do think there's a moment when we just know we're done, when we stop trying.

And that's the thing: I don't want to stop trying. I don't want to be done.

After a while, Leo gets up and puts on the quiet music we leave on all night for John. The dog pads off to bed, reassured, and Leo goes over to say goodnight. 'Don't even think about waking before six,' he tells John, giving him his night biscuits.

Then he straightens up and looks at me. 'Would it help to dance?' he asks.

Leo and I barely knew each other the first time we went dancing. It was just meant to be a drink in a pub. But a drink turned into several, which turned into late spaghetti and meatballs in a tiny Italian near Leo's old flat in Stepney Green, which turned into rum in a bar full of dental students who'd just finished exams. We all became friends and the students took us to a club in Whitechapel where everyone was dancing as if the end of the world was nigh.

'Is this OK?' he shouted in my ear. Leo. Thirty-five years old, beautiful and so funny, in his quiet, deadly way. 'We can go somewhere less mental if you want . . . ?'

'No chance!' I yelled. 'I'm happy!'

And I was. Everything was so easy with Leo. He was so easy. Watchful, perhaps hurt in the past, but straightforward in a way that made me regret all the high-energy men I'd dated in the last few years, with their need for attention, for admiration, their noise. Leo didn't seem to need anything from me, other than me. I held his hand tightly. It was cool and steady, even in that overheated underground space.

Then he said, 'Right, let's dance.'

'I'm pretty good,' he warned me, which I took to mean 'I'm terrible.' But, oh God, could he dance. A man with rhythm is one of the sexiest things on earth, I've always thought, and Leo, in his slim jeans and T-shirt, his glasses and his uncertain haircut, was pure fantasy. He just slipped through the air, through the hot bodies around us, as if waterborne. I watched him, awed, until he took hold of my waist, in a matter-of-fact manner, and moved me around the sticky dance floor as if I too were the sort of dancer people stopped everything to watch.

'As far as I'm concerned, you're going to get the all-clear,' he says now, as we dance slowly, quietly, in our darkened kitchen. His voice is tired but defiant. 'There is no other possible outcome.'

Before we go to bed, I check on Ruby. She's bundled up in a corner of her bed, face down, arm hooked around Duck. I breathe in the smell of my sleeping girl.

We all but gave up on conceiving. Three years of hopes raised and dashed, endless appointments with real doctors, witch doctors and everyone in between. We'd had every test known to man, but nobody could give me a concrete reason for my inability to get pregnant. The only thing they seemed to agree on, in the end, was that I was very unlikely to conceive naturally, if at all.

Eventually, we took out a loan and payed for an eye-wateringly expensive 'miracle IVF' that Leo's sister-in-law had had. It worked. Another part of my body might have been growing a low-grade cancer, but in my womb, a child was forming.

A second chance, I think now, reaching out a hand to check for the gentle rise and fall of my daughter's ribs. Please, Dr Moru, give me a second chance tomorrow, so I can love my husband and daughter in the way I promised.

I will let him go, if I get the all-clear. No matter how hard, I will let him go.

Chapter Three

LEO

When Emma finally sleeps, I go back out to the shed. I pick up the notebook and hold it between two fingers, as if it's a contaminant.

Her instinct was spot on: I have been writing her obituary. Sitting, scribbling on the tube, strangers trying to read over my shoulder. Writing late at night, when Emma's gone to bed and it's just me and John Keats and a black opening of fear.

I understand why she wouldn't want me to do it, of course, but these words aren't meant to be a betrayal. They're meant to be something beautiful. A hymn to this woman I love so deeply, so completely.

The writing hasn't just helped treat my mental state; it's reassured me that there's no chance Emma could ever be forgotten, or otherwise overlooked. That matters to me.

Do whatever you need to do for yourself, she said when she was first diagnosed. *Join a support group, get a therapist. This is going to be every bit as hard for you as it is for me.*

So I did what I knew, and it helped.

Back in our bed, one of her sleeping hands is outstretched to my side of the bed, as if her subconscious knew what I was up to but has already forgiven me.

Chapter Four

LEO

Next day

The news about Janice Rothschild's disappearance comes in on a news wire soon after I reach the office.

I'm checking our competitors' obituary pages when Sheila, my colleague, sounds the receptionist's bell on her desk. *Ding!* She always does this when someone has died. Publicly, we all agree it's a terrible practice; privately, we find it funny.

Ding! We all look up. 'Oh, no.' Sheila says. She's staring at her screen. 'Sorry, ignore the bell. Reflex action. But – oh, God.' She picks up her mobile, checks for something, then returns to her screen.

We wait. Sheila does everything in her own time.

After a few moments she sits back and passes her hands over her face. 'Janice Rothschild has disappeared. Just walked out of rehearsals for her play. Three days ago; nobody knows where she's gone.'

Kelvin, my editor, says, 'Really? What play?'

Even for Kelvin, whose emotional range is slim, this is poor. Janice Rothschild and her husband Jeremy are among Sheila's closest friends: Kelvin knows that. We all know that.

Kelvin's question is answered by Jonty, another colleague, whose emotional range is far too broad. 'She's rehearsing *All*

My Sons,' he says. 'I have tickets to see it in July. I absolutely can't stand it, Sheila, please tell me you're joking?'

Sheila massages her temples, ignoring them both.

'This is awful,' I say, quietly. 'Sheila, I'm sorry.'

She ignores me too. 'I – oh, God,' she mutters. 'Poor Jeremy. It says on the newswire that she'd seemed depressed in recent weeks but I . . . I just can't believe that. She's always been so . . . so fine.'

My editor remembers his job. 'Very worrying indeed. But – ah . . . Do we have a stock on file?'

A stock is a pre-written obituary. We keep thousands of them in our filing cabinets, but Janice Rothschild, who is only about fifty and without any reported health concerns, has not even made it onto our 'just in case' list. She's in a BBC adaptation of *Madame Bovary* right now, for goodness' sake – I watched it on Sunday evening. Emma went to bed soon after it started, saying she wasn't a fan of Janice Rothschild, but I thought she was excellent.

Sheila leaves her desk to call Jeremy.

Kelvin calls the pictures desk. 'Can we please get a selection for Janice Rothschild? Maybe include a few of her in *Madame Bovary* . . . What? Oh, sorry – we've just heard she's disappeared. I know – a bit shocking. Anyway, can we get a few of her with her husband? Just in case?'

Jeremy Rothschild presents the *Today* programme on Radio 4; he and Janice Rothschild have been married for decades. I look up his Twitter account, but he hasn't said anything in seventy-two hours. Everyone else on the obits desk is doing the same. As one, we look up Janice's Twitter, which has been silent for three weeks, and Jonty goes off to make tea. 'She is delightful,' he says, angrily. 'I really will not cope if she's taken her own life.'

I put my headphones on, unable to listen to my colleagues

any longer, and spend a few minutes looking at #Janice-Rothschild. It really is breaking news; there's only a little more than five minutes of tweets. I watch an achingly funny clip of her guest-starring in *Ab Fab*, and a very moving one of her overcoming chronic vertigo to climb a rock face for Sport Relief. By the time she reaches the top, everyone's crying, even the cameraman.

None of these early tweeters seemed to have any idea why she's disappeared. I run a quick check on our archive but only find one potential clue: a picture of her leaving a psychiatric unit nineteen years ago, a few weeks after giving birth to their son. Since then, nothing. She's one of those relentlessly funny, upbeat women; the sort you wish you were friends with when you see them sparring with Graham Norton on TV. I wouldn't have had a clue.

Sheila returns to her desk with a large bag of Wine Gums. She says she's been unable to get hold of Jeremy. She doesn't offer the sweets around. Instead, she eats, mechanically and in solitude.

'Do not ask me to write a stock for her,' she says, after a while. 'I do not believe she could commit suicide. I'm not getting involved.'

'But you know her so well,' Kelvin tries, after a pause. 'It would be a really personal piece.'

'Which is precisely why I won't do it.' Sheila's voice is crisp. 'I'm not condemning a perfectly healthy, very precious friend to death.'

Kelvin nods his assent. He is the editor, and I'm his deputy, but nobody's in any doubt that it's Sheila who runs this desk.

Kelvin gives the obit to me, and I get writing. I know my colleagues at all the other newspapers will be doing the same thing; that we're all now working against the clock, checking regularly for an announcement that a body has been found.

I try not to think about Sheila's refusal to 'condemn' her friend to death. Is that what I've been doing, writing Emma's obituary?

On the news floor TVs, I can hear someone from the Metropolitan Police confirming that they're looking for a missing woman in her fifties. Then an actor, who has no idea where Janice is, saying he has no idea where Janice is.

Sheila eats Wine Gums non-stop and sends a lot of text messages, before announcing she's going out. 'Need to find somewhere that will serve me a brandy at ten thirty a.m.,' she says. 'I've already got lunatics emailing in amateur Janice obituaries.'

People seldom believe me when I tell them our desk is the most cheerful desk on the news floor; that our laughter is often a matter of irritation to our neighbours. But it makes sense, if you think about it properly. Current affairs and politics are perennially gloomy spaces to inhabit, whereas we spend our time celebrating extraordinary people. Besides, an obituarist's currency is life, not death, and my mind is always trained on the qualities of my intended portrait: the colours, the light and dark; the choppy textures. There is a sadness to it, of course, but it's gentle. Even writing advance obits is bearable if the subject has had a long life.

But this kind of advance obit, this preparation for a death that shouldn't be happening – the tragic car accident with an army of press camped outside the hospital, the sudden terminal cancer diagnosis, or an unexplained disappearance – this is the worst part of the job.

Especially when you're waiting for an appointment with your wife's haematologist.

*

Sheila finally hears from Jeremy around lunchtime. She leaves her desk quickly, and is gone for a long time.

'No real news,' she says on her return. 'It's one of the actors from her play who leaked the story. Shot his mouth off in a pub – as if he didn't know it'd spread across London like the plague. There's a whole scrum of press outside Jeremy's front door. He's raging.'

I'd sooner throw myself under a bus than get on the wrong side of Jeremy Rothschild. He's a national treasure, all right, but his ability to disembowel politicians is unnerving. He also once punched a paparazzo, although that I can understand.

'He has no idea where Janice is,' Sheila admits, sitting down. 'She left the house for work three days ago. They're rehearsing at Cecil Sharp House in Camden, and apparently the producers normally send her a car, but she wanted to drive that day. Rehearsals were going fine; she seemed fine – then she went to the loo and never came back. Her car was clamped and taken to the pound. No images of her on the tube.'

'But it's Camden,' Jonty says. 'Surely there's street cameras everywhere?'

'Primrose Hill end of Camden. By Regent's Park. Hardly any cameras there.'

Kelvin shoots me a far-from-subtle look, checking my Janice stock is ready to go. Grudgingly, I nod. Sheila sees the whole thing, but doesn't object. She knows we have to do it.

'They'll find her,' she says. 'And she'll be fine. I don't buy the depression story. I had supper with them a few weeks ago. She drank a fair bit, but then again so did I. We were singing Queen songs until two in the morning, it was disgraceful. She was on good form.'

'No hint of strain in their relationship?' Jonty asks. 'You don't think she's just left him?'

'I do not,' she says, and there's a warning in her voice.

Jonty doesn't take the hint. 'So there's literally nothing untoward?'

'Nothing,' she snaps, and the matter is closed. I watch her tidy her desk, throw out the remaining Wine Gums and raise, then lower, her shoulders. This means she is shelving any feelings she might have about Janice until such time as she knows more. She's one of the few people I know who's genuinely able to do this.

Sheila is only about ten years older than I am but she's already had high-ranking positions in both MI5 and the diplomatic service. To my great pleasure she chose me as her drinking buddy when she joined our team a few years back, and our lunchtime trips to the Plumbers' Arms remain the high point of my working day. Sheila can put away three pints in an hour and still be the most cogent person in the room.

Nobody is quite sure how, or why, she came to work with us, but I have a feeling she'll just disappear one day, as quickly and mysteriously as she arrived. There'll be someone else at her desk one morning and I'll have to spend the rest of my life imagining what she's doing. My money's on her heading up a multi-billion-dollar drug cartel somewhere. Driving around in an armoured Humvee, getting presidents and monarchs in her pocket.

'By the way, I saw Emma,' she says now, as we all return to our computers. 'Yesterday.'

'Oh yes?' Sheila has a habit of jumping from topic to unrelated topic without a moment's notice. She leaves us all behind in team meetings.

'She looked upset. It's none of my business, of course, but I do hope she's all right.'

Emma hasn't mentioned this.

'She was nervous about her scan results,' I improvise, because I don't want one of my colleagues to know more about my wife than I do. 'We're seeing her haematologist this afternoon.'

I start a message to Emma, to check she's OK, when Sheila pipes up again: 'She was at Waterloo Station.'

'Yeah. She works down in Plymouth two days a week,' I say, without looking up. Sheila knows this. We were talking about Emma's huge commute just a few days ago.

'That's why I was surprised to see her at Waterloo – don't trains to Plymouth run from Paddington Station?'

I stop messaging and think about it. 'Actually, you're right,' I admit. 'She was doing fieldwork in Dorset yesterday. Hence, Waterloo.'

Oddly, Emma didn't mention her trip last night, so I'd forgotten to ask how it went.

'Oh, lovely,' Sheila says. Her voice is friendly now, as if it's just me and her in the pub. 'Where in Dorset? I love that coastline.'

This is not only irritating, but most unlike Sheila.

'Wherever it is that her friend's collecting phytoplankton samples,' I say. 'I can't remember where.'

'Probably out from Poole Harbour,' Sheila says, nodding.

What? How does she know about bloody phytoplankton, on top of everything else?

'It was quite late in the morning,' she adds, going back to her screen. She gives me a curious sort of a smile – something not far from sympathy – and then returns to her screen.

Jonty looks up from his desk. He's noticed too.

What is she up to? Sheila and I often discuss Emma in the pub, in wider conversations about family lives, but this is different. I feel like I'm getting a glimpse of the interrogator she once was. (There's no way she was doing a desk job at

MI5.) She's polite and friendly; but there's an implied meaning that I neither like nor understand.

'She said something about how phytoplankton do a daily migration to deep waters,' I say, eventually. 'I guess she was waiting for that to happen.'

I don't offer that Emma's been struggling with timekeeping lately – sometimes a warning sign of her depressions – but it's no matter. The conversation seems to have reached its conclusion.

At 3 p.m. I get up to leave for the hospital, and nobody knows quite what to say to me. 'All the best,' Sheila calls, as I go. 'I'll be thinking about you both.'

Chapter Five

LEO

I don't like hearing people complain about the NHS, but as we wait forty, fifty, sixty-five minutes to be called into Dr Moru's office, I sink into fury. I try to read a former MP's obit one of our Westminster contributors has sent in, but I'm too anxious and angry to concentrate. A silent television suspended over the waiting room shows us footage of absolutely nothing happening at Jeremy and Janice Rothschild's house, a handsome Georgian terrace in Highbury.

Beside me Emma sits quietly, also studying her phone.

She's got nearly two inches of hair now. She's always had it short; short and wavy, sitting just at her jawline, but many months will pass before it's that length again. Today, she wears it with a slim black grip. She is beautiful. Even after months of toxic medications, of killer beams fired into her body, of endless blood tests and tears and phone calls and quiet terror, she is still beautiful.

I lean over to tell her this, but my eye is caught by her phone.

'What the fuck?' I whisper.

She's on Amazon, looking at coffins.

'I want a wicker coffin,' she whispers back. 'If I die. And a natural burial.'

I stare at her phone, transfixed. The wicker coffin she's looking at retails at just under £500 and is pictured in a sunny bluebell wood, with a posy of wildflowers on top.

'Emma, no!' I say. 'Stop it!'

'It's lined with organic cotton,' she says defensively. 'Anyway, I'm going to be fine. This is merely research.'

'Emma,' I whisper, rubbing my forehead. 'Please, don't.'

'We all die eventually. It's much better to die with your ducks in a row.'

'I . . . OK. Do what you need to do.'

A hot hollow opens in my chest. I really could lose her.

Emma, probably sensing this, puts her phone away and tucks her hand into mine, but I can't stand it anymore. I march up to reception, ready to explode, just as her name is called.

Chapter Six

EMMA

The problem with lying to your husband is that it changes everything and nothing.

I love Leo. Not in a part-time or conditional way; it's the real deal, an essential love, as much a part of my biological function as my liver and spleen. I love his Leoisms: the strange snacks he makes for himself, the meticulousness with which he folds clean clothes, the hours he spends trying and failing to play the opening bars of Bruce Hornsby's 'The Way It Is' on my grandmother's old piano. The way he looks at me across his long nose, in bed, and makes up filthy limericks as if he's reading the shipping forecast.

I don't think it's any exaggeration to say he saved my life.

When I was pregnant with Ruby, friends warned that parenthood would erode our grand love affair. I understood what they meant, once our daughter arrived: the chaos and sleep deprivation, the sensation of being on the back foot – always, and with everything – the loss of adult conversation or intimacy; but I came out of that first year more certain than ever that Leo was the best man I'd ever known. We'd survived a cancer diagnosis, a pregnancy, postnatal depression, and yet there we still were, quietly walking in step. When we weren't razed by exhaustion, we still belly-laughed in bed before going to sleep. We still kissed each other as if we were falling in love.

I was desperate to come clean with him; to tell him about the kind of woman he was married to.

But the reason I couldn't was the same then as it had always been. Leo would never, could never, come to terms with it. There are a small handful of men who perhaps could, but my husband is not one of them.

And even if he were a different person, with a less complicated past – the sort who might be able to forgive what I'd done – he would never forgive my attempts to conceal it. Leo was lied to from the day he was born, and he can't tolerate dishonesty in any form now. Last year he fired our nanny because she told us she'd taken Ruby to the park, when in fact they'd gone to her boyfriend's house. By the time I got back that evening he'd paid an HR consultant to check that the nanny's deception constituted gross misconduct, and had removed her from our house.

It was the right thing to do: we couldn't give Ruby to someone we couldn't trust. But the intensity of his anger extinguished any hope that I could one day tell him the truth.

Dr Moru tells us before we make it through the door.

'It's good news!' he beams, and, without any professional hesitation, hugs me.

'I'm OK? I'm OK?'

'You're OK. For now.'

Leo whispers, 'Oh thank God,' and removes Dr Moru, pulling me tightly to him.

'The PET scan is clear and the restaging biopsy looks good. So do your bloods,' Dr Moru says, sitting back calmly at his desk, as if he hadn't just thrown his arms around a patient. He starts talking about the next few months but eventually stops because Leo is pulling tissues from the box on his desk and jamming them into his eyes.

I hold my husband's hand while he recovers. I know he's been afraid, of course, but the sheer expanse of his anxiety, revealed now in plain sight, is painful. 'I'm sorry,' he says, in his normal voice, as if there aren't tears pouring down his cheeks. 'Please just ignore me.'

They will continue to monitor me at six-monthly intervals, Dr Moru says, but for now we can allow ourselves to be optimistic about my future.

'You should write about your experience on your page,' he says, merrily. He's openly admitted to having looked me up on Facebook. 'Those fans of yours would love it!'

I've read endless cancer memoirs in the years following my diagnosis; some written from the warm shore of survival, others cut short by an end note from a bereaved relative. Some talk of healing and growth, others of grief and suffering, but every account, every single one, has talked about love. About how, as we approach the end of our life, we find ourselves turning towards the things and people that are most meaningful to us so that we may face death with equanimity and courage.

My cancer journey, by shameful contrast, started four years ago with the rekindling of an obsession that could end my marriage. It's been about fear of discovery and deep regret. It is something I could never commit to paper, or Facebook, or anywhere else.

We don't go immediately to Ruby's nursery. We stop instead to drink wine at a pub on South End Green. I order a cheeseboard and we lay into it with a single-mindedness that is probably unsettling to onlookers.

I can't stop smiling, imagining the little smear of myself

stored on a histology slide somewhere, free of invading cells, entered into a database and now forgotten. Even in the beautiful cellular imaging we have access to today, B-cell lymphoma cells look evil.

'What are you going to do?' Leo asks, smiling at me. He's so happy. I'm so happy.

I ask what he means.

'You said you had all these plans, if you beat the bastard cancer. All these things you wanted to do.'

I think about it for a while. Really, I just want to focus on loving him and Ruby. I tell him that.

He kisses me, and then kisses me again. I notice a much older woman at a corner table, smiling at us. I smile back. He's my husband, I want to tell her. Older women are always smiling at Leo. I think it's those outlandishly long eyelashes of his. Perhaps the way his mouth turns up naturally at the corners, as if he's trying not to laugh at something.

'I like your plan,' he says. 'But what about your crabs? Didn't you want to nail them down?'

I smile. 'Sure! I'll just go up to Northumberland and find the colony, now I'm not tied to the hospital. Should be easy.'

'Oh, behave,' he says. He waves at the barman, gesturing for another two glasses of wine.

Nearly twenty years ago, when I was an undergraduate, I found a dead crab on a beach in Northumberland. I photographed it, sensing how unusual it was, but the beach walk took an unexpected turn and I finished the day in hospital. Several years passed before I found and developed the film.

When I did eventually hold the photo in my hands, I was studying for a marine biology master's at Plymouth University. I took it straight to one of my tutors, a decapod expert.

She looked at it for a long time before taking off her glasses and saying, 'Good Lord.'

There was a grapsid crab species, native to Japan, she told me, that had probably invaded Europe via the ballast water of a Japanese container ship. The first was found in La Rochelle in 1993. In the years that followed, it had spread along the French and Spanish coasts, eventually travelling north to invade Scandinavian waters.

'But it hasn't reached Britain yet,' she told me. 'Unless you found the first one five years ago.'

That crab was called *Hemigrapsus takanoi*. 'But this one doesn't really fit the spec.' She frowned. 'It's got some very unusual features.' She showed me how *Hemigrapsus takanoi* had patches of bristles – setae – on their pincers, and spots of colour across the carapace. They also had three distinct spines.

'But yours has four. Look! Four spines! The bristles cover the whole chelae, and the spots are red, which I've never seen before. This could be quite a significant finding.'

I was copied in on many emails between my tutor and her decapod colleagues around the world. Much of what they said was beyond my understanding, but there was one thing on which they all seemed to agree: it seemed as if I had unwittingly come across a new form, a different phenotype of *Hemigrapsus takanoi*. A phenotype so distinct, it was well on its way to becoming – or in fact could be – a new species.

Quite something, for a master's student.

I returned to the Northumbrian coast soon after, and when I didn't find anything I returned again, and again. Over the years I must have gone forty, maybe even fifty times, combing the sands of Alnmouth, Boulmer and beyond. My tutor had suggested that, if this really was a new species, the only way it could have evolved was in total isolation, away from the other *Hemigrapsus takanoi* in the North Sea. So I scoured every remote cove, every wave-beaten spur, every inaccessible rocky shore between High Hauxley and Berwick – but I never found another one.

I still go. When my mood is low, it's what I do; Leo's always encouraged it. I check into a tiny B&B in Alnmouth and I walk and search and walk and search. I'm conducting my own study at Plymouth, too – I won't give up. I will find 'my crab', as Leo calls it. One day.

'You're right.' I spear the final piece of Tunworth and offer it to Leo, who eats it straight from the knife. 'It's been ages since I went up there. Let's work out when I can go again.'

I eat the last cracker, even though I'm full. 'In fact, maybe we could all go together. Ruby wouldn't survive my crazy walks, but you two could do beachy things.'

Leo swallows the cheese, kissing his fingers. 'I'd love that. Let's do it. In fact, sod it, let's do it next week! I have to take some holiday before I lose my entitlement.'

'I . . . Well, maybe. Let me check with work. But if not next week, soon.'

He doesn't notice my moment of panic. He's far too happy.

Full of cheese, we collect our girl and take her up to our favourite summer spot on the Heath, where London tumbles away towards a dusty horizon and the long grass offers opportunities for endless three-year-old's adventures. I tell Ruby I no longer need to go to hospital for special medicine and she tells me she is a beetle called Mr Cloris.

Leo takes several photos of us, although he's been doing this since I was first diagnosed. On the Lymphoma Facebook group everyone complains about how their families won't stop taking pictures of them, as if we won't guess the subtext. But how can we object? If we die it's them who'll be left with only images to hold.

When Ruby goes to bed later on we have more wine, sitting out in the garden, and Leo tells me how relieved he is. I feel alive and precious and rather beautiful, which means I must be drunk. Leo strums quietly on his banjo, before sagging slowly into exhaustion. By five to ten he is lying face down in the grass, asleep. This happens a lot. He was asleep before 10.15 on our wedding night.

I message my friends and colleagues, Leo's brother and parents, and my one-time housemate and oldest friend, Jill. I lie back and study the sky, tracking the orange bloat of light pollution until it fades into inky space, marked by a single star. Messages of relief ping into my phone. More stars appear, further and further way; distant smudges.

I think of my father, who showed me the Plough just before being posted to Montserrat with his Marine commando when a volcano erupted. On his return, he told me the mission had gone well, but didn't seem to want to resume our astronomy conversations. I'd often find him looking up at the sky, but he seldom spoke.

I go in to check Ruby is breathing, and return with a blanket for Leo. (I had to do this on our wedding night too, when I found him napping in a corner while our guests danced.)

Only then, when there are no further tasks to do, do I feel brave enough to think directly about the phone call.

It stopped me in my tracks at Waterloo yesterday morning, coffee undrunk in my hand; commuters swarming around me. His voice was distant, as if he were calling from a mountain thousands of miles away.

I asked him to repeat himself, but he knew I'd heard.

I didn't make it out of Waterloo, let alone to Poole Harbour. The departures board scrolled on through the morning, the commuter rush receding, and I stood still in the middle of it all, immobilised.

I only made it out of there when Jill called.

'This could kick off,' she said. 'You should be prepared.'

So I went home, quickly, before Leo got home from work, to empty my personal file.

Just in case.

I stuffed the contents in an old shopping bag, in the corner of the dining room furthest from the door. Somewhere Leo would never look.

Not that he would even think of looking, of course.

Some thirty-six hours later, a woman without cancer, I sit quietly in the soft dark of my garden and allow myself to reread the messages he sent after the phone call, which I'd screenshotted before deleting, the photo hidden deep in my phone.

Please don't think I'm going to just leave this, he'd written. *I'm not. I need to see you. In person.*

And then, when I didn't reply: *This isn't a joke. I will turn up at your house if I need to.*

The elderly lady who lives next door to us is brushing her teeth in her bathroom window. She looks out at the dark tangle of trees that span our gardens, lost in thought about another time, another life maybe.

I cannot, must not see him. I know this. The risk is far too great.

And yet, *OK*, I find myself replying, a few minutes later. *I'll meet you.*

Chapter Seven

LEO

My editor, Kelvin, is a shy man. Meetings are held over the safe distance of our block of desks, and our annual appraisals are conducted digitally. He wouldn't do well with a one-to-one.

For this reason I'm surprised when he emails to suggest 'a chat this morning'. I turn to ask when and where, because he sits right next to me, but his jaw is clenched and he's typing at speed, so I type a reply to suggest the coffee bar in five minutes.

We repair to the atrium at the centre of the newsroom floor, where geometric blocks of light filter through a glass roof. Kelvin shifts, struggling to meet my eye. Around us are the sounds of keyboards, low conversation, the news flickering quietly on giant screens suspended from the ceiling. I wonder if I'm about to be sacked, and for what. For being unsustainably average? I write decent obits, but they lack the intellectualism and forensic gaze of Sheila's, or the Wodehousian humour of Jonty's.

'Very pleased about Emma,' Kelvin says, after clearing his throat. 'I'm not afraid to say I think your wife is fantastic.'

I mean, at least he's honest.

I wheel out a few trite sentences, largely because I have few words for the relief. She'll have to be tested from time to time, of course; there's always the prospect of secondary tumours secreting themselves around her lymphatic system – but the odds are on our side. Relapse rates are fairly low, and Emma is relatively young and healthy.

Kelvin fiddles with his coffee. 'We wrote a stock,' he says, eventually. 'For Emma. We haven't saved it in the system – didn't want you stumbling across it. But we did have to get something written. We wrote it during her chemotherapy.'

I swallow, thinking about the last few months. Uneaten meals, mouth ulcers, tiny wrathful spots on Emma's skin. Ruby getting strep throat and Emma sobbing because she wasn't allowed near her.

'I'm sure this is an unappealing subject,' Kelvin adds. 'But we would publish an obit, of course, if she died.'

Emma's still known for her BBC series, a lovely three-parter about the ecology of the British coastline: how conditions have changed for the creatures living in our estuaries and rocky shores, our beaches and dunes. A development researcher from the BBC had 'discovered' her, chairing a panel at a British Ecological Society event. He had been charmed by her wit and nonconformity, as most people are, and invited her down to discuss programme ideas.

I saw some of the resulting proposals, which described my wife as a SPARKLING NEW TALENT. She found it embarrassing; I found it very funny.

A year later she co-presented a three-part series with an established BBC naturalist and – in my very subjective opinion – radically outshone him. Before the final episode had aired, she was recommissioned for a second series. Viewers loved that she was funny even when barnacled to a cliff, waves smashing below.

Emma is not a celebrity, of course, and to this day I don't see her as famous: she's a self-confessed nerd, an academic. Her only motivation in taking the presenting job was to share her love of that magical place where the terrestrial world peters off into the unknowns of the ocean. She hated the attention and did the bare minimum of publicity interviews when *This Land* was in its prime. Even now she won't come to newspaper parties. She says we're all vultures.

But the fact remains that, long after she disappeared from TV screens, we're still stopped in the street so that she can sign autographs, or discuss cliff zonation with socially awkward men. She was even asked to do *Strictly*. (She said no.)

I imagine most papers would run an obit if she died.

'Now that everything's looking – well, good,' Kelvin says, 'I wonder if you'd be happy to take a look at what we've written?'

'As it happens, I've already made a start.'

Kelvin looks uncertain. 'You have?'

'Yes. It was a sort of personal project, really, but I'm sure one of you could knock it into shape.'

A pause. Then Kelvin says, 'It can't have been an easy task, with cancer treatment rumbling on in the background.' His face greys with effort: this is way too touchy-feely for him. 'But I'm sure any obit you've written for Emma will be significantly more personal and honest.'

I almost laugh at the irony of his trust in me. The fact of the matter is, my obituary for Emma is full of holes. It's not honest at all.

Emma had an agent, back when she was presenting; a zealous and fiery woman called Mags Tenterden whom Emma worshipped. Mags was in negotiations with the BBC over the third series when Emma was, very suddenly, dropped from the programme, an old-timer booked in her place. There was an apocryphal story about changes in the commissioning team, but no reasonable explanation for Emma having taken the fall.

I was with her when she got the phone call. I don't think I'll ever forget her face.

I wondered, at first, if they just didn't want the uncertainty of a presenter with low-grade cancer and a child on the way, but it turned out Emma hadn't told them about either.

In an act of baffling cruelty, Mags Tenterden dropped Emma from her client list the following week. I think this unspeakable abandonment was the final straw, because, in the months that followed, Emma had one of her longest ever depressive episodes. She went off to spend three whole weeks on the lonely coast of Northumberland, isolated except for my weekend visits. Occasional emails would arrive, strange passages of abstracted prose about the secrets of the ocean, but mostly she was completely closed down, even when I visited. 'I'm just looking for crabs,' she'd said, one evening, in her B&B. 'That's all I can cope with right now. Just looking for crabs.'

Her normal route out of what I've always called her Times involves what she describes as a 'kickstarter' stint on medication, but she was too afraid to take antidepressants with a baby on board. On her return to London she told me she was 'just going to have to tough this one out'.

She had begun to recover by the time Ruby was born, but was then razed by severe postnatal depression. I don't think she fully came back until Ruby started sleeping through at thirteen months, and the low mood still comes and goes to this day. Her hoarding is certainly getting worse.

None of this appears in the piece I've written.

'I'm sure she'd be flattered,' I tell Kelvin. 'But she did explicitly ban me from writing a stock. She doesn't know I've been writing one.'

‘Ah. Well, I’d be happy for you to send some notes to Jonty or Sheila . . .’

‘I’ll send it over to Sheila. Or maybe Jonty,’ I add, remembering Sheila’s unaccountable interest in my wife the other day.

‘Excellent!’ Kelvin looks over his shoulder. The man’s longing for the lesser demands of a quiet computer screen, so I thank him for bringing the matter up discreetly, and let him go.

Emma miscarried twice while we were trying to conceive. When we returned from the hospital the second time I put her to bed and went down to make tea. On my return I found her with tears peeling soundlessly down her cheeks, and John Keats with his kind, canine nose on her old appendix scar.

‘I’m fine,’ she was telling him. ‘Absolutely fine, John, don’t you worry about me.’

Not even the dog is privy to her inner landscape. I’m allowed in, her friend Jill’s allowed in, and that’s it.

For this reason I find myself hesitating before typing up my stock notes to send to Jonty. Even though it goes against everything I know as an obituary writer, I feel a duty to keep my real wife to myself. Why not just give the world the version of Emma they already love? The laughing TV presenter with her windmill gesticulations, the adopter of rescue dogs with names like Frogman and Jesus; the granddaughter of foul-mouthed, chain-smoking Gloria Bigelow, one of the earliest female MPs?

There is more than enough of that Emma to share with the world.

I send Kelvin an email and tell him I’ve decided I’ll write Emma’s stock after all.

*

In the weeks to come I will think back to this afternoon, these last few moments before the world starts to spin at a different angle, and I'll envy myself this fantasy – this belief that I am one of only two people who knows about Emma's inner world.

This belief that I know her at all.

Chapter Eight

LEO

Emma has an old friend from university, Jill, whom she meets once a month for dinner. They studied marine biology and lived together in St Andrews, and although their friendship has always seemed slightly off-key to me, Emma's fiercely loyal to Jill.

I'm seldom invited to their dinners, which is probably for the best because although I like Jill well enough, I don't really understand her. She's one of those people who speaks in written sentences, rather than in normal English, and it makes conversation quite difficult – as if you're in a play for which you haven't been given a script. I also find her sense of humour to be on the aggressive side of dry, even though Emma seems to find her hilarious.

In spite of all of this, I think Jill and I would have been just fine if she hadn't turned up on our front doorstep, three years ago, and moved into our house.

She arrived on Ruby's due date. Just walked up our garden path with a large overnight bag and a box of dark chocolate truffles as I escorted a waddling Emma out for brunch. (I intensely dislike dark chocolate truffles, although I appreciate that's neither here nor there.)

'A very good morning to you both,' she said, as if we'd

been expecting her. 'I'll get settled in while you're out. Kick off with some light manual labour.'

Emma had taken my hand and led me off down the road. 'I told you I wanted her to help out,' she said, gently. 'When the baby came.'

What she had actually said was that she was worried about her postnatal mental health, and that she'd like to have Jill on standby in case things got bad. There had never been any mention of Jill moving in.

Jill stayed for two weeks after Ruby's birth. There we were; shell-shocked, exhausted, having to squeeze around a third party in an already tiny space. Ultimately, I think Emma regretted inviting her, too – as the postnatal depression rolled in like a combat tank, it was me she clung to, not Jill.

In the end I had to chalk it up to some intense expression of friendship I couldn't, or wouldn't, understand. Sympathy for Jill, perhaps, who had apparently longed for a baby herself. Maybe a pact they'd made as young women. Either way, it was no time to start an argument with Emma. Jill eventually returned to her flat and I said nothing.

Jill and Emma's monthly rendezvous is tonight, so I've retreated to our tiny study to get on with Emma's stock. It will take time to turn the grief-stricken passages in my notebook into something publishable, but I have whiskey and fig rolls and at least two more hours before Emma will be home.

Our house is sheathed in a thick veil of foliage, which I am quite certain is causing damage to the fabric of the building, but Emma refuses to do anything about it. Through the ever-narrowing frame hanging around our window, I see a silky mauve sky, from which light is fading fast.

I reread the opening section, rolling one of Ruby's marbles around my desk.

Marine ecologist and television presenter Emma Bigelow, who has died at the age of ??, was an enthusiastic collector of abandoned dogs, and widely credited with putting Britain's coastal ecosystems on the popular conservation map.

*She was a role model for women in marine biology, winning awards and fellowships that had for decades prior been reserved for men. 'Worth twenty of the insipid corvid-worshippers that normally front this sort of programme' (*The Times; *October 2014), Bigelow presented two series of the BBC's popular* This Land, *from 2013–15. An anonymous Instagram account was set up after the first series, dedicated to clips of her trademark windmill-like gesticulations. Bigelow was delighted.*

After two series Emma Bigelow returned to her teaching posts at the University of Plymouth and University College London. 'I'm more sea squirt than I am human,' she said at the time, 'so I'm very happy to be back in the intertidal zone, although I'll miss the free lunches terribly.'

I haven't mentioned that she said this to me in floods of tears, or that when she did so I was running around beating my chest, threatening to sue the BBC for unfair dismissal.

Emma Merry Bigelow was born into the peripatetic life of a military child, stationed variously in Plymouth, Taunton and Arbroath. Her father was a Royal Marine chaplain and her mother, who died shortly after Bigelow was born, a Classics graduate.

I stop reading.

I'm not satisfied with this.

Good obit writers sound like they knew the deceased: it's what we're paid to do. But those of us who spend our lives reading them – who discuss them on nerd forums and go to obit conferences, who read the obit books and articles and compilations – we can tell the difference. Had I not written this myself, I would have put good money on the writer of this obit never having met Emma. None of her unique magic is here.

While I think about how best to fix this, I make a list of the details I need to check.

Did Emma go straight into her master's after her undergraduate degree?

What were Emma and her dad's exact movements when she was a child? (I know her father served with several different Marine commandos, but I've no idea which ones, or when.)

How exactly did her mum die?

John Keats is asleep in the Queen Anne chair behind me, even though he's banned from the furniture. I watch him sleep, one paw twitching like a tired eye, and weigh up the pros and cons of just texting the list of questions to Emma, with an apologetic note blaming Kelvin.

It takes seconds to reject the idea. She's reopened the door on life; the last thing she needs is a reminder of her own mortality. Just this morning she went running, and afterwards sent me a picture of her shiny red face. *I AM ALIVE!* she wrote. *FUCKING ALIVE!*

I'm also far too ashamed to admit to her that I don't know

exactly how her mother died. She's only ever said it was a birth complication, and it's never felt right to drill down for details she hasn't offered.

Emma has a plastic folder of important bits called FOLDER OF IMPORTANT BITS. I've never looked inside but I imagine it's exactly the same as my own box file: birth certificate, degree, letters, that sort of thing. The folder lives at the top of her filing cabinet, which she keeps locked, but I give the door a light nudge anyway. This would be a far easier means to the same end.

The door rolls quietly upwards. It makes the tiniest hair-split noise, but it's enough to wake the dog. He and I both stare inside.

I can't remember the last time I saw the inside of this cabinet. Emma never leaves it unlocked; she's terrified of a burglar making off with her non-computerised research. If we go abroad she comes down here to get her passport out personally: *you'd just forget to lock it*, she always says, which is absolutely correct.

I wonder if she's slipping into one of her Times. It's not like her to leave it open.

After a pause, I reach up for the folder, which clicks open.

John Keats looks worried, so I put on a jungle album from our Spotify favourites. *Ghosts of My Life*, it's called, by someone called Rufige Kru.

The folder is all but empty.

There are a few recent things; her PhD; a thank you letter from a charity she's been sending money to for ten years; the last paper driving licence counterpart Emma had before they became obsolete. A photo of Emma and her father outside an enormous naval ship, an old work ID of Emma's. But nothing else.

The dog is still watching me.

This cupboard is seldom open, but I've seen this folder often enough. It's always been overstuffed, just like mine – life is perplexingly full of vitally important papers that never actually get used. The files we use to store them expand and fatten to the point of bursting: they don't slim down to almost nothing.

I pull out her work ID, still attached to a well-worn lanyard.

EMMA BIGELOW, it says. *BIOLOGICAL AND MARINE SCIENCES*. I smile at her photograph. Even with the required impassive expression, my wife looks at once subversive, beautiful and amused.

I stand back to get a good view of the cupboard. She must have moved the papers to a different shelf.

Only she hasn't. Everything else is labelled and accounted for. I could open up all the lever arch files in front of me, but what would be the point? She's not going to have hole-punched her birth certificate.

I go upstairs to look at the piles of stuff in our bedroom, but there's no pile of papers there.

They haven't been left in the mess on the landing.

They aren't in the empty box she's recently started using for haphazard document storage, perched halfway up the stairs.

I know the papers were there a few weeks ago, when we went to Paris to celebrate the end of Emma's chemo. I was right next to her in the study when she got her passport out. And I remember grinning at the state of her folder, because it was even more full than mine.

I'd have noticed those papers, if she'd got them out: this is not a big house. I'd have had to shift them to put down a cup of tea, or to stop Ruby covering them with paint or glitter glue or bogies: there's something about their absence that feels a little odd.

I don't know it yet, but this moment is the moment I start spying on Emma.

I go down into the dining room; a sea of paper. It's all Emma's granny's; she died years ago but Emma still hasn't sorted through her things. There's only about four square feet of floor space available in here; the rest is stacked knee-high.

I climb from one clear patch of floor to another, looking around me. There is no pile of Emma-related papers. It's mostly musical scores and violin studies and yellowed bank statements that should have been thrown out decades ago. Most of the paperwork is stuffed into shopping bags from the eighties – white Sainbury's with orange lettering; Tesco with thick blue stripes. Everything is covered in a substantial layer of dust.

. . . Except for the old Marks & Spencer's bag in the corner, which I see when I climb over to the furthest floor clearing. It's also from the eighties, when their bags were bright green with *St Michael* in gold cursive. And, although most of the bag is as dusty as the rest, there are several shiny gaps where the dust has been disturbed by someone's fingers. In the last few days, by the looks of things.

I pause. This mission is beginning to transcend its fact-finding scope.

But this bag.

It's in the furthest corner of the room, half-under Emma's grandmother's old desk. It's concealed from the view of anyone standing in the doorway by a brass fireguard; I can only see it now because I've climbed so far in.

To put something in this bag, in this corner, would be to deliberately hide it. Why would Emma want to hide something?

I reach over and pick it up.

The very first thing I see is her master's certificate from Plymouth University. The next paper is the letter she got from Berkshire Police when she was caught doing 40 mph in a

30 limit in Slough last year. Briefly, I smile. This letter made her furious – I'm surprised she kept it, but equally, I know how hard she finds it to throw anything away. She really is her grandmother's granddaughter in that regard; hoarders, the pair of them.

Next is the leaving card her crew and colleagues from the BBC series sent her after she was mysteriously sacked. *We will miss you so much! I will never look at a breakfast buffet in the same way! Really hope we can work together again soon!*

Next is Ruby's passport, then two of Emma's – one of them current, the other expired, with the corner clipped off by the Passport Office.

I open the expired one, smiling in anticipation of an old photo of her I might not previously have seen, only to find the name and photo page ripped out. I flick through but there are no stamps. I return to the missing page. It's been done in an amateur way, with tears still visible, as if perhaps someone was in a hurry.

I check the photo page of the other passport: this one is definitely hers. EMMA MERRY BIGELOW.

I stare at the expired one. Is it Emma's? If so, why would she rip it up?

Slowly, tentatively, unease begins to snake through my veins. A large part of me is still quite sure there's a sensible explanation for this hidden bag of things, but I'm struggling to imagine what it would be.

I flick through a pile of Emma's industry achievements – acceptance letters from academic journals, a prize, fellowship and chair appointments.

Next there's a university section, from which I pull a piece of paper topped by the University of St Andrews crest. But this is a letter, not a degree certificate.

I start reading, *Dear Em—*, and then stop.

Partly because there's a blotch of black marker pen gouged through most of her name, which I'm surprised by, but mostly because I have a strong sense that this is where the line is. On one side there is trust in Emma, on the other, surveillance.

After a second, I carry on.

I have tried to make contact by phone but have been unable to reach you.

I can only reiterate what I said to your grandmother: I wholeheartedly encourage you to continue with your degree in Marine Biology, even if you feel unable to do so immediately. We would be delighted to welcome you back next academic year (or even the following year, if next September was too soon).

I should add that I was deeply saddened to learn of the challenges to your mental health that your grandmother described. I can only imagine how unappealing academic study might feel at this time. But many of us here in the department feel strongly that you have an excellent career in marine biology ahead of you, and will do anything we can to help you through the process of returning to the course.

Along with my colleagues I send you my very best wishes. Please do call or email at any point should you wish to discuss – now or at any time in the academic year.

Warmest regards,
Dr Ted Coombes
School of Biology

Before long, I find another University of St Andrews crest. I read this letter – also defaced by black marker pen, as if Emma couldn't bear to see her name there.

It is an official letter of discharge from the university, acknowledging Emma's permanent departure from her undergraduate degree. It requests that she destroy her student union card, and wishes her well. The date is November 2000, which I calculate as being the autumn term of her third and final year.

The dog is standing in the dining room doorway, watching me.

I try to think.

In one of the tidal deposits of Stuff on our landing, there is a picture of Emma on her graduation day. I adore it: her solemnity and defensive stance, the corner of a smile. There has never been any question that this is a picture of her graduating from St Andrews University.

I put down the paperwork and go upstairs to locate it. I find it quickly but, unlike mine, there's no information on it, no cardboard mount with the name of the university or department engraved. Just Emma, my lovely Emma, wearing a black academic gown with a light blue hood, trimmed with gold brocade. No mortarboard.

After a long wait, I go back down to the study and search online until I find the academic gown details for St Andrews undergraduates.

The page loads slowly. Outside, the foliage sways in a gust of wind and fists of ivy pound at the window. The house, warm and overloaded, creaks and sighs as the pixellated images clear.

St Andrews science undergraduates wear a purple hood trimmed with white fur. I scan the other categories – arts, postgraduate, education – but not one involves a light blue hood with gold trim. I look again, and again, until I have no option but to accept it: Emma did not graduate from this university.

I have the sensation of a shelf being removed from my abdomen.

John Keats, still watching me, thumps his tail against the armchair; a short rap of support, or perhaps warning – I'm not sure. I kneel down in front of him, staring into his deep amber eyes, and tell him that there must have been a misunderstanding, even though I don't see how there could have been.

Two whiskeys and six fig rolls down, I return to the paperwork in the dining room. There's no longer any excuse for my actions, but I have alcohol in my system and I'm too unsettled to care.

I pull the stack of papers out again, and split it open at random. The thrill of wrongdoing makes me fast and efficient: I'm once again the man who went hurtling through his parents' private papers, all those years ago, focused wholly on uncovering the truth.

I find myself reading a letter from the Naval Archdeaconry to Emma's father, telling him it was his last chance to write to them before they would have to start the process of dismissal.

I read it a couple of times but this makes no more sense than the letters from her university. Emma's father died in Zaire before this letter was even written.

Upstairs I hear what sounds like a child's foot on a grouchy floorboard, so I push the papers back into the M&S bag. But as I do, a smaller piece of paper – a compliment slip, bearing the BBC logo – pirouettes to the floor. On it, a handwritten note: *Hey doll, I'm sorry I missed you this morning. Call me. I don't want this to be goodbye . . . Robbie x*

I slide it back into the bag, and put the bag back where I found it.

In the kitchen, I drink another whiskey. All seems quiet now in Ruby's room, but my thoughts are layering too fast; I can't pause any of them long enough to interrogate them, let alone make sense of what I've just seen.

Without any real attempt to stop myself, I tiptoe into our bedroom and open Emma's laptop. We use each others' laptops all the time, but have never, would never – until now – do so for the purpose of spying. I don't even know what I'm looking for. Just that I want to find something that will halt this creeping anxiety.

She has fourteen tabs open, which is typical. The vast majority concern things like genetic population structure of weird-sounding decapod crustaceans, but there are three others: email, Facebook, and what appears to be a dispute with eBay about a parcel that never arrived.

I can't quite bring myself to look at her email, not yet. That feels like the ultimate betrayal, beaten only by looking at her phone.

Facebook is open, at her fan page. She has more than three thousand likes. There's nothing going on there, and I'm about to shut her laptop when a notification pops up with a message from someone called Iain Nott. *Ive sent u 4 msgs and no reply so bored of woman on tv thinking there superior would it hve really cost you so much to reply?*

Instantly angry, I open the message to compose a crushing response. But in doing so, I inadvertently open her inbox.

I nearly look away, for the same reason I didn't want to open her email, but I can't. It's full of messages from men.

I can see the first line of each message.

Mikey Vaillant: watching you on the iPlayer, minxy. You're

Erik Sueno: YOU LOOK NICE I WANT TO

Charlie Rod: Here's my number, please call me, I'd really

Iqbal Al-Jasmi: Hey girl

Skinny McSkinnyface: slag

Robbie Rosen: Hey doll, been thinking about you,

I stare at the screen for a long time.

Firstly, I want to know if the Robbie in this inbox is the same Robbie that wrote the note. Must be, surely – 'hey doll' is hardly a stranger's greeting. Who is he?

And I also want to know why she hasn't told me about all these messages. When I asked her last week she said she'd had a couple in the last few days, but there are six here – *six* – and these are just from today.

I'm torn between fury at these men, and shock that Emma hasn't told me about this. Why would she keep it to herself?

Why would she keep anything I've found this evening to herself?

I feel mildly dizzy. I delete all of today's messages and block the senders, but for each one I delete, another appears in its place, from previous days. I stop, snap her laptop shut and march myself downstairs, where I pour a final whiskey.

My mind cycles through a thousand scenarios, jumping from the university photo to the perverted men to the passport, the hiding of the papers, the handwritten note from some bloke at the BBC. Like Emma's Facebook messages, every time I feel I've ascribed an explanation to one discovery, there's another to account for, and my brain can't keep up.

I sit down and drink, until I hear a creak from Ruby's room.

'Daddy? Daddy . . .'

Chapter Nine

EMMA

I call Jill on the way home, to tell her I've just had dinner with her.

'I see. And what did we eat?' she asks. It sounds as if she has her mouth full. Jill has put on quite a lot of weight in the last few years. It worries me, but I could never bring it up – we both just pretend it's not there.

'Whatever you're eating now,' I tell her. 'That's what we ate.'

'I'm gnawing at a leftover chicken bone, like a hound.'

'Perfect.' I pull my cardigan around myself. It's cold for a June evening; an offensive wind swerves between the old houses of Hampstead Village, pushing down crooked alleyways. 'Let's say we went to that chicken place in King's Cross.'

'The waffle one?'

'Yes, perfect.'

'Might it be too much to ask that we actually go there together?' she asks. 'Soon? I haven't seen you since the late medieval period.'

'What? We had film night two weeks ago!'

'Fine. Early Tudor period.'

'Stuart period at minimum.'

Jill laughs. 'You're hard work, Emma.'

'Not as hard as you.'

The 268 whines slowly down Heath Street, buffeted by the wind. I clutch my handbag to myself for warmth and make a mental note to organise a real dinner for next week.

'How's work?' I ask. Jill now consults on deep sea fisheries and hates her boss.

There's a pause, while she swallows her chicken. Someone in a grossly expensive sports car roars needlessly up the hill. Jill says, 'I'm still planning to resign someday. But never mind that; are you OK?'

'I'm . . . No. Not OK.'

'I take it you went to see him?'

'Yes.'

'And?'

I hesitate. I don't want to talk about it with anyone, even my oldest friend, but Jill's had my back from the start. When we were just two students at St Andrews, heads full of foolish dreams, wallets empty of money, she saved me. Through the years that followed, she was there. And then, when I got myself into trouble during a trip to Northumberland four years ago, she not only covered for me with Leo but did a thirteen-hour round trip by car to rescue me. No matter what ditch I fall in, Jill has always been there to pull me out.

The least I can do is tell her about tonight.

'As difficult as you'd expect,' I say. 'Worse, possibly. Some awkward small talk, followed by a very uncomfortable conversation about his wife.'

There's an intake of breath down the line. 'Really? What did he say about her?'

'Mostly just grilling me. He was obsessed with the idea that I'd been in touch with her. I told him I wouldn't dream of it, but I'm not sure he believed me.' I hold my hand out in front of me. It's shaking again.

'What makes you think he didn't believe you?' Jill asks. 'Was he angry?'

I think about this for a moment. Not angry, exactly, but I was frightened, sitting opposite him. He was intense; all over the place – it had felt like an interrogation, not a conversation. I had plenty of fears of my own about the situation, but I hadn't dared voice them.

I try to explain this to Jill, but it's difficult to convey.

Tap, tap, tap. My boots hit cooled paving stones; a chocolate wrapper skitters down the hill. I turn off Heath Street and up a narrow lane.

'I'm so sorry.' Jill's voice is pained. 'I hoped it might be more positive.'

I sigh. 'It's my fault. I should never have agreed to meet him.'

'But how could you not? You've been beside yourself with worry. Oh, Emma. I can't stand it for you.'

'Bless you. Thank you. I can't stand it either – I didn't get to ask any of the questions I wanted to ask.'

'But did it help?' she asks, after a tactful pause. 'For you, I mean?'

'No,' I say firmly. Then: 'Maybe.' Then: 'No.' Then: 'Oh, shit. I just don't know. I feel crazy. I'm going to try and get an emergency appointment with my therapist tomorrow.'

'Well, I'm here if your therapist can't fit you in,' she says, as I knew she would. 'Why don't we meet for lunch near your work tomorrow? I need to spend a few hours at the British Library, I'll even be in the area.'

'Ah, that's a lovely idea, but I can't. I've a meeting with one of my PhD students from twelve thirty til two.'

'Cancel it,' she says, immediately. 'You need some space to process this, Emma. You meeting up with him is huge.'

I promise to think about it. I value Jill's company greatly – a night on her sofa with a bottle of wine and a power ballad playlist on loud is one of life's great tonics. The problem is that our entire relationship has been shaped by the catastrophic wreckage of my early twenties, and there's no hiding, when I'm with her. Sometimes I don't want to lean into all that pain; I prefer to just pretend it's not there.

'The main thing that came out of tonight is that there's no way forward,' I say. 'He might have been a mess, but he was abundantly clear that he won't be coming to any sort of "arrangement" with me. Apart from all the usual reasons he said it would be a betrayal, and he's done with betraying his wife. All he wanted was to find out if I'd been in touch with her.'

'Oh, Emma.'

'I think he's probably going to cut off contact again.'

'Mmm,' she says, quietly. 'I wouldn't bank on that.'

'No, seriously. I think we're done. For good, this time. Which means I'm going to have to go back to sitting on my hands. Thinking about it every bloody day, never really moving on. But at least I know, Jill. At least I can just get on with loving my family.'

We end the call soon after, because I can't turn up in this state. I'm not sure Leo is Jill's biggest fan, but even he knows I'd never come home in tears after a dinner with her.

If you're an organism living in the intertidal zone, you face a life of extremes: scorching sun or icy submersion; salinity stress, crashing waves, frenzied coastal winds – it's one of the most perilous environments in nature, my tutor Ted told us, in our very first seminar. If you think you've got it hard, imagine life as a limpet!

It's a line that both Jill and I have never quite forgotten, so when Jill texts *Hang on in there, little limpet!* a few minutes later, I smile. *Managing two separate lives is herculean by anyone's standards, especially when you've just finished months of cancer treatment. But, my friend, you are tougher than you know.*

She messages a third time as I turn into the alley that cuts through to my road. *And I'm here if you're ever feeling less than tough.*

I delete this and all of the evening's messages. To be extra sure, I go into my contacts and rename the man who has once again broken my heart as 'Sally'.

I see him as soon as I emerge from the alley.

A male figure. Standing in the street in front of our little terrace, looking at our house.

I stop dead. Neither of our neighbours have any lights on and Leo, as usual, has left on every light in every room. But, irrespective of the lights, I know instinctively that he's there for us. For me.

I drop back into the alley and peer around, clutching my bag. He's wearing a baseball cap, under which long-ish hair spills out at the back. Tall. Rangey, I'd say, although he's wearing a lightweight parka and it's hard to tell. I can only see the side of his face, and it's too dark to make out much detail – but I don't think this is anyone I know; anyone with a good reason to be visiting my house at this time of night.

I pull back again and get out my phone to call Leo, fingers fumbling. Is Leo safe inside? Ruby? I peer round one final time before calling, just as the man turns and gets into a small car, parked next to mine.

He drives off, turning left down Frognal Rise.

I wait for a long time, but he doesn't return.

I remember the man outside my work at Plymouth. Same

build, same baseball cap low over his face. Fear worms in my chest.

Is it the same person?

I scroll through my mental Rolodex of the men who've messaged me lately on Facebook, but it's been several days since I looked at my inbox and besides, none of them use real photos.

After a long wait, I leave the alleyway and run towards the house, heart in my mouth.

As I reach the gate, I see something yellow lashed to next door's front gate. Something angular, fixed – I stop in the middle of the street. It's a For Sale sign.

Of course. They told us last month they were putting their house on the market.

I allow myself to smile. The man was just looking at a house he'd seen online. Nothing more. There are many millions of baseball-cap-wearing men in the world. The weirdo in Plymouth, hundreds of miles away, has nothing to do with this man – this perfectly innocent man, who could quite feasibly end up being my new neighbour.

I slide my phone back into my bag and stand at the bottom of the steps up to our miniature front garden, waiting for my breathing to slow down. There'll probably be a stream of people coming to stare at the house in the coming days, before viewings begin. I'd better get used to it.

Then it comes to me, suddenly – perhaps because I'm already primed for threat, perhaps because it's so unusual – that our dining room light is on too, along with all the others. Leo's been in there.

My heart starts racing again. Why?

Because he needed to find something of his.

Because Ruby went in there before bed.

For any one of a million reasons, none of which involve

him climbing across stacks of Granny's stuff to find the papers I hid last week, which he couldn't possibly know were missing because he doesn't even know they exist.

But I must get them out of there, I realise now. Out of the house. I should never have kept them under our roof in the first place: even with my cupboard locked, it was never worth the risk.

I'm going to have to do something about this whole hoarding business. I think Leo's right.

Tomorrow morning, before Leo and Ruby come down, I'll put it all in my bag and take it to work. I'll lock it in my drawer until I can bring myself to throw it all out, which I should have done years ago. Those stupid things, those testaments to the final moments of my old life: they could destroy everything I hold dear now. What was the point?

As I open the front door I can hear Leo talking to Ruby, who's recently started arriving downstairs at ten o'clock, claiming she's been awake since bedtime. (She never has.) I imagine my little girl right now, pink-cheeked with the sleep she claims not to have had, negotiating hard with her beloved daddy.

Ruby is at the centre of my universe. I'd die for her, immediately, and without quibble – but that makes no difference, I realise, in the context of where I've been this evening. Of the papers hidden deep in the expanse of my grandmother's haphazard archives.

He's still there. He will always be there, and there will never be any resolution, for me, because he is the love of my life.

The love of my other life, I remind myself, tiredly, but that refrain is losing power now, and my heart knows it.

Chapter Ten

LEO

Emma was sitting across the aisle at her grandmother's funeral in Falmouth, the first time I saw her. I remember her voice hitting all the wrong notes during the congregational hymns and her not seeming to care; her laughter as she recounted her grandmother's predilection for handsome young men. She had short, curly hair that she tucked behind her ears, and a yellow felt coat, and in that church full of winter black she was like a bright torch.

After they buried Gloria, Emma broke off to watch the gig boats racing across the Fal estuary. There was a strong north-easterly wind, scrambling in over the hills behind St Mawes, and she looked straight into it as it caught her hair and gusted it up and away from her face. I thought about the yellow coat that Jess, my ex-girlfriend, had bought once, wanting to spice up her wardrobe, and how it had never really worked. I remembered the night she asked me if I still loved her and I said yes and then woke her up at 1 a.m. to say, actually, I'm so sorry, but I don't.

I watched this woman, on whom a yellow coat looked perfect, and hoped she wasn't smiling about a lover.

Then I felt bad, because this was her grandmother's funeral.

*

The problem was, I'd fallen for Emma before even seeing her in the flesh.

I can cover any kind of obituary, but my specialty is politicians. This is largely because I spent a while on the politics desk before moving to obits, so it was assumed that my Westminster knowledge was heavy-duty. (It's adequate.)

It was actually an undertaker who alerted us to Gloria Bigelow's death, which tends only to happen when the deceased doesn't have much by way of a family. I'd heard of her, a rare female MP in 1950s London, fond of backbench tirades, but she'd been absent from political life so long that nobody had thought to write an advance obit.

I'd called Gloria's granddaughter, Emma, to ask for a few details. We spoke for more than two hours. By the end of the phone call, I was intoxicated.

She invited me to the funeral, which, again, is not something that happens often – and something we invariably decline when it does, especially if the funeral in question is all the way down in bloody Cornwall – but I said yes, because I had to meet her. I even went to Soho at 9 p.m. to get a haircut at one of those cheap late-night barbers.

I was late to the funeral service – I barely made it through the door in front of her grandmother's casket – so I didn't get to talk to Emma until the reception at the Greenbank Hotel, where I engineered a meeting by the sandwich buffet.

'Hello. I'm Emma Bigelow,' Emma said, sticking out her hand. Somehow, I managed to introduce myself as Gloria.

'Really?' Her hand had paused above the egg mayonnaises. 'I felt you must be Leo.'

'Oh fuck. Yes. Leo.'

She laughed. 'I wouldn't put it past my grandmother to fake her own death and then turn up in disguise at the funeral.'

‘Really?’

‘Absolutely. It would be just her cup of tea.’

I picked up a bottle of red and topped up her glass, determined to make her stay.

She did, but a lot of other people wanted to talk to her. For a long time I stood next to her by the sandwiches, watching her talk to politicians, friends, even, to my surprise, an ex-prime minister.

‘Granny had it off with him a few times,’ Emma said, as the man walked away. I stared at her. ‘Hated him, hated his politics, but he was an animal in bed; she couldn’t resist him.’

‘I don’t believe you,’ I said, eventually. ‘No, you’re pulling my leg.’

After a while, she laughed. ‘OK. As you like it.’

A man with a sumptuous beard came over to talk to Emma about his days conducting the amateur orchestra Gloria had played in for more than twenty years. ‘She was terrible,’ he said, fondly. ‘Quite literally never stopped talking. Never practised. But she played beautifully; I couldn’t throw her out even if I’d wanted to.’

Emma nodded, proudly. ‘My grandmother was terrible in so many ways.’

I leaned against the wall, listening to them talk, compiling a mental list of the adjectives I’d use if I were writing Emma’s obituary. Formidable and mesmeric, I chose, eventually. She was a force of nature.

I went to the gents at some point, and saw in the mirror that my tongue was stained purple. I tried to scrape it clean. ‘Emma,’ I said to my reflection. ‘Emma, I would like to take you out for a drink.’

Of course I said no such thing, but we talked for hours, long past the point at which the other guests had left. The hotel staff laid up for dinner around us, and the winter sun shot flames through the estuary water.

She told me she lived in Plymouth but was going to be down here for another week: she was a marine ecologist, and had agreed to help with an estuarine creek study one of her colleagues ran. Something involving suspended particulate matter and biogeochemical compounds in the Fal River creeks.

I did not know what this meant, but I liked the idea of her in a hazmat suit, taking perilous samples from a deadly river and storing them in cryogenically sealed containers.

When I shared this with her, she roared with laughter and said she would most likely be wearing wellies and fingerless gloves – 'But I'll track down a space suit if you prefer.'

She was flirting with me, I realised.

I displayed such an insatiable interest in coastal ecology as the evening wore on that Emma invited me to join a creek-side walk she'd been asked to lead the following morning. It was in Devoran, a nearby village with an old quay and 'fascinating wildlife'.

Around us the boat masts clanked under a darkening sky. I had a ticket for the train back to London that night, and nowhere to stay in Cornwall, but I said yes.

'I'm staying in a yurt while I'm down here,' Emma announced, as the hotel staff finally flushed us out with bright lights. I had no idea what, if anything, she was trying to convey. (In fact, I had no idea what a yurt even was. I was unaware of the middle-class predilection for glamping, and I'd never been to Central Asia.) 'My dog's staying with me, too. His name's Frogman.'

We walked the length of the hotel's little pier. The air was painfully cold now, and the water a deep black story. I tried to imagine a dog called Frogman.

'I've loved talking to you,' she said, suddenly, and I heard a bashfulness in her voice that made me wonder if 'formidable' had been an unfair descriptor.

'I've mildly enjoyed it,' I shrugged.

She smiled.

I smiled.

She pulled the yellow coat tightly around herself. 'I'll see you at Devoran Quay, ten a.m.,' she said, and left.

I booked into the Greenbank, which was beyond my pay grade at the time, and lay in bed, replaying Emma's stories about her work, and about her grandmother. The next day, I called in sick and went on the nature walk. Nobody else turned up; it was just Emma, me and Frogman, an overwrought terrier.

Emma strode along the edge of silvered mudflats in a long skirt and wellies, damp seaweed bladders crackling underfoot, her commentary gilded by the cry of wader birds. She picked samples of pennywort and sea spinach for me to eat, humming tunelessly under her breath. She taught me about mud worms and slime tubes, pollutants and litter, weeds and waders, and she had brought soup in a flask, which was lucky, because I hadn't thought as far ahead as lunch. (This sort of thing still annoys her now.)

It took me hours to register that she'd only brought two soup cups. That there was no 'Nature Walk' poster on the tree at the top of the quay, even though there were posters for just about everything else. Even then, I couldn't quite believe she might have made the whole thing up to engineer another meeting.

And yet – and yet – 'Of course there wasn't a Nature Walk!' she said, when I asked how often she did this. 'I just wanted to see you again!' She laughed, watching me, and slid one of her hands out of its fingerless glove. It stayed on her lap.

'That was devious,' I said, eventually. I folded my arms and fixed my eyes on hers.

There was no way I was touching that hand. Not yet.

We sat on the bench in silence, sipping soup, until the shadows lengthened and the cold air began to sting. Then we went back to her yurt, where she had a hairdryer and straighteners and a fridge for gin and tonic. ('I'm not on a spiritual retreat here,' she said, when she caught me looking.) She told me about her father dying before she went to university, about the years she'd spent living with her grandmother in Hampstead. She sat close to me on the sofa, often looking me straight in the eye, her face inches from mine.

We talked until, eventually, I couldn't take another moment. I reached out and traced a finger down the side of her face, down her neck, and she shivered under my fingertip.

We sat in absolute stillness, staring at each other.

'God,' she said. 'You're lovely.'

'I am,' I agreed. I felt as if I might have a stroke if this didn't happen soon.

She looked away. 'The thing is, I'm . . . not lovely.'

I thought about this for a moment. 'I'd like to dispute that.'

She studied me for a while, and said, 'Oh.' She seemed uncertain.

'I have to be honest, Emma. I would not be here, in a yurt, in a field, in the middle of the night, with nowhere to stay, and my boss sending pointed messages about my "food poisoning", if I thought you were unlovely.'

'Oh,' she said again. 'Well, that's nice. But you see, the thing is . . .'

'The thing?'

She sighed. 'There is a thing. Not a huge thing. Well, a mid-size thing . . .'

'You're in a relationship?'

'No! Of course not!'

I looked around the yurt, full of books and pots and bits of what looked like laboratory equipment. Frogman watched me. How could a woman this clever, this funny, this beautiful not be with someone?

'Are you sure?' I asked.

She picked up my hand and took it back to her cheek, closing her eyes for a moment as it touched her skin. 'I'm sure. It's just that I . . . that I . . . I'm complicated.'

I laughed. 'Luckily, I'm very simple.'

She laughed, too. 'I like you,' she said, and then leaned in and kissed me.

The tenderness of it. The sense I had of everything changing, as we came to lie on the bed, taking off clothes, at first slowly, then faster, faster.

In the months that followed I returned to that conversation from time to time. I wondered why this woman, who seemed so open and willing to love, would have described herself as complicated. What was it she had been trying to say? I asked her a couple of times, but she just said that she had a long history of relationship-sabotage. 'I won't sabotage this one, though,' she said, and I believed her.

How could I not? She told me all the time that she was madly in love. She wanted to move to London to be with me more. Even though her career belonged on the coast, and she taught at Plymouth University, she managed to get a second job at UCL, lecturing aquatic conservation postgrads on estuarine and coastal ecology. She cut down her Plymouth work to two days per week and put in long hours on trains and the M4. All for me.

She suggested we sell my flat in Stepney Green and her

place in Plymouth, and that we make her grandmother's house our home. She mentioned having children. And it was she who proposed marriage, one night in a Turkish restaurant in Haringay, over a bottle of crap wine we'd bought at the all-night shop next door.

'Marry me,' she blurted, just as I put a large forkful of ali nazak into my mouth.

I stopped chewing.

'What?'

'Leo! You can't say "what!" I just asked you to marry me!'

I downed my glass of water, to clear the aubergine. 'And you can't just ask me to marry you when I'm eating a kebab.'

'Why not?'

'Because you can't!'

'Well,' she said, 'I just did.'

We sat across the table from each other, defiant.

'Are you serious?' I asked eventually, because I always crumbled first. I still do.

She started laughing. 'I am. I just wanted to get it over with.'

I picked up my wine glass. 'You "just wanted to get it over with?"'

She was shaking with laughter. 'Yes. I – sorry . . .'

And then I was laughing too. I couldn't drink my wine at all. 'You're unbelievable,' I said. 'Is this actually happening?'

'I'm afraid so. I love you more than anything else in the world, Leo, and I never thought I'd want to get married but I do; I want desperately to be able to call you my husband. So please say yes.'

We both stopped laughing and stared at each other, just like that first night we spent together.

'Yes,' I said quietly, and joy spread through me like a sunrise. 'Yes.'

She got out of her chair, climbed into my lap and kissed me, then hid her face in my neck. 'Sorry,' she whispered. 'It lacked finesse. But I couldn't wait a moment longer. I love you. I love you. I love you so much, Leo.'

She gave me a ring made of plastic and we carried on eating our cold kebabs and drinking our warm wine, and I had never in my life been so happy.

There was nothing to arouse suspicion. No sign of secrets kept or information withheld. When she sank into the first of her Times I had no reason to suspect that there was anything going on, beyond the fact that she suffered from depression. And who wouldn't, if they'd lost both parents before leaving school?

Now we lie in bed together, hours after her return from dinner with Jill. Emma is fast asleep, I am awake and overstrung. I find myself returning to that first conversation, that red flag she waved, which I was too love-blind to reach out and grab. Why didn't I heed it? Or at least question her further?

There's a part of me that still hopes this is a misunderstanding; an overreaction, perhaps, but my gut doesn't believe it to be either. My gut thinks: she hid papers somewhere she thought you'd never look. And at least half of them didn't add up. She's got a bunch of men harassing her on Facebook and she hasn't said a thing to you. None of this feels innocent.

Ruby had come downstairs before I had a chance to go back to the green shopping bag, and then Emma came home.

What else is in there? What else do I not know about my wife?

Uncertainty hovers like bad weather out at sea. I either admit to my trespass into her hidden corners, or I watch, and wait, and hope it'll blow in a different direction.

Neither feels right.

Chapter Eleven

LEO

Ruby is using apple juice to arrange her mother's sparse new hair into tiny spikes. 'I'm turning Mummy into a monster,' she tells me. 'One of the bad ones which is dangerous and poisonous.'

'You are,' I agree. 'It actually really suits her.' And then, apropos of nothing, I look at Emma and say, 'St Andrews undergraduates wear purple for their ceremony, not blue.'

We've taken Ruby to an outdoor Tom Jones concert at Kenwood House, with my brother, Olly, and his family. Olly and Tink have two untameable young boys. Oskar is being yelled at in Norwegian by his mother because he has climbed the scaffolding sound tower in the middle of the audience, and the Kenwood House Event Security Team are now in attendance. His younger brother, Mikkel, is missing, so Olly and I have been running around calling his name. The Kenwood House Event Security Team are in attendance on this matter too.

I just stopped at our picnic blanket to check Mikkel hadn't returned, but found only Emma and Ruby eating quiche and singing the *Sesame Street* song.

Emma frowns at me from under Ruby's hands. 'Sorry? St Andrews what?'

'St Andrews students graduate in a purple hood, not blue,' I repeat, slightly breathless. I drop down to sit on my heels, half looking at her, half scanning around for Mikkel.

'I don't understand,' Emma says.

It's been three days since I found the paperwork from her Folder of Important Bits hidden in a corner of the dining room.

Every night since, I've opened my mouth to confront her as I've climbed into bed. But every night, at that very moment, she has rolled into me and slid a sleepy hand around my middle, and I've been too afraid to jackhammer the night – and, quite possibly, us – wide open.

But this is the problem: Emma hasn't told a harmless lie, nor have I misunderstood what I saw. She has deliberately misled me about her university education. Why would she do that? Why would anyone do that? If it were just this that I'd discovered, I'd be surprised. A little shocked. But it's not just the university thing. It's everything.

Ruby's trying to comb the spikes out of her mother's hair with sticky fingers, and Emma flinches. 'That hurts!'

'I apolgise,' Ruby says solemnly, before resuming. I will be sad when she learns to say this word properly.

Emma reaches round and bundles Ruby onto her lap. 'You're a tyrant. Kiss me now.'

Is Emma trying to distract me?

In the distance, I see my brother dragging Mikkel through the patchwork of picnickers. Thankfully, he's taking him to join the fracas with his elder son at the sound tower.

'It was your graduation photo that caught my eye,' I say. I sound peevish. 'In the photo you're wearing a blue and gold hood. Whereas St Andrews' colours are purple with white fur. I noticed the other night, and I've been feeling a bit confused about it.'

Emma offers Ruby a Tupperware of breadsticks and some green-coloured dip. 'Really? Well, they can't have been purple when I graduated. I wore whatever the academic outfitters said I had to wear.'

Ruby inserts a breadstick carefully into my ear.

'Sorry, Leo. I don't understand; why is my graduation photo a thing?'

'Because I . . . When did you graduate from St Andrews?'

'You know when I graduated! 2001.'

The support act has finished, and the cascades of speakers flanking the stage spill funk while men in black get the stage ready for Sir Tom. Olly, Tink and, thankfully, both boys are heading in our direction. The crowd are swarming to the toilets and the bar; those left behind are packing up picnics, ready to stand and dance.

'I nearly didn't make it,' she says, suddenly. 'I had a grief blackout about my parents at the end of my second year; I nearly quit my course. But I managed to reverse the process before they physically removed me from campus.'

There's another pause, while I try to decide whether or not I believe her. Behind her, the sky lies in stripes of soft blue and magenta.

'And as for the robes, I haven't the faintest idea, Leo. Surely their colours change, over the years?'

What she's saying makes sense. If I'd had more time with her Folder of Important Bits, I might have found yet another letter from St Andrews accepting her back onto her course. And I could call the university, or even the academic outfitters, and ask if the colours for the Bachelor of Science have changed over the years. Christ, I could call Jill if I really wanted to, and ask if Emma finished her degree.

But the unsettling truth is that I don't want to. What if I

find out she's misled me? Now, after I've given her a chance to put it right?

I found out I was adopted by mistake. A few weeks after we met, I'd proudly taken Emma up to Hitchin to meet my parents, and during lunch I'd gone up to the spare room to get some old photo or trinket; I can't remember what. Mum and Dad's bedroom was being recarpeted, so the spare room was full of boxes that normally lived under their bed. I saw a folder labelled LEO – BABY STUFF and opened it, because why wouldn't I? I expected photos, maybe a hospital wristband, a cardboard envelope of pliant baby hair.

Instead, I found my birth certificate, with the name ANNA WILSON for 'mother' and 'UNKNOWN' for 'father'. My parents, sitting downstairs, were called Jane and Barry Philber.

I'll never forget my search through the rest of the folder: the adoption paperwork, the endless local authority correspondence and – shockingly – a letter from an agency, asking if my birth mother could contact me. Told them no, someone had written on it.

Told them no.

I remember the sound of the ice cream van pulling up at the park; the benign tick of my parents' clock. I remember recognising fury in the glutinous mass of thoughts as I considered the task ahead of me. I didn't want to smash apart my foundations and start excavating. I wanted Jane and Barry Philber to be my mum and dad.

With hindsight, however, I've come to see that the most agonising thing about that day was the jolt of recognition I felt as I tore through the adoption paperwork. It had never crossed my mind that I might not fully belong in that family, and yet –

in my heart, my nervous system, somewhere, everywhere – I had known. Those papers had simply legitimised my lifelong feeling of non-belonging.

I drove Emma down the M1 in shattered silence. 'You deserved better, Leo,' she said, when we got back to London. There were tears in her eyes as she closed her arms around my clenched body. 'So much better.'

'Where's Tom Jones?' Oskar asks, humphing down onto the picnic rug. He bitterly objects to discipline, especially when a security team is involved. 'Uncle Leo, will you teach me one of his songs?'

I smile. 'I'm sorry,' I say to Emma, and I open the cool box. 'What you're saying makes perfect sense.' She shrugs, as if to say it doesn't matter at all. 'I think I'll teach you "Sex Bomb",' I tell an appalled Oskar. 'And I'm getting your parents a beer, which they're going to need after your shabby behaviour.'

My brother sits down next to me. He's angry. I pass him a beer, wordlessly, and put a hand on his shoulder. Oskar makes a lunge for the beer, something Olly would normally find funny, but today he just snatches it away and says, 'Seriously, Oskar. Don't push it.'

Emma and I sit in awkward silence while Olly and Tink bicker about who's to blame for what just happened.

Ruby climbs into my lap. 'I love you, Daddy,' she says. 'Except when you're stinky.'

'I love you too,' I smile, kissing her hair. 'Except when you're stinky. But you've been very good this afternoon. Thank you.'

'Seriously?' Olly snaps, turning round. He's talking to me.

'Seriously what?'

'Are you really praising your compliant child when mine are behaving like delinquents, again?'

He's not joking. Oskar and Mikkel have kept their parents close to the edge for many years: I think Olly may finally have boiled over.

'Olly,' I say, carefully. 'Olly, Ruby's three. She's been here for two hours without complaining or running away. You must remember the boys being three. You must remember what an achievement that is. It was no reflection on you or your children.'

'Fine,' he says. He's furious. 'Whatever.'

'"Whatever?" Olly! Stop it! This is not a thing!'

'Don't provoke me and then play innocent,' Olly says. 'It's offensive.'

Without warning, Emma cuts in. 'Olly, stop being an arsehole,' she says, loudly. We both turn around. She's looking straight at my brother, cheeks reddening.

'Sorry?' Olly wasn't expecting this.

'I said, stop being an arsehole.' Emma continues to look straight at him. Her voice lowers. 'Leo's just run round half of Hampstead Heath looking for Mikkel, who he loves, and who he's never once judged, just like he's never judged you as parents. You know that, Olly, so will you please stop using him as a scapegoat.'

Everyone, even Ruby, is silent. Oskar watches his father with fascination.

After a weighted pause, Olly nods. 'You're right,' he says. I can't believe what I'm hearing.

He turns to me. 'Sorry, mate. That was out of order.'

'Apologies,' Emma whispers, a few minutes later, when Olly and Tink are talking to their boys. 'You're more than capable of fighting your own battles. I didn't mean to belittle you.'

I study her face. 'What would you have done if he hadn't backed down? Were you going to swing a right hook?'

She shrugs. 'If I'd had to. I won't allow Olly or anyone else to treat you like that.'

At this I laugh. Emma has always been ferociously defensive of me; comically so at times. I put my arm around her, as the looped fairy lights begin to glow and the audience begins to chant for Sir Tom.

'You are the best person I know,' I tell my wife, and I mean it.

Ruby lies across our laps and tells us it's time for a sleep.

I choose to believe what Emma's said about her graduation photo. I choose to believe there is a perfectly reasonable explanation for her removal of her papers to the dining room, and that the confusing things I found were confusing only because I wasn't seeing them in context.

My wife is everything I have always believed her to be. She loves me, I love her, and to allow myself to go searching for dark corners would be to betray all that is good in the life we have created together.

Chapter Twelve

EMMA

'Time for ice cream,' Ruby calls, as I root around amongst whorls of hair and dust under a trampoline. I took her to the gymnastics club for the morning, but mostly it's been me bouncing up and down while she shouts feedback. Now Duck has been posted through some trampoline springs.

'OK,' I call. Above me, an enormous dad jumps onto the trampoline and I have to flatten myself against the floor. Quickly, I get Duck and commando-roll out. 'OK. Ice cream.'

Ruby grabs Duck and kisses his velvety beak hard.

Unbidden, the whispers about Leo rise inside me again, as I lead my daughter over to the shoe rack. I'm not sure he believed my story about the academic gowns, but I was too blindsided to think of anything better.

What tipped him off?

For a terrible moment I thought he'd found my paperwork in the dining room, so I improvised something about 'nearly-but-not-quite' leaving St Andrews. But Leo is honourable, almost pathologically so – it's one of many things I admire about him – and even if he had somehow found that pile of papers, he wouldn't read them.

Ruby sticks out her feet so I can put her shoes on, and I find myself too tired to insist she has a go at doing it herself.

It was always my intention to tell Leo. That first night we spent together in my friend Casey's yurt, I was desperate to tell him. But I held back, as I lay with him afterwards. I held back, and promised myself I'd leave it a few weeks.

Then Leo discovered that his parents had adopted him. A few days later, during a furious phone call with them, it got worse: Jane admitted that Leo's birth mother had in fact died of heart disease two years ago. He couldn't even meet her.

As I held him through the dark knots of that time, it became clear that I couldn't tell him about my past. Not then, when he was already contending with so much – and, perhaps, not ever. I started seeing a therapist, who, to this day, remains the only person other than Jill who knows everything, and she encouraged me to review the situation once things had calmed down in Leo's own life. We agreed that the end of the year felt about right.

And so nine months later, I looked sincerely at my boyfriend – by then my fiancé – and I knew, with crystalline certainty, that I could not tell him. Not because too much time had passed, but because I knew him well enough by then to know he wouldn't be able to cope with it, no matter how hard he tried. Not just my revelations, but the fact I'd kept the truth from him in the first place. That, for Leo, in the aftermath of his parents' dishonesty, would be the ultimate betrayal.

I crashed out of St Andrews University in the autumn term of 2000, aged twenty, and didn't resume study until I was twenty-three. I chose the Open University second time around. They didn't teach marine biology, but I was happy to make do with straight biology – it would be enough to get me into a master's somewhere. I hadn't the stomach for the things I'd loved first time round: freshers' week, halls of residence, earnest late-night pigeon politics with someone wailing Jeff Buckley in the corner.

I hadn't the stomach for any human company, beyond that of my grandmother. I studied alone, either in the British Library or in bed, and when I was done I booked a graduation ceremony in Birmingham, because Granny had said she hadn't been there in ages and would love to go for a night. When my graduation day rolled around, though, she was ill, so I graduated alone. But I still scanned the congregation when I stepped down from the stage with my certificate, like a solo traveller in the arrivals hall of an airport: that absurd hope we hold, as humans, that we're not alone, even when all the evidence tells us we are.

For a split second I actually thought I saw him – Dad – a head of close-cropped hair in one of the side tiers, a face in shadow. But it was someone else's father, sitting next to someone else's mother, clapping someone that wasn't me.

I had my allocated one celebratory drink on the top floor of the foyer at Birmingham Symphony Hall, with a kind woman from the alumni development stand. She asked me what my plan was now. I drained my wine and told her my first port of call would be to change my name.

She'd raised her glass. 'Good for you!' Then: 'I'm sorry?'

'I'm going to change my name,' I repeated. It was the first alcohol I'd had in a long time. I noticed someone had discarded half a burger in the plant pot next to us. 'I'm going to call myself Emma Merry Bigelow. Bigelow is my Granny's name and she's fierce. And Merry – well, I'd like to be more merry. I don't ever want to think about my old name again. OK, well, have a good afternoon. It was kind of you to come over.'

And off I went, through a deserted convention centre and

down to a canal, where I wandered for hours next to the still water, silver birch leaves fanning weightlessly across the path.

My phone rings as I shepherd Ruby across the trampoline club car park. Ruby notices my frenzied scrabble for the handset, but doesn't say anything.

It's Leo's mother. She often calls when Leo hasn't replied quickly enough to her text messages, and it's always on a Wednesday, because she knows I don't work on Wednesdays.

'Jane!' I cry, hand on chest. I have to try to calm down. He's not going to call: he said no contact, and he meant it.

'Oh, Emma, good. How are you? I just wanted to let you know that Barry came down with flu on Sunday,' she says, without stopping to hear how I am. 'Proper flu, he's very unwell indeed.' Her voice is taut and I know straight away what this is really about.

I tuck my phone into my shoulder and strap Ruby in, mouthing silently to my daughter that, yes, we are going to go and get an ice cream. Above us the sky is pale and troubled; the breeze is spiny with the promise of more rain.

I get into the driver's seat after the call ends, just as my phone buzzes again.

'Dear God, Jane,' I sigh, picking it up.

'Dear God, Jane,' Ruby sighs, in the back.

It isn't Jane.

I need to see you again, says a notification on my screen. After a pause, I swipe it open.

Please, he writes, in a second message.

'Mummy. Mummy! ICE CREAM.'

I scrabble around and find Ruby a copy of *The Marine Professional*. 'Here.' I hand it to her. 'I think you should learn about conger eels.'

'OK,' Ruby agrees, but only because I've taken her by surprise. I have maybe thirty seconds before I need to start driving in the direction of an ice cream.

We agreed there was nothing more to say, I write. *Why do you need to see me?*

He starts a response. I wait.

He replies: *I'm going up to Northumberland next week. I need to sort through some things in the cottage. We could meet up there, if you're nervous about getting together in London.*

I close my eyes. Yes. No. Yes. No.

I have a conference in Newcastle next week. It would be easy. Less than an hour's drive.

But Leo. Ruby. My promise.

Chapter Thirteen

LEO

'Leo, can I have a word?' someone asks. I look up: it's Jim McGuigan, our editor-in-chief, dropping breezily into Kelvin's chair. He's a disconcertingly energetic man.

The rest of the team are at lunch. 'Of course.' I save my work. I'm writing up a cold war double agent one of our readers tipped us off about earlier. He recently died in Moscow after a successful retirement hustle importing Jaffa Cakes and Yorkshire Tea.

'It's regarding a piece you wrote,' Jim says. 'About Janice Rothschild.'

'Oh?'

Patrick, the charming man who runs the Court and Social desk, pauses his typing so he can listen in. Jim gestures for us to duck into the meeting room across the walkway for some privacy.

I follow.

I was asked by one of our weekend supplements to write a short feature about Janice, which they published a few days ago – nothing that sounded like an obit, of course, just a look at her life and career to date. She's still all over the news; there's been no sighting of her and the police appear to have drawn a blank. Readers want to hear more about her life.

We receive complaints all the time on the obits desk, mostly because grieving relatives frequently believe it's our role to nurture their loved one's personal propaganda machine. When we don't write a misty-eyed hagiography, and instead publish a truthful account of the deceased – crime, bigotry, sexual misdemeanours and all – they tend to send furious letters. But the Janice feature I wrote last week is unequivocally positive, and the piece was well received online. I'm surprised someone's objected.

'It was actually Jeremy Rothschild who complained,' Jim says, as I sit down at the empty meeting table. 'He was upset that you included the story of Janice leaving the psychiatric unit after they had their son.'

I frown.

He frowns back, with Senior Management steel.

One of the first things I did when writing this feature was to go back to the piece I found in our archive. It was very short – no more than a few photos of Jeremy and Janice leaving a psychiatric unit for mothers and babies, and a caption saying exactly that. The paper that published the photos has no morals, but they're protected by an army of lawyers and they were smart enough not to speculate. The photos are more than enough to suggest Janice suffered a psychiatric emergency after giving birth.

I referred to this in the feature, of course. It would have been negligent not to mention a previous mental health crisis when she's disappeared into thin air, and besides, the pictures are in the public domain – they're hardly a secret. I'm quite sure other newspapers have found and written about them.

I say as much to Jim.

He nods, as if he understands, but says, 'The photographs were devastating for her at the time – for both of them. Jeremy felt it was an insensitive inclusion at a time like this.'

I cannot believe I'm hearing this from a newspaper editor.

'Are you telling me you'd want me to cover it up?' I ask, after a pause.

Jim seems to have some sort of conflict with himself before shaking his head. 'No. Of course not. To be honest, I'm as surprised as you about this. I suppose he must just be in a bad place – not thinking rationally. But he's a good friend.'

Of course. They're probably members of some expensive club, somewhere; them and the rest of modern journalism's top tier. I notice how scuffed my shoes are. Jim is wearing very nice brogues.

'I was straight with him,' Jim says. 'I told him that a retraction or apology would be out of the question. But I do think someone else should write the obituary, if Janice turns out to have . . . passed.'

I smile, briefly. Obituary writers are probably the only people on earth who aren't afraid to say dead or died. It can be quite a sport watching other people flounder around with words like *passing* and *loss*.

'We haven't done anything wrong,' Jim says. 'You haven't done anything wrong – if it's the truth, we publish. But he's a friend, and he's very worried about his wife, and I don't want to rub salt in the wound by having you write the obituary. That's all.'

'OK,' I say, eventually. 'But I'm surprised. I mean, for starters, we don't byline our obits. He wouldn't know who'd written it.'

'Oh, I think he would. Your obituaries are brilliantly distinctive, Leo.'

In an industry entirely lacking in positive feedback, this is hands down the most lavish praise I have ever received. I try not to beam.

'Fine,' I say. 'I'll hand it to Sheila.'

It's not right, though. How can Jeremy Rothschild, who embodies everything that is rigorous and impartial about journalism, object to us mentioning a part of Janice's life that is already known? We're a national newspaper! I pick at a lump of wool on my jumper, wishing I'd used the little comb Emma gave me for de-bobbling last week.

'Great,' Jim says. 'Thanks.'

We get up and walk back to obits.

Jim's gaze wanders to the haphazard Pinterest of deaths on the whiteboard above my desk; the spidery mess of my handwriting. Beside one of the names on my OBITS TO WRITE UP list are the words *Shit! Apparently not yet dead!* – also in my handwriting. He seems to linger on this.

'Keep it up,' he says, undecidedly, before leaving our corner of chaos and death.

I go for a pint at the Plumbers'. It's full of colleagues, staring at their phones and pretending the others aren't there. Sometimes I wonder if journalism has changed that much, or if we're all still on Fleet Street at heart, drinking ourselves to death while we wait for a lead.

I call Emma, but she doesn't answer. I suffer a brief surge of anxiety as the business of her graduation rears its head again, but I'm able to deflect it. I have the option of calling St Andrews University, or even Jill, if I want to dig deeper. Instead, I have chosen to trust my wife.

I do a quick scroll through Twitter in case any deaths have slipped through our net.

Then Twitter disappears, and Emma's name takes over my phone screen.

'HI!' she shouts, when I answer. 'Sorry! I'm at Milk with Ruby!' Milk is our local family cafe. It's maybe my least favourite place on earth, but they serve ice cream sweetened with some weird-sounding substance that makes all the middle-class parents feel better about themselves. There's also a children's tool station, and Ruby, unlike her parents, is really into DIY.

'Thanks for calling back,' I say. A tourist in the street stops to take photos of the words 'CASK ALES' on the window glass, as if he has discovered a bonafide sixteenth-century alehouse right here on Lower Belgrave Street.

'EVERYTHING OK?' Emma shouts.

'Ish. Jeremy Rothschild made a complaint about me. He didn't like a piece I did about Janice at the weekend, and I've been told not to write her obituary.'

'I mean, I don't care who writes her obit,' I add, when Emma doesn't say anything. 'It's more just the principle of it. Felt like my editor was taking a shit on me to keep his mate happy. Which I didn't appreciate.'

Emma calls something to Ruby. Then: 'Sorry, I was struggling to hear you. A complaint from who?'

'Jeremy Rothschild,' I repeat, as quietly as I can. But of course she can't hear me.

'Sorry, darling, who?'

'Jere— Oh, look, it doesn't matter.'

'Hang on, did you say Jeremy Rothschild?'

'Yes.'

'What the hell?' She sounds angry.

Here she goes. Already smiling, I decide against the second pint.

'I was honest about Janice's mental health crisis after she gave birth to their son. He didn't like that. Thought it was insensitive.'

'You're fucking kidding me!'

'Nope.'

There's a long silence.

Then: 'Leo,' Emma says. 'Please don't ever stop being the sort of person who wants to tell the truth. Jeremy Rothschild sounds like a complete megalomaniac.'

I take another draught of my pint, smoothing down my trousers. I don't go as far as wearing a suit at work, but even these not-particularly-smart chinos are out of my comfort zone.

'Hmm. How was trampolining, anyway?'

'Good,' Emma says. She's stopped shouting; the cafe sounds quieter. 'Listen, Leo, your mum called me.'

'Oh dear. Why?'

It's been nearly ten years since I found out I was adopted, and my relationship with my parents is still bumpy. I didn't talk to them for the first few months. I felt that if we were ever to recover I'd need some time away, so I asked them for a bit of space – just a month or two, I told them, nothing permanent – but Mum wouldn't respect it. She wrote and messaged incessantly.

She's very smart, my mother, and until that point I'd thought her to be quite robust as well. But my silence broke her. She developed an emotional destitution that she still can't seem to rein in.

For Ruby's sake, I've worked hard at patching things up. But it's still there between us. It was my right to know who I was, and I don't understand how my parents could see it any other way.

'She called to say your dad has flu,' Emma says, before pausing to go and rescue a child whose hand Ruby is trying to hammer.

'Proper flu,' she says, on her return. 'He's pretty sick.'

'Poor Dad.' I sigh. 'Although I can't help thinking this is another test.'

Mum's started laying down little challenges in recent months, to see how I respond. Last month it was a message via Emma to say her pension had been stopped and nobody knew why. It made me furious, really, because I do care – of course I do – but I knew her motive was to see if I'd offer to help.

'It probably is,' Emma agrees. 'But either way, you should ring her. Maybe you could whizz up there to help them for a day or two? She said he fell ill on Sunday, so if you wait until next week there shouldn't be any risk of you getting it.'

'Urgh.'

'Leo,' she says quietly. 'They're Ruby's only grandparents. And they're good people, no matter how wrong they got it.'

'Oh, I know. OK, I'll call her. Will you be able to do the nursery drop-offs and pickups?'

She starts to say she can, then stops. 'Oh, hang on. It's my conference at Newcastle University next week. Sorry, I should have checked the diary before calling you.'

We bat this back and forth for a while, and in the end Emma offers to take Ruby to Newcastle with her. She's only speaking on Monday morning and Thursday lunchtime; she says she can take Ruby up to the Northumberland beaches on Tuesday and Wednesday. Ruby's never actually been to 'Mummy's crab beach,' and there's no way I'm taking her into a house with flu.

'But are you sure?' I ask. 'You can't hunt for crabs with Ruby.'

'I can't, no, but we can do lots of rock pooling and sandcastles.' She's had to raise her voice again; the cafe seems to have filled up with screaming babies.

'All right. Why not? Then we can go together in the summer holidays, like we said.'

'It's a plan!' she shouts. 'I'll book flights for me and Ruby later.'

After the call, I go to WhatsApp her. I want to thank her for making me feel better.

She's online, writing me a message, so I wait to see what she has to say first.

Hi. Just spoke to Leo. I'm coming up to Northumberland next week so yes, we can meet. I'll be in touch again to make a plan when I've booked.

I start a reply: *Not sure that was for me!* But before I press send, I pause. Who was it for?

One of the staff at Newcastle Uni? Or maybe Susi, her friend from school in Scotland? Doesn't Susi live somewhere up round Tyneside, these days?

My phone buzzes. *Sorry! That was for Susi, not you!*

I head back to work.

The afternoon passes in a fog of word counts and Emma, obit planning and Emma; phone calls and Emma. I finish the double agent's obituary and make a start on a woman who choreographed the British Olympic synchronised swimming team for three decades. I also discover that one of the military chaps I wrote up last week – we call them Moustaches – had lied about his World War Two military cross. I decide I haven't the energy to break the news to his family, who are pushy enough already, so I just shelve the obit entirely.

I think about that WhatsApp again.

She was writing to an old friend, I tell myself. There's nothing more to say.

Other than it didn't quite read that way.

Later, when I'm getting into bed, she zooms off to the loo. 'Code Brown!' she whispers.

For reasons I don't like, I check WhatsApp, and find she's online. She is not writing a message to me.

I sit still in bed, tiredness expanding radially into alarm. Why I am doing this? What is wrong with me? Emma is well! She's in remission – I prayed for this! And now I'm lurking on bloody WhatsApp at eleven o'clock at night, because I've decided she's planning clandestine sex with someone in Newcastle? During a work trip, accompanied by our daughter? Seriously?

I swing angrily out of bed and march downstairs. The woman has just survived cancer! I've got to put a stop to this, I tell myself, once and for all – even though I see the flaw in what I'm about to do, the unforgivable weakness.

I can see the old green shopping bag has disappeared from the dining room as soon as I'm halfway across the floor, but I fight through to the little clearing in front of it anyway, in case my eyes are deceiving me. There is a new patch of floor showing, where the bag was previously.

John Keats shuffles through and wags his tail. 'Hi mate!' I say, but my voice, like everything else, is pitched wrong.

'What are you up to?' Emma sticks her head round the door.

'I was looking for an obits cutting book.' I make a show of scanning around this room of hoarder's chaos, even though I would never store anything in here, and Emma knows it.

'That's a strange thing to be looking for at this time of night.' She's using a cotton wool pad to take off her mascara.

'I know. But Kelvin's doing a compilation of our most memorable obituaries and . . . It was easier for me to use my personal collection.'

'I see. Hey – I just booked flights to Newcastle for me and Ruby. She's going to explode with excitement!'

Something settles in my abdomen. Of course. Her passport. It was in the shopping bag. So was Ruby's.

The bag will reappear tomorrow, and I have to stop behaving like this.

Chapter Fourteen

EMMA

Dawn.

I seldom cry upon awakening anymore, but today it happens before I have the energy to pin my defences. I cry silently, hands pressed into my eyes.

He's not here, nor will he ever be. I will never wake up with him again.

And the sheer grief of it; the motionless weight, is more than I can handle today.

After I caught Leo trying to find my papers in the dining room last night, he tossed and turned for hours. I feigned sleep next to him, wondering how much he had seen, how much he knew.

What would happen if he confronted me? What would I say?

Sometimes I don't know who I am anymore; where the line is between real and longed-for. Sometimes I imagine my husband demanding the truth, and me genuinely unable to answer because I no longer know.

When he finally slept I went to retrieve my papers from their temporary hiding place under Ruby's bed. I should never have put them in the dining room last week. I should have shipped them straight out of the house, and I should have taken more bloody care to lock the cupboard so Leo wouldn't have gone looking for them elsewhere.

This is how criminals get caught. They make mistakes under duress.

One by one, while Ruby slept, I removed papers pertaining to my degree, to my parents' deaths, the police paperwork, to him. I removed the 'sweetheart, you need to sort your life out' letter Jill had written to me four years ago, after I'd gone missing and she'd driven up to Northumberland to rescue me. I took out anything that might make Leo think I was anyone other than his loving, faithful wife, and I cursed myself for not having been strong enough to get rid of all of it before. It was one thing hoarding a houseful of knick-knacks, but this paperwork? It was sentimental, superstitious; utter stupidity. Keeping it didn't connect me to the unbearable losses of that time in my life. It just left me vulnerable to losing the beautiful family I had now.

Later, at work, an unknown number calls my phone. I'm with my coastal geohazards postgrads, talking about fluvial and tidal flooding in the Thames estuary. It's warm outside and the windows are open: hard to imagine storm surges and submerged flood plains.

When I spot my phone flashing in my bag, I ignore it. But when it happens again I excuse myself and go out to the corridor.

'Hello?' I say, just as the line goes dead.

I check my missed call list. There are three of them, all in the last hour, all from an unknown number.

'Oh, piss off,' I say to my phone, but my voice is uncertain.

I've always felt that there's something slightly malevolent

about a missed call from a withheld number. But when it came up at a friend's dinner party last year, I discovered I'm largely alone in this. Leo and most of our other friends declared themselves completely unbothered by the idea of an unknown person trying and failing to get through: it was only me and Stef, a friend from work, who seemed to find it unsettling.

Perhaps it's just those of us with something to hide. Stef has had multiple affairs.

Before I return to my postgrads, I glance out of the window to the square, conspicuously empty now most of the undergrads have gone home for the summer. There's just a couple of people eating sandwiches on benches, a girl walking up and down on the phone.

And a man, who appears to be staring up at the window I'm standing at. Not somebody I know. He's scruffy; could easily be a student, but there's something about him I don't like.

His hat. He's wearing a baseball hat. Like the man in Plymouth, like the man outside our house.

I glance along the corridor, but there's nobody else standing by a window. Nobody else he could be staring at.

My skin prickles; something cold opens in my chest. Is he looking at me?

By the time I return to the room with my postgrads, he's walking away. I catch the back of him heading out towards Gower Street, and he doesn't return.

I'm more vigilant than normal when I leave the building at the end of the day, but I'm surrounded only by the silent flow of people leaving Bloomsbury, eyes glued to their phones, nobody talking. Nothing feels quite right.

I don't want to be here. I want to be by the ocean.

Somewhere vast and ethereal with the sun making wrinkled skin out of the surface of the sea.

Next week. Next week is Northumberland, with its huge skies and happy tides. With Ruby, with the sea: closer, perhaps, to him.

Four more days.

Chapter Fifteen

EMMA

Ruby and I leave for the airport on Monday. My daughter, inspired by a book at nursery, has it in her head that we're going to stay on a tea plantation in Darjeeling. She wraps Duck in a muslin and warns him the days will be hot but the nights rather cold.

I leave her to lecture him on climactic conditions in the Rangbhang Valley, sitting on the train seat beside me. I get out my phone. It's only 8.30 but I'm exhausted already.

I dial his number.

'Emma?'

'Hi.' I focus on the front page of the copy of *Marine Biologist* magazine I've been trying to read, where a shoal of tiny pipefish float calmly in a wrecked ship.

'Hi.' His voice drops.

'Is this a bad time? Is someone there with you?' I roll the magazine into a tube.

'No.' He sighs. 'I'm alone. I'm just not used to talking freely with you.'

'I see.'

There's a silence, so I continue. 'Look, I know you've got a lot on your plate. But you haven't responded to my messages and I'm on my way up north as we speak. Newcastle for a conference this afternoon, then Northumberland for two nights. Are you still in Alnmouth? Are we still meeting?'

'I am still in Alnmouth,' he says. 'And I very much want to see you, yes.'

'I've got a cottage for Tuesday and Wednesday nights. It's less than a minute from yours. The lane that goes down the side of the post office? It's number fifteen.'

'Right.'

'Come over when Ruby's asleep. Any time after eight. I don't mind which night.' I roll the magazine into an even tighter tube. 'We're leaving Thursday.'

'OK,' he says, after a pause. 'I'll come round on Tuesday night. But Emma, I . . .'

I wait. Ruby is still chatting away about tea plantations.

'Oh, look, I'll tell you when I see you,' he says. 'I don't want to do this on the phone.'

'Are you sure? Do you have news? Are you all right?'

'I'll see you on Tuesday,' he says, and ends the call.

I close my eyes and tell myself everything will be OK. I've survived twenty years of this back and forth with him, after all.

Chapter Sixteen

LEO

When the Queen dies, a global response plan named Operation London Bridge will be set in motion by her private secretary. Prime ministers and presidents will find out first, but the international press will follow soon after. At my newspaper, we have twelve days' coverage ready to go. At the BBC they have prerecorded TV packages ready, and staff carry out emergency drills every few months. The armed forces are on standby, your local village radio station is primed. Just say the word.

Obituary writers, on the other hand, need to operate at this level of preparedness for just about everyone. If a singer cancels his stadium tour, you can guarantee I'll be writing his stock – what if he's losing a battle with addiction? We have moles in politics, in finance, in theatre, film, the church and beyond. Basically, if you're not looking good, we'll be writing you up.

Someone always slips through the net, though. Someone we just weren't ready for. Today it's Billie Roland, celebrated mistress of half the cabinet in the early eighties. Heart attack in the middle of the night – she lay there for three days before her son let himself into her flat and found her.

I haven't a clue why we didn't have her written up in

advance. All I know is that she had a dizzyingly busy and fascinating life, and that we are woefully behind. Everyone apart from Sheila is off, we've had to completely reshuffle tomorrow's obituary page and the poet who was meant to have sent us his buddy's obit by midday has disappeared into thin air. I'm racing against the clock to get Billie a half page vertical filed by our print deadline at 4 p.m.

It's therefore completely unjustifiable that I'm googling the production team who worked on Emma's BBC series. I've told myself it's because I'd like to get one of them to say something about her for her stock obit, but, really, I just want to identify who 'Robbie' is.

Hey doll, I'm sorry I missed you this morning. Call me. I don't want this to be goodbye . . . Robbie x

It's not that I think this is a lover's note, left on an empty pillow – Emma would never have an affair with someone who called her 'doll' – but there's something here. Some connection I don't know about. And I can't help thinking there's a reason why I don't know.

I angle my screen away from passers-by and pull up the production crew on IMDb. I find him straight away: Robbie Rosen, the series runner. Less than thirty seconds after that, I discover via Twitter that he's now an assistant producer at BBC Scotland in Glasgow. Gin and tea; my cats, *Friends* jokes and occasional telly stuff, his profile says. He looks about sixteen, and is wearing good make-up.

I half smile. Emma definitely hasn't had an affair with this boy. But there's still reason why his note has been kept in her file. She wanted to remember it, to look at it again some time.

Why? Who is he?

With some effort I tear myself away from his Twitter page to finish Billie Roland's obituary.

*

Half an hour later, we're done, and my mind returns to Robbie Rosen of BBC Scotland.

Glasgow University's End of Life research unit is putting on a death conference on Thursday. I didn't book because there wasn't anyone of note speaking, but they've since confirmed Di Sampson, who writes quite literally the best obituaries in the world. I know they'd find me a place if I called them.

. . . For what reason? I ask myself. So that I have grounds to pop along to BBC Scotland afterwards? Interrogate some poor kid about a programme he worked on half a decade ago?

Somewhere across the newsroom floor, there's a cheer and a scatter of applause. I look up, but they're out of sight, somewhere in features.

What I do see, though, is Sheila, watching me.

'Leo,' she says. 'Everything all right?'

'Yes . . . ?'

She returns to her screen, but sends me an instant message: *You're a little red in the face.*

I reply, *because it's too hot.* It's nearly 30 degrees outside. London is sweltering and thirsty.

I'm always here if you want to talk, she writes.

I look up at her again, and she's just watching me, levelly, as she did when she was asking all those questions about Emma. I wonder if she used to do this during interrogation. It's bloody unsettling.

After a long stare, she mimes, *pint?*

I shake my head, because it's not even 11 a.m., so she sends another note.

You sure? You're a man with a lot on his plate.

I write, *Sheila. You seem oddly certain I'm having a crisis. IS there something we need to talk about?*

And for a second – just a second – she pauses. And I think, she knows something about Emma.

I look up at her again.

What? I mouth. I almost don't want to ask.

Sheila starts typing.

Nothing, she writes. *But I know Kelvin's asked you to write a stock for Emma, and if that's what you're doing, I suspect you'll be feeling all sorts of unpleasant things.*

Then: *Sorry. I was actually just trying to be helpful. You know that's not my strong suit.*

I realise I've been holding my breath.

I have got to put a stop this. It doesn't matter what happened with my parents, my adoption: that's past tense. This situation with Emma is my present, and I must deal with it as a functional adult would. I need to talk to her, properly, and soon.

And while I'm at it, I must stop reading into everything Sheila says. She's met Emma twice; they have no contact beyond me, no friends in common. Sheila simply saw Emma in Waterloo Station, an unexpected place, and was being nosy.

I write back and tell her again there's nothing to worry about – I really am just hot – and I go to get some water.

. . . And yet, I still can't quite let go. As I cross the newsroom floor I think about Emma's papers, which have not reappeared in the green shopping bag. I've searched the house for the university letter: gone. The letter about her father: gone. The note from *Robbie x*: gone. I started flicking through the skeleton paperwork that remains in her cupboard, but I had no idea what I was looking for; what she might have taken out. And the further I looked, the deeper I was pulled into the black song of the past, into my parents' spare room that day.

We are Emma and Leo. We're a good couple. A great couple. So great our friends find us annoying; we're not that couple whose relationship is riddled with secrets.

Aren't we?

I decide in that moment that I'm going to Glasgow, and I will speak to Robbie Rosen.

Knowledge is power, we tell ourselves, only that's a lie, too. I'm already way out of my depth.

I pick up the phone and call Glasgow University. I bring up Easyjet to book a flight. I message my university friend Claire, who works at BBC Glasgow, and ask if she's around for coffee on Thursday afternoon. She responds straight away: *YES! Fantastic! Can you come to the BBC? I'll sign you in!*

Finally, I log into an email account I've had for years, from my hack days. It's not my real name. I email Robbie Rosen and ask if he's available on Thursday for a quick chat about Emma Bigelow, because she's been ill recently and I'm writing up a stock obituary. Forty minutes later, he replies to say he can.

It's as easy as that.

Chapter Seventeen

EMMA

Something in me breaks when Leo's sad. I can't rest until I've solved whatever the problem is; I stop at almost nothing. But of course, it never works; it just drives him mad. It's probably the only time he loses his temper.

Thankfully, Leo is nothing like me. When I have a problem he trusts me to deal with it howsoever I see fit. He's never once questioned my need to escape to Alnmouth when dark clouds gather – he calls these my Times, and knows to take a back foot. 'Go and reset,' he'll say, kissing me, at King's Cross station. 'And remember, I love you.'

But his generosity only makes the guilt more acute. He has no idea what I'm risking, every time I come up here. He thinks I come only to heal.

Alnmouth, three and a half hours from London on the fast train, is where the dark curl of the river Aln empties into the North Sea. Dad and I came to this part of the coast every summer when we lived in Scotland. In my memory our holidays were ripe with everything I'd craved: laughter, spontaneity, the company of other human beings. I remember us rockpooling for hours with the family in the caravan next door, shared picnics on the edge of the dunes. Me laughing myself silly in the playground as light faded from the estuary and the wind whipped up the scrub grass on the saltmarshes. Golden times.

But there was nothing golden about my visit to this place four years ago. The wind was ferocious for the entire visit, rain flouncing in and out from the sea, and I couldn't dry my clothes quickly enough. By the last day I was desperate to get back to London, and Leo.

That final morning was the one time I failed to make my checks. A fatal error. I went out to the beach, unthinking, with a plan to kill the last few hours crab-hunting on the exposed rocks beyond the golf course.

And then, suddenly, right there – amid the wrack-strewn boulders – there they were.

Metres from me, frozen to the spot. Both of them.

The police came quickly. I missed the last train back to London, but Jill drove all the way up to collect me, and Leo never knew a thing.

Today, though, it's serene and beautiful, and warm enough for Ruby to ask if she can paddle. 'Of course,' I say, removing her shoes. The sun has really thrown me. It has no place in my rotten plans for the next twenty-four hours.

Ruby runs delightedly across the corrugated sand, jumping over tiny abandoned sandcastles; miniature Lindisfarnes and Bamburghs, covered in shells. She stops a couple of times to poke at coiled lugworm castings ('Sand poos!') and then gallops at speed into a large tidal pool, with no concern for its depth or her trousers.

I abandon our things under the dunes and go after my daughter, who's already emerged from the pool and is now running down to the sea. Above her, blue sky is combed through with cirrus and the air is summer-holiday warm.

Jeremy Rothschild is coming to our rental cottage tonight.

Ruby runs into the water, hopping and squealing.

I was in Waterloo Station when he called to tell me Janice had disappeared. Already late, I was hurrying to catch a train to Poole Harbour but, after that news, didn't even make it off the station concourse. I just stood there until Jill called and warned me this could 'kick off.' That's when I realised I had to go home and hide my paperwork.

I don't know what's happened, Jeremy had said, over and over. *I just can't understand it, Emma. Janice was fine.*

A few days later, I told Leo I was having dinner with Jill. Jeremy and I met face to face.

We went to a shisha lounge on the Holloway Road, because there was scant chance of a paparazzo spotting us there. Neither of us wanted a shisha pipe – we had no idea what to do with it – but the friendly manager, perhaps sensing the weight of the occasion, had brought one 'on the house!' A terrible scene ensued while he demonstrated how to use it, and we sat in bleak silence.

We ordered grainy coffees and talked in truncated sentences, mostly about the police search for Janice, until he looked me in the eye and asked me – in a tone I really didn't like – if I had been in touch with her.

Of course not, I told him, but he didn't believe me: I could see it in his eyes. He asked me again, and then again.

'Is that what this meeting is about?' I asked, eventually. 'You think Janice has disappeared because of something I've said? Or done? Seriously, Jeremy?'

Jeremy took the shisha pipe and sucked for a minute. He looked ridiculous. 'Yes,' he admitted. 'But before you get too haughty, or defensive, you might want to ask yourself why I'd worry about that.'

There wasn't much I could say in response.

'I just needed to see you,' he said, more levelly. 'Ask you in person. I'm sure you'd do the same, in my shoes.'

And he was right. I would.

Sensing the meeting might soon come to an end, I'd asked, and then begged, for the same thing I always begged him for, and he said no.

Soon after, we'd walked off in opposite directions.

Since then there have been several text messages, plus his request to meet up here in Alnmouth. No further information about Janice and no explanation for his complaint to Leo's editor, even when I sent him a furious message about it. He ignored that completely, as if my husband's work was a matter of such infinitesimal importance he hadn't even read to the end of my message. And I'd hated him, for a few days, until the old longing returned and I said, yes, I'll come and see you in Northumberland.

I'd go anywhere, if I thought there was half a chance of him relenting. Anywhere at all. He knows the power he holds over me.

The sea is a film of green glitter, with my daughter hopping and shrieking at its edge. I smile as she comes sprinting over to me, gasping when she jumps up into a freezing clamp around my waist. 'Mummy!' she yells. 'Too cold!' I stagger across the sand, zigzagging, and she clings on. I kiss her head, already salted by the air.

Jeremy has always held power, I think, as my daughter jumps down and runs off. Even now, with Janice missing, I'm like a stray dog, following him around, desperate for crumbs.

Ruby stops to investigate a bright drift of gutweed. She pokes her toe at the green slime, bristling with disgust and pleasure. 'Is this seaweed?' she asks, even though she knows.

'It is,' I confirm. '*Ulva intestinalis*. Which means gutweed. Weed that lives in the tummy of people called Ruby.'

Ruby snatches her toe away, squealing.

I watch her jump across to a spray of tiny black pebbles, dragging my sleeve across my eyes before she notices my tears. I don't want this, I think, furiously. I don't want to be thrown back and forth between two lives. I want to be normal. Like the family we passed in the car park, unloading spades and windbreaks from their campervan.

But Leo is at work in London, trying to believe I am having an innocent beach holiday with Ruby. And I am soon to welcome Jeremy Rothschild into a house in which my daughter sleeps.

Tiny wavelets are defeated by the rising shore. Out on the sandbar, a group of Arctic tern screech and lift off into the briny air.

Chapter Eighteen

EMMA

Jeremy knocks a little after 8.30, by which time Ruby is in a deep sleep. He stands on the cobbles outside, surrounded by tubs of geraniums, looking intently at my face.

Desperation loops and coils inside me as I move aside to let him in. His jacket brushes my arm as he passes, and I flatten myself against the wall to stop it happening again.

I've planned a speech, but I can't remember a single word.

'Through here?' he asks, pleasantly enough. I nod, trying not to attach meaning to his tone. He's been very clear in his messages: he has something he needs to discuss with me, something Janice-related. I cannot allow myself to hope for more.

The Rothschilds have a house on the main street. It's one of the bigger ones, with an arch through which horse-drawn carriages once passed. They call it 'the cottage', which has always made me laugh.

'Please do take a seat,' I say. Jeremy is too big for this rental sitting room, with its low ceilings and tiny wingback armchairs. But he's always been too big for every space we've shared, I think, watching him settle. Too big, too smart, too well-resourced: I stand no better chance trying to win him over than the politicians he takes down every morning.

Just before he arrived I put a teapot in the sitting room to avoid an awkward wait by the kettle. My father taught me that. 'If it's going to be difficult, prepare the backside off it,' he used to say. He thought the line was funny. I was never sure about Dad's sense of humour, but the men in his commando units found him hilarious. 'Best Padre in the business,' one of them said to me. 'Always there for us. Total legend.' I'd smiled, as if pleased, but I ached for the closeness these men had with my father.

'How have you been?' I ask. I pour him a cup of tea.

When I look up, his eyes have filled with tears. He seems unable to speak. He gestures with his hands, a sort of apology, and I put the teapot down and hand him a tissue. He tries to take a deep breath but an ugly sound comes out of his throat, and then he covers his face with his hands.

He sits in front of me and sobs. My fitness band tells me my pulse is at a near-death 178 bpm.

'Forgive me,' he says, eventually. 'Forgive me.'

I go over to crouch down in front of him. 'Oh, Jeremy.' I give him more tissues. 'I've been so worried about you all. I can't imagine how terrifying this must be.'

He says nothing, but the tears continue to fall.

'What's happened?' I ask, gently. 'Why has she left?'

Eventually, he blots at his eyes. 'I wouldn't be here if I knew the answer to that question,' he says. 'But I appreciate that you've been worrying too.'

'Of course I have.'

He straightens up, smiling briefly at me, and I go back to my side of the coffee table. It's not comfortable being this close to him.

'She had been very anxious,' he admits, eventually. 'It had been getting worse since Charlie left for university last autumn. But I'm not convinced anxiety's the reason.'

I wait for him to carry on.

'Are you sure you've not been in touch with her?' he asks.

'Jeremy, we've been over this. I'd have everything to lose, calling your wife. Why are you still asking?'

He sighs. 'I'm asking because she's written to you.'

I stare at him. 'Who? Janice?'

He nods.

'So – so she's alive?'

'Yes. Or at least she was three days ago. She sent us a letter.'

'Jeremy! I – oh, wow! Thank God!'

He nods, slowly. 'It's definitely from her, but she doesn't sound good. Oddly conversational. But detached, you know? As if she'd taken too much medication.'

'What did she say?'

He pauses. I'm surprised he's told me even this much. He's always kept Janice well out of my reach: the times we met after my cancer diagnosis four years ago, he wouldn't even use her name.

'She said she's alive. Apologised for disappearing. Said she needs to be alone at the moment.'

I wait.

'It was a relief, of course. A huge relief. But it's very worrying. To just walk out on her life, then wait two weeks before writing to us – and even then, to sound like she's just updating some distant relatives . . . That's not her. She can't be well.'

'So will the police still help? If they know she's alive?'

Jeremy picks up his tea again. 'Yes, but it's scaled right back now. We've told them she's vulnerable but they're less interested. Which, I suppose, is understandable, but it's very hard to take.'

I nod. What a desperate situation. If Leo just disappeared – no warning, no note, nothing – I don't know what I'd do.

I search for something to say. 'Ah . . . So – where was the letter posted?'

'No idea,' Jeremy says. He looks at a criminally awful watercolour on the wall, one of many the rental cottage owner has painted.

'No postmark?'

Jeremy shakes his head. 'Letters tend not to get post-marked anymore.'

'Really? I didn't know that.'

'Well, you do now. But as I said, there was also a letter for you in the envelope.'

There's a caution in his eyes. 'I've read it, obviously. Just in case there was anything that might help us trace her. So I can tell you now that it's not what you're hoping for.'

He leans forward to retrieve the letter from his back pocket, which I take, wordlessly. It does not sit well with me to hear him talk about my hopes, when he's spent years battering them.

'I'll leave you to read it,' he says, getting up. 'Get back to the cottage.'

'Hang on.' I put the letter on the coffee table. 'Before you go, I'd really like you to explain why you complained about Leo to his boss.'

This surprises him: I think he's actually embarrassed. For a few seconds the only sound in the room is the wind tracing in from the sea.

'You're right, I did complain,' he admits. 'And I hope it didn't cause him too much trouble. But none of the other papers dug up the story about the postnatal psychosis. I panicked.'

'Well, then the other newspapers' journalists are crap. Why punish Leo for doing a thorough job?'

'I'm sorry. It took me so completely by surprise that I thought you must have come clean with him. About our history. I thought he was trying to send me a message.'

'I could never tell Leo,' I remind him. 'You know that better than anyone else.' Besides, the idea of Leo sending a coded message to Jeremy via a newspaper article is ridiculous. I tell him that.

'Well, my wife has gone missing,' Jeremy says, flatly. 'Forgive my inability to think cogently.'

I take a breath. 'Let's start again. I'd like to read this letter with you here. Will you stay a bit longer?'

He thinks for a moment, then sighs, 'OK.'

'Mummy?'

Ruby stands in the doorway. My warm girl; a little puff of blonde with eyes scrunched against the light.

I cross the room at the speed of sound. 'Hello! Why are you up?'

'I didn't go to sleep,' she says, rubbing the thick sleep out of her eyes. 'Hello,' she adds, looking at Jeremy. She sits on my hip and stares, with the unabashed curiosity of a child. She inserts one of Duck's knotted corners into her mouth. I can't think quickly enough.

Jeremy stares at Ruby, his body still. His face, which I once thought very handsome, is bloated and ugly in the aftermath of tears. 'Hello,' he says, quietly. Then he smiles. 'You must be Ruby.'

'What's your name?'

He glances at me, I shake my head. 'Paul,' he tells her, extending a hand. 'I work with your mummy. It's very nice to meet you, Ruby.'

She looks at his hand but doesn't shake it. 'How do you know my name?'

'I've heard all about you! Your mother's very proud of you,' he says.

I feel faint. Jeremy Rothschild is talking to my daughter. I have a letter from Janice on the coffee table.

Ruby squashes her lips together, considering this man, with his red face and surprising knowledge.

'My big name is Ruby Cerys Bigelow Philber,' she says. 'Do you want to know what my short name is?'

'I do.'

'Ruby Booby!' She falls about laughing, and Jeremy gamely joins in.

Then: 'Who's that?' she asks, pointing at his phone. He's just checked it again, for perhaps the tenth time since he's arrived. It's the same each time he touches it. A photo, the time, and a couple of bars of service.

Jeremy looks down. 'My son,' he says.

Ruby holds out her hand for the phone. 'Please can I look at him?'

'Ruby . . .'

'Please?' she adds. I tell her no, but Jeremy is already up. 'It's OK,' he says. 'Here you go.'

I sit back down with Ruby. Together, we look at the man on the screen. He has one of those enormous foam fingers they wave around at American sporting events; a broad smile bursting out from under a cap. 'What's his name?' she asks.

'Charlie,' Jeremy said, and I see the pride in his eyes. 'His big name is Charlie Ellis Rothschild.'

'Where is he?' Ruby asks, looking at Charlie Ellis Rothschild.

My heart. My heart might never recover from the sight of my little Ruby, talking to Jeremy Rothschild.

'He's in London at the moment . . . But generally he lives in Boston, which is a big city across the sea.'

'Why does he live across the sea?'

'He's studying there. At university.'

'Uvines . . .' Ruby says, trailing off. She purses her lips again, considering Jeremy. Then: 'Does he miss you?'

'I hope so!'

'I don't want to live across the sea,' she tells us, after a pause. Then: 'Does he like you?'

At this, Jeremy laughs out loud. 'I think he does, yes. He's a bit angry at the moment, but he still likes me.'

'Why?'

I want nothing more than to remove Ruby from this room, and then Jeremy from my house, but I want to hear his answer. I want to know every ridge and furrow of the Rothschilds' family life. I always have.

'Why is he angwy?' Ruby asks, in her wheedling baby voice. She wraps her hands around the arm scroll of the sofa, swinging back and forth.

'His mother has done something he didn't like,' Jeremy's voice is soft.

Ruby nods sympathetically. 'Sometimes I get angry with my mummy,' she says.

'That's the problem with parents.' Jeremy smiles, and I see how hard he's trying.

I can't take my eyes off him. The deep creases of exhaustion and sadness under his eyes. The creped skin under his chin. I wonder if his radio guests would be quite so afraid of him if they could see that skin up close; its vulnerable softness, its humanity.

'Right, I'm taking you back up to bed,' I say. Ruby nods, and says to Jeremy, 'Are you having a sleepover with us?'

He shakes his head. 'Definitely not.'

'OK. Bye bye,' says my daughter, after another long, hard stare.

'Bye bye,' he replies.

I mouth, please don't go, but he isn't looking at me.

*

When I get back downstairs he's gone, the letter left on my armchair. I run out into the lane, but it's empty. The sea, below me, is miles out; a band of darkening mercury. The remaining light silhouettes two people and a dog on the beach. A ball being thrown, clouds racing north to Scotland. No sign of Jeremy.

Sorry, he texts, as I stand there. *I couldn't do it with Ruby there.*

Another text: *I've told you all you need to know, now. Please contact me immediately if you think there are any clues in Janice's letter we might have missed.*

Then, in a final text: *Ruby's perfect. I'm sure you're a great mother.*

I go back inside and tear open Janice's letter. I feel unhinged.

Dear Emma,
I know this letter will come as a shock. But I had to write to you. You crop up in my thoughts often.

It's about that crab we spotted all those years ago. On Alnmouth beach remember. Of course you remember. I have watched your television series and know you've never stopped looking for it. Anyway, I think you should look on Coquet Island.

In Shakespeare, islands are like magic, and he knew what he was talking about.

Coquet Island is the only place on that coast that's completely out of bounds to human beings

& I paid a fisherman to take me out there once to look at the birds and although you're not allowed to land there I saw many things including, I'm sure of it, one of your crabs . . . I guess you only really get bird lovers going out there so nobody'd notice an unusual crab, they're all there for the puffins and roseate terns

I'm sorry I've kept this information from you for so long. I should have told you years ago. I mean it I am so sorry.

sorry again Emma

Janice

I take the letter to the kitchen, where I sit and read it again. Then again.

I haven't spoken to Janice in nearly two decades, but Jeremy's right – nothing about her sounds right here. The lack of punctuation, the repeated apology – the very existence of this letter, this friendly communication with a woman she hates, feels wrong.

But it's her. Jeremy's right about that, too. It's definitely her, I know her handwriting. And, unless she's broken her silence about how intimately we're connected, nobody other than the three of us know she was with me the day I found the crab.

This letter is off, I message Jeremy. *I agree.*

He replies immediately.

You can understand my concern about her mental state. Is there anything I've missed? Anything that might tell us where she is?

Despite my complicated feelings about Janice, I can't help feeling guilty as I scan through the letter again. There are few things she'd be more horrified by than the idea of Jeremy and me discussing her mental health.

Nothing obvious, I write. *Apart from the fact that she's talking about Northumberland, but I'm guessing that's why you're up here – to look for her?*

Jeremy replies: *Yes. But I don't think she's here. We get a message if anyone deactivates the alarm at the cottage, but there's been nothing. Besides, if Janice had been up here, somebody would have spotted her. I've asked practically everyone in Alnmouth, nobody's seen her. And I've checked, just to be certain, but there's no possibility she could be hiding on Coquet Island. It's still off limits to everyone other than RSPB wardens. I'm not giving up, because I can't, but I really don't think she's here.*

I reply to say I'll let him know if I think of anything.

I read the letter again as the room fills with darkness, then I look up Coquet Island on my phone. There's every chance Janice is right about the crabs: it's a perfect place for an isolated species to start changing, undisturbed by other populations, and it would make sense that a dead specimen could wash up on Alnmouth beach from there. I don't know why I didn't think of this before.

But is there any chance she's on the island, too? Jeremy said not, but is it a cry for help? There's an old lighthouse there; I guess she could have broken in. But a woman who wants to disappear would not be able to get there without paying someone. And someone who'll take money to ferry you to a forbidden island is not the sort of person who you can trust not to sell the information to a journalist.

Jeremy's right. I don't think there's any way she could be there.

I reread the letter three, four times. I can't believe she's written to me, after all this time. How strange she sounds.

I try to eat some toast but I'm too wired. I go and stand outside the front door, hoping the cold sea air might ground me, but before long I'm shivering.

Later still, I lie awake, thinking about the shock of Jeremy Rothschild and my daughter in the same room. I think about Janice, about Charlie, a young man in London, praying for news of his mother, and it breaks my heart.

From time to time I think about Jeremy, alone in their

house, reaching over for his phone in the middle of the night, just in case Janice has sent a message.

I thought this family was unbreakable. I just don't understand what's happened.

When I do finally sleep, I dream that a man in a baseball cap walks into my room, trying to talk to me, but I am paralysed. I see the entire room in detail, can hear the herring gulls calling outside, but I can't say anything, can't move. When I wake properly, Ruby is sprawled, star-like, next to me. She must have crept in as dawn broke.

Jeremy hasn't texted.

I look at Wikideaths. Nobody of note.

Chapter Nineteen

DIARY OF JANICE ROTHSCHILD

Seventeen years earlier

April 16th, 2002

Impossible to describe how dark this week has been. Life has changed forever. How will I ever feel safe again?

Am so angry. So fucking angry, so frightened, still so shocked.

Writing this in bed, looking at the picture of the three of us in the hospital when Charlie was a newborn. J and I look so happy – even with that scowling nurse who hated us lurking in the background – but you can see it in my eyes; the way I hold Charlie. I was terrified of something like this happening. Even then, with the joy of that tiny scrap in my arms.

One week ago today, it was. Took Charlie to the sandpit at the park. Just a normal day, C playing happily. Then Bec arrived; talked to her for a bit. Ate most of her cookies and didn't panic about my weight: progress.

Then realised C was gone.

Horrific. Nobody knows the first thing about fear until they find their child isn't there anymore.

Was running around the park, calling then shouting then screaming, into the public toilets, big kids' play area, out of the front exit of the playpark because some fuckwit had left it open.

People looking at me, why is that woman screaming, he's bound to be somewhere, calm down, god poor child stuck with a crazy mother like that, hey, haven't I seen her on the telly?

Was screaming HELP ME, HELP ME, and all I could think was that I knew this would happen, I knew.

Going to have to try to come back to this tomorrow. Have been having panic attacks, can feel breath going wrong. That's what it's done to me. Can't even write about it here.

I don't know what to do. Someone help me. Help me.

Chapter Twenty

LEO

Present day

Robbie Rosen is seven and a half minutes late. Claire, the old friend who signed me in, has long since returned to her desk. The only other person in the BBC canteen is a woman cleaning the now-empty serveries.

I stare out of the windows at the Glasgow skyline, pierced by blackened church spires. It's stopped raining but droplets of water are still beetling down the floor-to-ceiling glass, and rain has pooled on empty plastic tables on the roof terrace outside. Further down the river, traffic queues on the motorway bridge.

I found the death conference oddly unsettling this morning. Emma's illness has made death feel personal, suddenly; as if I've been stripped of my vocational ability to separate a person's beginning and middle from their end. I was relieved when it was over; for once I didn't stop to talk to anyone.

A young man the shape of an apple walks into the canteen. Tight jeans he'd probably be better without. He has a fashionable beard, but for some reason it doesn't quite hit the mark – I think because his face is so youthful, so pink and plump. He sees me and raises his eyebrows in greeting.

We sit down and he asks if I know how Emma's doing. He was 'really upset' to hear she was so poorly.

I tell him I've heard on the grapevine that Emma is doing well, and he seems genuinely relieved. Then I give my rehearsed speech about how I'm writing Emma's stock obit and wanted to talk to someone on the production team for *This Land* about Emma's time in front of the camera. I explain I've been just round the corner all day, at a death conference of all things, haha! 'I thought it'd be easiest to drop by. Just ask a few questions.'

He tells me sure, it's no bother. Behind him, fingers of sunlight poke through the clouds.

'Can I assume that you and Emma worked quite closely?' I ask, pulling my notebook out. 'You're the right person to talk to?'

'Oh God yeah, we were together all the time,' he says. He's stroking a thumb self-consciously along his chin; a gesture better suited to an older man. 'It was me who used to drive her around, check her into hotels, sort out her meals. We'd mess around while the cameraman and the director argued about how to shoot the next scene. Got on like a house on fire.'

I nod, as if to say, *I thought as much!* 'I suppose it's a much more relaxed relationship than that between, say, her and the director.'

'Totally. I mean, to be honest, I was really doing an AP's job, or at least a researcher's job – definitely not a runner's. But yes, I was with her most of the time. Bloody telly!' he adds, as if I'm one of the inner circle. 'We're all working at least two levels below our pay grade.'

He wants me to sympathise, but I haven't the time.

'So – would you say she confided in you?'

There's a fine-spun pause.

'I mean, yes, of course,' he says, carefully. 'Although I'm not going to tell you all her shit!'

'What shit?' It bursts out of me and hangs in the air between us like a bad smell, refusing to disperse. I throw in a laugh and say, 'Only joking,' which just makes it worse.

He backtracks. 'I suppose what I really mean is that as the runner you kind of see everything, don't you? I'm sure it's the same in your industry. So yes, she confided in me, but to be honest I saw everything that went down on that show, whether I was told or not. You buy respect by keeping your mouth shut.'

'So no real gossip,' I say, grinning, as if his answer doesn't matter to me at all.

'No, no gossip in particular,' he says, but I can see it – there is something.

I know I'll lose him if I push this now, so I invite him to tell me a few anecdotes from the series.

He doesn't tell me anything I didn't already know. He mentions the lightning bolt that took out their tripod on a clifftop in Devon, the day Emma fell into a rock pool during a piece to camera. There are many details of their relationship – chatty, giggly – and he's particularly emphatic about her not being an 'arrogant dick'. ('Most presenters are such arrogant dicks,' he explains.)

'To be honest, though, that second series was overshadowed by Em being dropped, straight after she'd recorded the voice-over. We were all so gutted, and her poor agent, Mags, was furious, but it was out of our hands. Commissioners are dicks too, by the way.'

'I imagine it hit Emma very hard.'

'It did,' he says, remembering. 'Emma went a bit mad and sacked her agent, Mags – Mags took it very badly.'

I've been noting this down in shorthand, but then I stop,

rereading. 'Actually, Emma's agent sacked her. Not the other way round. I've – I've read about it.'

'No, Emma definitely ditched Mags. I saw her at the RTS awards a few weeks later, she was still shocked. A little bit furious, too, if I'm honest.'

His phone rings and he excuses himself. He wanders off across the canteen, rapping his knuckles occasionally on the deserted tables. A man in a BBC Logistics sweatshirt sits down nearby, unwrapping a sandwich.

Emma told me she'd been dropped by Mags. She cried in my arms, for hours. The next day she went to Alnmouth to search for her crab, and didn't come back for three weeks. When I visited her at the weekends she told me her heart was broken. And not just her heart, her pride.

Rosen returns to the table. 'Where were we? Oh yes, Emma ditching her agent. And commissioners being dicks.' He leans back in his chair, and I realise how much he's enjoying this. I suspect he's rather overlooked in his job.

'The worst thing about Emma's dismissal was that they did it because some Big Knob BBC presenter insisted they sack her. I mean, who hates Emma that much? And why? It must have been someone pretty famous to have that sort of leverage.'

After a shaky sip from my teacup, I express my own surprise. 'I've heard nothing about enemies,' I admit.

'Well . . . This can't go on the record – nor can anything to do with the BBC, of course –' I nod. 'But not everyone loved Emma,' he says. He's really energised now.

'Oh?'

Then my phone starts ringing, and it's my wife. I immediately cancel the call, but not before her name and face have flashed up on my screen. Rosen thinks my name is Steve Gowing, and that I have never met Emma Bigelow. I look at him carefully, but his face remains impassive. I think – I hope – I've got away with it.

Either way, though, the interruption has broken our spell. 'Oh, look, I should get going,' he says, and I know from my years as a hack that he's lost his nerve. 'Can we leave it there? Those stories should be enough, right? It's just that I have a meeting soon.'

I could have scripted it.

I give it one more try, but he won't say any more. He tells me he's got to get back to work; reiterates that the stuff about Emma's dismissal is one hundred per cent off the record. Then he shakes my hand and is gone.

I stare out at the clouds creasing over the city, the dark dragon green of the River Clyde. I think about this morning's conference, all the earnest talk of community remembrance spaces and respectful deaths. I had sat there, thinking about this encounter with Rosen, and had decided it would go really well. My journey of doubt and insecurity would come to an end in the BBC canteen, and we'd get on with our lives as a family without cancer.

The fact is that this meeting has made me feel much worse.

My phone pings, but it's only Mum, checking my arrival time later. I'm going to stay with her and Dad tonight so I can help around the house tomorrow, give Mum a break from flu carer duties.

It's all part of the family story we enact, these days. In this narrative I have completely forgiven them for lying to me about who I was, and everyone loves everyone again. Mum is the director, Dad and I the weary actors. But it keeps us ticking along. And who knows; in ten years I might even have convinced myself it's all true.

*

I hand my visitor's pass to the receptionist on my way out, and stop by a gigantic pool of rainwater. The air is cold; it smells of minerals and fresh earth – here, in the middle of the city, as if I'm in the Trossachs. I get out my phone and try to work out how to get to the airport. I don't want to think about anything else.

I've just ordered a cab when Rosen runs outside. 'Oh, hi!' he calls. 'I wanted to . . .'

I wait, as he pulls a jumper on.

'You're her husband,' he says, when he's done. He's annoyed, but also pleased with himself. 'I thought there was something weird going on. Then she called you! I remembered her husband was an obituary writer so I looked you up. What the hell? You told me your name was Steve.'

After a pause, I nod. 'I . . . I'm sorry. It's not appropriate for us to behave like that anymore. Journalists, I mean. I don't know what I was . . . I'm sorry.'

He watches me. 'I don't know what's going on,' he says. 'But I know she adored you. She talked about you all the time. Why are you here, asking about her?'

I swallow.

'I don't know what's going on either.' I stare at the giant rainwater pool, rippling in the wind. 'Her health is fine – she got the all-clear. But I think something's going on at the moment. Something bad, that she won't talk to me about. I also think it's something you might know about. That's why I got in touch. I'm sorry I misrepresented myself to you. I . . .' I take a long breath. 'I'm worried. About her, about us, about whatever it is you won't tell me. But I know that doesn't excuse me sneaking around like a scumbag reporter from a scumbag newspaper.'

Rosen is watching me, fascinated. He wasn't expecting this at all.

'Why are you here asking me questions?' he asks. 'Why aren't you asking her? Did you two split up?'

I shake my head. 'No. And I have asked her, but she keeps deflecting me. Everything's fine, apparently.'

'But why don't you believe her? If she's told you everything's fine?'

I explain to him that in the process of writing Emma's stock I've stumbled across some very confusing documents. 'They were all concerning things that pre-dated us, though,' I say. 'But her sacking Mags Tenterden – that's news to me. It's happened while we were together, and she's lied about it.'

'Well, I mean, I could have got it wrong,' Rosen begins, but then trails off. 'No. I didn't get it wrong, I'm sorry. Emma definitely sacked Mags.'

I beg him not to tell Emma I visited him. 'Not until I get a better handle on what's going on. I just need to . . . I just need to establish that she's not actually in some sort of trouble.'

Rosen looks anxious. 'Look, can I ask why you emailed me, not one of her close friends?'

'Because Emma and her close friends are as thick as thieves, and I thought they'd go straight to Emma and tell her I'm digging around. And I didn't want to upset her with the news that I've been writing her obit when she's only just got the all-clear.'

Rosen thinks about this for a while. Then: 'Are you genuinely worried about her?' he asks.

I nod.

'OK,' he says, slowly. 'OK. Listen – my loyalty's always going to be to Emma, but I've had my concerns about what was going on back then. If she was in some sort of trouble I'd never forgive myself for covering it up. Especially if it's kicking off again.'

Especially if what's kicking off again?

‘She had a visitor, one time. When we were filming in Northumberland, for the second series. I was up until the wee hours every night, photocopying shooting scripts and – well, on our last night I saw her talking to a man in the hotel bar. Late, when she thought we’d all gone to bed. And I saw them in a cafe in London a few weeks later. Near Broadcasting House.’

I sink my hands in my pocket. My fingers are shaking. ‘Do you know who the man was?’

There’s a long silence.

Then: ‘Jeremy Rothschild,’ he says quietly. ‘You know? The broadcaster?’

Recent memories replay at a screaming speed, while everything else becomes slow and silvered. A taxi pulls up at the edge of the road and my phone starts ringing.

He must be wrong. Emma has never met Rothschild. She speaks about him the same way she’d speak about Justin Webb or Mishal Husain, the other *Today* presenters – she enjoys him slaughtering politicians, doesn’t rate his wife as an actress and that’s that. Unless – ? No. No.

I stare at the wet tarmac beneath my feet, trying to make sense of what he’s saying.

‘The only reason I’m telling you,’ he says, ‘is that she was always upset after his visits. Like, exhausted, blotchy face, as if she hadn’t slept all night. I don’t know what they were talking about, but it worried me. Especially the time I saw them in that cafe in London; Rothschild looked quite angry. Emma had only just found out she had cancer; she had a lot on her plate. I was concerned.’

I can’t speak.

‘I’ve sometimes wondered if it was Janice Rothschild who got Emma sacked. She was a big BBC name, she’d definitely have had the clout. She’s been one of their stars forever.’

His face changes: he's worried he's said too much. 'Look, you mustn't say this came from me,' he begins, before I cut him off.

'I won't. I promise I won't. But Robbie, I need to know more. Why would Janice get Emma sacked? What was going on with Emma and Jeremy Rothschild?'

He shrugs again, helplessly. 'I really, truly don't know. I guess Janice might have got wind of their meetings, and . . . ?'

'I see.'

I don't see. Emma and Jeremy Rothschild at a table together doesn't even begin to make sense.

'I'm only telling you because the whole thing worried me at the time. I had a nasty feeling about their relationship – whatever was going on between them, it wasn't good for Emma at all. And now with Janice going missing, I really don't like it. I know the police have said Jeremy Rothschild isn't a suspect in his wife's disappearance . . . But you can't help wondering, can you?'

A thin line of anxiety rises in me. This hadn't crossed my mind.

'He knocked out a pap once, a few years back,' Rosen says. 'Did you know that?'

'I did.' Robbie can't have been much older than ten when it happened.

'At the time everyone was, like, Jeremy was seriously provoked, yada yada, but if all of us lashed out when things got hard, the world would be a pretty violent place, wouldn't it? I think he's got a dark side.'

'Food for thought,' I say, forcing a smile. Then: 'Look, thank you. I appreciate your honesty. Especially when I've been so dishonest with you.'

Rosen shrugs. The rain starts again.

'One final thing. You wrote Emma a note – just a line

about not wanting to miss out on saying goodbye to her – but she's gone out of her way to keep it safe. Why do you think that is?'

I see a flash of pride, amid the unease.

'She had a huge amount to deal with on that series,' he says. 'Cancer, IVF, pregnancy, whatever was going on with Jeremy Rothschild. She told me I'd been her rock. I guess she just wanted to keep hold of something good from that time?'

This, at least, makes sense. Emma finds it hard let go of anything. We have an entire house of her stuff to prove it.

'There's nothing else,' he says. 'I'd tell you if there was. And maybe it was all just a storm in a teacup.' He makes a temporary hood out of the back of his jumper, which is soaked in seconds. 'Look, I'd better . . .' He points back inside with a thumb. I nod, and stand there in the rain, trying to decide what to do.

My phone rings again.

After a while, the taxi drives off.

Chapter Twenty-One

LEO

A few years ago I dreamed my mother was a Venus fly trap. I told Emma the next morning and we laughed, because, as metaphors went, it was gold. It's nearly 9 p.m. now and Mum is hugging me on the doorstep of the house in which I grew up, hugging and hugging and telling me it's been too long, she doesn't see enough of me. '. . . Must have been at least fifteen months, because of course you decided not to come for Christmas, and . . .' With each complaint her arms tighten resentfully, and I allow it. Anything to stave off the lethal undertow of my thoughts.

I flew from Glasgow to Luton after meeting Robbie Rosen. As my plane climbed through somnolent clouds I tried to envisage an innocent place for Jeremy Rothschild in Emma's life – a place I could accept, that wouldn't harm the fabric of us, but I couldn't come up with a single thing. Innocent stories are never kept secret, my journalist's brain whispered.

The thing is, my 'journalist's brain', if that's what you call it, isn't always to be trusted. Far too many times it has decided that some man or other is in love with Emma. The current suspects are Kelvin and Dr Moru, neither of whom I'm concerned about, but there have been others.

It started when she'd been presenting *This Land*, and I'd found a chat forum full of men talking about her. I've always known Emma's sensational, but it was something else to hear other men talking about her in that way.

When I told her about it she went large on my 'adoption issues'. Apparently I'd had a terror of being abandoned from the moment I lost my birth mother, and now – according to Dr Emma Bigelow – I was projecting the very same abandonment fear onto her. 'I am not going to leave you,' she kept saying, as if I'd told her I feared she would.

I didn't desire further amateur psychoanalysis, so I never brought it up again. When I see men looking at her nowadays, I pretend it's not happening.

But she's right: I don't like it. Just last week, on the way back from the Tom Jones concert, there was a man in a baseball cap staring at her while we waited at a zebra crossing. Just staring, as if she wasn't quite obviously with her husband and child.

She was looking down the hill and didn't notice him, but it took everything I had not to walk up and kick him in the balls.

But this business with Jeremy Rothschild: it's not some freak eyeing her up on the street; it's real. And I don't know what to do.

If she can so easily lie about her degree, about Mags Tenterden and the many other things in her folder that made no sense, who's to say she couldn't have had an affair with a man she's never even told me she knows?

I bought three miniature bottles of aeroplane wine and passed out just as we came in to land.

Emma called soon after, but I didn't pick up. It was still light and the air was warmer than it had been in Glasgow; everyone disembarking the plane seemed happy – perhaps the miracle of a budget airline landing on time. I smiled at them in the baggage queue, as if I was happy too, rather than mildly drunk and miserable. I took a taxi all the way to my parents' in Hitchin and shared funny stories with the driver about family life. I could see myself in the mirror, looking like a man who had his shit together. Crew neck jumper, recent haircut, stylish luggage which Olly and Tink got me for my fortieth.

Emma texted as we turned into my parents' road. *The sun disappeared after breakfast so we went to Alnwick Castle. Ruby more interested in gift shop. Flight was fine, just landed at Heathrow. Call me! xxxxxx*

Everything is OK, I repeat to myself now, even though it's not. I spot a glorious sunset through the landing window as I follow Mum up to see Dad; orange and blood red layered on tired grey, with streaks of pink straight from an eighties disco. The bell of the local church strikes the hour and somewhere a family is barbecuing.

When I arrive in their room, Dad's trying to prop himself up in bed. 'Oh, Leo,' he says, gesturing in frustration, or perhaps resignation. He refuses analgesia on the grounds that he'd 'rather know', but tonight he's surrounded by painkillers and he looks frayed. 'I'm seventy-one and I feel like I'm a hundred. To hell with this.'

'To hell,' I agree, sitting down. We don't hug these days. He's lost weight, I notice, although he did have a fair bit to spare. My father is one of those men who pretends he is extremely proud of his overeating; patting his belly like a friend, boasting that he eats more in one meal than most small families eat in a week. Emma says that Dad's feelings are stored in his stomach.

Mum hands him a bowl of crumble, which he eats so fast I can't imagine he's tasting it. 'Making up for lost time,' he says, laughing and coughing. On cue he pats his belly, a still substantial mound under the duvet, and looks at Mum for comment, but she's hanging up his newly washed dressing gown.

This is my father. He makes jokes, he sidesteps awkward conversation. He wrote to me just once, in the six months of silence after I discovered I was adopted. *We were just following the advice of the adoption agency*, he had written. *They said it would be easier for you not to know. It was a different time, I'm sure you can understand.*

I couldn't, actually, and a few weeks later I had replied with a long list of questions he never answered. Nowadays he gives me a slightly longer pat on the shoulder, as if we have passed into a special understanding.

The room settles to silence. Mum's looking at a picture of Olly and me on a wintery beach somewhere, as toddlers. Olly, who was not adopted ('our miracle!') has his hand tucked into Mum's pocket, while I stand off at a slight distance, watchful. My skin is darker than my brother's, my hair dark brown to his white blonde. It had never crossed my mind to question this.

My parents have hundreds of pictures from our childhood, in a large box under the stairs. The first time I came back here, after discovering I'd been adopted, I went through the whole thing: alone, in silence, on the floor of my childhood bedroom. It was as if someone had handed me a photographic archive of my alienation. Everything I'd felt, but never understood, was there. My little brother, with his round face and chunky limbs; me, with my angular jaw and slight frame. How could I never have thought to question this? And it wasn't just the physical differences; my expression in so many photographs betrayed an outsider's unconscious longing.

I could have understood why every atom of me felt different, I wrote to my parents. *I could have had a counsellor when I was still young. But you took that decision out of my hands.*

The next day I do what I came to do: I clean the house, I do a supermarket shop, I put on a couple of loads of laundry, and I let Mum sit on the sofa and complain that I'm not allowing her to do anything.

Dad falls asleep after his lunch, and a few minutes later, Mum goes up to join him, 'Just for forty winks.' By 12.45 p. m. the house is quiet.

I check in with Sheila, hoping there might be some crisis involving a famous dead person I can bury myself in, but she says everything is fine and I should enjoy my day off.

So I sit alone in my parents' sitting room and force myself to contemplate the possibility of my wife having an affair with Jeremy Rothschild.

I think about the short shrift Emma has always given Janice Rothschild as an actress. The fact that she never comes to industry parties, even though she loves a good booze-up. Has she been avoiding him?

And then Rothschild complaining about my Janice feature, barring me from writing an advance obituary. Was I getting too close for comfort?

I imagine the actual act of sex between Emma and Jeremy Rothschild, and it makes me want to retch. I don't believe it. I can't believe it.

And yet, nothing I've taken for fact seems reliable anymore. Here I am in the house of my parents, who are not, biologically, my parents. And now my wife, the woman who pledged to love me until death, turns out to have lied about everything: there are untruths scattered across our relationship like landmines, and I don't see how I can move through or beyond them.

At 2 p.m. I leave for London. I feel unarmed and vulnerable, as if in a combat zone wearing nothing more than a shirt. This is not how I ever imagined feeling about the family I chose. This is not how I imagined feeling about my wife.

Chapter Twenty-Two

EMMA

Leo doesn't call until he's left his parents' house and boarded the train to London, nearly seventy-two hours since we last talked. It's the longest we've gone without contact in ten years.

'Hey!' I say, darting into the water analysis lab. It's a mistake: there's a bunch of postgrads around the SediGraph, chatting and laughing at top volume as if they're at a bloody house party. In desperation, I go into one of the cold stores.

'Hey,' Leo says, with the verbal fixity of someone who can't permit so much as a millimetre of emotion.

'Hi darling. Are you OK? Did you and your mum part on decent terms?' I stick a finger in my other ear to drown out the cold air fans.

Leo pauses. 'Oh, we're fine. Listen, I was just thinking about Mags Tenterden. Your old agent.'

Leo is very bad at lying. He has not been 'just thinking' about her.

'Oh yes?' I transfer my phone to the other ear, hoping I'll perhaps hear another story on that side.

He says, all rushed, 'I did get it right, didn't I? She dropped you as a client? It wasn't the other way around?'

I close my eyes, where flames lick.

Please, Leo. Don't go there, my love.

But he is going there, and it's coming, now, no matter what I do. If Leo doesn't already know the answer to this question, he's close. And if he's close to the truth about Mags, he's close to all of it.

Over the years I've raged at myself for lying about Mags. It was one thing to conceal a past Leo could never forgive; it was quite another to start a whole new line of deception in the present tense. But what else could I have said to explain my hysterical state? What possible reason could I have had for leaving Mags, whom Leo knew I adored?

'Mags did drop me,' I say, hopelessly. 'You must remember.'

There's a long silence, which means he knows I'm lying. This call was very possibly my last chance.

I lean against the specimen storage shelves, shoving my free hand deep into my pocket. It brings to mind an image of Leo the day we met, leaning against the wall at Granny's send-off, hands in pockets, watching me with a quiet smile on his face. I'd fancied him so much I'd barely heard the kind words of the funeral guests.

'Fair enough,' he says. 'I was just wondering.'

'OK. Well . . . See you later, then?'

'I'll be back for bathtime. Just need to sort out a couple of things in town before I come home.'

'OK,' I say. My eyes are filling with tears. I love you, I want to say, but I don't.

Chapter Twenty-Three

LEO

Mags Tenterden's offices are in one of the new blocks at King's Cross. I pause by the canal before going in, looking at the crowd of well-dressed young people lounging by the water on cushions. Why are they not at work at 3.45 p.m. on a Friday in June? When I was twenty-five I was slaving away on a hot newsroom floor for twelve hours straight, too fearful even to take a piss.

Behind them, children run shrieking between choreographed plumes of water. There is live music somewhere, and the workers queueing for late lunch at the street food stalls have their sleeves rolled up. Everyone is having a nice day.

I turn back to Mags' office building and my stomach churns.

'I don't have a great deal of time,' Mags tells me. She's aged only fractionally since I saw her last, but seems even more fashionable than before. Her silver hair is cropped, and she wears large red glasses with a dress that is all Scandinavian angles. 'Sit,' she adds, pointing to a chair.

I almost laugh at her frosty welcome. When I first met Mags at the BBC transmission party for *This Land* she warned me 'not to be a pain in the backside' if Emma's career took off. It had taken me so completely by surprise I'd been unable to swallow my G&T and just stood there, cheeks bulging like a hamster.

'I won't be long,' I reply.

She watches me. I expected her to have a clichéd agent's office, covered in yellowing photos and dust-gathering trophies, but this place is like a waiting room in a design consultancy. Blonde wood, architectural steel, white-painted walls and prints in slim black frames. There is nothing to suggest that this woman represents close to a hundred actors and television presenters.

'When you and Emma parted ways, was it her decision or yours?' I ask.

Mags sits back in her chair, visibly surprised.

She recovers quickly. 'It was Emma's decision, of course,' she says. 'May I ask why?'

That weightless feeling again. I think a tiny part of me still believed Mags would trash Robbie Rosen's story. 'It's complicated,' is all I manage.

'I was shocked,' Mags says. 'But she didn't sign with anyone else, so I supposed she meant it when she said she was done with TV.'

I nod wordlessly. Outside the sky is a perfect blue.

Jeremy and Emma. Emma and Jeremy. The picture of them sharpens focus, obscenely.

'What's this all about?' Mags repeats. She leans forward on her elbows, watching me. I think she's had her teeth whitened.

'Emma told me you let her go,' I reply. 'She was heartbroken. She went off to spend three weeks on the coast, recovering. I don't – I don't understand why she said one thing and you're saying another.'

Mags frowns. In the background I can hear phones and a

giggled conversation in some corner. Mags' agency is the oldest and largest in the entertainment business, their website says.

'I can show you the termination letter she sent if you don't believe me,' Mags says. 'I remember it well. I left her a voicemail – asked her to have a proper think about it – but she wouldn't talk to me. I emailed her, even wrote her a letter, but she was having none of it. Just sent me a note saying she was done with television.'

She scratches her elbow. 'I still receive fifteen per cent of her BBC Worldwide royalties, though, so it wasn't all for nothing.'

Emma had sobbed on my shoulder and told me she'd been dropped. What was she really crying about? What was going on? I feel dizzy just contemplating the possibilities.

Mags is studying me carefully. 'Emma was having a bad time. Bear that in mind, won't you?'

'Yes,' I say vaguely. I'm too hot. I undo a button of my shirt, and look pointedly at the aircon unit above Mags' desk, which is not switched on. 'By "a bad time" you mean her cancer diagnosis – right?'

Mags picks up a pen that she rolls between the finger and thumbs of both hands. 'I actually meant her being sacked from the BBC. But yes, the cancer news was bloody terrible, too.'

'Right. Well, on that subject, can I ask if you know why the Beeb sacked her? She told me at the time it was all a bit vague and nobody could really explain it – a new commissioner, something like that. But I've since heard it wasn't vague at all.'

Mags continues to roll the pen. 'Have you two split up?' she asks.

I tell her we have not. Then, after a brief internal struggle, I level with her.

'Look, Mags – I apologise. I'm poor at lying. The reason I'm here is that I've discovered Emma has misled me about a great number of things. I'm getting my facts straight before speaking to her later.'

Mags thinks about this for a moment. 'Sounds difficult,' she says. 'But it's not appropriate to involve me.'

She places the pen on the desk, then picks it straight back up. I think this is rattling her.

'I agree it's not appropriate,' I say. 'And this isn't how I'd behave, normally, but I'm desperate. Will you at least tell me why the BBC got rid of her – if you know, that is?'

'Of course I know.'

'But you won't tell me?'

'No. If Emma didn't tell you, I won't.' The set of her jaw tells me she means it.

'Well then – I guess I'll get going.'

'I think that's a good idea. Nice to see you again, and goodbye!' says Mags.

In another time, I might have smiled, but not now. I sag in my chair. 'Oh, look. Please will you help me out?'

'I can't.' Mags looks at her watch. 'And I really do have to get going. Leo, I urge you to go home and speak to Emma. That's the best I can offer.' She throws me a stinging smile and then snaps her laptop shut.

There's nothing for it.

'Your husband,' I say, as she places the laptop in a sleeve. 'We have a stock obituary on file for him.'

She stops what she's doing, but says nothing. Mags' husband was the political editor for ITV for years. He hasn't been an honourable sort of a man.

'A mutual friend told me several things about him. I'm pretty sure I'm the only person they confided in, so none of it has made it to the stock yet.'

I jam my hands between my legs, where they dance and jitter. This had seemed like a good idea on the train, but I'm not that sort of hack. I never have been – it's why I ended up in obits.

'Oh, forget it,' I mutter. 'I'm sorry. That's blackmail.'

Mags is watching me with disgust. She doesn't say a word.

I scrape back the chair. 'People do awful things when they're desperate, don't they? Just – forget I was here.'

'For fuck's sake,' Mags snaps. She almost throws her laptop back onto her desk. 'The reason the BBC—'

'No,' I say quickly. 'Forget what I said about your husband. I'm not that kind of man. It's OK.'

Mags bats me off. 'I won't have Emma tell everyone I got rid of her. It's borderline libellous – in fact, I've half a mind to talk to our lawyer about it—'

'Oh no, please don't,' I begin, but she's not interested.

'Listen, Leo.' She waits for me to stop bleating. 'The reason the BBC had to let Emma go is that someone informed them Emma had a criminal record. They investigated and it turned out to be true.'

After a pause, I lean forward. 'I'm sorry. She had a what?'

'You heard me.'

'But – what for? I mean, what *for*?'

Mags purses her lips. 'Stalking.'

I cradle my head in my hands. 'What? Who? Who did she stalk?'

Mags Tenterden leans back in her chair, remembering that time. 'She stalked Janice Rothschild.' Her voice is quieter now, almost apologetic. 'I know this isn't easy to hear.'

'It's . . . not.'

'It was Janice who tipped the BBC off. Emma resigned as my client because she didn't want to put me in a difficult situation – Janice has been with this agency since she came out of RADA in the nineties.'

'Oh, God.'

Mags watches me for a while.

'Leo, I'm afraid I really do have somewhere to be. I'll have my assistant show you out.'

Chapter Twenty-Four

LEO

I stand on our overgrown front path, imagining Ruby, full of stories about the 'rarpoplane' and what she 'needs' before bed (chocolate biscuits). I try to imagine the conversation Emma and I are going to have. Spokes of anxiety turn.

I called my brother when I left Mags' office. Olly, unlike me, has an intrinsic sense of belonging in this world and seldom jumps to the worst conclusion.

'We all keep things to ourselves,' he said, easily. He was loading his dishwasher. 'And yes, I keep all sorts of things from Tink.'

'Such as what?'

'Such as secrets.'

'You just made that up to make me feel better.'

There was a long pause. 'OK, well I have never told Tink, or anyone else, about the time Mum came into my bedroom and found me cracking one off over a picture of Samantha Fox,' he said squarely.

I laughed for the first time in twenty-four hours. 'That's beautiful. But I'm talking about the big stuff, Olly, not teenage masturbation.'

'Mate! Listen to me. Emma's lied about her degree and something to do with her agent. It could be a lot worse.'

'Really? You'd be OK with Tink making up a degree course that didn't happen? Getting sacked for stalking and then fabricating a whole story about it? And what about her hiding a long-term weird and quite possibly sexual relationship with Jeremy Rothschild? You'd be happy if it was Tink?'

Olly made a noncommittal noise. 'Mikkel,' he called. 'Leave him alone!'

'The worst thing is that Emma's gone out of her way to cover it all up. She's removed paperwork from the cabinet, hidden it somewhere else, then told me I'm being paranoid. And she was texting someone in Northumberland the other day, trying to arrange a meet-up. She said she was messaging Susi, her old school friend, but I just don't believe her. Not now.'

At that, Olly had stopped loading his dishwasher. 'Did you say Northumberland?'

'Yes. Why?'

He exhaled slowly. 'I'm sure it's nothing, but Jeremy Rothschild has a house up there. One of my colleagues goes there on holiday every year, they rent a cottage next door to his place. Alnwick, I think? Alnmouth maybe?'

'Oh fuck,' I said. 'Oh fuck, Olly.'

I slide the key into the lock and pull the door silently behind me.

She'll be bathing Ruby by now. I know Duck will be perched on the Victorian school chair in the corner of our bathroom, just where Ruby likes him to be. I know what the room will smell like, I see the window with its warm condensation sliding towards the rotting sill.

Normally these thoughts make my heart soar, but now I crave only knowledge. I tiptoe to the kitchen, where I take my wife's phone out of her bag and open her messages.

It's mundane stuff at first: work chat, mum chat, friend chat. The rumble of dread is too loud for me to question the ethics of what I'm doing. I go through each message chain methodically before moving on to the next.

Sixth down the list is a message to Jill, sent this morning. Emma tells Jill she's nervous about seeing me later. *I wish I could just tell him*, she writes. *I feel so bad.*

Jill: *You can't tell Leo. You decided that a long time ago. None of the reasons have changed.*

Emma: *Oh, I know . . . But I can't bear it*

Jill: *I think you need to go home and have a nice dinner together, and deny whatever he thinks he's on to. It'll pass. He loves you too much to blow everything up over some half-baked intelligence.*

I stare at the phone. What does this mean?

And Jill, why is she telling Emma to lie to me? My heart brims with rage. How dare she encourage Emma to conceal things from me? *Deny whatever he thinks he's on to*, she's written, as if I'm some fool. What the fuck?

I continue to scroll, feverishly now, through Emma's messages. I don't have much time. I need to look for people she's never mentioned – decoy names. Names like . . . Names like this. *Sally*.

I open up the message chain, and my fingers are like jelly.

It's him.

Two hours ago, he messages to say he's thinking about her. *Would be good to meet up again soon*, he adds. *Feels like there's a lot more for us to talk about.*

Twenty-four hours ago, he writes, *Are you OK?*

Then forty-eight hours ago, when Emma was in Alnmouth, he sends three rapid messages, apologising for having left suddenly. He says he 'couldn't do it with Ruby there'.

Couldn't do what? I seethe, repulsed.

Emma has a started a reply. It sits in the dialogue box, as yet unsent.

Jeremy, respectfully, I'm going to have to ask you to stop messaging me about Janice. I can't shake the feeling that you hold me partly responsible for her disappearance, and that really bothers me. I understand: she's disappeared, you're terrified, you're wondering if you could have protected her better, if I might hold some sort of key. Similarly, I know that, whether any of us like it or not, we are bound together – you are the father of my child, for God's sake – and that you have your own views on how we should navigate this mess, but awkward meet-ups are not the solution to our problem. You know what I wan—

The cursor flashes, ready for her to continue.

I scroll back and read again. I get to the end again. Then I read the middle section, five, six times over. My fingers hover above the phone, almost as if to delete the words, before starting to tremble.

I turn around and crash straight into Emma's suitcase, which falls over.

Within seconds, a thundering and scrabbling is heard, as John Keats gallops down the stairs.

'Leo?' Emma calls. 'Is that you, darling?'

I look at the dog, who's going round and round in circles because his daddy is home and everything is so great. My eyes fill. This is it, I realise. The end of a loved and longed-for family life. All the times I complained about mess or noise, all the times I worried about unknown television viewers and their imagined crushes on Emma, when actually she was having an affair with Jeremy Rothschild.

And then I sink into the chair, allowing myself to think about the child in the bath upstairs, my little pea, my baby. The idea of her resulting from a sordid, hot-breathed affair is more awful even than the thought of Emma having sex with someone else. It is an anguish I can't contain. I stand up, circling. I have no plan.

'Daddy?' A little squeak of a voice, some splashing. John wags and wags, pressing his wet nose up into my hand. He can't understand why I won't get down on the floor for rough and tumble.

'DADDEEEE!' Ruby yells, from upstairs.

I can't face her. There's a howling somewhere within myself. The very idea of my girl being –

No.

My body moves towards the front door, then I'm out into an evening that smells of expensively planted gardens and cooking. I walk quickly down the lane to Hampstead Grove and then Heath Street, where wealthy women with thickly drawn eyebrows sip from misted wine glasses.

I never belonged in Hampstead. I wonder if I ever really belonged anywhere.

Eventually I swerve into a pub near Belsize Park. I order a pint, then a second one, and take both off to a corner table, as if I'm waiting for a friend. I stare at a wall of hop kiln tiles and drink mechanically, in the way that sometimes makes Emma touch my arm and say, hey, do you want to talk?

'She loves me,' I say, to the pub. It's a lovely Victorian public house with oxidised mirrors and stained ceilings, into which stories and songs have been baked for decades since the last paint job. I finish my first pint in minutes, grateful for the anonymity of London. Here, you can harm yourself in plain sight, and nobody will ever stop to ask if you're OK.

We were at a pub when Emma found out she was pregnant with Ruby. We'd met in Soho after work, because there were still three days to go before Emma was due to take a pregnancy test and we both needed a distraction. Emma went upstairs to the loo while I ordered at the bar, but by the time I'd taken our drinks outside and found a patch of windowsill to lean on, she still hadn't reappeared.

Everything OK? I texted her.

Seconds later, she appeared next to me, white as a sheet.

'Look,' she said. She turned to block out the other drinkers with her back, and handed me a plastic stick. I stared at the stick for some time before I realised what it was; what the two blue lines meant.

'I bought the test on the way here,' she said. 'And it was there in my handbag just now and I know it's three days before I should be doing the test and a pub toilet really isn't the place to do it but I couldn't resist.'

I tried to take the stick, but she held on fast. 'I've just weed on it,' she said.

It wasn't the first time we had stared at a positive pregnancy test together. And I knew this pregnancy was only days old, that there was every chance it wouldn't get far. But as we stood there, under hanging baskets of geraniums, surrounded by hipsters and market traders and office workers, I had a gut feeling this was it.

Tears filled my eyes. 'Wow,' I said. Emma didn't reply, but when she turned her face up to mine, I saw she was crying, too.

She hugged me hard, burying her face in my shirt, and warm tears bled through the cotton onto my chest. Behind us, a bunch of young men were falling about laughing, singing a tuneless song with the lyrics 'Blake smells of fish, Blake smells of fish.'

I remember our journey home later, how quiet she was, how she held my hand as we sped north on the tube. How she stopped me in the street, just before we went into our house, and said, 'I love you so much, Leo,' and how I smiled because I knew she meant it.

She did love me. She does love me. I haven't just made it up.

But then I think of all the people I've written up in my time as an obituarist. The aristocrats with their happy marriages and long-term sexual relations with the housekeeper. The gangsters with girlfriends in every city. The married academics with their student lovers, the artists with their orgies. Many of these people claimed, towards the end of their lives, that they loved their spouses deeply; that their marriages had never suffered because of their infidelities.

Maybe it is possible to love someone and have basic physical sex with someone else? Maybe it is even possible to love two people?

I try not to think directly about Ruby, because I can't, but the truth about her has already lodged itself somewhere in my skin. Jeremy and Emma met late at night at around the time she got pregnant. This, after years and years of us trying without success to have a baby.

They saw each other in Northumberland this week. They've been messaging each other. Emma calls him 'the father of my child'.

There is no one on earth to whom I'm related by blood, I realise. Absolutely no one.

Chapter Twenty-Five

EMMA

I don't take Ruby downstairs. I know something has happened by the way John Keats slinks into the bathroom with his tail rammed between his legs. He only does this when he's seen human behaviour he doesn't understand.

I help Ruby into her pyjamas, listening for a sound from the kitchen, but none comes. A quiet space of fear grows in my chest as I read Ruby her bedtime story. Since asking me about Mags earlier, Leo hasn't replied to any of my messages.

The kitchen is like a held breath when I make it downstairs. Leo's weekend bag is there, but mine is on its back, stranded like an overturned beetle. John Keats stands at my side, pointing his anxious nose at the wireless speaker through which we play jungle.

'Leo?' I say, to nobody. Ruby's preschool plant, in the corner, is now quite dead. She's watered it to an early grave.

I hold myself still, trying to think what might have happened to Leo.

John pants. 'It's OK,' I tell him. 'It's OK, John.'

Then I spot my phone on the worktop, and hear a small wail come out of my mouth.

It is not OK. My phone was in my bag when I took Ruby up for her bath.

Leo, no.

And there it is, when I pick it up: my half-written message to Jeremy. The cursor blinks benignly at the end, awaiting instruction.

. . . you are the father of my child, for God's sake . . .

The room falls silent. Soft pink clouds twist over the trees in the garden. A cat is sitting on the back wall, washing its paws.

'No,' I say quietly. 'No.'

I read my draft again, twice, three times, and imagine Leo doing the same, the agony in his body, the disbelief.

'I'm sorry, I'm so sorry,' I whisper, before scrabbling to dial his number.

Hello, this is Leo Philber, says his voice. His lovely voice. *Sorry I can't take your call. Please leave a message, and I'll come back to you as soon as I can.*

We laughed about 'come back to you'. I said it was American; he said it was what all the cool young journalists said on their voicemails these days, at which I had laughed very hard indeed, and he'd been unable to keep a straight face.

I try to think. Maybe he hasn't read it? But of course he's read it. And besides, Leo would never have invaded my privacy in this way if he wasn't already close to the truth.

The phone screen clears, suddenly, starts ringing. I nearly cry with relief – but it's not Leo, it's Jill. I cancel the call.

I try messaging.

Leo, are you there?

Tick: the message leaves my phone.

Two ticks: the message arrives in his.

Two blue ticks: he's reading it.

Relief breaks over me, although I don't know why. I have no hope of undoing this.

My darling, please come home. I have to explain this to you

Two blue ticks. I try to picture him, the reading glasses he never cleans, smudged and sad. Maybe he's out on the Heath as the evening greys. Or on the tube, paused at an underground station before the train swishes onwards to – to where? Oh God, Leo.

Jill calls again. I cancel it. Seconds later, she tries again. I cancel it again; I'll ring her tomorrow.

I start another message to Leo, trying to explain, but stop. What can I say? The message he's found goes so much deeper than Ruby's parentage. There are important reasons why I've shielded him from it; these years of collusion and misery between Jeremy and me. How can I tell him now, in a text message?

He goes offline. I send another message, asking if he's still there, but it doesn't deliver.

In the middle of this, Jeremy texts. *Are you OK? I don't have any news. Just checking Janice hasn't been in touch.*

I delete it, and sink slowly into a chair. I use my phone to put something on the speaker called 'Smooth: New Directions in Ambient Jungle', so John can calm down.

Jill calls yet again, and this time I pick up. 'Hey,' I say. 'I'm sorry but I can't talk. Leo's been reading my phone and he's disappeared. Can I call you tomorrow? Are you all right?'

'I'm fine. But I have to talk to you, Emma—'

'I just can't,' I interrupt. 'I'm so sorry. I promise I'll call in the morning.'

You need to call me back tonight, Jill writes, straight away. *It's important.*

I reply, *I'll call you tomorrow, I promise.*

I stay still for a long time, until darkness swallows the room. Planes whine and drag across London, circling into Heathrow and Gatwick, and a fox topples a dustbin. The air cools, but my heart won't slow.

I try Leo at 1.37 a.m. His phone rings out.

I try again at 2.04.

At 2.30, he messages, finally. *Sleeping in the shed. Please don't come out. I need space.*

I go to check Ruby is breathing.

Chapter Twenty-Six

LEO

The next morning I wake with a pounding head and a mouth full of sickness and regret. I have no idea how many pints I had last night, how many chasers after that. I do remember climbing over the wall so I could get into the shed because I couldn't decide if I had actually left Emma, and I felt it would be wrong to spend the night elsewhere without making a proper decision. No matter what, I won't just disappear on Ruby.

A trapped fly vibrates in a cobweb near the end of my dusty sofa, and outside John Keats is barking at the pond. I'll have to go inside in a minute, but I have no idea what will happen when I see Ruby. I'm afraid I will just pick my little girl up and run out of the front door.

She's mine. She has to be mine. For at least the first year of her life people would say to me, 'Oh, she's the spit of you! She's gorgeous!' and my chest would crack with pride. For the first time, I belonged to a unit. A real family, no secrets.

I think about Ruby's soft hair, her stubby fingernails, that crafty little laugh. Then I think about Emma and Jeremy Rothschild and it's so foul and wrong and unbelievable and preposterous that for a moment I really don't believe it's true.

But as I sat in the pub last night, before the alcohol smudged my memory and judgement, I remembered things. Emma's baffling long-term hatred of Janice Rothschild. Her fury the other day when Jeremy complained about me to my editor-in-chief. And of course her Times. Years and years of them.

Emma lost her mother a day or two after birth; her father just before she sat her A-levels. His commando had been sent to what was then Zaire to help evacuate British nationals from Kinshasa, and he didn't make it back.

Her father had been an unhappy man, she said, and mostly absent, but she had loved him, as any child does. A picture of him sits on our landing; the only thing Emma's managed to put on the walls since we moved in. The loss of both parents has always seemed like a plausible explanation for her spells of sadness. But I began to wonder last night, with a downward drop of dread, if her Times were even real. What if they were an alibi, so she could go up to Northumberland and have sex with Jeremy Rothschild? Did she move Jill into our house when Ruby was born because she was afraid Jeremy would turn up to claim his daughter?

I swallow hard.

When I'm able to get up I open the door a crack, and am near-blinded by shafts of early sun. Spider webs glow on the ground like jewelled plates, broken only by paw prints. Soon the dew will be burned off and the day will reach full heat, full speed.

I pause again, uncertain if I'll throw up.

John Keats is watching the pond with impatience, but bounds over happily when he sees me, as if he is used to me sleeping in the shed. I pull him back inside. 'Jeremy,' I say to him. 'Jeremy? Do you know Jeremy?'

He beats his tail on the floor.

'John. Where's Jeremy?'

The dog, confused, excited, turns in circles. He has no idea, but he doesn't like to miss out on a game.

I tell him we need to go inside. I stand up, but don't move. I tell him to lead the way, but he starts jumping around, barking. I kneel down and hug him, which is the only way of stopping him once he's overexcited.

It takes a while before he settles. I sit back on my heels, looking at him. 'I don't think I can do this,' I admit. 'I'm not ready, John.' The only conversation I can have with Emma, now, is to confirm the details of her affair, and to tell her I can't be with someone who has cheated on me, and I'm not ready for that.

I fight tears as I message Emma to say I need more time. I stick my head out of the shed. There is no movement in the kitchen; they must be upstairs.

That decides it. I give John a kiss, and sprawl heavily over the back wall, into the brambled alley that separates our gardens from those we back on to. Nobody ever uses this narrow lane, and the gate at the end has been locked for years. For the second time in twelve hours, I climb over it, only this time I'm watched by a delivery man, sorting through parcels in the back of an unmarked van.

'All right?' I say to him.

'All right,' he replies. In the distance, John Keats is barking again.

Chapter Twenty-Seven

LEO

Few newsrooms are empty at the weekend, and ours is no exception. Features is dead, of course, but today the news desk is frenzied, and politics is doing brisk business too. A protest has tipped into violence and skirmishes are breaking out across Westminster. Apparently the Foreign Secretary's car has got stuck in an angry crowd. I hurry past the busy desks, unwilling to engage.

As I round the corner, I see Sheila at her desk.

'Oh!'

'Oh,' she echoes. She removes her glasses.

It takes me a little while to realise she's embarrassed. Her computer is switched off and there is a novel in front of her, and it's ten past ten on Saturday morning. Eventually she places her book on her desk and swivels her chair to face me properly.

'You look terrible,' she says. 'Are you OK?'

I shake my head.

'Oh, Leo,' she says quietly, and it comes to me, finally, that she has known all along. Humiliation comes at me like a landslide.

'How did you know?'

'The Rothschilds have been friends for years,' she says. 'Jeremy and I in particular; he's always confided in me.'

I remain silent, mostly because I don't trust myself to speak.

'I'm sorry, Leo,' she says. 'I was never comfortable about you being kept in the dark.'

I've never heard tenderness in Sheila's voice. It fills me with despair.

'Is that why you kept asking about Emma being at Waterloo Station?' I demand. 'You were trying to tell me something?'

She looks down at her book. 'Not really. I was passing through Waterloo on my way to interview someone, I saw Emma in the middle of the station, all at sixes and sevens, and I wondered what had happened. The next day we all heard about Janice disappearing. I realised that Emma must have just found out from Jeremy when I saw her.'

'And . . . ?'

'And, Leo, I felt angry for you. It wasn't right that you didn't know about them. That you had no idea just how close to your own life the Rothschilds have been.' She sighs. 'I suppose I asked about Emma because I hoped she might finally have come clean. But of course, she clearly hadn't, and you just thought I was being nosy.'

I slide into someone's seat: I'm still by the family and community desk, several metres from Sheila. The desk's occupant has a Post-it reminder: PERSONAL TRAINER 6PM DON'T BE LATE.

'You should have told me,' is all I can say.

Sheila spires her fingertips. 'I would have done, if I could. But I have loyalty to both parties, Leo. I had to promise Jeremy that I would never breathe a word of this to anyone.'

I stare at someone's flashing voicemail light. Jeremy Rothschild doesn't deserve your loyalty, I want to say. But she's known Jeremy far longer than she has me.

Sheila continues: 'I knew you'd find something when you started writing Emma's stock. I saw you googling her university, Leo. Her TV series. I knew how upset and confused you'd be. I've found myself very conflicted.'

Someone in news turns on the giant TVs and the floor fills with noise. I get up and go to sit at my own desk.

'I want to kill Jeremy Rothschild,' I say, even though I've never been even half capable of violence.

Sheila sighs. 'God knows, you must dislike him at present, but he's not a bad man. He's actually been very good to Emma.'

'I bet he has!'

'He's not a bad man,' she repeats.

'Fine, Sheila. I get it. You've known him for years, you don't want to take sides.'

She smiles, apologetically.

'But, Ruby,' I say, and my voice shatters. 'What do I tell Ruby, Sheila? How can I be her father now?'

Sheila looks stern. 'You'll be her father in the same way you've always been,' she says. 'Of course. Look, this is not where you should be. Come to my place. I'll give you some food, and then I think you need a good sleep. You look frightful.'

I've never been able to imagine where Sheila lives. She's so private I don't even know what part of London she travels in from every day – she just says 'north of the river'. I imagine a flat somewhere sensible, maybe Queen's Park or Barnsbury.

But Sheila is unlike anyone else I have met, and for this reason it is not a huge surprise when she tells me we can walk to hers in twenty minutes. And when she stops outside a townhouse on Cheyne Walk, north of the river by approximately five metres, I start to smile. Of course she lives in a grand house right on the river. Of course.

It is stylishly decorated inside; that sort of bookish, old-fashioned good taste Emma and I have striven for but never quite attained. Persian rugs and bookshelves; antiques from an ancestor's Grand Tour. A pleasant smell of leather, flowers, ancient velvet.

'Wow,' I say, miserably. What a coup it would have been, in another life, to get an invitation to Sheila's house. To be able to tell Jonty that Sheila is probably a multi-millionaire in property, that she has a neo-classical statue with a huge penis on her mantelpiece.

'My father's house,' she says offhandedly. 'Too many rooms for a single woman. Sometimes I – it gets too much.' She gestures towards her bag, which contains the book she had come into work to read.

I've never imagined Sheila to be lonely. Whenever I think about her, out of work hours, I imagine her entertaining large crowds and hosting visitors from all over the world. Being here with her, on a Saturday, feels like reading her diary.

She shows me a room upstairs, in which there is a large white bed and a wall hung with charcoal studies. 'I'll bring you something to eat in a minute,' she says, and disappears. I try to find something to lay on the sheets so I don't get them grubby, but I have nothing else with me. Eventually I sit down on a thick rug next to the bed, unable to make a decision about anything.

When Sheila comes up with chocolate Hobnobs a few minutes later, I am fast asleep. I get up briefly, at her request, and allow myself to be shepherded into bed. She puts a calm hand on my head for a few moments, and then I'm gone again.

When I wake the light is beginning to slope and particles of dust wait in the air. It's 5 p.m. I can hear Sheila moving around downstairs, and for a few moments I can't quite remember why I am here.

It doesn't last long. I check my phone and my stomach rolls; there are nine messages and five missed calls from Emma.

Please call me.

Please come home.

Leo, I love you. Please talk to me.

There's a knock at my door. 'Hi,' Sheila says. She's dressed as if she's spent the afternoon doing yoga. I find this mildly surprising, even though these days everyone apart from me seems to do yoga. 'How are you bearing up?'

'I want to die,' I say.

She considers me for a few moments before smiling. 'I think you need to speak to Emma first. Are you ready to call her?'

I shake my head.

'You're welcome to stay over,' she says. 'But you have to let Emma know you're alive, and you have to meet her tomorrow. Monday at the latest. The two of you have to decide what happens next. You can't just disappear on your daughter.'

I close my eyes. My daughter.

Sheila comes over and puts her hand on my head again, as she did when I went to sleep. Maybe she wasn't an interrogator after all. Maybe she worked in a more human department of MI5, if such a department exists.

'You'll work it out,' she says. 'Leo, I've never known anyone love their partner more than you love Emma.'

'But that only counts if it's reciprocated, surely?'

After Sheila has left the room I sit with my phone in my

hand, staring at the charcoal studies on the wall. I feel hollowed out; an empty space.

My phone starts ringing. Surprisingly, it's Jill.

Jill is the last person I want to speak to, but there's a part of me hoping she might be able to tell me that this is all a mistake, that I have added two plus two and made nine.

'Jill?'

'Leo,' she says.

'Everything OK?'

'Yes, fine. I'm just trying to get hold of Emma. It's really urgent. I tried her last night, she said she'd ring back, but she hasn't. I must speak to her, Leo. Can you help?'

'No,' I reply. 'I can't. I'm not at home.'

'Still?'

'Yes, still. I found out Emma's been involved with Jeremy Rothschild for years. And I found a message last night in her phone, saying that he was Ruby's father. And I know you know about this, because I saw your messages too. So, please don't waste my time denying it.'

Jill is absolutely silent.

After a very long pause, she says, simply, 'Oh.'

'For Emma and Ruby's sake, I stayed the night in the shed. But I've gone back out again. I'm not ready to face Emma.'

'Right,' Jill says. Then: 'Sorry. Just for clarification. Are you telling me you've left Emma?'

'No, I'm not. I'm saying I need a couple of days to think, so I've gone to stay with a friend. OK?'

'OK,' she sighs, and ends the call.

I doubt I will ever understand Jill.

I message Emma, asking her to meet me at the house at 9.30 on Monday morning, once she's dropped Ruby off at nursery. I apologise for walking out, but admit that I am not handling it, and don't want Ruby to see me until I'm calmer.

She replies instantly to say *yes*, and *thank you*, and *I love you*. Shortly after, she sends another to say Ruby is fine.

Then that's done, and it is only ten minutes past five, and I have no idea how to fill the hours before my body will let me check out again.

I go downstairs to find Sheila drinking red wine in her garden. I have never seen Sheila drink red wine; when we go to the Plumbers' she always drinks continental lager, occasionally brandy. I also never imagined her drinking alone in a garden full of lush, boldly planted flowers at 5.15 p.m. Everything is out of place.

Wordlessly, she pours me a glass and we sit in silence as the afternoon bleeds into evening.

Chapter Twenty-Eight

EMMA

I take Ruby to nursery on Monday morning, swinging her hand and singing the hokey cokey as if everything is fine. Today is plant handover day and she carries the bag all the way there.

I hand the plant back to Della, Ruby's key person, saying Ruby has loved looking after it.

'Wow!' Della says. 'It's really shrunk!'

She winks. To try to kill a few painful hours yesterday I took Ruby to Ikea to buy a replacement, and Della is no fool.

I pause by the door as she puts it on a table, remarking to a colleague that the plant has come back looking substantially smaller. 'They're all the same,' says the colleague, oblivious to my presence. 'Middle-class parents. Can't ever admit to being wrong.'

This final heaping of shame does it. The tears come, and I flee.

As I walk off down the road, at speed, I hear a car pulling up to the kerb next to me. I take no notice until I hear the door open and my name called.

I turn to see who it is.

Chapter Twenty-Nine

LEO

At 9.55 a.m. I call Emma to find out why she is not here. Although she's late for everything, always, this was one appointment I trusted her to make.

Her phone rings out.

I try again at 10.30. Then at 11.00.

Is she with Rothschild, getting her story straight? The thought makes me want to throw my teacup at the wall. I don't, because it's rare Huguenot porcelain left to Emma by her grandmother. Instead I find an Ikea one and smash that. I have never done anything like this before, and it does not make me feel any better.

I sweep up the fragments and call the obits desk to tell them I'll be working from home. Kelvin seems unbothered but Sheila calls me straight away.

'What's happened?' she asks. I can hear her moving away from the obits desk. 'Did it not go well?'

'Emma didn't turn up,' I tell her. 'We were meant to meet here at nine thirty. No sign of her. She's not answering her phone.'

I can almost hear her frowning. 'That's strange. I thought she was desperate to explain herself to you?'

'She was. She's done nothing but message me about how

sorry she is, how she needs to explain, how much she loves me. But this morning: zilch.'

'Keep me posted,' Sheila says. 'Please?'

At 11.15 I call the nursery, suddenly panicking that Emma has taken Ruby and done a runner. I speak to Della, who assures me that Ruby is there, and that Emma dropped her off at 8.45 'with a very perky-looking plant'.

I update Sheila. She replies with a puzzled emoji, and Sheila is not someone who dabbles with emoji.

Unease drums in my stomach. I try Emma's right-hand woman, Nin, first at Emma's UCL department and then, when she doesn't answer, on a mobile number I find in Emma's Rolodex. She tells me Emma called in sick this morning, but spoke to someone else. 'Is she OK?' Nin asks.

'Who knows?' I say. I laugh oddly, and end the call. Nin probably thinks I've killed her.

That huge space is opening up in my chest again: I have to do something. I write a note for Emma on the kitchen blackboard and leave the house. I go and buy milk. When I return, it is midday and she's still not here.

I force myself to take John Keats for a walk on the Heath. I watch people running round the athletics track, and John steals another dog's ball.

When I return, it is 1.30 p.m. and she's still not here. I make a sandwich I can't eat.

I check in with Nin again. She says she supposes Emma could have gone to a marine ecology event in Plymouth, but she doesn't sound convinced – pulling a sickie just so she can sneak off to her other employer is not the sort of thing Emma would do. I hear myself agreeing with her, but what do I know about my wife?

'Will you let me know?' Nin asks, and it's then that I

really begin to worry. 'When you find her, will you message me?'

I promise I will.

I sit down with a notebook and make a list of the places Emma might be.

Jill's
Jeremy Rothschild's
Her therapist's
Marine conference Plymouth
On the Heath/ladies' pond
With one of her Mum Friends
With one of her other friends.

I feel better when I've finished this. There are many people and places to check, and by the time I've got through them, she'll probably be home.

I find the Plymouth event first and give them a call. Several people are no help at all, but eventually I'm passed to someone who says he works with Emma when she's in Plymouth, and she is definitely not there. 'We'd have loved to have her here today!' he says.

Her therapist tells me she cannot talk to me about Emma, but that if I am concerned I must call the police, and maybe Jill. I end the call as quickly as I can. That woman will know far more about me than is comfortable.

I try the two mum friends for whom I have numbers, but she's not with them. They sound borderline excited that I've lost my wife. I promise more and more people I'll keep them posted. Nin texts for an update. On the edge of all of their responses, I notice, is an unspoken suggestion that she might perhaps be having a serious depressive episode – something more weighty than the Times we are all used to – and that I should escalate my search if she doesn't appear soon.

I try Jill, but there's no reply. I text her, asking her to phone me.

Sheila calls again.

From the moment I got off the plane at Luton four days ago until 9am this morning, Emma has done nothing but text me. She's been desperate to talk. What has happened? I begin to feel the first movements of real fear inside me.

I try Jill again but she's still not reachable, so I decide to go and pick Ruby up early. I feel uneasy knowing that Ruby is only semi-accounted for herself.

Ruby is wild when I pick her up, almost as if she knows something serious is going on. She dances sideways up the street, before having a bellowing meltdown when I refuse to buy an ice cream from the fancy gelato place. She tells me she hates me, and even kicks my ankle.

I bend down in front of her on the pavement. Where is your mother? I want to shout. What has she done? Instead I pull her to me and hug her tightly. We piggyback all the way up the hill to our house, which is helpful, because the strain of carrying a three-year-old up a long hill is just about enough to keep my mind busy.

The house is empty. John Keats is in his bed listening to the jungle I left on for him; he thumps his tail lazily before falling back to sleep. Nothing in the kitchen has been moved.

Ruby passes out on the sofa so I take her up to bed for a nap. As I emerge from her room I think I hear the front door – thank God! Thank God. But when I race out to the landing, I see it's just a leaflet for a kebab shop.

I call Emma again, while Ruby naps, and this time I hear it: the sound of a vibrating phone. I have only called her from downstairs today. In my panic I hadn't even noticed that her handbag is on our bed, and her phone is in her handbag. It's there with her wallet and an overstuffed A5 envelope with nothing written on the front. I can't say for certain but I'm pretty sure this envelope was in her bag on Friday evening, when I got her phone out.

The envelope holds her passport, and Ruby's. Not overly suspicious; they took a flight together last week, and it's typical of Emma not to have unpacked her bag yet. But then I find the letter from St Andrews University about her leaving and, after that, a slew of other documents, including an acceptance letter from the University of Plymouth, offering Emma a place to study for a masters in marine biology. *While we normally only accept postgraduate students with a degree in marine biology,* it reads, *your first class undergraduate biology degree at The Open University earlier this year, and the accompanying recommendation from your tutor there, has satisfied us that you will make a strong addition to our thriving postgraduate research team.*

Then I find a letter from Highbury Magistrate's Court, confirming a non-molestation order. It bans Emma from being within two hundred metres of Janice Theresa Rothschild, and it is seventeen years old. I read it once, twice, three times, but I haven't made a mistake: if Emma broke the conditions of this notice, she would face immediate arrest.

The penultimate document I see, before my phone starts ringing, is a birth certificate. The name on it is Emily Ruth Peel, a woman I have never heard of, although she shares a date of birth with my wife.

As I open the final piece of paper, I know already what it will be.

Official Deed Poll, the document says at the top, before confirming that Emily Ruth Peel changed her name to Emma Merry Bigelow in 2006.

Chapter Thirty

LEO

Ruby is very excited about the police station, before I put her in a corner with CBeebies on my phone, but the police are not excited about me. People often take time out after arguments, the officer on the desk says. We get it all the time.

She says she'll be in touch, but that Emma won't be registered as missing until she's been gone forty-eight hours.

This whole thing feels like someone else's life. It can't be mine.

When we arrive back it's early evening and there is no sign of Emma, but Olly and Tink have just arrived with Oskar and Mikkel, who are here to distract Ruby. I feel like we've been upgraded to Defcon 1. My phone pings incessantly with message previews from friends, asking if I've found her yet. I can't bring myself to open them.

Upstairs, the kids are playing a game that sounds quite dangerous. I leave them be. Tink is making some sort of soup or stew, and Olly is sitting at my kitchen table, listening to the full story for the third time.

'What's your worst fear?' he asks, suddenly.

'My – what?'

'Because from where I'm sitting, you've just had devastating news about Ruby's parentage, but you seem far more worried that something might have happened to Emma.'

I think about this. 'I've been worried about her lately. She's had a lot of stalky messages from men on the internet. Some dropped calls. And I hope it's nothing, but there was a weirdo staring at her the other day, after the concert. Just staring right at her, as if he knew her.'

Olly seems perversely pleased. 'Well then – you haven't given up on your marriage,' he tells me. 'Which I'm relieved to hear. Leo, listen, I'm sure the internet men are just lonely. And everyone gets dropped calls – I still think there's likely to be a reasonable explanation for all of this.'

Tink turns round from the worktop. 'Sweetheart. Leo's found out he's not Ruby's father. He's discovered that Emma was called Emily Peel until she was twenty-six years old. I don't think it's reasonable to be talking about innocent explanations.'

Olly shrugs. 'I believe in Emma,' he says, simply.

I get up once again to open the front door and look down the street. I check my emails, my Facebook, my work emails – but, nothing. I've never known powerlessness like it.

What I keep coming back to is this: she left the house with only her keys, which means she was planning to come straight home. Significantly, the last sent message in her phone was to me, this morning, reconfirming she'd meet me at 9.30 a.m.

A bird is singing chromatic scales in next door's sycamore. 'Help,' I say, suddenly standing up. 'Olly, please help me, I have to do something.'

'Right, OK.' He's grateful for a task. Tink watches us quietly. 'Look, let's start by writing down a proper list of all the things that could have happened. I know we've been through all of them twenty times, but maybe writing it down would help.'

Illness, we write – maybe a post-chemo reaction, or, God forbid, a relapse of the cancer – or accident. But we agree it's too late for a chemo reaction and too early for a relapse. An accident seems unlikely, on the short journey from nursery to our house, but, just to be sure, I called the Royal Free and the Whittington Hospitals earlier, and she hadn't been admitted to either.

I propose abduction next but Olly, quite reasonably, dismisses it. 'This is Hampstead Village,' he says. 'Why would you abduct Emma when you could grab a millionaire?'

Stalker, I suggest. After a pause, Olly asks to see Emma's Facebook messages.

I leave the room and get her laptop. I set it down in front of Olly, and Tink comes to look over his shoulder.

Emma's had a steady stream of messages since I last saw her inbox. Most of them are actually quite sweet, but there's enough sexual and aggressive stuff in there to make Tink turn away after a while.

'Fucking dark ages,' she says.

Olly looks grim. 'I might not have been quite so blasé about the dropped calls if I'd seen these.'

We agree I should tell the police about this, but the number they gave me rings out, even though I try it five, six, seven times.

As I press redial for the eighth time, something occurs to me. I cancel the call and pick up Emma's phone, which I'm charging on the worktop. I open her messages with Jeremy again.

'Look.' I hand Olly the phone. 'Look how many times Rothschild's tried to arrange to meet her in London. Maybe he turned up? Maybe he turned up here and saw her in the street and . . .'

'And what? Kidnapped her? In broad daylight? A well-known public figure?'

'Olly. We're talking about a man whose wife has disappeared without trace. Now it's Emma who's gone, and we know he's been in touch with her in the last few days. Do you not think that's significant?'

'If you mean, do I think Jeremy Rothschild has done away with Emma and his wife, no, I don't.'

Then he says, 'But you should probably call him. Just to check.'

There's a long pause after I tell Rothschild who I am. 'Oh,' he says eventually. 'Leo. I wondered if you might call.'

'Firstly, fuck you,' I say. 'Secondly, are you with my wife?'

'Sorry?'

'Are you with my wife? It's a simple question.'

He says he isn't, but he sounds unnerved.

'Then this conversation is over,' I snap. 'Goodbye.'

'I'd like to talk to you,' he interrupts. 'I had a call from Sheila this morning. I know you've uncovered some difficult information concerning me and Emma, in the last few days – would you be willing to come over?'

'Are you serious?'

He pauses, as if trying to decide something. 'Emma's stopped communicating with me in the last few days,' he admits. 'I've been trying to talk to her about something. I . . . I thought perhaps I could tell you.'

'You want me to pass on messages to my wife?' I ask. 'Is this a joke?'

'It isn't,' he says. 'Look, Leo, I'm not sure you're completely up to speed - I really think we should talk. And I appreciate it's a bit of a drive, but I need to be here in case Janice calls. Plus, I've got to keep an eye on my son.'

'I'm looking after Ruby,' I begin, but Olly interrupts, telling me – loudly enough for Rothschild to hear – that he can look after her.

'Go,' he whispers. 'Might be helpful.' I know he's right because I'm thinking the same, even though I'd actually like to go and murder Jeremy Rothschild.

'I – maybe, I – oh, bloody hell. Fine, I'll come. After I've put –'

I swallow. 'After I've put my daughter to bed.'

'Come via Kentish Town,' he texts, a short while later, as if we're meeting for a friendly beer. 'There's an Arsenal match on; Holloway Road will be at a standstill.'

Chapter Thirty-One

LEO

An hour later I am standing outside a large, very handsome house. Rothschild opens the door, and instead of delivering a devastating right hook I have to ask him for money for the parking meter. I left home without my wallet and there's extra football parking restrictions tonight.

Then we're standing in his spacious kitchen, looking at each other, and he's saying thank you very much for coming over, and I don't reply because I haven't the faintest idea what to say and I'm worried I might break down.

'She's my girl,' I manage, eventually.

Rothschild says nothing.

'Mine,' I repeat, and to my fury, my eyes fill with tears. 'I don't want you anywhere near her.'

The kitchen is perfectly silent for a while. Outside twilight is falling and the plane trees in the park move silkily, on a breeze we can't hear. I imagine this house is fitted with very expensive windows.

When Rothschild finally speaks, his voice is careful. 'I have tried to help her, over the years. From a distance.'

'We don't want or need your help.'

'I understand. And I don't know what you've been told, Leo, but I've done my best for her. I'm not the villain: I feel for her.'

I stare at him. 'You feel for her? You "feel" for a child you fathered?'

He stops. 'A child I – what?'

'All I want you to know is that I have raised Ruby; she loves me, and you are not to come anywhere near that. I also want you to know that I despise men like you, with your entitlement. Fathering a child and then taking zero responsibility for what you've done – you selfish establishment fuck.'

Rothschild – who, as the son of a docker, probably didn't deserve 'establishment' – is looking quite lost. 'What in the name of God are you talking about?' he asks. 'What child?'

'Don't. Really, please don't.'

He takes a deep breath, as though he's making a conscious effort not to lose it. I notice their back garden, lit by pretty fairy lights, is full of alliums. I want to go out and hack every graceful purple globe off at the stem.

'Shall we start again? Did you just suggest I'm Ruby's father?'

'I didn't suggest. I know.'

He raises his hands in front of him. 'I have no idea where this has come from, but you've got it wrong, Leo.'

'I don't think so. It came from Emma. Her friend Jill corroborated it, as did Sheila. So please stop lying.'

He runs a hand over his face. 'You're serious, aren't you? You think I've had an affair with Emma. That Ruby's my child.'

'Listen to me,' he says. He presses his hands on the kitchen island, which is still scattered with Janice's things: lip salve, a Liberty print diary, a woman's watch. 'Emma couldn't possibly have told you I am Ruby's father, because I am not. And if Sheila corroborated that "fact", she couldn't have understood what she was being asked.'

'And Jill? Her friend?'

Jeremy pauses. 'I can't speak for her.'

He picks up Janice's watch. 'Janice and I have been married twenty-five years,' he says, curling the watch between his fingers. I realise that he, too, is close to tears. 'Infidelity has never even crossed my mind.' He takes an unsteady breath, then looks straight at me. 'So. Just to be clear, if you wish to continue to accuse me of having had an affair with Emma, you can leave.'

We stand in silence for a moment, while I try to think.

The truth is, I don't want to go. This man knows too much. And I think I believe him.

'I invited you here because I need to stay in regular touch with Emma. At the moment, however, she's ignoring me,' he says. 'And I thought if I were able to explain the current situation, you might be willing to persuade her to suspend hostilities. But I have my limits. What's it to be?'

When I say nothing he turns and marches over to his sink. He splashes cold water over his face and dries it with kitchen towel, before turning back.

I look straight at Rothschild, searching for guilt, but I can't see any.

'You aren't Ruby's father?'

'How many times do I need to tell you?'

'I'm sorry,' I say. 'I just need to . . .' I get out my phone and call Sheila, who answers after one ring.

'Leo. Any news?'

'Not yet. The police have taken the details but I don't think they're all that interested. Look, I'm at Jeremy Rothschild's house.'

'Oh. Oh right.' She waits for me to expand.

'Is he Ruby's father?' I ask, turning away from Rothschild, as if this will stop him hearing me.

There's a pause. Then Sheila says, 'I'm sorry?'

I repeat the question.

'Leo, what on earth? Of course not. Unless I've missed . . . Christ, I mean – No, Leo, absolutely not.'

I think she's telling the truth, but none of this makes sense.

'So when I said to you that I knew about Emma and Jeremy, what did you think I was talking about?'

She doesn't answer immediately.

'I think you've probably only worked out half of the facts.' Sheila's voice is suddenly toneless. She's in spymaster mode. 'If you're at Jeremy's house I suggest you have a frank conversation. Although, let me be clear, you have got the wrong end of several sticks if you think he's Ruby's father.'

Ruby. Oh, thank God. I close my eyes and lean against Rothschild's worktop.

I couldn't have borne it. No matter what Emma has done, no matter who she really is – the loss of my daughter would have defeated me.

'OK,' I say. 'Thank you.'

Sheila ends the call without comment, as is her fashion.

Jeremy is still watching me, when I open my eyes. He's put the watch down, but it's still there in front of him, a sad talisman.

'I apologise,' I say. 'There was a message from Emma to you in her phone. A draft. It said, I know you are the father of my child. I'm not sure how else I was to interpret that.'

He nods, almost as if he saw this coming. 'I can understand why you'd think what you did.'

He doesn't offer anything else, but I sense that it's on its way.

'I know for a fact that Emma hasn't had any other children,' I continue. 'I was there when Ruby was born. Things started to go wrong and they had to get her out with forceps. I clearly remember the obstetrician telling me this was common for a woman's first delivery.'

'Yes,' Jeremy says, staring down at Janice's watch. 'I believe it is.'

'And as you well know, I've seen photos of Janice shortly after she gave birth to your son, Charlie, so Emma can't be referring to him either, when she talks about this child.'

Rothschild doesn't say anything. It's not even 8.30 p.m. and the man looks exhausted. I've been in the hellish uncertainty of trying to find my wife for less than twelve hours; I can't begin to imagine how he's borne it for two weeks.

'So I have to ask what has been going on,' I tell him, and my voice finally crumbles. 'I don't know who you are to my wife. Why would she call you the father of her child? And why has she changed her name? This whole thing is awful. Just unreal.'

'It must be a terrible shock.'

I wait for him to say more but he doesn't, so I go and sit at his table. 'Please,' I say, and I gesture for him to sit down. 'Talk to me. Why are you trying to reach her? What's going on?'

After a long pause, he lowers himself into a chair opposite.

'Can you start off by telling me where she is?'

Rothschild pauses as he pulls in his chair. 'What do you mean, where she is?'

'Where Emma is.'

He looks confused.

'You mean you don't know?'

'No! What's happened?' He looks genuinely worried. 'Is that what you meant when you mentioned the police to Sheila just now?'

'She's gone,' I tell him, and a vault of panic opens up again. I thought this was how I'd find her. 'She disappeared nearly twelve hours ago. She went to drop Ruby off at nursery and never came home. She left her wallet and phone in our bedroom . . . That's why I called you. I found messages from you asking for a meet-up. I thought . . . I thought . . .'

'That I'd – what? Kidnapped her? Killed her?'

'I don't know. I just want to know where she is.'

Jeremy takes this in, across his handsome oak table. I wonder how many dinner parties it has seen. How long it will be before people sit around it again.

He comes to life. 'Of course. I'll tell you everything I know. Do you think she's vulnerable?'

'She's had depressive episodes in the past. But I wouldn't say she's been in a particularly bad place lately.' I watch his face. This conversation must be horribly familiar. 'Why? Do you really not know anything?'

Jeremy shakes his head. 'I promise you, I have no idea where Emma is. None at all.'

'Then what's happening? You must be out of your mind about Janice, and now Emma's missing too – I don't understand any of this. Why did you say you needed to be in touch with Emma? What's going on?'

What is going on is that I have lost my wife, my Emma, and gained in her place a stranger called Emily Peel. Although, in this moment, I don't even have Emily Peel.

The streetlamp across the road from the Rothschilds' house glows brighter as darkness creeps.

'OK.' Jeremy says. 'I'll tell you what I know. But only Emma can tell you exactly what happened, and why she did the things that she did. Some of them I can understand, others I don't think I ever will. But, for what it's worth, here's my side of the story.'

PART II

EMILY

Chapter Thirty-Two

EMILY RUTH PEEL

Twenty years earlier

The night we met was like something from a film, Jill said at the time, but it's hard for me to look back on it as anything more than a sordid night of student drinking.

Jill and I found him lying on a pavement on the Kinnesburn Road, at around 6 p.m. He was surrounded by his friends, who were laughing hysterically. 'Dickheads!' he was shouting, as if his friends were responsible for the fall. I doubted they were. He looked drunk; they all did. I thought they must be postgrads: they were at least ten years older than everyone else.

We gave them a wide berth because we'd already decided they were fools, these overgrown boys with their all-day drinking and attractive faces, but he caught my eye and begged me to help him because his friends wouldn't, and we ended up getting drawn into their gang and drinking in the Whey Pat until closing time.

It was around nine, maybe ten, when Jill cornered me. 'How do you do it?' she whispered in my ear. Her breath was damp and gin-fumed. 'They're eating out of your hand, but you're not even trying. Damn you, Emily, share your secrets!'

'They're not eating out of my hand! Don't be ridiculous!'

Jill went off to wee, muttering about taking lessons.

I realised she wasn't entirely wrong when I returned to the group. A fight broke out about who was going to sit next to me, and, without any conscious plan to do so, I found myself leading a conversation that had everyone in stitches.

The ability to charm strangers is one of many things you learn as a military child. You need to be fearless and funny when you start in a new schoolroom – and there are many new schoolrooms – but you also need to seem as if you don't care at all.

I didn't really know any other way of being. Not then.

Jeremy came up to me at the bar when it was my round. 'Sorry,' he said, with the sort of indulgent smile that suggested he wasn't sorry at all. 'Pack of beasts, aren't they?'

If anything, I'd say he was proud of them. He looked oddly familiar, I thought, but I couldn't quite place him.

There was Jeremy, there were two Hugos – 'fat Hugo' and 'twat Hugo', a Briggs and a David. Jeremy told me they'd graduated ten years ago but came back annually for a 'boys' weekend'. He told me he worked for the BBC, in London. He was attractive and obviously intelligent. Unlike his friends, however, he wore his brainpower lightly: I rather liked him.

Jill and I drank hard. Jill was rolling out her foulest language, which was how she flirted – her secret weapon against girly girls. She spent a lot of time with one of the Hugos, but when he started chatting up a waif in a deerstalker, she barrelled off to talk to Briggs.

They flirted with me, too, but only one seemed determined to win. I felt his eyes on me, watched him dispatch his competitors one by one, and by midnight we were sitting above West Sands in the velvet darkness, hands inside each other's clothes, the unseen sea pitching in and out. I told him what I was going to do to him later, and in that moment I entirely bought this version of myself.

He left my house at 6.45 in the morning. 'I've got to get back to London,' he said. 'Train's at 7.45 from Leuchars and I don't even know where the others are.'

'Do you have a mobile phone?' I asked. I couldn't afford one, but lots of other students were getting them.

He smiled, as if this was an adorable question. He was thirty; he lived and worked in London – of course he had a mobile phone. 'I do, but it's dead, and I don't know my number. Give me yours and I'll call.'

I scribbled our landline on a piece of paper, even though I doubted I'd hear from him again. Then I pulled my duvet around myself, luxuriously, as if this was the sort of thing I did all the time. 'Well, see you! It was fun.'

Jill came into my room a few moments after he'd left. Mascara was flaking under her eyes, her pyjamas were stained with red wine.

'Er, morning,' she said. 'Everything OK?'

I nodded, smiling.

She turned to look out of the window. 'I'm afraid he's married,' she said, watching him walk up the street.

I sat up. 'What? No he's not!'

'Oh, yes he is,' she said, sitting on my bed. 'Sorry to have to break this to you, Em.'

After a moment, when I realised she wasn't joking, I closed my eyes. 'No.'

'Affirmative, I'm afraid. He told me last night.'

'When?' I stared at her. 'Why didn't you tell me?'

'You didn't ask him . . . ?'

'What, if he was married?'

'Er – yes?'

I shook my head. 'No. I just . . . Isn't it reasonable to assume a man's single, if he's trying to kiss you?'

Jill started laughing. 'Do you know anything about men, Emily?'

'Oh God. No.'

She nodded, sympathetically. 'I take it you had sex?'

We'd been at it all night. 'I wish you'd told me,' I said, but I just sounded petulant.

'When, Em? When was I meant to tell you? You two disappeared from the pub without warning! What was I supposed to do?'

I groaned. She was right.

'Just tell me you used a condom!'

'Of course,' I said, miserably. 'Oh, God, I feel horrible.'

She climbed in next to me. 'It's what's commonly known as a bummer, Em. I'm sorry.' She slid down the bed and pulled the duvet up over us. 'I suggest we sleep it off and then go and eat several burgers.'

So that's what we did. But she was in a strange mood all day, and I felt I'd somehow let her down.

He didn't call, and I was relieved. It had been exciting, for a few hours, to feel wanted – to be willingly selected by someone older, someone at the helm of his own existence. But he had stood at an altar and said 'I do' to someone else, in front of all of their friends.

And had Jill not told me, I would never have known: that's what made me really angry. No remorse. No quiet doubts. He had put himself inside my body, this married man, and his only thought had been of orgasm. His, mine, his again, mine again.

I thought about her often, as the days passed: his wife in London. Had he done this to her before? Did she know? Had she ever confronted him? Did they have some sort of arrangement?

Eventually, I put him out of my mind and told myself I'd never be so stupid again. I got on with my course. There were essays, there was fieldwork, there was reading; endless reading, and of course there were parties. I was a second-year undergrad; I sat in the inside lane of normal, my strange childhood moving further away with every passing day.

I was happy.

Until one cold morning in early March, when I was sitting in the library reading about marine hermaphrodites, and it occurred to me that I hadn't had a period in a long time.

Chapter Thirty-Three

It'll be OK, I thought, sitting on the lip of our mildewed shower. It'll somehow be OK.

I was nineteen years old, a blue line was forming on a screen but still I felt there must be a solution. I might be broke and orphaned, but I was an educated, middle-class woman: I had choices. This was the privilege into which I was lucky enough to have been born.

Wasn't it?

Jill knocked on the door. 'Are you doing what I think you're doing?' We'd been into town to buy the test that morning.

I nodded, taking in our tiny bathroom; the cracked floor tiles, the over-mirror light that had never worked. A can of hair removal cream with gruesome pink foam around the rusting collar, an empty bottle of shampoo covered in long black hairs.

My precious, hard-won student life.

'Emily?'

'Sorry,' I called. 'Yes. And yes.'

A pause.

'You're pregnant?'

'I'm pregnant.'

Another pause.

'Right. Well, we need to . . . Let's – oh Em, let me in.'

Jill came and sat on the floor next to me.

'We used a condom,' I said. 'I don't understand.'

'Who was in charge of condoms? Him or you?'

'Him.'

'Well. He was very drunk.'

We stayed there as the winter day darkened, then Jill got up to make toasted cheese sandwiches.

'It'll be OK,' she said, as she went. 'We're in this together.'

It was not OK. By the time I'd thought to take a pregnancy test, I was fifteen weeks and a day: termination was still possible, but when I read about what would be involved this far into the pregnancy, I couldn't face it.

Yet the idea of having a child felt no more real than a moon landing. Where would I go? Who would help; where would I live? How would I afford it? (I couldn't possibly afford it.) How could I finish my degree? (I couldn't possibly finish my degree.)

And my friends. My cherished new friends. Dad and I had never lived anywhere for more than a few years, and even then I'd had to stay at Granny's when he was away with the Marines. My student friends were the first solid group I'd had. Whether they knew it or not, they were front and centre of the life I'd always dreamed of; the life that began when I arrived here as a fresher.

The wind blew and the North Sea hulked around the land, indifferent and vast. I took to walking along the shore every morning before lectures, singing loudly to keep my thoughts at bay, watching the sea change minute by minute. It could be sleek as steel when I arrived but furious and rolling by the time I left, and I found some comfort in that: no state was permanent. But for all its changes and its rising and flattening and booming and sparkling, it never gave me any answers.

Can I do this? I asked it, each morning, and each morning it said nothing.

There was an expanding layer of fat around my middle, and my face was bloated with hormones and worry. I didn't feel sick, but the exhaustion was like being trapped underwater, my thoughts oily and slow. In desperation, I finally visited a clinic to discuss termination, but left before my name was called.

My short time in the world of average was over: I would be a mother by the age of twenty.

'If you're going to keep this baby, you're going to need help,' Jill said. 'Financial help, logistical help, the works. You need to get in touch with him.'

'How?'

She frowned. 'Well, unless you have his phone number, which you don't, I think there's only one way of doing it.'

We looked him up. Jeremy Rothschild. He was actually quite well known – I wasn't wrong when I thought he'd looked familiar. He was a radio presenter, listened to by millions every morning – I'd heard his voice in Dad's house for years.

His wife was an actress. I recognised her face, too.

We composed a letter. On the envelope I wrote the BBC correspondence address I'd heard a hundred times on children's BBC: Television Centre, Wood Lane, London W12 7RJ.

There was no way he'd get back to me.

Three days later, Jill burst into my bedroom and hissed, 'Fuck, Jeremy Rothschild's on the phone.'

'What? What did he say?'

'He's on the line now! Downstairs! Fucking get out of bed!'

'Emily,' he said, in a pleasant, untroubled voice, but I don't think either of us believed he was having a relaxing afternoon.

'Hello,' I said. And – a self-betrayal – 'Um, sorry.'

'Don't be. The last few weeks must have been hellish for you.'

I wasn't expecting that. For a moment, my eyes filled with tears, but Jill poked me until I agreed, carefully, that it had not been an easy time.

'I can barely imagine,' he sighed. 'The situation is complicated at both ends, but I'm sure it's a lot worse for you. Anyway, let me try and explain my end of it, so we can work out what to do next.'

'OK,' I said, and I turned on speaker phone and sat under a blanket with Jill while he talked.

Chapter Thirty-Four

My mother died in childbirth: a postpartum haemorrhage was spotted too late, and within days of becoming a father Dad was widowed. Granny, my mother's mother, often came down from London to help, but she was an MP and could never stay long.

I have a couple of still-life memories of my early years. Both of them are on a beach, somewhere near our little Dorset home. In one memory I am rockpooling with Dad: he shows me a beadlet anemone and I am delighted. In the other it's raining and we are sitting in the pouch of a shallow cave. As we watch turnstones searching for food among the beach pebbles, Dad sings about being rescued and saved. His voice is soft, achingly sad.

Many years later, Granny told me he was singing a sea shanty. She said my mother had been buried at sea, as was her wish, but Dad had not been able to bear the idea of leaving her out there alone. So the two of us used to drive down to keep Mum company whenever he wasn't working. The little girl and her grief-shattered father, walking up and down in the pulling tides of loss.

Dad was a parish priest. It was all he'd ever wanted to do – he'd had a proper calling, I believe – but he left his parish to train as a Royal Marines chaplain when I was four. I have vague memories of arguments between him and

Granny. She'd tried to stop him, she later told me, because he'd made no provision for me during deployment. Not because he didn't care, but because linear thinking was no longer available to him. The arguments were wasted, though; apparently nothing she said would sway him. I think the siren song of danger was the only prospect substantial enough to dilute his grief and loneliness. That, or perhaps the belief that he might be nearer to my mother at sea.

After training he took a chaplaincy post with the 45 Commando in Arbroath, near Aberdeen, and we moved into spartan family quarters. I was nearly six and I hated it, but I made do. Dad was still Dad, after all. He picked me up from school and took me to the coast, where we'd poke around in rocks and swim in icy water. We grew potatoes in our tiny garden, we went camping in the Grampians. He sang to me, and looked after me when I was ill.

When I was nine we transferred to a commando in Somerset, and when I was twelve he went with his 'lads' to Iraq. I stayed with Granny for the duration of his tour. Another first day at another new school: I was exhausted.

Dad was minister to a bunch of Marines protecting Kurdish refugees on the northern border with Turkey. It was a peaceful deployment, his letters said, until they abruptly stopped. We later learned there'd been a confrontation with a local militia, and a young woman and her child were hurt. Just like my mother, this young woman had died in Dad's arms.

He was signed off work for three months after that, because the Naval Archdeaconry wanted to look after him. In actual fact, this isolation – the very thing he'd spent so many years trying to avoid – sent him to an alcoholic grave.

There were no dramatic scenes, and he continued to take

me to the coast whenever he was sober enough to drive. He continued to cuddle me, to tell me he loved me – he sometimes even made me sandwiches for school. But the drink towed him under rapidly, and he never went back to work. I think he foresaw his end because he managed to buy us a tiny house in Plymouth when I was fourteen. I was lucky – by the time I was fifteen he was capable only of buying alcohol.

The Naval Archdeaconry did their best to help him, but Dad never took the hand they extended. Drink was clearer and easier, and it was available from the shop at the end of the road, rather than a weekly counselling session twelve miles away.

My father was a lonely and humble drunk. He spent most of his time in the front room, watching television, drinking, sleeping. He ate when I fed him. Whenever I tried to do something about it, the drinking got worse, so there were no desperate scenes with hidden bottles. He was just never sober, and I was too frightened to push him over the edge.

The Archdeaconry had to let him go in the end. They'd agreed a recovery roadmap that would ultimately have had him serving his commando in Zaire, but he repeatedly failed to turn up to meetings and ignored their letters. He couldn't do it.

He died of alcohol-related heart failure a few days before my A-levels started. His training at least bequeathed him the good sense to call an ambulance before he lost consciousness, but he died on the way to hospital. They told me he wouldn't have known a thing, that he had gone out with a half smile on his face. It made me wonder if he could already see my mother.

By the time I left school, I had only my grandmother. She was a formidable character, but she was eighty.

Jeremy Rothschild was my only long-term hope.

Chapter Thirty-Five

'David's married,' Jeremy said, as if I didn't already know.

'My housemate told me. The morning after. If I'd known, I would never have . . . I'd never have . . .' I stopped.

I thought back to the way David had gone after me, that night. What Jeremy must have thought of me, when he saw us kissing. When he got my letter.

He was silent for a moment. I wondered if he was angry, or embarrassed. Or perhaps resigned? Maybe this wasn't the first time he'd had to deal with the aftermath of his cousin's one-night stands.

'That's why I wrote to you, rather than David.' My voice held, and Jill gave me an encouraging smile. 'I didn't want his wife to find the letter. This situation is bad enough without someone else's marriage being ruined.'

'Very considerate of you. Especially given the circumstances.'

Good start, Jill wrote, on the back of an envelope. *He seems nice.*

'Look,' he continued. 'Emily. I am so sorry that this has happened. It shouldn't have done.'

I agreed, although there was no spirit in my voice.

'Can I send money? That's not why I'm calling,' he added, quickly. 'But right now, in the immediate term, before we make a plan, would money help?'

Jill and I looked at each other. 'Is this . . . ?' The words dried in my throat. 'This isn't . . .'

'Silence money?' Jeremy asked, softly. 'God, no, Emily. Look, my cousin is an overgrown child. He's irresponsible, incredibly stupid and unfortunately very good at charming people. But he's not a bad man, no more than I am. I'm calling to work out how I can help.'

'OK.' We talked around in circles for a while – including, briefly, about Granny, who it turned out he'd interviewed when he was starting out as a journalist: 'She shredded me,' he admitted, and I could hear him smile. For a moment I smiled, too, because Granny took great pleasure in shredding people, especially ambitious young men.

I told him she didn't yet know I was pregnant. She was old, and had led a life of excess. 'She smoked like a chimney,' I explained, although he probably already knew. 'She worked too hard, she drank, she never said no. She seems healthy enough at the moment but I don't feel I can rely on her. Not in a long-term way.'

There was a pause. 'From what I remember of your grandmother,' Jeremy said, 'she would be quite furious to hear you say that.'

'She would.'

'OK, look.' His voice changed. Jill leaned in to the phone, even though the volume was loud enough.

'Janice,' he said, then paused. 'I'm sorry. This is difficult. It's not something I – we – talk about. But Janice and I are . . . well, unable to have children. It's been a very difficult few years. Awful, actually.'

Cautiously, I said, 'I'm sorry.' I waited for him to go on.

'A while back we started the adoption process. We're about halfway through the second stage, which means that in as little as two months we could be approved and ready to find a child.'

Oh God, Jill mouthed.

'And although I'm sure we can work out an arrangement where David pays you an allowance, probably through me, so as to protect his wife, who of course has no idea – I wonder if that's enough or if you might consider a different kind of solution.'

Oh God, I mouthed back at Jill.

I asked Jeremy to expand, even though there was little doubt where he was heading.

'What I mean is that you sound very much like a woman who does not want to have to stop her life and bring up a child,' he said. 'Although please do correct me if I'm wrong. You may be thrilled at the idea.'

I stayed silent. What did a woman who doesn't want to stop her life for a child sound like?

'What I'm trying to say, although, God knows, it's not easy – is that Janice and I would be open to a discussion about adopting the baby. If the idea held some appeal. And I appreciate it might not.'

SHIT, wrote Jill, on the envelope.

I wrote a tick next to 'SHIT'.

'Emily, I don't expect you to know what to say straight away. I nearly wrote all of this down in a letter, in fact, so you'd be able to digest it alone, and not feel pressured to say anything.'

I wished he had.

Jeremy waited a few moments, but continued when I didn't say anything. 'Legally, it wouldn't be too complicated, because David and I are cousins. We'd all still have to go through the proper system, of course, but as I said we're already on that road.'

'So – so you've told David? He knows?'

Jeremy's voice softens. 'He does, yes.'

'And he doesn't . . . He doesn't want to . . .'

He sighed. 'I'm afraid not. But he'd be happy for us to adopt the child, if that was something you ever wanted to consider.'

'Right. OK.' My face burned. I was no more than an inconvenience, a silly pregnant student he hoped would go away.

'I'm sorry,' Jeremy said, quietly. 'I know that's hard.'

Jill held my hand for a moment. Then she started scribbling on the envelope again. *Why this baby?* she wrote.

'Er – why this baby?' I asked obediently.

'What do you mean?'

I looked at Jill. I had no idea what she'd meant.

Weird it's his cousin's? she scribbled.

'Would you not find it difficult – strange, even – bringing up your cousin's baby? I mean, what if David's wife found out?' I added, as the wheels of my brain began to turn again. 'How would he feel, seeing the child all the time? What if he changed his mind and said he wanted to bring it up himself?'

Jeremy didn't say anything for a while. 'I can't answer any of those questions,' he replied, eventually. 'Janice and I were up nearly all night discussing the things that could go wrong. David says he'd be fine with the arrangement, but there's no guaranteeing how he'd feel when he met the child. You're right to ask, and I'm right not to pretend I have the answer.'

Even Jill had nothing to say to that.

'All I know is that this feels like an arrangement that would make perfect sense. The baby is family. We'd be able to take him or her at birth – I mean, if you agreed, which might never happen, and that would be fine, of course . . . What I mean is, we'd be getting a baby we felt we knew. And after the time we've had, that's appealing.'

'You don't know me,' I said, childishly. I was out of my depth now.

'I don't! But I liked you, that night. I thought you were bright, and very kind. You told me a bit about your father.'

'Really?'

'Really. Not much, but it sounded like you cared for him beautifully when he was in the grip of the drink. I suppose I just got the impression I was talking to a decent young woman.'

'I wasn't expecting this,' was what I said, eventually.

'Of course. Which is why I think I should go, and let you mull it over. Unless it's a flat no, in which case, please say.'

He waited, but I didn't say anything. Then he gave me his email address, so I could send a Flat No if a phone call felt too intimidating.

'Or, if you're open to the possibility, we'll arrange a time to talk further. I'm sure you'd have many questions. There wouldn't be any rush to start talking to social services, or the adoption agency.'

They'd thought this whole thing out already. They knew exactly how it would work; what would have to happen. How they could take this baby in my womb and make it their own.

'I . . . OK.' I said, and then I started to cry, and Jill took the phone and told Jeremy it was time to end the call.

He didn't sound surprised someone else had been listening in. 'I'm glad she has a friend in her corner,' he said, before ringing off. 'Do take care of her.'

I liked that. And I liked him. Not many public figures would be so open about their personal lives.

But appreciating someone's honesty was a long way off handing them your child.

Chapter Thirty-Six

There was a young woman called Erica whom Dad used to visit, back before the Marines when he was just a parish priest. She was a single mother, nineteen years old and alone in the world, entirely dependent on state benefits. I was only two or three at the time, but I read about her in Dad's diaries after he died.

Erica's life as a single mother seemed to break my father's heart. In the pages of his diary he often asked God how he could better be of service. He wrote about taking her to the supermarket, about topping up her electricity meter with his own money, and about the way he'd see her sitting in the park sometimes, eyes blank with unhappiness.

But what really got to me was a line he wrote about how her baby cried all the time. That image of a sweet baby – my sweet baby – stuck in a damp bedsit with a mother who had no idea how to look after her (I was certain my baby was a girl) kept me awake at night. A baby who could otherwise have lived in a warm, comfortable house with proper grown-ups like Jeremy and Janice Rothschild.

Jill said I was being ridiculous, that young single mothers on benefits had babies all the time, and these babies were perfectly happy and did not cry all day long, any more than they lived in damp bedsits. And she was right, of course, but it was easier for her. She hadn't read my dad's diaries, and she had a whole family to lean on.

She reminded me that Jeremy had promised he'd get David to pay me an allowance if I decided to keep the child. He and Janice had already sent me a mobile phone – I knew they wanted to help.

But what if David didn't want to pay me an allowance? What if he just said no? He was a lawyer, he'd find a way out of it if he wanted to; Jeremy couldn't force him. And I was a twenty-year-old with no backup; no more able to take him to court than I was to swim the Pacific.

The Rothschilds had a holiday house in Northumberland, Jeremy told me, when I finally called to ask more questions. A village called Alnmouth, near where Dad and I had stayed when I was a kid. One of Dad's lads at the 45 Commando had a static caravan in Beadnell Bay, a few miles up the coast.

I imagined a little girl running around on that wide, shimmering beach with a bucket and spade as I had once done; her dad showing her how to look for blennies and prawns in rock pools, teaching her about dahlia anemones and sponges and seaweeds, just like Dad had me.

Janice and Jeremy would watch as she played, smiling, explaining, guiding – maybe adopting another child, so she'd always have a sidekick. They would have a car, a fridge full of food, and they'd give her that basic, cellular sense of safety that comes with a healthy bank balance.

Jill gave this short shrift, too: she said there was nothing to stop me taking my daughter to the beach myself. 'You'd be a brilliant teacher!' she insisted. 'Your dad was just an amateur rockpooler; you're on your way to being a pro!'

She would help me, she said, the day she took me out for a 99p baguette to try to persuade me not to give the baby away. 'We can turf Vivi out and have a nursery in her room. We can ask to be in separate tutor groups so I can look after the baby while you go to seminars. And I'm sure you could take a baby into lectures!'

In the end I had to ask her to stop, and she did, because she knew what I was really afraid of: that this baby would have a childhood as lonely as my own.

It was the call from Janice that made up my mind.

Led by one of the PhD students, a small group of us from my department had converged on rocky shore at low tide one Tuesday lunchtime to survey a stretch of exposed rock. We were armed with quadrats, hand lenses and cameras and I felt unusually hopeful, surrounded by friends, working in the hard spring air.

The tide was out, the North Sea thoughtful. Clouds massed on the horizon, where huge tankers lumbered north to Russia and Canada. I was standing on a rock, surrounded in all directions by dank bladderwrack, when my phone rang.

'Emily?' said a woman.

I recognised her voice straight away. Jill, Vivi and I had rented one of her films the other day: she only had a small part but she did it very well and we all agreed she was 'cool'.

'Yes,' I said. 'Janice?' Although I normally forbade myself from doing it, I felt my hand ascend to my belly, where it rested protectively.

'Yes,' she said. Then: 'Alan, fuck off!'

There was a scuffling sound.

'I'm so sorry,' she said, when she came back on the line. 'I'm looking after my friend's dog; she's having an operation. I made the mistake of giving him a biscuit earlier and now he won't leave me alone.'

I liked her immediately. Granny had always had dogs, and she was always giving them biscuits and swearing at them.

'Look,' she went on, 'I won't take up your time. I just felt it was strange that we hadn't spoken yet. I just wanted to say – even though I know Jeremy will have said it a million times – that you mustn't feel any pressure whatsoever to give your baby up to us. Or to anyone. This is your child, and, God knows, I know how special it must be to be carrying it.'

To my surprise, I laughed. 'Special isn't the first word that crosses my mind,' I said. 'I mean, it is special, but it's . . . terrifying.'

Janice laughed, too. Nobody had laughed about my situation until now. It was actually quite refreshing.

'It's been a bit of a shitshow for you, hasn't it?' she said. 'I always feared David would do something like this. I could kill him. But all I wanted to say is that we really, truly do not want you to feel trapped. We'll do our best to make sure you're OK whatever you decide to do. I just needed to tell you that myself.'

We'll do our best. They had no control over David Rothschild, and she knew it.

My coursemates, focused on what lurked under rocks and in pooled water, fanned across the shore, surveying, discussing, documenting. A trawler ploughed towards the harbour with a late catch.

'Thank you,' I said. 'But – honestly – I don't feel pressured at all. Jeremy's been great.'

'He is great,' she agreed. 'He's been incredible these last few years.'

I stroked the modest mound of my belly again.

'Well, I'll leave it there,' Janice said. 'But you've got my number now, so call me any time. Or Jeremy. We're here for you, no matter what you decide.'

The sky brightened momentarily, and an offshore wind played with my hair. 'Thank you. I really appreciate it. I'll call you soon.'

A few days previously, a lecturer had told us about a species of seahorse that stays in monogamous relationship for the rest of its life. Everyone had been charmed, of course, but all I'd been able to think about was how the father of my child had not even stayed for breakfast. He had had sex with me; he had kissed me, and then he'd left to get a train back to London and his wife.

Jeremy must have told him how frightened I was. He must have said that I had no parents, no money and no idea what to do. David knew Janice had sent me a mobile phone, and presumably he had the number. And yet, nothing.

Not for a second had I entertained hopes of him leaving his wife and setting up home with me. I wouldn't have wanted that even if he did. What I needed, simply, was someone to talk to from time to time. And if that wasn't available – which, of course, it wasn't – I'd settle for financial security.

Not even that was on the table.

Janice and Jeremy were the only people who seemed to care about me at the moment, besides Jill and Vivi, and the few coursemates I'd told – but what could they do? What did they know?

I needed a grown-up in my corner.

I sat for a while on a rock, thinking about how it would feel to let these people into my life properly, to allow them to help me, to know this sweet baby girl would have a good life with good people. I had no doubt they'd love her. I had no doubt they'd make sure she had everything she needed.

A shower clattered over the beach, backlit by the sun, and my coursemates' hoods went up. Rain started trickling down my neck so I pulled my coat around my body and tried to do up the zip, but my stomach was too much for it and it broke.

That did it. I gave in and cried, with the rain. The meagre income I received from the woman renting Dad's house in Plymouth was barely enough to cover my rent up here, let alone maternity clothes. I couldn't even afford a coat to keep this bump warm and dry. And if I couldn't afford maternity clothes, how could I possibly afford to keep a child alive? A couple of my closer friends came and huddled round: they'd been keeping an eye on me.

'It'll be OK,' they kept saying. 'You're amazing, Emily, you'll get through this!'

They were lovely. They also had no idea what they were talking about. I was four months pregnant and alone.

As the shower passed over us and moved inland, I stood up and told them I was fine.

They went back off to their prawns and blennies, their crabs and their whelks, reiterating the meaningless things people always say: I was 'amazing' and 'brilliant' and 'stronger than I knew'.

I singled out Jill, who was far away with her hand plunged into a freezing pool, and scrambled over the rocks.

'I'm seriously thinking of doing it,' I said, when I reached her. 'Of saying yes.'

Jill abandoned the top shell she'd been examining.

'I really would be there for you if you decided to keep the baby,' she said. 'Seriously.'

'I know. And thank you. But I think I want them to have her. I want her to have a good life, Jill. I want more than anything for her to be happy. And I don't think she would be with me.'

'Really?' Jill's voice was sad. 'You really don't think she could be happy with you?'

'I don't. No.'

After a long pause, Jill took my wet, cold hand in her own wet, cold hand, and nodded.

We stood there, surrounded by kelp, watching cloud shadows stripe the shore. And for the first time in weeks, even though tears were falling soundlessly down my cheeks, I felt something that might be hope.

Chapter Thirty-Seven

After I said yes to the Rothschilds, I began the obligatory counselling and interviews. I filled in forms, I shared medical records. I made cheerful jokes with everyone and anyone, and when they dried up I'd head back outside, walking up and down the shore at St Andrews, fractured and craving anaesthesia.

Janice kept a respectful distance in the first few weeks, but eventually asked if I'd like her to call to check in from time to time. And I did want her to. She and Jeremy were the only people who actually wanted me to be pregnant. Who had some idea of what I was going through, and what lay ahead.

She had the local greengrocer deliver me fruit and vegetables every week, and sent me a book about pregnancy, along with a maternity coat, as if she had somehow been there the day my bump had burst through my zip. She always seemed to know the right moment to send chocolate, or a pair of pyjamas.

She lifted my mood. She listened.

She offered to take me maternity shopping in Edinburgh. It wasn't a bad idea, but it intimidated me. This semi-famous woman, this stranger, who wanted to be the mother to my baby. What would we say, without the safety of a phone? Would there be excruciating small talk? Or would she want to discuss things I couldn't quite fathom yet, like how and when to hand the baby over? Would the agency even approve of us meeting?

The problem was, I was exhausted by then, sick of doing it alone. I didn't want to talk about marine ecosystems or who was shagging whom on my course, I just wanted to talk about foetal movements and pelvic girdle pain and which girls' names I liked most.

So I said yes.

Janice took me to John Lewis in Edinburgh and bought me a maternity pillow. We went for lunch in a proper restaurant. She bought massage oil and iron supplements. She put me on the train to Leuchars at the end of the day and told me I was a bloody brave young woman and should be proud of myself.

'Please come again?' I begged, as I boarded the train.

She smiled and said of course, as if it were no bother to travel hundreds of miles. And she did, the very next week. And the week after.

I looked forward to her visits. She was becoming a friend.

I had made the right decision. I knew that, even in the middle of the night when I was faced with the reality of my body, with the miniature human beginning to kick and tumble. She would have a better life with the Rothschilds. Not only were they good, kind people, they were ready for her, and I was not.

Granny called often to try to make me change my mind, even though she knew it was pointless. She sounded defeated every time we ended a phone call, and my grandmother was not the sort of woman to sound defeated.

She gave up eventually. We agreed I'd go and stay with her for the summer when my second year finished, and I'd have the baby in London in early September. Then I'd stay at her house until I felt ready to rejoin my coursemates in St

Andrews for our final year. She even had one of her toy boys paint the spare room for me.

Sometimes, I would wonder if Granny was actually right – that we could, somehow, do it together. Or I would think about what Jill was still saying, which was that we could muddle together to bring up a baby in our little student house. Vivi, our housemate, stayed up all night smoking pot and talking to her boyfriend in Korea – she'd be able to do the night feeds, no problem! But when I woke, and heard Jill entertaining some man in her bedroom, or spoke to Granny on the phone and heard her age in every word she spoke, I knew it was hopeless. Jill was twenty. Granny was eighty.

In the Easter holidays Janice invited me to stay at their place in Northumberland, so I could 'relax'.

I had never forgotten how beautiful it was down there, with those enormous sandy beaches and endless rock pools and castles jutting out from the coast like dreams. I said yes.

I arrived in Alnmouth on a bright Wednesday morning in late April. Janice wasn't due until later, so I let myself in with a key she'd hidden in the coaching arch. A coaching arch, I thought. A coaching arch! The house I had inherited from Dad in Plymouth was barely wide enough to accommodate a front door.

Inside it was beautiful. There were sheepskins and huge kilims and those thick creamy sofas you only ever saw in magazines. I showered in a sparkling cubicle that looked as if it had been installed that morning.

Later, I sat in the silence, looking out over the estuary at dripping farmland. This is going to be your holiday home, I told my baby. This is where you'll learn the sea. The baby must have woken from a sleep just at that moment, because something shifted on the right-hand side of my pelvis.

Sudden tears burned my eyes. She would come here with a bucket and spade, just as I had. She would beg for ice creams and waffles and deckchairs she'd be far too busy to sit on. She would play on the swings down by the estuary, would be taken for tea at the pub up the road, would ask, all the way up the M1, *Are we nearly there yet?*

'Hello?' Janice's voice called from downstairs. 'Emily?'

I swallowed. 'Hi! I'm here!'

'Great!' Janice shouted. 'Lets go for a walk, it's wild out there! Sunny and windy and glorious! I have food!'

We sheltered in an old sheep hut to eat the food Janice had brought. Outside, a storm raged back and forth across the beach.

We talked easily as rain pelted the old stone tiles. In my heart, hope grew.

We spotted the crab skeleton at the far end of the beach, soon after our picnic lunch. Medium-sized, dead, alone on the strandline amid deposits of driftwood and dried spiral wrack. There were razorshell fragments stuck to its abdomen, a bleached twist of trawler net hooked around a lifeless antenna, and peculiar, signal-red spots on its body and claws.

Tired now, I sat down to examine it properly. Four distinct spines crossed its carapace. Its claws were covered in bristles.

I looked into its unseeing eyes, trying to imagine where it might have travelled from. I'd read that crabs rafted long-distance on all sorts of vessels – pieces of plastic, hunks of seaweed, even the barnacled hulls of cargo ships. For all I knew this creature could have travelled from Polynesia, surviving thousands of miles just for the chance to die on a Northumbrian beach.

I should take some photographs. My tutors would know what it was.

But as I reached into my bag for my camera, my vision took a sudden pitch. Light-headedness dropped like marine fog and I had to stay still, hunched over, until it passed.

'Low blood pressure,' I said, when I was able to straighten up. 'Had it since I was a kid.'

We turned back to the crab. I got up onto hands and knees and photographed it from every angle.

The dizziness returned as I put my camera away, although this time it ebbed and flowed, imitating the waves. Pain was beginning to gather in my back, accompanied by a darker, more powerful sensation near my ribs. I knelt down again, tucking my hands in my lap, and the dizziness billowed.

I counted to ten. Murmured words of concern, laced with fear, tumbled around above my head. The wind changed direction.

When I finally opened my eyes, there was blood on my hand.

I looked carefully. It was unmistakably blood. Fresh, wet, across my right palm.

'It's fine,' I heard myself say. 'Nothing to worry about.'

Panic rolled in with the tide.

After I'd sat with my head between my knees for a few minutes, Janice called the maternity ward in Edinburgh.

'Yes, she's sitting down. No, not like a haemorrhage . . . But enough for there to be blood on her hands when she put them between her thighs . . . Yes. More than just spotting . . . No loss of consciousness. She just got a bit dizzy and had to sit down but now she's . . . Hang on. Emily. Are you still bleeding?'

I checked again. 'No.'

'No. She's twenty-one weeks pregnant. Yes . . . Emily, have you had any pain or cramping?'

'In my back, yeah . . .'

Janice paled. 'Yes, in her back. What do you think? Do we need an ambulance?'

I stared out to sea. There was an island, a couple of miles south, jutting out of the sea. A small wink of white on its furthest tip – a lighthouse, perhaps. It was as lonely as I felt. I might be losing my baby.

'Well, she's OK now, but I hardly think . . . OK . . . Right . . . Do you have their number? Oh, it's no matter. I'll get her there.'

She sat down next to me. 'They said you should come in to get it checked. Because you're so far from Edinburgh they suggested you go to the maternity unit in Alnwick. OK? It's not far at all.'

The wind blew, clouds scudded. *I cannot bear it. I cannot bear it.*

The sun passed briefly over the island, over the tiny lighthouse.

'I want to go to Edinburgh,' I said, after a pause. 'I . . . I don't like hospitals. I'd rather go to the one I'm used to.'

'Of course,' Janice said. 'Once we're in the car it should be less than two hours. But are you sure, Emily? What if the bleeding starts again?'

Terror. There was terror in her voice.

'I am sure,' I said. I didn't want to be with her anymore. I didn't want to be anywhere near this woman, who already felt that this was her baby. 'And I'd like to go on my own. On the train. I feel fine now.'

Chapter Thirty-Eight

I took the train back to Scotland, sitting on my coat. Janice had begged and pleaded at Alnwick station, but I stood firm. I wanted as many miles as possible between her and my baby.

My baby.

I'd never allowed myself to use those words. But all the normal rules were out, and I stroked my belly all the way.

The bleeding didn't restart, but I must have checked nearly twenty times between Alnwick and Edinburgh.

'Please be OK,' I whispered to her, as we sped north. 'Please be OK.'

'Try not to worry, Emily,' the midwife on the delivery suite said. Her tone was neutral, but I knew it wasn't good when she took me straight off to a private room.

A few minutes later my community midwife, Dee, came in. 'I saw your name on the board,' she said. 'Are you OK, sweetheart?'

That's when I started crying. I cried all the way through my examination, and when she attached me to a machine that monitored the baby's heart ('Looks good!' she smiled, examining the printout) I sobbed. It was only when Dee took me for an ultrasound and I saw her there, asleep with her tiny head against my navel, a miniature hand tucked under her cheek, that I believed she might survive.

‘Everything looks fine,’ Dee said. ‘I’ll need to get one of the doctors to take a wee look, but the baby looks happy and everything else is as it should be.’ She zoomed the ultrasound into my baby’s chest. ‘Sometimes these things just happen.’

I watched the chambers of my girl’s heart moving quietly, and I couldn’t do it for another moment.

I grabbed her hand, just as she went to leave, and said, ‘Please, Dee. Help me.’

After Dee had got the whole story out of me she went to call Granny.

‘Let’s just say, your grandmother’s going to take care of this,’ she smiled, upon her return. ‘She’s calling the agency now. You don’t have to hand over your baby to anyone, sweetheart. I just wish you’d told me what you were planning. I can’t believe you’ve been going through all of this on your own.’

Granny called an hour later.

‘All sorted,’ she said, as if she’d just cancelled the plumber.

I breathed out.

‘I also took the liberty of calling the Rothschilds,’ Granny said. ‘I’m sure the agency will, but I wanted to nip this in the bud.’

‘And?’

‘I was nice, but I told them not to contact you again. I don’t want them putting any more pressure on you.’

‘They haven’t put any pressure on me,’ I said. ‘Not once.’

‘Hmm.’

‘How did Janice take it?’

‘Bugger Janice.’

‘Granny. Come on.’

She sighed. 'Devastated,' she admitted. 'But that's not your concern, Emily.'

There was a pause. 'We'll do this together,' said my eighty-year-old grandmother. 'We'll do it together, Emily, and if you think I'm too old, you've forgotten who you're dealing with.'

In spite of my misgivings about her age, I moved to Granny's house in London two weeks later, too exhausted to sit my second-year exams. It might be years before I went back to university, I realised, and I didn't much care.

Granny had done hours of research on benefits and tax breaks, and worked out complex budgets involving her own pension and the modest rent I received from Dad's house. Our situation wasn't excellent, but it was a lot better than terrible, and she was full of rambunctious excitement.

I loved my growing baby. The love crept through my veins like an infusion. I dreamed of days on the Heath with my girl. Walking with Granny, or maybe Jill, once she'd graduated, because Jill's parents also lived in London. I even allowed myself to imagine befriending other mothers at an antenatal class. I tried to imagine sleep deprivation and I wasn't afraid. I'd be able to offset it with the cake and coffee I'd be having with all these new friends.

But then one day in September my baby came, and it wasn't like that.

It wasn't like that at all.

Chapter Thirty-Nine

Four days postnatal

It was a Tuesday afternoon, and I hadn't slept in days. I stood at the window of Granny's bathroom, looking out at the sky, recording what I could see on a sheet of toilet paper.

The sun was burning at midday height, but around it, the sky was iron-black. The front of Granny's house looked over a walled garden, inside which magnolia trees and lilac bushes slid with the breeze. But the sky itself was still as a portrait: no wind; just hammered-in sheets of black where there should have been clouds and light.

I slid up the sash for a better view, or perhaps a clearer understanding. It must be an eclipse, but there was an energy to it – something occult, that didn't feel right for an astronomical phenomenon. Besides, the sun was not obscured. It was fat and fiery, a disco ball on the black ceiling of Hampstead.

I wanted to dance under it. I'd loved dancing, once. I'd been good at it.

I rode a wave of love, of euphoria, of deep and absolute clarity as I walked back downstairs to my grandmother and my baby girl. We'd got back from the hospital an hour ago, and my caesarean incision burned at the bottom of my empty belly. Something nasty snagged when I tried to lift my left arm, and my breasts were like unexploded bombs.

But it was all manageable. I was a woman who'd just had a baby, and we were purebred fighters, made of steel, forged in fire. We could overcome anything.

In the kitchen I found a salad, my grandmother, and my daughter. My perfect girl. And, oh God, she was perfect; a tiny ornament, a plum, a goddess in miniature. I hadn't named her yet, but I would, when things slowed down. There were baby clothes to buy, and I needed a breast pump, and I'd promised to help several women on the postnatal ward. A lot of them were really struggling.

'You don't know what fear is until you become a parent,' a mother had said to me yesterday. She'd been in the bed next to mine on ward A300. 'You really have no idea.'

I told her I understood but that it was important not to be scared, especially now, at the height of her feminine powers. I tried to talk about it again later, but she was asleep and didn't wake up even when I got out of bed and poked her. I asked the midwives if she was alive and they said she was just exhausted because this was her fourth child.

I'd wanted her to know that nobody need be afraid: we were women, us mothers, we were warriors. Nothing could get in our way.

Granny was holding my little girl in the worn armchair she kept in the corner, in the place any sane person would put a dishwasher. She smiled at me, above my baby's soft head.

I went and crouched in front of her. My daughter. She was a beautiful thing; downy and warm with small red hands and feathery eyelashes. She slept for two hours and then woke to feed, just like they told me she should; she latched on well and seldom cried. I couldn't wait to take her out for a walk. Granny had said I should wait a while but Granny was being infuriatingly cautious at the moment. Her daughter had died shortly after giving birth to me, so I supposed it was old trauma. But Granny had always been so fearless!

'I really think we should go for a walk,' I said now. 'The neighbours will want to meet her. And besides, we need to talk. I'm worried that you're anxious, Granny, I want to help.'

'Oh, I'm fine,' she said. 'But you mustn't overstretch yourself. The Heath isn't going anywhere and Charlie's in no hurry.'

Charlie was Granny's dog. She must have shut him in the garden, because I hadn't seen him since we got back. He was raven-black like the sky outside.

'Hey, by the way,' I said. 'The sky—'

I paused. The sky had returned to normal in the space of a few minutes.

'Did you see the sky?' I asked, sharply. Something did not feel right. Something did not feel right at all. The light outside was bright, now, but brassy, as if there was a nuclear cloud above us.

Granny craned round, trying not to wake my daughter. 'Did I see the sky do what? It's not going to rain, is it?'

'No, it went dark. Well, black, actually, but now it's . . .'

I stopped. People in authority took babies away from women who started saying crazy things. I'd nearly lost my girl to adoption; I wasn't going to lose her to a bunch of hormones.

'Obviously, I'm just being stupid,' I said, and put the salad in the fridge. I didn't have time to eat.

A wave of unspecified dread broke over me as I turned back to Granny, so I smiled. I'd been feeling euphoric, since my daughter had been born – all-conquering, glorious. I wasn't ready for the emotional crash everyone said to expect.

Hormones. Just hormones: not everyone got the baby

blues. Besides, it had been the weird midwife who'd warned me about this emotional dip, the one who sometimes used strange dialectical words I didn't know. Almost like a code – as if she was testing to see if I was a member of her cult.

I crouched down again in front of my daughter and then stood up, forgetting to hold onto something, because the panic reappeared. I gasped at the pain in my abdomen. 'I might go for a drive,' I said. 'If she's still asleep?'

Granny frowned. Behind her, the radio played quietly. Exotic-sounding voices from across the Atlantic, maybe in Hawaii, or Malibu.

'If she's still asleep?!' Granny said. 'Oh, Emily, you need to rest. Why don't you go and have a nap now? You can't drive. Not for another five and a half weeks.'

I'd forgotten about the driving ban. But that was just for the really poorly mothers, whose C-section wounds got infected, or something like that. I was healthy and well. So incredibly well; my body was doing all the things a new mother's body should with the most beautiful precision. I loved it.

The door!

I went too fast to answer it, and jarred my wound again. It was the midwife, wearing a strange uniform like a 1970s postman. I let her in, but the sight of her made me anxious. She acted as if we were old friends, but I'd never seen her before.

I answered her questions carefully. While we were talking, the same subterranean dread I'd had in the kitchen with Granny resurfaced, pulling me towards a crevasse. I talked my way through it.

The midwife asked some rather probing questions, and in the end I had to ask her what exactly her training was, which offended her less than I expected. My thoughts began to pick up speed. Who was she? When was she leaving? I wanted to dance. I needed to get a breast pump.

After a while we had a look at my little girl.

'Oh, you're a lovely boy,' she said, undressing my daughter. 'Look at you!'

'She's a girl,' I said tightly. I didn't have a good feeling about this woman.

The midwife stopped and looked over her shoulder at me. 'Is there any chance of a cup of tea?' she asked, after an extended pause.

I was more than happy to oblige: I felt murderous and oddly afraid. We'd been sitting in stasis for what felt like hours and this woman hadn't even acknowledged how busy I was; how much of my time she was taking up. Had she actually met a new mother before?

In the kitchen I checked the sky. Granny and the midwife talked in low voices, punctuated by squawks from my daughter. I started making toast but abandoned it because the smell was disgusting.

A cat jumped into Granny's garden and started wandering around a flower bed, looking for somewhere to shit. I ran outside to chase it away – cat shit was bad for babies – but by the time I got out there, it had vanished.

Everything felt sharpened, but nothing felt right. The sky was normal again; no nuclear mushroom cloud. The euphoria melted down, and now the fear was biological.

Granny came and got me from the garden.

I went over to my daughter, who was lying on a special play mat with dangly arches that Granny had bought. I removed her blanket to tickle her, only to discover she was naked apart from her nappy.

'She'll freeze like this,' I snapped, and left the room to get a sleepsuit. Imbeciles! If I wasn't so busy, I'd report this midwife.

Granny followed me out to the hallway. 'Emily,' she said, in the voice she probably used to use in the House of Commons. 'Darling, I need to ask why you keep calling Charlie "she".'

'What?'

'Charlie. Your baby. Why do you keep calling him "she"?'

I took myself off up the stairs. 'I haven't the time for this,' I said. Granny had hung a new picture on the landing, but it needed dusting already.

When I got back down to the sitting room, Granny was holding my daughter. 'Emily,' she said, in that MP voice again. 'Do you think you had a daughter?'

'What is this?' I exploded, but the fear had reached deep inside me now, and it was hard to think straight. 'What are you doing, Granny?'

Granny looked at me for a long while and then undid my baby's nappy. 'You had a son,' she said. 'You called him Charlie. He's a boy.'

And there, tucked inside the nappy, were a tiny boy's genitalia.

My breath stopped in my throat. I bent down and, wincing with pain, I did up her nappy, and started to put her sleep suit on. But before I could do up the poppers, I had another look inside her nappy, and the room darkened.

'See?' I muttered, but my voice was inaudible. 'The sky.'

I snapped the poppers closed.

His head was a different shape to my daughter's, and his hair thicker and darker. He was now wearing one of her sleepsuits, but he wasn't the child they pulled from my womb yesterday, or last week, or whenever it was she arrived in the world.

The dread opened up before me, smooth-sided and sparkling blue.

'What have you done?' I asked. The two women in the room watched me.

'What. The fuck. Have you done?' I repeated, in a whisper, but it was no use; the boy had started to cry – as any baby would, if they'd been taken from their mother.

'Who did this?' I asked. 'Who took my girl and gave me a boy? Where is she? Where is she?'

'I totally understand that you think you had a girl,' the midwife said, crossing her legs at the ankle. 'But you had a boy, and you called him Charlie. It's all here in your maternity notes. Please don't worry, though, women undergo all sorts of hormonal changes after birth; it's not unusual for this sort of confusion to occur. I can see you've been quite . . .' She made a show of looking at my maternity folder. 'Quite busy, and distracted, since you had him, and your grandmother agrees. How have you been sleeping?'

I replied, or at least my mouth did, but my thoughts were racing. Who was involved in this? How had it happened? My money was on the hospital midwife, who'd used the strange words. Was she even a midwife? Had she been wearing a lanyard? I stared at this boy, Charlie, who was beginning to look hungry.

I had to find my daughter.

I forced my aching body up and went over to my grandmother. 'Granny,' I said. 'Someone has taken my daughter, and you need to help me. We have to call the hospital. And the police. Straight away.'

Until that moment I'd thought Granny was my ally, but she looked me in the eye and said, 'Emily, there hasn't been a mix-up, and nobody has taken your daughter. This is your son, Charlie, and you had him on Friday. I was there when they got him out and he hasn't been out of my sight since. I think we need to see a doctor, just to make sure you're OK.'

The midwife was out in the hallway, on the phone to someone. Everything was imploding. The crab with the signal-red spots and bristled claws was in our garden, and Dad was on the phone to the midwife, telling her this baby was not biologically mine.

'Granny . . .'

'Yes. I'm here. Talk to me, my love.'

Her betrayal was worse than anything I could have imagined. I couldn't meet her eye.

'You're a liar,' I whispered, although she seemed not to hear me. 'A born liar.'

The baby was wailing, Granny was saying my name, and there was a man nearby, I think the postman who used to deliver letters to me and Dad when I was tiny, back at the beginning of the eighties when they still wore peaked hats like Postman Pat.

I was twenty years old, my baby had been stolen and I had no one on my side.

The midwife left and I gave in and fed the baby because how could I not? He felt wrong and my breasts wept to feed another baby when my own was missing.

The midwife had somehow concealed a surveillance camera in the carriage clock on Granny's mantelpiece. There was another above the door, and I suspected a whole suite of them in the kitchen. Hundreds of secret lenses swivelled back and forth as I paced the house.

The sky darkened further as the sun began to sink on the day, on me. Granny's house was full of flowers and sweet cotton bibs and knitted socks. There was a breast pump, but

I couldn't remember going out that afternoon to buy one and Granny said it had been there all along.

A GP came round in the early evening. She told me she was calling the community mental health team, so I called 999 and told them a group of people in Hampstead had stolen my baby and were now trying to pretend I was having a psychiatric crisis. I don't remember what they said to me.

The sky was maroon-streaked and the camera in the Edwardian clock was watching me. Granny was feeding Charlie with a bottle, which he didn't seem to mind. I implored her to stop this conspiracy but she just told me she loved me, and then we both cried.

The people who came round that night didn't have my daughter. It was two women, a social worker and a psychiatrist, they said, and they were there to carry out a Mental Health Act assessment. One of them smelled as if she'd just finished a cigarette. I said I had to go to the toilet but really my plan was to climb up to the roof terrace and try to find a way down via our neighbour's house, which was covered in scaffolding.

Or maybe not the scaffolding? If I couldn't get my daughter back, did I want to live? I could just step off the roof into the black arms of the evening. It would be quick. This lovely boy, Charlie, would be back to his mother in no time, and – and . . .

Someone grabbed my foot as it disappeared up the ladder to the roof hatch. There was a baby crying downstairs.

A depthless dark broke over me as I sat in a room that looked like Granny's kitchen and answered questions. I had lost my baby. They were all in on it.

People talked to other people, somebody else came to speak to me, something about the Mental Health Act.

Eventually I said I'd go to this hospital for mad mothers they kept going on about, but only if they let me bring my real baby.

Later, or perhaps the next day, they sent the crazy ambulance.

I shouted at Granny, *I will never forgive you*, and she was crying, which was understandable given what she'd done, although she was saying, 'I can't lose another one, please, I can't lose another one,' which didn't make any sense because it was my baby who had been stolen, not hers.

Chapter Forty

North London & UCLH NHS Foundation Mental Health Trust Mother and Baby Unit, Camden

I lay on the bed and monitored the faces at my door; bodies in uniform watching. In a chair right next to the bed, Charlie was being bottle-fed by a woman with a lanyard round her neck. His actual mother, perhaps? This place was horrifying. Doors were locked, everywhere, but the door to my own room remained resolutely open and there was no lock at all on my bathroom door. There were spy cameras and babies crying.

Another woman, who'd greeted me at the front door, came in at that moment. She told me for the second time her name was Shazia – as if I cared! – and talked to me about tranquilisers. She told me I needed a night's 'protected sleep'.

'It's this child who needs protecting,' I said. 'He's been stolen from his mother; he's less than a week old. Someone else has my baby. Do you know if the police are involved yet? No? Well, either way I'm not willing to zonk out on pills. I don't think you understand how awful the last few days have been . . .'

'I do understand,' she said, and in spite of myself I liked her voice. 'I do understand, Emily, because it's my job to look after women in your situation. I know you're afraid, and I know you're angry, and above all I know this is not where you want to be.'

When I refused the drugs she said she'd come back in half an hour.

I cuddled Charlie for a while, because he was lovely, and I was afraid of this place, but I cried for her – my girl, whose name – whose name was . . .

Had they drugged me already?

I asked the woman in the chair where my grandmother was, and she seemed surprised, because apparently I'd said I didn't want Granny anywhere me. In the end she agreed Granny could come tomorrow morning. 'We need to assess you properly first,' she said. She, too, had a nice voice. I suppose they were accustomed to making women feel safe before swapping their babies around and pretending we'd all gone mad.

As the day came to an end I felt so afraid I realised I had to be either dead or unconscious if I were to survive another minute. I gave in to Shazia's pills. 'Just rest,' she said. She had hair like black satin. 'Charlie's fine. He's going to be in the nursery tonight. He's taken beautifully to the bottle.'

I floated on a slack tide.

They kept me in that barely-conscious space for days, but insisted it had been less than twelve hours, that it was now Saturday lunchtime. I had been admitted the night before.

Shazia handed me Charlie and it came to me that I loved him with a force almost indistinguishable from pain, but by mid-afternoon the black sky had rolled back in and I cried for my daughter.

I don't know how long it took me to balance. I know only that as the days passed I stopped thinking about a daughter and began to accept as fact the things they told me: postpartum psychosis, delusions, mania, euphoria, mood swings. There was a lot of pain and mess. Nobody could explain why it had happened to me.

When I stopped being so busy doing everything but nothing, I began to talk to the other women in the unit. There were eight of us in total. Three seldom left their rooms; the rest of us spent most of our time in the lounge, trying to make sense of what was happening to us.

Things sharpened, then lost focus, but the food was always disgusting.

In the room next door was Darya. She loved her daughter desperately but could not find any reason to live. One day there was a commotion from her room; people shouting and running. After that she was shadowed by nursing assistants all day. Her husband would visit and I'd hear them talking in Russian, and he would start crying the moment he left her room.

In conversations with Shazia I remembered that I'd believed the baby to be female when I was pregnant, which went some way to explaining things. But of course it was Charlie – it had always been Charlie, with his black bead eyes and patchy hair, the victory-punch fist that escaped his swaddles.

I started looking after him all day, and a week or two later they let me have him at night. When he cried I would hold the soft angles of his body close and pray for him to be safe. The world was full of danger and I had no idea how to protect him.

Oh, for the life of a limpet, I wrote to Jill. Surrounded on all sides by shell and hard substrate. Only ever looking down, never up. A limpet's contribution to reproduction involved only the release of larvae. Our tutor had been wrong: life was not remotely tough for limpets.

*

'I curse this stinking illness,' Granny sighed, during one of her visits. She'd brought flapjacks and a novel, only to find me miserable after another setback. 'It's obscenely unfair that it should happen to you, of all people.'

A nurse took her to one side and told her off. 'It bloody well is unfair,' she replied, loud enough for me to hear. 'You have no idea what this girl's been through. Did you know she was orphaned by the time she sat her A-levels?'

The nurse didn't have a great deal to say to that.

When Granny came back, she told me Janice Rothschild wanted to visit.

'I told her to piss off,' she admitted. 'But it felt unfair to keep you in the dark. What do you say?'

I didn't know. I had no idea if I was ready for people, with their perfumes and hairstyles and opinions. Even the prospect of Jill felt overwhelming. Janice, on the other hand, had become a friend to me, at a time when no one else I knew could understand my life. Upon learning I was pulling out of the adoption arrangement she'd written an incredibly kind letter and enclosed some of the outfits she'd bought: there had been no recriminations.

And surely the Rothschilds would be on the road to adopting another child by now? They might already have one, come to think of it.

I said yes.

Janice brought a beautiful dressing gown in a stiff cardboard bag with woven handles and reams of tissue paper. She spoke easily and kept conversation simple, and for a while I forgot she was a woman people asked for autographs. She said she was sorry if I ever felt pressured into the adoption plans, that she worried it had somehow contributed to my crisis.

She told me she and Jeremy hadn't found the right baby

yet, but she seemed very positive about the whole thing. It made me feel fractionally better.

The days passed, the air was damper and cooler. I changed nappies and fed my baby. There was therapy; there were crafts, there was sleep – although never enough. I washed rompers in the laundry room, I watched television. Above all, I ached to be like the other women here, with their partners and husbands, their tentative hopes for life on the other side. I had no plans. The next fifty or sixty years loomed before me, blank as a winter sea.

With help from Granny I wrote to my university, telling them I wasn't coming back. I was touched to hear from my tutor. He tried to persuade me to stay on, so I had Granny write a reply saying no. The offer to stay was both kind and completely unrealistic.

Charlie started smiling. He slept on my chest on slow autumn days. Jill sent me a book of tropical fish for him and we'd flick through the pages together, looking at coral reefs, emperor angelfish, purple queens. He held on to my finger and closed his warm gums over the tip. His newborn hair fell out and soft blonde wisps grew in its place. My whole body ached with love.

The mists did still descend but they were transient now; occasional visitors.

I started to believe that I might, in fact, recover.

It was then – when I thought I might be out of the woods – that it happened.

Chapter Forty-One

DIARY OF JANICE ROTHSCHILD

November 1st, 2000
E's grandmother says I can visit. Seems desperately upset and stressed about the whole thing.

Been reading about postpartum psychosis. I know E will get better. But what then? Grandmother 80ish and E's recovery will probably be slow and difficult. I worry for Emily and I worry for Charlie.

Having a lot of thoughts about how much better off this baby would have been with us, but obv can't voice them to anyone. Especially J. He thinks my visits are a terrible idea.

BUT: we have a meeting with the adoption agency about a newborn who might be available quite soon (They'd said it could take years! Amazing!) so J going easy on me.

He's right, tho – I probably shouldn't be going to see E. Thing is, I like her. Kind of reminds me of me, at her age.

Anyway. Must get stuff together and go visit her.

November 2nd, 2000
Oh God. Oh God, oh God.

Last 24 hours playing over and over in my head.

The most horrifying of all horrifying things.

Yesterday I went to visit Emily at the MBU and found her trying to smother Charlie.

Was frazzled when I arrived which probably hasn't helped with the stress – J and I had had a fight before I left: he actually asked me if I was trying to change Emily's mind about the adoption. (What kind of monster does he think I am?)

I was walking down the corridor towards Emily's room and thought I heard laughter and a game of peekaboo. But it must have been someone else, because when I walked through her door, she was trying to suffocate Charlie with a pillow.

I screamed, managed to stop her. Alarms going off, chaos, they took me away but I could hear her crying and begging them to give Charlie back as I left the ward.

I honestly thought she was getting better – a lot better – but she must have relapsed. I know she loves him. She wouldn't dream of hurting him in her right mind.

Would do anything to get that image of the pillow out of my mind. I just can't stand it.

J was right. I should never have visited her.

Chapter Forty-Two

EMILY

I knew nothing until the moment Janice Rothschild was in the room, screaming 'STOP! Emily! Stop!'

I froze. People ran in.

Janice said something to a nurse, who tried to take Charlie away, so I held on. Janice was taken out of the room. She was crying. One of her hands was over her mouth, as if she'd just been sick, or witnessed something too terrible to comprehend. Seconds later, Shazia arrived.

I didn't know what was happening, only that it was bad. They'd reduced my antipsychotic drugs two days ago. Had I done something crazy? I tried to rewind the last hour but nothing was there, just a red sea of panic. A guitar riff played over and over in my ears, as if to stop me remembering.

'Help me,' I said. 'Shazia, what are they doing?'

Shazia, who seemed shaken for the first time since I'd arrived here, crouched down next to my bed, where I was sitting, holding onto Charlie.

'We have to talk to you,' she said. 'Away from Charlie. Can you give him to me, Emily?'

I started crying. 'Why? What have I done? Why can't he stay? Why can't I hold him?'

Shazia put both hands on my knees. 'Will you trust me?'

she asked. 'Will you trust me to take him away so I can talk to you for a few minutes, and then bring him back to you?'

I sobbed as I put my tiny boy into her arms. I knew without having to ask that I had no choice in the matter.

'What happened?' Shazia said, when she came back without him. 'What were you doing, Emily? What do you remember?'

I told her I didn't know. I told her this again and again, my voice upwelling with panic. What did everyone think I'd done? Why had Janice screamed at me?

'What's wrong with Charlie?' I asked. 'Is he sick?'

She told me they'd checked him over and he seemed fine. By then I was sobbing again. Whatever it was I'd done, it was serious.

After a while Shazia took my hand and let me into room where we found the psychiatrist who came every morning. There was an unknown man, too, who said he was a social worker. He had huge liquid eyes, and I could see in them that I'd done something wrong, no matter how much he did that one-sided smile people did when they felt bad for you but couldn't afford to be warm.

Shazia sat me down and told me Janice had found me trying to smother Charlie.

There was an opaque silence. I stared at them, they stared back. And I started to say 'No,' when I saw it: Charlie, on my bed, a rectangle of pale blue over his face. My heart stopped as I framed and reframed the image, but there was no editing it. The hands holding the blue rectangle were mine.

The three people in the room watched me. There was a clock with a battery running low, the second hand kicking uselessly between 3 and 4.

I ran through the image once again. Charlie's face, smiling, then disappearing from view as I lowered a blue rectangle over his face. A cushion? A folded jumper?

I let out a strange sound. It was my pillow.

'Janice is – she could be right,' I whispered, incredulous. My life creased beneath my feet. 'I think – Oh God, no.'

'Oh God no, what?' Shazia prompted.

I closed my eyes. 'I think she's right.'

'Are you sure?' Shazia asked. I opened my eyes. 'I mean—'

The social worker shot her a look, and she stopped. 'Just tell us what happened, as and when you remember the details,' she said, gently.

I thought about it again, about that pillow. Was my intention to smother him? Really? That little boy, who was already the love of my life?

There was a sharp movement in my abdomen, a fire-like pain. That was exactly what my intention had been. The pillow down on his face, so he'd be safe, away from me and this cruel world.

I screamed at them for reducing my medication. *I told you I wasn't ready. I told you!*

Shazia somehow got me to sit back down.

We had to go back through it several times. Each time more detail emerged, and each detail was unbearable. I would have done it, if Janice hadn't walked in. I would have done it.

'You told me women with this condition don't hurt their babies,' I kept saying. 'You told me I was safe to keep him.'

'It's incredibly rare,' Shazia said, helplessly. 'And when it has happened, in the past, the mother has never meant it . . .'

'Of course I didn't mean it,' I cried. 'Oh God, help me. Help me.'

Later, I was taken back to my room, and Charlie was given back to me. He was asleep. One of the nursing assistants stayed in the room and I knew without asking that she wasn't allowed to leave.

'I'm sorry, I'm sorry, I'm sorry,' I told my sleeping baby. 'I love you. I love you more than anything in the world. I love you.'

I wanted to die.

My meds were changed. I slept for two days. When I woke up I called Janice.

'I want to go through with the adoption,' I told her.

They tried to stop me. I had endless meetings and consultations; even the other mothers tried to talk me out of it. But the bottom line was this: I wanted Charlie to be safe. I wanted him to have a good life – a great life, even – and he couldn't have that with me.

I lay awake at night with the guitar riff that had started when Janice caught me, reverberating over and over like a scream. No drug they tried me on made anything bearable, and all I could do with Charlie was cry, and tell him I was sorry.

My heart burned with self-loathing. It shrunk to a small hard mass, and, when the staff finally accepted I was giving Charlie to Janice and Jeremy, it shattered.

I suspected then that it would never heal, and it didn't.

Chapter Forty-Three

DIARY OF JANICE ROTHSCHILD

December 7th, 2000
Our baby boy's here! He's home!

No curtain call comes close to this feeling. I'm mad with love and joy and excitement and terror and exhaustion and adrenalin – even if Charlie sleeps tonight, there's no way I will. WE HAVE A BABY! Our perfect boy!

David of course v happy about 'this little plan', already signed the foster papers. Was anxious about what might happen when he met C, but he popped round earlier and although obviously thought C was cute, I didn't see so much as a second of recognition, or uncertainty – nothing. Just drank champagne, talked bollocks and left. Classic D.

God, though. The handover = awful. I wasn't expecting to see E but she handed him over herself. I suppose there isn't a rulebook for a situation as unusual as this, but still – was harrowing. She couldn't catch her breath. Kept kissing his head, smelling his hair, trying to breathe. Was sobbing by the time she made it to the door. Just dreadful. So much guilt, and E's nurse Shazia was super shitty with us, which didn't help. Not sure why. E begged us to take him, what were we supposed to do?

Right until the end, kept expecting her to run out screaming that she'd changed her mind. Didn't happen, of course, but we did get papped.

Fuckers. J says no paper could print the pics because Charlie's a minor, but I'm worried. If they do get printed, they'll ask me about postnatal psychiatric illness in press interviews for EVER. What would I say?

So many variables. So much guilt. Keep thinking about E. Beyond limits of my imagination to envision how she must be feeling. Feeling unable to bring him up. Handing him over to someone else. But then I remember that awful, awful day, and I know she's done the right thing. For all of us.

4am

Haven't slept. I'm frightened now. I keep checking my phone in case she rings to say she wants him back. Nothing to stop her doing that. The law is on her side right up until the court order is signed, and that could be more than a year away.

Not sure I can do this. Live with this much fear.

December 12th

A female 'journalist' called me today. Told me they had photos of me leaving a mother and baby unit and were planning to run a story. Would I like to talk?

Was another moment I'll never forget. The moment a woman blackmailed another woman over her postnatal mental health.

J's been trying to shut them down all afternoon but the paper and its shitty little lawyers were ready for us – they're adamant that they're going to print.

December 15th

The 'story' is no more than a photo of us leaving the unit, with a caption that reads, 'Jeremy and Janice Rothschild leaving a mother and baby unit, for mothers suffering perinatal psychiatric disorders, earlier this month.' The photo is so big it takes up most of the page.

The press came and stood outside for a few hours. They've already gone. One filthy arsehole still lurking, but he'll lose interest. I detest them.

The adoption agency isn't keen on this turn of events, but we had a call just now to say they've had a meeting and are happy for us to continue, 'subject to regular assessment.'

December 19th

Fear keeping me awake at night. Fear of Emily changing her mind, fear about Charlie, fear about myself. Am so tired of being terrified the whole time. I keep thinking about what might be going on in Emily's head. What might be unfolding.

Will she want him back?

The whole thing is just awful.

Chapter Forty-Four

EMILY

One year later (December)

The evening after Charlie's adoption finally went through the courts I left Granny's for the first time in months.

Some time later I found myself outside Janice and Jeremy's, in the middle of a downpour. It was a beautiful four-storey Georgian house, right on Highbury Fields. Their huge front door sat expensively between pillars, and an engraved sign by the letterbox said NO FLYERS, because they were too important and cosmopolitan for handymen and pizzas.

You could see right through the window to their kitchen, and a big marble island larger than my grandmother's dining room. Jeremy was sitting at it, reading something on a laptop.

I stood still in the rain and watched him for a while. His tie was off, swirled round his computer, a glass of red wine nearby. If Charlie had started talking, this was the man he'd be calling Daddy. This house, these people, were his life.

At one end of their huge dining table stood a highchair.

I dug my fingernails into my palms, breathing with the pain. Occasionally in the last year I'd been to a support group for mothers who'd given their children up for adoption, and heard many of them talking about 'trusting' or 'breathing with' the pain.

As of 2 p.m., my baby was no longer mine, and there was

nothing I could ever do to change it. Breathing exercises were an insult.

Momentarily I allowed myself to imagine it was me upstairs with Charlie, not Janice: giving him a bath, being splashed and playing with toys. Or perhaps in Granny's little bathroom, with the grumbling floorboards and the window that never quite shut.

The pain made me want to lie down and curl into a ball, right there on the rainy pavement.

I stood for a long time, freezing and wet, until Janice suddenly appeared in the kitchen, holding a child's bottle. Before even putting the bottle down she walked straight into the sitting room at the front, to look out of the window.

It had been dark for a few hours, and I was on the other side of the road, by a tree. But I realised too late that I was still too close to a streetlamp, and she saw me straightaway. She pressed her face closer to the glass and framed her vision with her hands, to get a better look. I didn't dare move. My hood was up, so she couldn't see my face, but she knew. I sensed her, just as she sensed me. Urgently, she turned to call Jeremy.

I ran, slipping into the shadows past the leisure centre, pushing unfit legs towards Highbury and Islington Station.

Stupid. I was so stupid. What had I hoped to achieve?

Jeremy reached me just as I got to the pelican crossing. I should have pulled free when I felt a hand on my elbow – I should have sprinted – but I stopped and turned around. Nobody but Granny and my GP had touched me in a very long time.

'Emily?'

I shook my head. 'No.'

'Emily . . .' He gently pulled me across the road so we were standing on the pavement. The rain drummed on my hood.

'She looked like she checks out of the window every night,' was all I could say.

'She does.' Jeremy hunched uselessly against the rain.

'Why? Have you two had some sort of trouble?'

Jeremy shook his head. 'No trouble. Charlie's perfectly safe. She's just . . . She's just been very anxious since we took him. She's been really afraid you'd change your mind.'

'So afraid she checks out of the window all the time?'

After a pause, Jeremy nodded. 'She's wonderful with Charlie,' he said. 'So you don't need to worry about the effect this anxiety's had, but . . . Anyway, now it's all legalised I think she'll be able to draw a line. Start to believe she really is a mother.'

I had not expected this. The scenes that played in my head had involved Janice and Jeremy smiling with joy at their sleeping toddler, coming downstairs to drink wine together and talk about all the funny things he'd done that day. It hadn't crossed my mind that she could be anxious. Especially about me. About Emily Peel, who'd lain in bed for months on end, hardly able to take care of her most basic needs.

'I've never been here before,' I said. 'This is the first time. And, obviously, the last.'

He started to say something but I interrupted.

'I will never get over what I did,' I said. 'It's ruined my life. But you don't need to worry, Jeremy. I'm not stalking you. It was just a . . . I don't know. The finality of the court order going through. I panicked.'

He nodded. 'I understand. But it mustn't happen again – Janice will call the police if you harass us, and I won't stop her.'

I closed my eyes against the rain for a moment.

'I'm so sorry, Jeremy. Please don't tell her it was me. It'll only cause unnecessary alarm.'

'Absolutely. I'll say it was a nutter.'

I nearly smiled. He nearly did, too.

'Just . . . Just tell me Charlie's OK,' I said. It was rising up inside me, again; the longing. The deep sea swell of it. 'Tell me he's well, and happy.'

'He is,' Jeremy said, gently. A bus with steamed windows pulled in behind him. 'Oh, Emily. He is very well, and very happy. You don't need to worry about him at all.'

I couldn't speak. Passengers spilled from the bowels of the bus.

'We will never tell him what happened,' he said, and his voice had become the kindest voice in the world. 'We'll just say that you were young and very challenged by life, and that you felt you couldn't keep him. He won't ever know about that day.'

'Thank you.'

He nodded. 'Is your grandmother looking after you?'

I jammed my hands in my pockets. 'Not really. She's had some virus, it's kind of taken her out. I'm not sure how much longer she's got, to be honest.'

'I'm sorry to hear that.'

'Yeah. Anyway, I apologise. Sincerely. You won't see me again.'

Without any particular plan, I turned and walked off into the rain.

My baby boy. My sweet tiny Charlie, now a little toddler with wealthy parents and a big house on the park. Kept from me by law.

And if I did one thing right in my life, I thought, walking on down the Holloway Road, if I really cared about him, I would never go near him again.

Chapter Forty-Five

EMILY

Four months later (April)

The playground wasn't busy.

There were two mothers sharing cookies while one of their toddlers played in a wooden boat. A lone father with a baby. A couple of teenagers in school uniform, eating fried chicken from a box.

On the edge of the sandpit, sitting under some lime saplings, I watched my son. Charlie was playing in a red train, metres from me. If I tried hard enough, I could recall the scent of his downy skin, convince myself it was carrying on the breeze.

'Yuga yuga yuga,' he muttered. Chug chug chug?

I love you. So much.

Janice was laughing with the other woman, laughing as if she had the best life anyone could imagine. Charlie's hair was almost white blonde, his cheeks still fat. I had to get out of here. I should never have got so close.

I didn't move.

Without warning, Charlie climbed out of the train and looked straight at me. After a moment's consideration, he smiled. My son smiled at me, as if he knew. As if he had never forgotten.

I got up and backed away, into the trees. 'Hello!' I whispered, turning to leave. 'And, bye bye!' But he followed me, over a little dirt bank, away from the train and the sandpit.

Through the saplings I could see Janice, still talking to her friend. She had no idea.

Quickly, before I had time to stop myself, I ran over to Charlie and held him, closing my arms around his solid little toddler's body, smelling his hair. 'I love you,' I whispered, to an avalanche of joy and pain. 'I will always love you.'

Then I went. I heard calling, then shouting, as she tried to find him. I skirted around the wooded area towards the east gate. I knew he was safe – this gate was shut, and to get to the main entrance he'd have to walk right past Janice. She'd find him under the trees any moment now.

I heard her voice become fainter, and then louder, and then, just as I slipped out of the gate, I heard her find Charlie where I'd left him. Noisy sobs, wails, *where were you, oh God, I was so worried . . . Oh God, Charlie, little one . . .*

I walked slowly, so as not to draw attention to myself. My heart raced.

I needed help.

It was the fifth time I'd done this. Just turned up in Highbury, when things got too difficult. Watched in plain sight while my son went about his life with Janice and Jeremy.

Janice seemed to have relaxed in the last few weeks; she wasn't looking for me anymore. I'd sat at the bus stop opposite the Trevi, watching Charlie trying to eat spaghetti in a table by the window. I'd watched them in the corner shop opposite the Hen and Chickens, I'd watched them twice in the park. I never stayed longer than a couple of minutes: just enough to calm my system; to dull my screaming nerves.

I need help.

I walked away towards Highbury Place, keeping my back to the playground, concentrating on my feet, one in front of the other.

Left foot, right foot. Left, right.

I need help.

Chapter Forty-Six

DIARY OF JANICE ROTHSCHILD

April

Held him in my arms, crying, kissing him, shouting at him. Felt judgemental gaze of other parents. Seriously? Shouting at a tiny child who just wandered off into the trees?

Picked up phone, which I'd dropped on ground when I reached C. Could not stop sobbing. Managed to tell J that C seemed unharmed.

Then J said he'd just found Emily Peel, as he ran across the park to help me.

Everything stopped. I couldn't believe it.

And yet, I could. I totally could. Fury came, fury like I've never known. Despair.

J took Emily to Islington Police Station. He's been all 'poor Emily' since we became Charlie's legal parents, but that's over now.

She'll be punished by the law, he said, in voice that makes politicians shit themselves. Promised he'd stop the press getting anywhere near this.

But how will we get her out of our lives? She lives less than half an hour away. She isn't going to give up, I feel it in my bones.

Just as I began to believe we were safe.

September 30th, 2002

A two-year restraining order. That's what she got.

Two years? For a woman who tried to abduct a child? I can't think straight or do anything. Panic attacks, can't sleep. Therapist wants me to get trauma treatment, she thinks I have PTSD. I can't let Charlie out of my sight.

Emily won the magistrate over with her bullshit about 'just wanting to see him'. He said there was no evidence she tried to abduct C, even tho E admitted that she's been harassing us.

Waited in the street outside Highbury Mag Court for her to come out. J couldn't stop me. He tried, but I wasn't in the mood for compliance. In the end he went home.

Took her forever to come out. She was alone. She's lost a lot of weight.

I quite literally wanted to push her in front of a bus. You asked me to be a sane and stable mother to Charlie, and then you stalked me? Seriously? You hid in a fucking bush in my local park and tried to steal him away?

How dare you – how fucking dare you?

You have taken so much from us by doing this. And I mean us. You have stripped Charlie of the safe home you asked me to give him. You fucking madwoman. You fucking lunatic.

Instead of all this I walked up to her, calm and composed, and quietly told her that I would make her pay for what she's done.

And I mean it. No matter how long it takes, I will make her pay.

Chapter Forty-Seven

EMILY

After my conviction I started at the Open University. Three blank years later, I graduated and changed my name. The woman who had terrorised Charlie's family was removed from record.

I hadn't gone anywhere near the Rothschilds, nor would I. Instead I used the consuming energy of grief to search for my crab. Whenever I had an empty few days – and there were many empty days, in those early years – I went up to Northumberland to look. I neither found anything nor gave up. I just kept going.

I finished my master's in Plymouth and eventually got a research post there. I began to lead a life that met the basic requirements of Normal. At times it even felt pleasant, providing I didn't think too much about where I'd come from. As the years passed, Emma behaved much as young Emily had learned to, and people enjoyed her company. They were entertained by her – I made sure of it.

I'm not sure I was happy, exactly, but I was busy and purposeful, and mostly surrounded by other human beings. That felt like enough.

*

Granny died, a few years later. A man called Leo called about her obituary, and I knew before I even met him that I was being given a second chance.

And that second chance was beautiful; more so than I could ever have imagined. My body moved on, my heart loved again.

But there was always a negative space, a shadow on the sand. That is the way with loss: you can't undo it, no matter what you have gained.

PART III

EMMA

Chapter Forty-Eight

LEO

Jeremy watches me.

I feel everything and nothing. We sit together, two men without their wives, linked by a nightmare I knew nothing of.

'I don't like the fact that you're learning all of this from me,' Jeremy says, after a long silence. 'It's not right. But if it helps you work out where Emma might be . . .'

I rub my hands over my eyes, at a loss. I don't know this woman Jeremy has described. This woman he has known nearly twenty years. I don't know anything about the way she thinks or what drives her decisions. Do I love her? Could I love her? Has she ever loved me, or has that just been a part of the performance?

Emma is Emily. She met Jeremy's cousin and became pregnant. She agreed to let the Rothschilds adopt the baby; she changed her mind, she suffered postpartum psychosis and tried to suffocate her baby. She then went through with the adoption, only to harass them, and then attempt to abduct the child.

'This is . . . . This is a nightmare,' I say, eventually.

Somewhere, in a back room, a washing machine beeps. I escape from the hell in my head for a moment to try to imagine Jeremy Rothschild doing laundry, but I can't. I can't think.

I know a little of postpartum psychosis. I had to write up that poor woman who jumped off a bridge with her baby, a few years back; the story still haunts me. But Emma? How could she go through a trauma like that and not tell me? Not tell anyone?

But she did tell someone, I realise, as the truth presses silently in. Jill, who turned up at our house just before Ruby was born, who wouldn't budge until Ruby was two weeks old. Jill, who never left Emma on her own with Ruby, even when they were napping together on the sofa.

Jill knew.

The thought makes me so angry, so desolate, I nearly get up and leave. But what then? There are so many questions I need to ask Jeremy.

I hold myself steady. I concentrate on my breathing, just like Emma taught me.

Emily. Emily Ruth Peel, with a grown-up child and a criminal record.

'What about this abduction?' I ask, eventually. 'What actually happened?'

'She hid in a copse of trees in our local playground, apparently 'just to have a look at' Charlie. He disappeared for a few minutes; Janice panicked and called me. I found Emma just as I ran across from our house to the playground.'

I rest my head in my hands. 'And this wasn't during the postpartum psychosis?'

'It was more than a year later, Leo. I believe she was very low, but she certainly wasn't psychotic.'

I imagine Ruby disappearing in a park. Me and Emma running, shouting her name; the sheer terror. It's incomprehensible that Emma could inflict that on another parent.

'What did Emma say at the time?' I ask. 'What was her defence?'

Jeremy prevaricates. 'Well, actually, she denied the charge of abduction. Claimed she was just watching him from the edge of the park. That he spotted her and came over for a few minutes; she did nothing to encourage it. Certainly, the magistrate believed her.'

A tiny crack of relief. 'Well, I'm inclined to believe her, too,' I say. 'Emma wouldn't just . . .'

Doubt swarms in before I can even finish the sentence. Emma is capable not of just small lies but fundamental deception. For starters, she was hiding in a bloody grove of trees, watching Charlie play without Janice's knowledge. Who am I to say that's not acceptable. That's many miles from acceptable. Who am I to say she wasn't planning to take him? That she didn't try?

I look back at Jeremy. 'What did you believe?'

He considers his response for a moment.

'I also struggled to imagine her actually taking him,' he admits. 'But the fact is, Charlie disappeared for several minutes, and when Janice found him, he was next to the gate Emma exited by. That's just too much of a coincidence for me. Especially given that she admitted to having covertly watched him and Janice several times in the preceding months.'

'But if the magistrate believed she wasn't trying to abduct him, why the restraining order?'

Jeremy's face stills. 'I'm sorry,' he says. 'Did you not just hear me tell you that Emma turned up to follow us five times in six months?'

He's losing his temper. 'Can you imagine how distressing that was? The abduction is neither here nor there. She harassed us.'

'But if she was only trying to watch him, it seems a little harsh to—'

Jeremy interrupts. 'Be careful,' he says. 'Be very careful, Leo.'

I apologise, but the atmosphere now hangs on a thread.

'The whole thing was extremely stressful,' Jeremy says. A tiny nerve pulses above his eye, visible only at close range. 'Janice was destroyed by it all. But what makes it worse is that Emma started up again, four years ago. Harassing us.'

'*What?*'

'I met with her, after her cancer diagnosis, because she was afraid she would die without knowing Charlie. But I couldn't – wouldn't – just parachute her into Charlie's life, no matter how grave her circumstances, which is why I said no. So she just turned up in Alnmouth one day, when the three of us were up there on holiday. Charlie was only fourteen at the time. Janice nearly lost her mind.'

I feel sick. 'You mean – she tried to take him?'

'No. He was at our house, thank God. Janice and I were out walking on the beach. She just came at us, over the rocks.'

I close my eyes. That time Emma didn't come back from Northumberland on the agreed train. Her phone, switched off, worry growing with each passing minute. Eventually, I'd thought to phone Jill, who said Emma was at hers. I had had no reason to doubt this. I remember only the relief of knowing she was with her friend.

I tell Jeremy a little of what happened, that night, and ask if the dates sound about right. He nods. 'Yes, that's when it was.' He looks out of the French windows, into the night garden. After a pause, he gets up and opens a cupboard, from which he takes a packet of crisps.

I didn't expect Jeremy Rothschild to eat crisps. I'm not sure why. They're Worcester sauce flavour, which I'm even more wrong-footed by. He offers me a packet, but I decline, so he sits back at the table and opens his.

'They didn't arrest or charge her, that time,' he says, thoughtfully. 'She apparently had enough evidence to suggest she was up in Alnmouth conducting some kind of informal marine survey. Crabs, I believe. But the police were called. Her friend Jill drove all the way up from London to bring her home.'

These lies. All these lies.

'And after that?'

Jeremy shrugs, takes another crisp. 'After that she left us alone again, and we had no contact until three weeks ago, when Janice disappeared. I got in touch with Emma to check she hadn't spoken to Janice, she said she hadn't, and, actually, I believed her. But Janice recently wrote Emma a letter, so I met Emma in Alnmouth to hand it over.'

'You couldn't post it to her?'

Jeremy shakes his head. 'I wanted to talk to her again. I needed to look her in the eye and be certain she hadn't been in touch with Janice.' He takes a pinch of crisps and eats them all. 'And if you're wondering why Emma went all the way to Alnmouth to see me, it's because she's never given up hope that I might give her access to Charlie. She's begged me again and again for a chance to meet him. I don't think she'll ever give up.'

I sit back in Jeremy's dining chair. Thoughts churn slowly, quickly. Jeremy keeps eating.

'But . . . Charlie must be eighteen now,' I say slowly. 'Surely Emma could just get in touch with him, if she wanted to?'

'You're right, she could. But she won't. Not without an in from me.'

'Why not?'

Jeremy finishes the crisps, and folds the packet into squares. He slides it under an empty coffee mug. I wonder how it must feel for him, knowing more about my wife – my life – than I do.

'As I understand it,' he says, 'Emma made a bargain with herself after the abduction incident. She promised she'd never enter Charlie's life uninvited again, no matter what. She knew how much the business in the park had traumatised us, and therefore, by extension, him – she was extremely remorseful about that. Anxious she'd ruined the peaceful childhood she dreamed he'd have. So she decided she'd only get in touch with him through one of us, rather than putting him on the spot. Janice was never going to agree to anything, so it's always me she's come begging to.'

I frown. 'You mean – you mean you've never told him Emma wants to meet him? You've kept him in the dark?'

Jeremy gives me a patient look – a sympathetic look – and I realise, with an extra sting of humiliation, that he knows about my own adoption. My question was far too loaded.

'Of course I haven't kept him in the dark,' he says. 'He's always known he was adopted.' He shifts in his chair. 'When Emma got cancer I had a conversation with Charlie. I didn't say his birth mother had asked to meet him, as such, but I did say that if he ever wanted to know more about her, or even to meet her, I'd help. He said thanks, and that was that – he's never said anything since. I won't force the issue.'

I try to imagine a lifetime of separation from Ruby and panic tightens my chest: what Emma's gone through is unimaginable. How deeply she must love this boy, to hold off writing to him. Even now, as an adult.

Neither of us say anything for a long time. It's so quiet in here that I can even hear the faint tick of Janice's watch, coiled on the kitchen island behind us. Our crooked old house is alive with creaks and loud sighs, banging pipes and ticking radiators. Everything is so beautiful here, so well-plumbed and fitted and streamlined. Why would Janice want to walk out of this sanctuary and not come back?

'Where's Charlie?' I ask, suddenly. It seems far too tidy for an eighteen-year-old boy to be living here. 'I thought you said you were looking after him?'

Jeremy looks over his shoulder. 'He's in his room. This whole business has been very hard for him.'

For a moment I'm quite floored by this. I am under the same roof as Emma's son. I want to race upstairs to look at him, talk to him, check that it's really true, that my wife really does have a grown-up child.

'He's at home from university,' Jeremy says. 'MIT, in the States,' he adds, and he can't keep the pride out of his voice. 'He had a great first year, then Janice walked out, only a few days after he got back for the summer. He's really suffering.'

Eventually, my thoughts return to Emma. To Janice, and these years of mess and misery that lie between them.

'Did Janice ever forgive Emma?' I ask, eventually. 'Did you?'

Jeremy thinks about his answer. Outside the alliums bob and sway under the fairy lights. I almost envy the Rothschilds the straightforwardness of their relationship with Emma. She harassed and stalked them; they'll probably never forgive her. But she's my wife, and I've loved her deeply, tenderly, for ten years. I have no idea how to feel.

'We were very supportive of Emma,' Jeremy says, eventually. 'Both in her pregnancy and the terrible time she had postnatally, but that doesn't excuse her later actions, Leo. Giving a parent reason to believe that their child is unsafe is a terrible thing.'

I have no option but to agree.

'It changed Janice. Quite fundamentally, I think. She lost her confidence, her spontaneity, her resilience – she came out of it so much more anxious, and angry. She doesn't trust people. Over the years she's gradually withdrawn from her social life; it's quite hard to get her out these days.'

I believe him, even though there's no hint of this in the Janice Rothschild we see on our screens. But what I'm really struck by is the absence of obvious damage in Emma. She's had a few Times, over the years, and the postnatal depression, but none of these have lasted long. She's not withdrawn, she's not angry. She's confident and trusting, and above all, she's always so energetic and happy. Has it all been an act? Is that even possible? Surely nobody could spend ten years acting.

Another thought emerges.

'Look,' I say, slowly. 'Forgive me for asking. But I don't suppose you think . . . I don't suppose you think there's any way Janice has anything to do with Emma's disa—?'

'Stop,' Jeremy says. 'Stop there.'

'I'm sorry. But you told me yourself that Janice threatened Emma after her court appearance. And I know that was years ago, but perhaps—'

'No, Leo.'

'I'm not suggesting Janice has done anything bad, or harmful to her, I just—'

'Leo. Did you hear me tell you how fragile Janice is at the moment? Did you hear me say that – from the very beginning – it's Emma who has been behind all the acts of aggression, of threatening behaviour? Janice hasn't retaliated once. Nothing, not even in the face of unforgivable provocation.'

'I accept that. But I—'

Jeremy carries on. 'May I also remind you that you did not know until last night that your wife was born Emily Peel?

That she has a child you knew nothing of? Leo, you are not sufficiently informed to be casting any aspersions about Janice, who, God knows, has suffered enough at Emma's hands.'

Here he is. Here's Jeremy Rothschild.

He walks calmly to the kitchen door. 'It's time for you to leave,' he says. 'My wife has had a breakdown and disappeared. I'm desperate with worry. And yet, in you come, wondering if she might have popped back to London to mete out some pathetic revenge on Emma. It's tasteless, Leo. Tasteless and really very poor.'

'Jeremy. Please. I apologise, I really didn't—'

'Oh, just get out,' he says, suddenly tired. 'Fuck off. Go.'

This is not how he ends his radio takedowns.

He stands by the kitchen door, not looking at my face, and seconds later I am standing on Highbury Place.

When I return to my car it has a parking fine stuck to the windscreen. After borrowing money from Jeremy to pay for the meter, it seems I failed to actually display the ticket.

Arsenal fans stream past me, singing, chanting, laughing. Sounds as though it was a home win tonight.

Chapter Forty-Nine

LEO

I pull out onto Highbury Corner. Rothschild had been so happy to spill the beans about Emma, her catastrophes and deceit, the harm she had caused. But it was a different story altogether when I asked one bloody question about Janice.

And then he just went for me, as if I were a lying politician. It was a humiliation I didn't need – the man had just put my entire marriage through the shredder, for fuck's sake.

'Fuck you,' I mutter, as I speed up Upper Street. (Why am I going this way? I don't even live in this direction. I turn right onto Islington Park Street, to cut through Barnsbury.)

'Fuck off,' I say, loudly, to nobody.

I hit a speed bump I hadn't even seen. 'Fuck!' I shout.

Tears are forming in the corners of my eyes now. Emma has disappeared. Emma doesn't even exist.

'FUCK!' I yell, and I hit another speed bump. This time the bottom of the car scrapes the bump, and a pedestrian turns to look at this stupid driver, this speeding fool, destroying his car.

'FUCK OFF,' I yell, at the pedestrian, but the tears are falling now.

I drive, crying, until I nearly hit a third speed bump and

realise I must pull over. Briefly, before I crumple over the steering wheel to sob and swear and scream and thump my wrist, I see the pedestrian turn around and run back down the street, away from my car.

Ten minutes later, I set off again. The rage at Jeremy has already subsided: he's no more than the messenger; I know that. It's my wife I am angry with. My wife, the woman who doesn't exist.

I would have understood, is what I keep thinking. Emma could have told me any of what Jeremy's just related to me, and I'd have accepted it all. How could I blame her for what happened when she was knee-deep in a psychiatric emergency? How could I judge her for watching her child in a park when the pain of missing him overtook reason? Wouldn't anyone make a clandestine visit, if they knew where their adopted child lived? I would.

She wouldn't have wanted to tell me she gave away her child: I understand that. God knows, she's seen me struggle enough with my own adoption. But I would have taken it without judgement. I was in love with her; I'd have kept my own past out of it.

(Wouldn't I?)

And I could have helped her forgive herself for the suffocation, piece by piece, or at least softened the edges of her guilt. You were ill, I'd have told her, day after day, year after year, until she was able to believe it.

(Wouldn't I?)

I accelerate up past Pentonville prison, floodlit and eerie.

The ugly truth is that there is a part of me that's horrified. A part of me that is frightened; a part that has even briefly wondered if Ruby is safe with her mother.

And that is precisely why she didn't tell me. Why she

appears to have told nobody, other than her oldest friend – because she knows that these same thoughts would cross almost anyone's mind. Is she a violent person, underneath it all? Does she still think about harming her child? Harming anyone else?

I bang my fist on the steering wheel again, raging at Emma, raging at myself for thinking exactly what she predicted I would.

I turn off Agar Grove into the noise and filth of Camden at nighttime. The streets are full of young people drinking, laughing.

As I inch my way north towards Chalk Farm and Belsize Park I allow myself to sift through the stuffed pocketbook of lies Emma must have told me. The trips to Northumberland – all those fucking trips she took, all the times I waved her off so she could have some time alone, looking for crabs, when she was just trying to stalk the Rothschilds.

The day Ruby was born; the sympathy the maternity team must have felt for me as I held my baby for the first time, dizzy with joy, oblivious to the fact that this was Emma's second child.

And, talking of precious days, what about our marriage? Is it legal, if Emma failed to tell the officials she'd changed her name? She said nothing about it when we gave notice at the town hall. And yet, a few months later, she stood opposite me at the registry office and said she knew of no legal reason why she, Emma Merry Bigelow, should not marry me, Leo Jack Philber.

Her criminal record. The stalking of the Rothschilds, even when we were together. The 'dinners' with Jill when she must have been doing God knows what; her refusal to come to any industry parties, presumably because she was avoiding a public meeting with Jeremy.

The traffic is stop-start all the way up Haverstock Hill. My fingers drum against the steering wheel, my leg twitches. Being trapped in here with these thoughts is unbearable.

When I pull up at my house I scan for Emma, just in case, but the only familiar car is Olly's.

My heart pounds. I'm exhausted. I have no idea what to think, what to do, what my next move should be. My heart is afraid for Emma – my heart which has loved her so long, and so deeply – but I am angry, I am in shock, and I do not see how I could ever trust her again.

And if there is no trust, there is no us.

As I lock my car I hear another car door closing behind me. I whip round, certain it will be Emma, only to find Sheila standing in my road, under a streetlight. Normally quite casual, she's wearing a trouser suit tonight. She could not look more like a high-ranking intelligence official if she tried.

'Sheila? What are you doing here?'

'I have some news,' she says. 'About Emma.'

Chapter Fifty

Olly and Tink are looking at something on Tink's laptop when we get into the house; Mikkel and Oskar are asleep under a blanket.

I introduce Sheila.

Olly eyes her with some interest. 'Are you the ex-spy?'

'Olly!'

'What? I've never met a spy!'

'I couldn't possibly comment,' Sheila says, which Olly loves.

I remove John Keats from the Queen Anne chair in the study and bring it through for Sheila. 'It's a bit doggy . . .' I trail off: Sheila isn't interested. She sits on the hairy chair. I take a seat on the floor.

'I went to your daughter's nursery and asked to view their CCTV,' she begins. 'It seemed expedient; it was the last place Emma was seen.'

I stare at her. 'And they let you?'

She nods, almost surprised. 'Of course. Anyway, I saw Emma leave at exactly the time they told you. She looked upset, just like they said. And you're quite right, she didn't have so much as a handbag on her.'

A sleepy John wanders in from the study, an ear stuck to the top of his head. He goes straight over to Sheila and sticks his head into her crotch.

Sheila removes him. If she has any feelings about this, her face doesn't betray them.

I am horrified and delighted. Not just by my dog and my brother, but by the thought of Sheila, marching into a nursery and demanding CCTV footage. It's exactly the sort of thing I've always imagined Sheila doing.

'I then watched a car pull up outside the nursery entrance. She got into it and drove away, quite willingly, I'd say: she didn't really hesitate.'

'You think it's someone she knows?' Olly asks.

'I do.'

Sheila pulls out her phone and swipes a few times. 'ZQ16 5LL,' she says. 'Silver Peugeot. Does this ring any bells?'

I frown. 'No . . . At least, I don't think so . . . Oh, actually, her friend Heidi has a silver car, a big estate thing . . . ? Roof rails? Bike rack on the back?'

'No. This is a small car. Never mind, I took the liberty of calling in a favour from an old contact at the DVLA.'

Olly and Tink exchange glances. Now they know Emma is probably OK, they're enthralled.

Sheila swipes her phone again, then looks at me. 'The car is registered to a Jill Stirling. Do you know this woman, Leo?'

Chapter Fifty-One

EMMA

Earlier that day

'You'll see,' is all Jill keeps saying, when I ask where we're going.

She's enjoying this. She doesn't say much, but I can see it in her face; her body language – she's alive with purpose. The radio's turned off but she keeps singing snatches of songs under her breath, and she's running a full commentary on the road conditions as if we're having a driving lesson.

It's been more than twenty minutes since she picked me up outside nursery. We've just joined the North Circular, on the outskirts of London. Ahead, the M1 is signposted, for Watford and The North.

'Look at the size of that man's bum!' she hoots, pointing at some poor specimen crossing the footbridge. 'A symphony of an arse!'

It is generous, but it definitely doesn't warrant this condemnation.

'I really think I should call Leo,' I say, after a pause. 'I know you said he needs more time, but it . . . It just doesn't feel right not to check in with him. Please can I borrow your phone?'

'No,' Jill says. 'I told you, I spoke to him.'

When she turned up outside Ruby's nursery earlier, I

thought Jill had just come to offer me some moral support before my meeting with Leo – a lift up the hill, perhaps, with a pep talk, a coffee and a hug. But instead she drove straight past our road and headed up and out across the top of the Heath, towards Golder's Green.

'I've got a meeting with Leo at 9.30!' I said. 'Stop! Jill, I can't talk now!'

'This is far more important,' she replied, with a strange smile; so strange I almost wondered if she had taken something. In our first year at St Andrews we'd tried mushrooms, but Jill had declared the experience of being out of control to be so intolerable she never tried any drugs again.

'Jill!' I cried. 'Seriously, I have to get out!'

When she ignored me, I undid my seatbelt at the pedestrian crossing by the entrance to Golders Hill Park and tried to open the door. What was she doing?

Like something from a hostage movie, Jill had activated the central locking. 'Don't be a lunatic!' she said. 'You can't barrel out of the car like Bruce Willis; you're an out-of-shape woman of nearly forty!'

'Jill! I mean it! Let me out.'

But she carried on driving.

She'd spoken to Leo, she said: he was still in shock and needed a couple of days to think.

She repeated this again and again until, finally, I was able to hear her. 'Which is why I came to get you,' she said. 'I thought it would be awful for you to go back to an empty house, thinking you were about to see Leo.'

I put a hand on her shoulder. 'Thank you,' I said, quietly.

We stopped and started for a while, passing by a rundown parade of shops, but I no longer made any attempt to get out. Leo did not want to see me. It would be Wednesday, maybe even Thursday, before he would be ready. By then he would probably have realised he'd never be able to trust me again, and that would be it: I'd have lost him. That precious man, the love of my new life. My beautiful Leo.

Now we are heading down the North Circular towards the M1 and I barely care where Jill is taking me.

For the fourth or fifth time I reach for my phone, to send a discreet message to Leo, but of course my phone is still in my handbag, on my bed. In my room, in my house, where I hoped to be able to persuade my husband just how deeply I love him.

The traffic thins and Jill puts her foot down.

Chapter Fifty-Two

We don't turn up the M1. We stay on the North Circular until Wembley, where Jill turns off, and I realise she's just taking me to her flat.

Of course.

Knowing Jill, she'll have bought ingredients for a big fry-up, or a huge bag of pastries. There'll be films we've watched in the past. Hot chocolate, lots of counselling and positive talk. I'm not sure Leo and Jill love each other quite the way I love them, but she knows he's everything to me. She'll buoy me up; tell me he'll come round. That we're meant to be together; we'll survive this.

I hope she does. I hope we will.

Jill lives in a vast city of new-build flats in Wembley, all landscaped gardens and identikit cafes, heavily marketed with slogans like 'find the new you' and 'your peace on earth'. It's worlds away from my disgusting little house and I always love coming here. Everything is so perfectly tessellated and tidy; Jill's fridge is full of Ziplock bags and her cupboards are full of neatly stacked plastic boxes which never contain out-of-date food.

Last month Leo found some smoked paprika seventeen years out of date in my spice rack.

Jill turns off her engine and looks in the rear-view mirror for a few seconds longer than seems natural.

I turn round to look behind us, but there's nobody here apart from a groundsman building a wooden cage around a young tree.

'Who're you looking for?' I ask, as I get out. She's scanning around the car park.

'What? I'm not looking for anybody,' she says. 'Right! Let's get inside and have a cup of tea.'

There's something going on. She hasn't just brought me here to cheer me up.

'Look, I really do think I should text Leo,' I say. I walk round the front of her car. 'It's 10.15, I'm nearly an hour late for our meeting. Please can I borrow your phone?'

'Later!'

There's a cold breeze today. I'm wearing one of those infuriating jumpers with sleeves that only stretch just past your elbows. I try to pull them further down my wrists as I follow Jill across the resident's car park, but I'm still cold.

I notice how each parking space has been painted a different colour to show just how playful life is in HA9.

Jill has been a faithful friend for more than twenty years, but, as I follow her into the lift, I sense a cool hand of unease at my back.

Chapter Fifty-Three

LEO

Now

I call Jill again and again as I cross north-west London towards her flat. It's 10.30 p.m. and the streets are still busy, even though the cold wind lingers. Council blocks flash past, windows neat squares of yellow, clothes flapping on washing lines in the dark.

Jill's phone continues to ring out. How could she have been with Emma for nearly twelve hours and not called me back? What are they doing?

Before she drove home, Sheila had given me Jill's address. If she was disappointed to learn that Emma's kidnapper was also her oldest friend, she didn't betray it.

'Good luck,' she said, before getting into her car and reversing out of her parking space.

I waved her down, just before she pulled away.

She opened her window. 'Thank you for doing this,' I said. 'You are truly wonderful, Sheila. I – I'm very glad I have you in my life.'

Sheila thought about this for a few seconds, then gave me a businesslike nod. She closed her window and drove off.

I pull off the North Circular at the signs for Wembley Park, and try to call Jill again.

This time, her phone goes straight to voicemail.

Chapter Fifty-Four

Earlier

Jill's bought pastries, not a fry-up. She busies herself heating milk for hot chocolate while I pee, wash my face, and mentally compose yet another message to Leo that respects his need for two more days, while somehow communicating that I adore him and that I lied to him all these years with good reason.

But of course, I have no phone, and Jill is being infuriatingly resistant to giving me hers.

I stand in front of her bathroom mirror, contemplating my face. I look exhausted; the skin round my eyes saggy and translucent.

What did I think would happen? Did I really believe I could bury these truths permanently inside myself, that Leo would never sense there was more?

Really?

'Look. Jill,' I say, when I return to the kitchen. 'It's so kind of you to do this, but I have to speak to Leo. Even if he doesn't want to speak to me, I still have to sort out stuff concerning Ruby. Please let me borrow your phone.'

Jill gets cocoa out of one of her neat plastic storage boxes. 'OK,' she says. 'Fine.'

She starts making a paste out of cocoa, sugar and milk, humming under her breath as if I'm not in the room.

'Jill.'

'Yes! Hang on, let me get these done, then I can—'

I go to the hallway where her coat and bag are hanging on their designated hooks. I get her phone out of her pocket and as she comes out I hand it to her, for the password.

'Emma! Could you not have—'

'Please just unlock it,' I say. 'Please, Jill. I'm desperate.'

She sighs, reaching for the phone, just as the intercom goes.

She jumps. Jill actually jumps, and her face changes completely.

'Emma . . .'

'Yes?'

Jill pauses. 'Listen, I didn't just bring you here for pastries and a heart-to-heart. I – there's something important you need to know. It's why I was trying to get hold of you Friday night.'

I close my eyes. 'Can it not wait?'

She doesn't reply. When I open my eyes she's buzzing someone into the building. She runs a hand up and down her jeans, and it comes to me that she's not just a bit nervous, she's terrified.

'What have you done?' I ask, quietly. 'Jill, what's going on?'

'Just wait a moment,' she whispers. She creeps over to her front door and puts her eye to the spyhole.

'Jill . . .' I'm whispering too, although I don't know why.

And then she straightens up and opens the door to a young man, standing outside. A man with my face and a male body. With longish hair that needs washing and a once-red T-shirt, sun-baked to pink. He stands in the doorway, looking at me with fear and curiosity.

I would know my son anywhere. Even if I hadn't spent years looking at pictures of him on the internet, I would know.

I stare at him. He stares at me.

My heart, pounding. All my life. This moment.

'Hello,' he said. 'You're Emma, right?'

I nod. Tears gather in my eyes. My child.

Seeing the tears, he balks. 'Oh, I'm sorry – I . . . I didn't mean to . . . I'm Charlie. Charlie Rothschild?'

I nod again, not trusting myself to speak. Grief falls inside me, a landslide.

'I've been trying to get in touch with you, actually, I . . .'

I have longed for you every single day of your life.

Charlie.

Jill puts a gentle hand on my back and retreats into the kitchen, and my son speaks to me. The landslide takes everything in its path. He says, 'I tried to reach out to you via Facebook, but I don't think you knew who I was – or perhaps you just didn't want to talk to me – you blocked me, after my second message, so . . . Look, I hope it's OK for me to be here?'

He has tanned legs in shorts, deeply scuffed leather trainers.

My boy.

Finally, the tears burst from me. He is my son, and yet, we're strangers. I scrabble in my pocket for tissues I don't have; Charlie has to hand me one from Jill's console table in the end.

I manage to say it is absolutely OK for him to be here. That it means more to me than he could ever imagine.

And then I sob into Jill's tissue, and the poor boy is floored.

Stop crying, I think, and then I cry harder, even though I don't want to do this to him.

I can't stop. I cry and cry, while my son stands in the middle of Jill's neat hallway, watching helplessly.

Jill's face is blazing with anxiety. She didn't plan for this.

I have to stop. With determination, I blow my nose, because they say that's the best way to stop crying, and it actually works. The landslide slows, the fragile bowl of my body holds. After a moment Charlie sticks out his hand to take my sodden tissues. It is a kind gesture. His fingernails are grubby, the hairs on his arm bleached by the sun.

I have never had the chance to nag him about his fingernails. I have never had the chance to clip his tiny baby talons like I did Ruby's, or to buy him toddler steps so he can reach the sink and wash his hands.

'I'm sorry if I've upset you,' he says.

'No, no, it's me who should be sorry.'

He smiles uneasily. 'Well, I think I've probably given you quite a shock . . .' He looks at Jill. 'Did you not . . . I mean, did Emma not know I was . . .'

'She didn't know,' Jill confirms, and although her voice is bright I can tell she's doubting herself now.

'I'm tougher than I look,' I lie. I have longed for this moment my whole adult life, and I will not throw it away. 'Ah – shall we sit down? If you're staying? I could make you a cup of tea?'

'I'll do the tea,' Jill says quickly, and I want to cry again, because I so desperately want to make Charlie a cup of tea myself. I want to make him a packed lunch, a birthday cake, a DIY pizza, a cheese sandwich. I want to give him water and juice and Calpol and his first ever beer.

Jill disappears into her orderly kitchen to shelve the hot chocolate and start the tea, while Charlie and I enter the foreign land of a shared room. He chooses an armchair; I take the sofa. He picks at the arm of the chair and I can see he's scared of being trapped in here, with my huge emotions. But he stays. He stays, and from time to time he even looks at me.

'So . . . How are you?' he asks. 'This must be quite a shock!'

From somewhere, I conjure a smile. 'It's the best shock I have ever had. I can't tell you how happy I am to see you.'

He nods, and I see how overwhelmed he is; what courage has been required to walk into this flat. 'Me too,' he says, politely. 'It's strange, but very nice to meet you.'

It's very nice to meet you.

Silence, which is interrupted only by Jill bringing our teas and some pastries, before excusing herself.

We both go for the same apricot Danish and then withdraw, laughing nervously. Charlie takes a swig of tea (very milky, one sugar, mug held by the handle) and I reflect guiltily on how ratty I was in Jill's car. She's doubtless found a way to cover for me with Leo, too, just as she did when I bumped into the Rothschilds in Northumberland four years ago. I don't understand what I've done to deserve her kindness, but Jill has always had my back.

'So . . .' I hesitate, afraid to ask Charlie anything that might frighten him away. 'So – you said you'd tried to contact me on Facebook . . . ? Is that right?'

Charlie tries a smile. 'Yeah,' he says, fiddling with his teacup. 'Yeah, I wrote to you a couple of times but you blocked me the second time.'

'I – what? Of course I didn't! I wouldn't! I'd have been overjoyed to hear from you!'

He looks doubtful. 'Oh, it's OK, I mean, it must have taken you by surprise . . .'

Leo, I think, suddenly. Leo's been into my Facebook messages, looking for answers to the clues I've left.

But why would he block Charlie? Does he know about him?

I look up. 'Can I ask what you said in your messages?'

'I just gave you my number and asked you to get in touch.' Charlie, my son, starts fiddling needlessly with his shoelace. (He wears his laces perma-tied, with the tongues of the trainers sliding off to the sides. He doesn't appear to be wearing socks underneath. He doesn't appear to be someone who irons his clothes, yet he's not scruffy, exactly, more just . . . eighteen.)

He sits up, suddenly. 'My name on Facebook is Charlie Rod. Dad said it was best not to use my proper name, because of him and Mum and whatnot. I did wonder if it'd be better if I used my full name to message you.'

Carefully, I tell him that I think he was probably blocked by mistake. 'I presented a TV series a few years ago,' I say. 'It was repeated recently, so I've had a bunch of strange people getting in touch, and my husband blocked them. He must have assumed you were one of them.'

He nods, knowingly, but I have no idea if he's just being polite or if he's actually looked up – maybe even watched? – an episode of *This Land*.

A silence opens up, but it's not painful. I sense he's coming round to the reason for his presence; the reason why now is the time he felt ready to meet me.

In the bathroom I can hear Jill's phone ringing. I'm pretty sure I hear a muttered 'Please, just go away,' but she doesn't answer the call.

'When I couldn't get hold of you, I tracked down Jill,' Charlie says. 'She comments on your Facebook posts quite a lot and I could tell by the things she said that you two are good friends. She's very nice,' he adds, and the admiration I feel for this young man soars. How many eighteen-year-old boys have the presence of mind to say something kind about a middle-aged woman they don't even know?

'Anyway, I said I was keen to talk to you and asked Jill to pass on my number. But Jill was like, why don't I get you and Emma together . . .'

'I hope you didn't feel pressured,' I say, because I know how Jill can be when she's got an idea in her head.

'Not at all. I just really wanted to ask you about Mum.' His voice is suddenly firm. 'That's why I needed to talk to you.'

I fix my smile. He mustn't see how disappointed I am.

'I know Dad's asked you,' he's saying, 'but have you really not heard from her? No emails, no messages?'

'She wrote me a letter,' I say, carefully. 'As you know. Your dad gave it to me. But beyond that, nothing. Or at least, nothing I've seen. We definitely haven't spoken, if that's what you mean.'

'Really?'

'Really.'

Charlie studies my face, then slumps back into his armchair. 'Oh,' he says. 'Fair enough. Well – I had to ask.'

He thinks for a while.

'I really wouldn't expect to hear from her,' I add. 'If that helps. The letter was surprising enough.'

I stop there, because I have no idea what Charlie knows about the relationship between me and Janice.

'I just had a suspicion Mum tried to reach you recently,' he says. 'Aside from the letter, I mean.'

I watch him, wary of saying the wrong thing. 'Why? You know we haven't been in touch for many years, don't you . . . ?'

There's a tiny shift. Charlie gets his phone out of his pocket (silicone cover, tatty at the edges) and checks it. The screen is blank. 'I do. But there must be a reason why she chose now, of all times, to write to you about crabs. It feels significant. I just wondered if she'd tried to reach you some other way. In case we'd refused to give you the letter.'

He's lying. There's something else.

'I can share the letter with you, if you want, Charlie, but I imagine you've already read it?'

'Yeah, I have.' He looks at the door, and I realise this is

about to end. This miracle is nearly over, and there's nothing I can do about it.

'So you've really heard nothing? Nothing at all?'

'Nothing at all.'

'OK,' he says. 'I suppose I should go. I've got a summer job, up in Queens Park. Easy to get there from here. But I'll be late if I don't leave soon.'

My heart begins to ache, and I smile, kindly and sensibly, so he knows I'm the sort of a person he could easily see again if he wanted to, not some maniac who tried to take him from a park when he was a toddler and will cry every time she sees him as an adult.

'Of course,' I say. 'I really am sorry not to be able to help.'

Next to me, on another console table, Jill has one of those leather boxes that hold a stack of notelets and a pen. I scribble down my number and then, as an afterthought, my address. 'You're welcome to get in touch if you need to ask anything else,' I say. 'Or if you just need to . . . talk.'

Charlie takes the note and stands up. 'Oh, I know where you live,' he says. He breaks off.

I stop. 'It was you. In the baseball cap.'

He winces. 'You saw me?'

I close my eyes. Thank God. Thank God. 'I did see you. And not just outside my house. I think I saw you outside both my workplaces. Plymouth and London. Was that you, too?'

He looks like he might pass out with embarrassment. 'Christ, I'm so sorry,' he says. Even his ears have coloured. 'I feel awful. I didn't mean to . . .'

He picks at a splodge of something – ketchup, I think – on his jeans. 'I only found out your name a few weeks ago. I wanted to . . . I really am so sorry. I just wanted to check you out, I guess. Try and get a measure of you, your life . . . I'm really sorry. I thought I'd been quite sly.'

I tell him not to worry. Him trying to take a quiet look at his mother is no worse than me trying to take a quiet look at my son, all those years ago.

He apologises again, but then looks at the door, and I know this really is it.

'I hope your mum comes back soon,' I say, desperately. I can't stand calling her his 'mum'. I want to be Mum. 'I'm sure she will. And in the meantime, please don't hesitate to call, or just turn up unannounced, I really don't mind. Anything I can do to help.'

He smiles briefly. 'Thanks. At least we know she's alive. But it's worrying. Anyway, look, thanks for your time. It's been nice to meet you.'

And then he's off, walking out of the room, and I want to throw my arms round him, tackle him, lock the door. But I just walk calmly behind him, smiling as he turns. The energy saving lights click on as he steps out into the corridor. 'Take care,' he says, and then he's gone.

Jill makes coffee and puts some brandy in mine, even though I tell her I don't want any. But I'm grateful for it, by the time it's in my hands. I am still, on her sofa, but inside me everything is tumbling. Did I get it right? Did he like me? Would he want to meet again?

No matter how desperate I've been to see him over the years, I've always agreed with Jeremy: the approach must come from Charlie, not me. But as the years have passed, I've slowly given up on that happening.

The incident on Alnmouth beach four years ago really was an accident. I always avoided going up there in the school holidays because I knew the Rothschilds would be there. But in term time, when I wanted to go up to Alnmouth, I'd turn on Radio 4 between 6 a.m. and 9 a.m. If Jeremy was on air, he had to be in London, and I was safe to go. If he wasn't on air, I stayed away.

But, of course, that was the one time I'd forgotten. I had a cancer diagnosis on my mind, a dismissal from the BBC, a pregnancy – I simply didn't remember to check; I just wanted to get up there, to the comfort of those vast beaches and racing clouds, the hope of a *Hemigrapsus takanoi* encounter.

I didn't see Janice and him until I was nearly upon them, and all hell broke loose. I will never forget her voice calling me every name under the sun.

My last hope had been Charlie's eighteenth birthday, when he could have got in touch even if Janice and Jeremy had hitherto concealed my identity, but – nothing.

And then, suddenly, he was here. In a flat in Wembley on a windy July day. My DNA curling in chains inside him, my parents', Granny's, the relatives and ancestors I never thought to ask about before Dad died. All there in the armchair for thirty beautiful minutes.

Jill's being unbearably kind, and has batted off my apologies for my earlier rudeness. 'I'd have found it strange too,' she said. 'But if I'd told you what was about to happen you'd have gone into a panic. As it was, you were totally natural. If I was Charlie I'd want to see you again.'

She listened to the entire thing through the bathroom door; eating her way through most of the pastries, by the looks of the pastry bag. She's adamant that I conducted myself impeccably, even allowing for the tears at the beginning.

The brandy is already muting the excess of my feelings. I feel tired, now, confused but euphoric.

'Listen,' Jill says. 'Stay as long as you need to. Let's have wine and watch awful films this afternoon. Get slowly drunk and make a night of it. You can stay over if you like – sounds like it would be a bad idea to go home right now.'

I close my eyes. Of course I want to stay, here in this flat where I met my adult son. Where there's possibility and hope.

But Leo. Ruby.

'I'll have to talk to Leo,' I say, eventually. 'I get it – he doesn't want to talk to me yet – but I've got to tell him he's Ruby's father. I was going to tell him face to face this morning. Besides, if I'm staying here I need to check he can pick her up from nursery. And drop her off tomorrow.'

Jill nods. 'Agreed,' she says. 'He does need to know he's Ruby's dad. Of course he does. But, Emma, he picks Ruby up from nursery every day. You never do! Can you not just give yourself a few hours to calm down?'

I think about this. Jill holds out her phone. 'You can call him right now if you want,' she says. 'I only tried to delay you from calling him earlier because I didn't want you to be a wreck when Charlie arrived.'

She looks tired; hot and dehydrated. I've watched her put a steady stream of carbs and sugar into her mouth since I arrived: something isn't right with my old friend, and it's about time I was actually present for her. Too much, lately, the insanities of my own life have taken centre stage.

'I'm just saying, you've been through something huge this morning. Do you not think you deserve a couple of hours to decompress?'

Reluctantly, because I know she's right, I nod. She wants to spend today with me, Leo does not. I'll have the wine. The food, the film, the tired laughs. I'll call after Ruby's dinner and hope Leo's willing to suggest a day we can meet.

That is my plan. I tell Jill, and she smiles. 'Well done, Limpet,' she says. 'Well done.'

Chapter Fifty-Five

Now

As the lift carries me up to Jill's flat it occurs to me for the first time that Jill might actually be a lunatic. That I might find my wife butchered in her friend's neat little kitchen, each part clearly labelled in a Ziploc bag.

The lift doors slide silently open and my feet pad along the carpeted floor of Level Six. I check my watch: 10.41 p.m. I want to be in bed. I want to be slowly drifting off while Emma reads her brainy magazines, fidgeting and driving me mad. I want Ruby asleep next door with Duck, and John asleep downstairs with jungle on whisper-soft volume.

Jill's face, when she opens the door, is a picture. I tailgated someone to get in the building; she had no idea. She has a wine glass in her hand. She's put on a lot of weight since I saw her last, but instead of softening her features it's somehow made her seem even less accessible, as if she's buried herself.

'Oh. Hey,' she whispers, as if there's a sleeping baby inside.

'Hi. Is Emma here?'

She hesitates, but I can see it in her face. I walk right past her and into the sitting room, where I find Emma on the sofa, drinking wine and eating toast.

We stare at each other for a few seconds. Then: 'Leo?' She looks surprised, as if it's strange for me to have turned up here after spending thirteen hours looking for her.

I look at the open wine bottle. They're halfway down it. A second, empty bottle, sits on a console table.

'What are you doing?' I ask. 'What are you *doing*?'

Emma's eyes flit over to Jill. 'Er – what?'

Then, suddenly, she claps a hand to her chest. 'Oh my God. I was going to call after Ruby's dinner. I did, but Jill's phone was out of battery so she put it on charge and then . . . I am so sorry, I—'

'You were going to call after Ruby's dinner? She eats dinner at six p.m.!'

Emma's looking at me like I'm talking a foreign language. Is she drunk?

'Leo . . . ?'

'What about calling me at nine thirty this morning? When we were meant to meet? Or maybe ten a.m., when you were already half an hour late? How about calling me at any time today?' My voice is too loud for this comfortable room, with its neatly ordered cushions and spotless surfaces. 'Do you give any sort of a shit about me, Emma? Does our marriage mean anything to you?'

Emma's hair is shiny in the glow of Jill's carefully placed lamps. I want to empty her wine all over it. She has shown no respect for me and Ruby, no consideration. She's allowed me to uncover her double life and then just deserted us to carry on running secret missions, as if we're no more than props.

'Leo,' she says, and I can see she's speaking carefully, so as not to sound drunk. 'I'm sorry. I was going to call after Ruby's dinner. But I . . . To be honest, I didn't think you'd want to hear from me. You said you needed a couple of days before you were ready to talk to me. I'm just respecting your wishes, darling, I . . .'

'I said I needed *what?*'

Her face changes, just fractionally, and I see her rewinding something in her head.

Slowly, she turns to look at Jill.

'Jill?' she says.

Jill's standing in the doorway to her kitchen, wine glass still in hand. Her knuckles, wrapped around its stem, are white. She's not enjoying my first visit to her flat.

'I had to help Emma with something today,' she says. 'I can't really talk about it, I'm afraid. But it was vitally important.'

I swap my car keys from one hand to another. 'Concerning the adult child she has? The one I knew nothing about? Concerning her relationship with Jeremy and Janice Rothschild? Her dismissal from the BBC when they learned she'd been convicted of harassment? I think you probably can afford to tell me.'

Silence.

There's music playing in the kitchen, something folksy and not really suited either to Emma or Jill. A mournful voice sings about a train disappearing down the line, down the line, down the line, guitar picking miserably along in the background.

Emma's hands have flown to her mouth. She stands up. 'No,' she whispers. 'Leo, no . . . Oh please no . . .'

'I've been at Jeremy Rothschild's house this evening,' I tell her. 'I was there because I was terrified, Emma, terrified something awful had happened to you, so I went to find out what he knew, because he'd been messaging you about meeting up. He told me everything.'

Emma sits back down, abruptly.

'No,' she repeats. 'No.'

'Yes.'

The song finishes and Jill disappears to turn the music off.

My wife's face is ashen. 'Leo, this isn't how you were meant to find out.'

I dig my key into my palm. 'I wasn't meant to find out that way, no. I was meant to find out through you. Ten years ago. Nine years ago. At quite literally any point in our relationship other than tonight, via Jeremy Rothschild.'

'No,' she whispers again.

'But instead of telling me, you disappeared to hang out here and drink wine. With no explanation, no regard for my feelings. Emma, what the hell?'

Emma looks at Jill, who has reappeared in the kitchen doorway. I don't think I've ever seen anyone look so uncomfortable. 'I was doing something important,' Jill says, but she sounds very uncertain. Then she looks at me. 'I got her and Charlie together.'

'Sorry?'

'I got Emma and Charlie together,' she repeats. 'And . . . Look, I'm sorry I went about it in such an underhand way but I had one chance to make it happen, and I took the decision to go for it.'

I turn back to Emma. 'You met Charlie?'

She nods.

I run a hand over my face. This is not my life. My regular, messy little life with my wife and child.

'But Leo,' Emma says. 'Do you mean . . . Look, did you, or did you not, tell Jill you needed a couple of days to think? She said you weren't ready yet. So I came here.'

I laugh, incredulously. 'I did tell Jill that I needed a couple of days. You're right. But I said that on Saturday morning. I said on *Saturday morning* that I needed more time. It's Monday night now. The "couple of days" have passed. We were meant to meet this morning.'

We both turn to Jill, whose face is puce.

'I'm sorry I fudged the details,' she says. 'I'm sorry to both of you – genuinely – but I think the really important thing is that we've got Emma and Charlie into a room together for the first time in nearly two decades.'

Exhausted, suddenly, I lean against the wall. 'I've reported you as a missing person,' I say to Emma. 'I called all the hospitals. Olly and Tink are at our house looking after Ruby. Even Sheila's got involved: that's how I found out you were here.'

'Oh God,' Emma gasps. 'Ruby doesn't think I'm missing, does she?'

'No.'

'Are you sure?'

'I'm sure. Although I'd probably have had to tell her tomorrow.'

Emma looks like she's going to be sick. 'Jill. How could you do that to a small child?' She stands up, then sits down again, perhaps realising how much she's had to drink. 'What were you thinking?'

Emma has told me before that in all the years she's known Jill, she has never – not once – seen her cry. So it's a shock for us both to see tears bulge in Jill's eyes.

'I just wanted you to meet him,' she says. Her voice is breaking. 'I just wanted to make it happen, without Leo or anyone else involved. Nothing was more important than that.'

'Not your decision to make,' I say, quietly.

Jill pinches the bridge of her nose.

'You're right,' she says. 'It wasn't. But I wanted to help Emma. That's all I've ever wanted to do.'

Emma and I exchange glances. Nothing about this scene is making sense.

Jill jams the heel of her hand into her eyes. She's determined not to cry. 'I'm sorry,' she says. 'I'm sorry, I'm sorry. I did lie to get you here. I did cause Leo a day of panic, which I regret – I just didn't think it through. I'm sorry, Emma. For everything. I'm sorry.'

Emma is at a loss. 'Jill, what's going on?' she asks, quietly. 'What's happening?'

After a moment, Jill crosses her arms over herself. 'Are you really so stupid?'

Emma looks at me again. She has no more idea than I do.

'I am pretty stupid,' she says, cautiously. 'Quite a lot of the time. But I don't know what you mean in this instance.' Her voice softens. 'Please, Jill. Talk to me.'

'I could have prevented all of this,' Jill says, eventually.

'Prevented what? What's "all of this"?'

'I knew David Rothschild was married. One of his friends told me. I could have told you, that night, but I didn't, because I was jealous of you, Emma. They were all after you. All of them. I wanted to make you feel stupid and small for a minute. But then you got pregnant, and your life fell apart. And that's on me. So yes, I've done everything I can to help you, ever since. But it'll never be enough.'

She yanks at the hem of her T-shirt, which has risen up. 'I think you should probably both go now. So you can bitch about me, and how badly I handled today, and how I ruined your life.' She's not even looking at us.

'Jill,' I say. I don't really feel like I should be speaking, here – this is a moment for her and Emma. But I can't just allow the last thirteen hours. I took Ruby to a police station, for God's sake. I called the hospitals.

'Jill, none of this explains why you shut me out of this. Why you basically kidnapped Emma. I've been beside myself. What were you thinking?'

Jill can't look at me. I don't think she has an answer. I don't think she's thought about any of this in a sane or rational way.

'I was planning on telling you that it was all my fault tonight,' she says, to Emma. 'I wanted to say sorry. I was just . . .' She looks around her, at the food cartons, the wine. 'I was plucking up the courage. I'm sorry, Leo. I'm sorry, both of you. Please, do us all a favour and go.'

Before we know it, she's walked to the front door and opened it. 'Take care,' she says, looking at nobody.

'Jill . . .' Emma says. 'Please, stop it.'

Jill just stands at her front door.

'Jill. Jill!' Emma says. 'You have to stop this! I invited him back to our house, I had sex with him. I didn't pay enough attention to condoms. It was my body, my decision. It wasn't on you. It has never been on you.'

But Jill can't hear her. 'I'm sorry,' she says, and when we don't move, she walks across the hallway and into her bedroom, shutting the door behind her.

We walk back down the corridor of Jill's silent apartment block again, as far apart as we can be.

I don't know what to think, or what to do. I don't think Emma does either.

The car park is bleak, a skin of rain on the ground, no sign of life save for an exhausted-looking young man in the strip-lit gym at the bottom of Jill's block. I look at my watch – 11.03 p.m.

I want today to be over, but I have a feeling it's only just beginning.

Chapter Fifty-Six

EMMA

We drive across north London in silence. Drizzle swirls in the peach glare of streetlamps, kebab shops bleed neon and cheerful music. In Willesden I watch a man fly-tipping an old fridge by a wheelie bin, looking round furtively for onlookers. Leo, who would normally have something to say about this, says nothing at all.

I watch him, from time to time. I've always really fancied Leo when he's driving. Not because he's flashy behind the wheel: the opposite, really. He's just so steady. I want to crawl into the warmth of his lap, feel his worn jeans under my legs, wrap my arms around his stripy top and fall asleep in his armpit.

'Leo,' I try, as we turn up Fitzjohn's Avenue.

'Please don't,' he says. And then, after a pause: 'I can't.'

I turn to stare out of the window again, at vast red-brick townhouses shuttered for the night, plane trees lining the street like old men, dripping and drooping.

Now I watch his clenched jaw as we turn off Frognal Rise into our road, and I know I'm going to lose him, this love of mine, just like I lost Charlie, and I'll have only myself to blame.

*

'I'll sleep on the sofa,' I say, when Olly and Tink have carried their boys into the car.

'No . . . I don't want Ruby to think there's anything wrong. I'll sleep in the shed. If she sees me come in, she'll think I've just taken John out for a pee.'

I stand in the hallway, trying not to cry.

Leo goes upstairs and comes back with his sleeping bag and a pillow. 'Let me get you a pillowcase,' I say, desperately, but he says no, he doesn't need one, and heads off towards the back door.

'Leo,' I whisper. I can't bear it. Here, in this house, is all that is good. All that has healed me, that gave me a reason to live.

He turns around. John, who was following him, turns around too. He sits down by Leo's feet, watching me.

'Leo . . .' Where would I even begin?

'I can't bear what you've been through,' Leo says, into the silence. 'I feel sick with grief for you, losing Charlie in such awful circumstances. For all you went through before and after. But, Emma, you didn't try to trust me with it. You didn't even try.'

He runs a hand through his hair. His lovely hair.

'I didn't even know your name,' he says, and he, too, is on the brink of tears. 'I have held you every night for ten years and I didn't even know your name.'

He turns round and heads for the garden door, just as there's a quiet knock at the front door.

Quick as a flash, Leo sinks to the floor and hugs John Keats, to stop him barking. 'It's probably Olly,' he says. 'He'll have forgotten something.'

He stays holding the dog while I go to the front door.

But, instead of my brother-in-law, I find myself face to face with my son.

I stare at him.

'Hi . . .' he says.

'Hello? Hi. Hi!'

Behind Charlie, at the bottom of our overgrown path, is Jeremy, in a parka and baseball hat combination he could only have borrowed from Charlie. The wind has picked up and the trees dance furiously, releasing an earlier rainfall on Jeremy's hat. Jeremy half-raises a hand in greeting.

'I'm sorry,' Charlie says. 'But I had to – there was something else I needed to talk to you about. Important. Should have brought it up earlier, but I . . . Well, something's come up this afternoon. Since I saw you.'

I turn to Leo, heart suddenly pounding. 'Leo, this is—'

'Charlie.' Leo's voice is soft. He stares at my first child, opens his mouth to say something, but no words come out. I see my features everywhere in Charlie's face. Leo must too.

'Come in,' my husband says, eventually. He lets go of John. John bounds at Charlie, delighted, dancing round him, knocking over a pile of books with his whipping tail. Charlie kneels down and plays with him, smiling and laughing for the first time today, and I realise I'm sitting on the floor, too, because my legs won't hold me anymore.

Chapter Fifty-Seven

EMMA

We all go into the kitchen. Leo puts the kettle on. Jeremy goes over to Leo and, after a pause, they shake hands. It seems as if Jeremy's apologising to him, although that makes little sense.

Charlie looks at the sleeping bag and pillow in a pile by the back door, but says nothing. 'You OK?' he asks, casually, as if I'm a mate he's bumped into in the student union bar.

I shrug – 'Bearing up, you know!' – because I won't undermine his belief that coming to see me was the right thing.

'We were just parking when you two turned up in your car.' He peers at Leo with interest. 'Were you out together?'

'No,' Leo says shortly, although his tone isn't unfriendly. 'Listen, I'll get out of your way in a minute, let me just sort out the tea.'

I hesitate. 'Actually, I'd like you to stay.'

I can't have any more secrets from him.

Leo pours tea. 'I don't mind going,' he says, levelly. He's so kind. So bloody kind.

Charlie looks to his father, who shrugs. Charlie says, 'As long as this can be confidential?'

Leo nods his assent and hands Charlie tea, but he hasn't put sugar in it and Charlie doesn't ask.

'OK then,' Leo says, sitting down, and I feel so proud of him. Nobody looking in on this room would guess that my husband was sitting with the stepchild he only found out about a few hours ago.

'Right,' Charlie says, as John Keats settles on the rug in the middle of the room. John's surprised by these late-night antics, but not unpleasantly so. He tucks his nose under his tail and watches us.

'So . . . what happened this afternoon was that someone left a message on our answerphone. Someone from the shop, in Alnmouth.'

Jeremy chips in. 'I asked them to call me if they saw Janice. Seems she popped in there this morning.' He pauses, and I realise this sighting isn't necessarily good news. 'It's probably inconsequential, but they said she bought two packets of paracetamol.'

Charlie rubs his hands over his face.

'I'm sure she's just in need of some pain relief,' Jeremy goes on. 'She gets bad tension headaches – but—'

'She could already have bought paracetamol from someone else,' Charlie blurts out, more to his father than to me. 'She could have a great big stockpile of it by now –'

'We're going to assume she hasn't,' Jeremy says. 'We're going to assume she was buying paracetamol much in the way you or I would. Nobody ever just buys one packet; we always buy two.' He turns to me. 'The shopkeeper is someone whose opinion I trust – we've known her for years. She said Janice seemed fine; no cause for concern whatsoever. In fact, she only told me Janice had bought paracetamol because I asked what was in her shopping basket. As well as paracetamol she bought bread, cheese, pasta, a few apples and a chocolate bar. And a bottle of orange squash. I don't think anyone contemplating the end would do that.'

Charlie checks his phone. He's a lot more concerned about this paracetamol than his father.

'But it means we at least know she is there. We're going to drive up tomorrow morning, after I finish work.'

'Sounds like a good plan,' Leo says, politely. I can see him wondering why they've turned up here in the middle of the night to share this with us, but he doesn't ask.

'Look,' Charlie says. 'The reason we're here is that – er . . .' He takes a breath. 'Well, the first thing to say is that I know why Mum disappeared.'

I look up, surprised, but not shocked. I knew there was something he wasn't telling me earlier.

'Dad didn't know. I should have told him before, but I promised Mum I'd . . .'

Jeremy rubs Charlie's arm.

'I promised Mum I'd keep it to myself. But I'm worried now. Dad's probably right that the paracetamol thing is harmless, but – I don't like it.'

He stops talking for a minute, takes another breath.

Jeremy removes the absurd baseball cap and puts it on his knee. 'What Charlie's about to share with you is very difficult.' He leans back on our sofa, into the light of Leo's reading lamp. He looks dreadful. 'Please don't be angry that he didn't tell you earlier. He's been put in a very unfair position.'

Charlie makes as if to speak, then stops again. He looks at his dad, who gives him an encouraging nod, and I have a flash of relief – of gratitude – for the trust and love that clearly exists between my son and his adoptive father.

After a pause, Charlie reaches down for his rucksack. He takes a small pile of notebooks out of his bag, each a different size. All are well-thumbed – diaries, I think, with a spark of admiration. I've often thought journalling was something that would have been good for me, but in nearly forty years have failed even to buy a notebook for the purpose.

Then: 'These are my mother's journals,' Charlie says. 'I've been reading them over the last few weeks.'

'To work out where she is?'

A complicated look crosses Charlie's face. 'Sort of.' He rearranges the diaries. 'I actually started looking at them before she disappeared. A big part of the reason she took off was that she found out I'd read them.'

'You mustn't blame yourself,' Jeremy says, quietly.

A terrible smell creeps across the room. John, the culprit, watches us all, nose between his paws.

Charlie is too polite to say anything, but Jeremy wrinkles his face in disgust. 'I only started reading the diaries because I was so worried about her,' Charlie's saying. 'I wanted to work out how I could help her.'

Then he looks at his hands, and says, 'I know about the smothering.'

I try to maintain eye contact, but it's too hard, the shame's too searing, and I have to look away.

'I cannot tell you how sorry I am, Charlie,' I say, after an age. 'What an awful, awful thing to have read.'

Charlie doesn't respond. He just looks down at the diaries again, needlessly tidying and re-stacking.

I add, 'I hope you know that I was dangerously ill. If I hadn't have gone to that unit they'd have taken me there under section.'

'I know about postpartum psychosis. I read about it a few years back, when I found out you'd been ill. Mum and Dad said my birth mother had "briefly had thoughts" about harming me. They didn't tell me anything actually happened.'

My skin crawls. What can I say? Sorry? It doesn't even

begin to cover it. The memory of that pillow, pressing down onto his smiling face. Years of guilt like an acid burn. The self-loathing, like a daily uniform.

The number of times I've had to run to Ruby's room, in case karma is waiting for me in the corner of my younger child's bedroom, and she's somehow suffocated or stopped breathing.

'If it helps, I've never come to terms with it,' I tell him. 'No matter how much therapy I've had, courses I've been on, groups I've joined, it never goes away.'

Charlie rests his forehead on his hands. John does another fart and Jeremy, without comment, gets up to let him out into the garden.

'The smothering is why I came tonight,' Charlie says, when his father returns.

Silence.

Then: 'You didn't do it,' he says. 'Mum made it up.'

After a second, I close my eyes. Of course Charlie wouldn't want to believe that of me.

'I'm afraid she didn't make it up,' I say. 'I'm sorry, Charlie – I don't want to believe it either, but it happened. I remember it. Every awful moment.'

He doesn't respond.

'I replay it in my head every day, and it's a living hell. But it's real, it happened, and I can't allow you to tell yourself it didn't.'

He watches me, almost sadly, and then shakes his head. 'No. Mum made it up. It's all here, in her diaries.'

I glance down at the diaries, the cracked spines, dog-eared corners. The top one bears a drink ring and tight, circular pen doodles. Charlie pulls out the third book down, and flicks through to a page near the end. It falls open naturally, as if it has been read many times. He hands it to me.

'This is going to be hard,' is all he says. He looks at Jeremy, who has sunk back into the sofa, lost in thought.

When I don't take the diary, Charlie puts it on my lap.

I pick it up.

Chapter Fifty-Eight

DIARY OF JANICE ROTHSCHILD

Six months ago

Eighteen years exactly since we formally adopted Charlie.

Guilt no easier. Fear no easier. Periods lying awake at night getting longer. Averaging 3.5 hours' sleep. Feel almost hallucinatory I'm so tired.

Problem is, I don't think sleep's going to come. BC what keeps me awake at night is the effort of trying to convince myself that Emily really was trying to suffocate Charlie.

I was certain once. When I walked into her room and saw the pillow over C's face, I was certain. They questioned me; still certain. Drove home, certain. Told J – certain. Didn't cross my mind I could have got it wrong.

When did the certainty begin to falter? Was there a moment when I began to question what I saw? If there was, I don't remember it. All I know is that I stuck to my script and didn't allow myself to think any further.

Until a few months ago. Her TV series was repeated; I was just flicking through the channels and there she was, marching along a cliff path, banging on about Cornish choughs.

Felt absolute dread, looking at her face on the screen. A turning point. I just stopped pretending. To myself, I mean. I just stopped lying.

She wasn't going to smother him. She was too well by then – she was playing peekaboo. I heard her saying it as I came up the corridor. I started to smile because I knew it was her and Charlie.

But then there she was with a pillow over his face, and I panicked. Was awful. Deeply traumatic; I had nightmares about it for months after.

If I'd stayed there for a second longer, tho, she'd have whipped that pillow away and said, PEEKABOO!

And then Charlie wouldn't have been my baby.

Don't know where this is leading. Am I ready to come clean? Career would be over. Marriage would be over. Might actually end up in prison? Not sure? Probably not. But suspect Emily could sue me. I would, in her shoes.

Above all, would harm Charlie, probably force him to cut me out of his life, and then what would be the point in living?

And why ruin everything? Emily completely believed it, and still does. She so fundamentally doubted herself at that time, she took what I said as gospel – I read her statements. I got her text messages, begging me to adopt Charlie because she didn't trust herself.

Emily's life has been fucked ever since, tho, and the part of me that's frozen over with horror at what I've done gets bigger every day.

Have interview with *Evening Standard* later about the power of female friendship. A fucking irony.

Might see if I can privately get some antidepressants or maybe anti-anxiety stuff.

So much rage and hopelessness. Eighteen years, and it hasn't got any easier, any better. I am still a monster.

Chapter Fifty-Nine

EMMA

I look up at Charlie, who's watching me, face blank. Outside in the dark garden, John is barking at the tree, which he likes to do when the wind blows it back and forth.

A hot hollow has expanded in my chest.

'Is there more?' I ask.

'Yes and no. She doesn't say anything as open as that again. Basically, this is the bit you need to read.'

'And you believe it?' My voice is stretched nearly to breaking. 'You think it's the truth?'

'I know it is. I confronted her.'

I stare at him. 'You mean, she admitted it?'

Charlie swallows, then nods.

I slump back into the sofa. I wish I could be closer to Leo, to cling on to him before I get swept away, but he's sitting at the other end of the sofa, and I have no idea if he'll ever hold my hand again.

Jeremy looks destroyed.

'Dad had no idea,' Charlie says, following my gaze.

I want to believe what I have just read.

I do not want to believe what I've just read.

Charlie leans back in our armchair. 'I started university last September. When I came home for the Christmas holidays

Mum wasn't herself at all. Very up and down, weirdly angry. Dad said she'd been that way since I'd left for Boston.'

John comes and scrabbles at the back door, which stops Charlie in his flow. Leo gets up and lets the dog in.

'When I came back for the Easter holidays she was even worse. Sort of ultra-needy, but also just – I dunno – just furious. Not just with us, necessarily, just generally.' He scratches his head. 'It was a dick move, but one night she left her diary by the loo in her en suite and I picked it up. Mum's written diaries my whole life and I've always respected her privacy, but – well, fuck it, I was worried.'

Charlie pauses. 'Sorry. Mum and Dad don't mind me swearing. Do you?'

'Of course not.'

'So I read a few pages. She sounded quite unstable. And I was about to put it back when I read something I didn't like. Essentially a reference to all of the stuff you've just read.'

He expels a long breath.

'I read it four or five times, but I couldn't see what else she could mean. It was about the smothering thing. It sounded like she'd made it up, but I couldn't quite believe it. I went back to Boston for my summer term, but I kept thinking about it. I suppose I was just hoping I'd misunderstood.'

He pauses. 'But when I came back for the summer, and went looking for her diaries again, I eventually found the entry you've just read.'

I wait. Nothing seems real. Not this room, not the people in it, not the story he's telling.

'She admitted it all, when I confronted her. She was in floods. Told me how she'd lost baby after baby, how adoption was their only hope in the end, and how they finally found me . . . And then you changed your mind and decided to keep me. I think that broke her.'

The wind picks up outside.

'So I get it. What an awful time she'd had, in the lead up to that day.' He looks at me, and I see sadness in his young face. 'But I still can't accept what she did. Let alone work out how to forgive it.'

The world is beginning and ending. I lean forward and rest my elbows on my knees.

Is this how it happened?

I was playing peekaboo with my baby?

When I look up again, Charlie's watching me expectantly, as if waiting for an answer. Leo touches my shoulder.

'Sorry? What?'

'I said, have you always thought you tried to smother me?' Charlie asks. 'Have you never doubted it?'

I bring up my memories of that day. A torrent of fragments surface, all the usual noise and misery. I find the moment of the pillow, over Charlie's face. I find the moment I was interviewed by the psychiatrist and the social worker and my nurse. I find the moment they asked if it had been my intention to suffocate my baby. And I find the moment where I looked into myself and said, yes, I think that's exactly what I was trying to do.

Why did I say that?

Why did I say *I think so*, rather than something more assured, like, 'Yes, that's exactly what I was trying to do?'

I try out the idea of peekaboo. Of wanting to play, not harm.

It fits. Playing, not harming.

Heat rushes through me. Please, no. Please let me not have given up my child for this.

'After I confronted Mum she begged me not to tell Dad – not until she'd figured it all out in her head. She said she was sorry, and that she would sort it out, sort herself out. She went off to rehearsals, then didn't come home. We haven't seen her since.'

After what feels like hours, I turn to Jeremy. 'And you never knew?' I ask. 'She didn't even hint at it?'

Charlie looks at the ragged form of his father. 'Of course he didn't know. Look at the state of him.'

There's an unbearable silence. Everything is imploding. Every single thing I told myself, every moment of torturous self-loathing: a story.

'I sort of thought after the letter she sent us that she'd be OK,' Charlie says. 'That she really did just need some time out. She texted Dad a few days ago and she didn't sound too bad . . .' His voice quakes. 'But I'm scared, now.'

'We came because I couldn't allow you not to know about this for another second,' Jeremy says. 'And we'll leave you in a moment, because, God knows, you'll need time to let it all sink in. But we have one question we need to ask you first.'

Leo gestures for Jeremy to go ahead.

'Janice mentioned a special place, in one of her diary entries a few months back. Her words were along the lines of "I'd escape to my breakdown bolthole if it didn't make me think of Emma." We wanted to ask if that meant anything to you?'

I try to unstick memories from the thick glue of shock. The places Janice took me for lunch in Edinburgh. The rock pools we explored on Alnmouth beach, the day I thought I was miscarrying. The train station later on, where I said goodbye to her. None of these feel like the sort of places she'd describe as special, less still would want to retreat to at her lowest ebb.

I relay this, and Charlie deflates further.

'Nothing? You can't think of anywhere?'

'I'm sorry,' I tell him. 'I can't.'

'Please,' he says. 'Please think. Is there really nowhere else?'

'I am. I'm thinking. I . . . No. Apart from a walk on Alnmouth beach we only went for lunch in Edinburgh. And of course she visited me a few times in the mother and baby unit, but she won't be referring to that. I'm sorry.'

Charlie looks desperate.

'OK,' Jeremy says, standing up. 'We should get going. Please ring us, any time of day, if you remember anything that might make sense.'

They make to leave.

I could have been your mother, I want to cry, as Charlie heads out of our sitting room. *You could have grown up right here in this house. You could have been my baby.*

But he's already in the hallway, this full-grown man, then out of the front door. He starts walking down our path, ducking to avoid the tangled foliage, saying thanks and goodbye over his shoulder because he doesn't want me to see how upset he is. I don't know when, or even if, I will see him again.

Jeremy stops on the doorstep, and turns to me. 'I will never be able to express how sorry I am,' he says. 'Never, Emma. I hope you believe me when I tell you I had no idea.'

I don't say anything. Right now I don't want to believe anything anyone tells me, ever again.

'It does make so much more sense, now,' he goes on. 'Her paranoia, the obsession with you wanting Charlie back. She must have been terrified you'd remember what really happened.'

But of course I hadn't remembered. I couldn't remember. You could have told me I'd robbed a bank and murdered all the cashiers, and I'd have believed you. I'd have created that memory, just like I created the memory of a smothering, because when you're that lost, your only anchors are the things people tell you.

After Charlie and Jeremy are gone, we sit in silence.

Yet again the world has shifted. My entire adult life has been nothing more than a story – and not even mine.

The story of a woman called Janice. A woman who allowed me to believe I had tried to smother my baby, because she wanted him for herself. A woman who took a restraining order out against me when I started following him.

She'd have had me sent to prison if she could. She had me sacked from my presenting job, knowing the humiliation it would bring; the financial loss. But worse than anything else, far worse, she stole my baby.

Leo shifts over, silently, to hold my hand, as I cry for all that could have been. For my baby Charlie, that smiling infant with his soft blonde hair, his simple, boundless trust in me. For his whole life, spent with someone else.

John falls asleep in his bed; Leo turns out the lights and sits with me in darkness, as the rain pelts our tiny old house.

I gave up my baby for a lie.

Chapter Sixty

LEO

Minutes – or maybe hours – after I fall asleep in the shed, Emma comes in and stands next to the sofa. 'Leo,' she whispers.

Silently, I shuffle up to make space. John Keats, who was excited about a night in the shed, is asleep under the duvet. God knows how he's breathing. I poke him with a foot and he moves around a bit, grumbling, but refuses to budge. Emma has to perch on the edge of the sofa.

'Leo . . .' she whispers again, and in that moment I just want to whisper, 'Hi!' and kiss her. I want us to laugh about our last meeting in here, when all we had to worry about was whether or not her chemo had worked and how awful my dairy-free chocolate was. I want to take our clothes off, not for sex, but for the pleasure of her night-warm skin on mine.

'I was going to tell you,' she says, in the darkness.

I turn on the lamp and look at her. She's still in her clothes, with a dressing gown on top. There are grey circles around her eyes and her skin is pale: she looks like she used to during chemo.

'I was going to tell you,' she repeats. 'You have to know that, Leo. I was going to tell you. The weekend we went up to Hitchin to meet your parents: I was going to talk to you when we got back to London. We'd been together a few weeks, it felt right.'

'And?'

'And you found out you'd been adopted. It blew everything apart, Leo, it took months for you to come back to yourself.'

'But when I did?'

'I knew you wouldn't be able to take it,' she says, after a pause. 'I held you through that time, Leo. I heard every word you said about your birth mother. About adoption, about people lying to you. It would have been like a bomb blowing your legs off, just after you'd learned to walk again.'

'But – but that was nearly ten years ago. Surely—'

She interrupts. 'If there had been one day in those ten years – one single day – where I'd believed I could share it without harming you, I would have done.'

I stare at her. 'So it's my fault?'

'No . . . I just . . .' She tries to take my hand but I can't do it. I can't sit here, holding hands with her.

'It's not your fault, Leo, no. But the truth is that if you'd had a different past, I would have told you.'

When I don't respond, she says, 'Put yourself in my shoes. Imagine you were me, with a past so awful you changed your name. Would you really, truly, have told your partner? When it fed directly into every traumatic thing that had ever happened to him? Would you really have done that?'

'Yes,' I say, without a moment's hesitation.

She sighs. 'It's easy for you to sit here now, saying that. But I was there, Leo. I knew better than anyone else what you could and couldn't cope with.'

'Seriously? We're doing that again? You know me better than I know myself?'

'That's not what I meant! I—'

'Emma, listen to me. Listen.' She looks at me. 'There isn't anything I haven't told you about myself. Nothing. I tell you everything, and I always have, because if we aren't honest with each other, what's the point?'

Neither of us says anything for a while.

'You didn't tell me you'd found all the papers I hid,' Emma says, eventually. 'I still don't know what else you've found out, or who you spoke to. You did all of that in secret.'

I sit up. 'You want to know who I spoke to? Robbie Rosen, for starters. And then Mags Tenterden. Over the weekend I was at Sheila's, who, it turns out, knows far more about our marriage than I did. And then I spent the evening at Jeremy Rothschild's, before finally tracking you down at Jill's.'

Emma balks. 'You went to see Robbie? Oh, God, Leo. And Mags, I . . .'

'While we're on the subject of our marriage. Is it legal?'

She looks away, and, after a while, shakes her head. 'Possibly not.'

'Possibly not? What does that mean?'

'It means I don't know for certain. But when we gave notice at the registry office, there was a box I should have ticked to say I'd changed my name. I didn't.'

Emma is looking at me, but I can't meet her eye. That was our day. Our happy, beautiful day, with its flowers and wine and cakes and friends and dancing and laughter.

When I saw her father's name on the marriage certificate, I'd been surprised, of course: his surname was Peel. But Emma told me she'd been given her mother's surname, Bigelow, to keep her memory alive, and I'd thought that sad and perfect and beautiful.

She lied to me on our wedding day.

'It was selfish,' she says, in the end. 'And wrong. I see now how cowardly I've been. But I loved you, Leo. Of course I wanted to marry you.'

I say nothing. I don't trust myself to speak.

'I didn't realise there'd be legal consequences when I proposed. I didn't think. All I knew was that I was intoxicated with you. I couldn't believe my luck. I was happy; so happy – I just wanted us to be married.'

I think about my wedding speech. About this woman I knew so well, loved so much. All those upturned faces, smiling and laughing, the raised glasses. To the happy couple!

After a while she takes a long breath and says, 'There was misery, Leo. There was misery and there was self-loathing; there was loneliness I still don't have the words to describe. But then there was you. You were everything. You still are.'

I close my eyes. I'm still so deep in shock I keep forgetting what Emma's been through. What she was carrying on her shoulders when we fell in love.

I think back to our very first phone call, when her grandmother died. How minutes ticked by, then hours; how 6 p.m. rolled around and we were still talking; how my colleagues turned off their computers and went home, smiling at each other, because they could see what was happening to me.

Three and a half hours. That's all it had taken.

Emma says, 'Life made sense again, when I met you, Leo. I remembered why people want to live.'

I glance at her, but she's not looking at me; she's lost somewhere in her past.

I think of Ruby. Lying on Emma's chest, marooned and tiny, bellowing with all her might. That dizzying moment, the beginning of everything. What was Emma thinking, as we stared in wonder at our baby? Was she even there?

'I also wanted to know how you managed to give birth without me knowing it was your second baby,' I say. 'The obstetrician told me forceps were common in a woman's first delivery. Was she briefed to lie?'

Emma shakes her head, slowly. 'Oh, Leo. No. The obstetrician meant it was my first vaginal birth. Charlie was born by C-section.'

I take this in. 'But you don't have a scar, you . . .' I stop. She does have a scar.

I close my eyes. I'm a man in my forties. I have a first-class degree; I've spent an entire career in pursuit of the truth. How could I have been so stupid? An appendix scar just above her pubic bone? I accepted that? For ten years?

'And yes, they were briefed to avoid any mentions of Charlie,' Emma says, gently. 'I think there was a sticker on my notes, or something on the door, or – I don't know. But they have a duty to protect the mother, Leo. Nobody was trying to make a fool of you.'

Grudgingly, I accept what she's saying to be true. If they knew even half of what she'd been through to get to that point, I imagine they'd have done anything she asked.

'And Mags?' My voice sounds weary. 'Why did you pretend she ditched you?'

Emma rubs her hands over her face. 'Because if I told you it was my decision, you'd have wanted to know why I was leaving her. And then I'd have had to tell you Janice had had me sacked. And . . .' She sighs. 'It was easier to just not tell you, Leo. I'm sorry. I know that sounds flippant.'

'It does.'

Emma looks around my shed, pokes the lamp where the shade is dented.

'Until tonight I thought I tried to suffocate my baby,' she says. 'I didn't trust myself to look after him, so I gave him away. Can you imagine giving Ruby away, when she was eight weeks old? Can you imagine the pain?'

'No.'

And I can't. I can't even come close.

She takes a long breath. 'Leo, you turned my life around. I don't know if you'll ever be able to understand why I kept it to myself, let alone forgive me, but – listen to me.'

She gets off the sofa and kneels down in front of me. 'It's real, Leo. Every single bit of you and me has been real.'

I look at her for a long time.

'Really?'

'Yes.' She touches my cheek. 'Nobody can pretend to love. Not for long.'

For a moment I allow myself to turn my face into her hand. Memories slide in and out. The day we both had food poisoning; the first time we met John Keats. Falling asleep on the Northern Line, arguments in taxis; burning endless dinners, kissing on the sofa, the 'hiking holiday' we spent in a pub.

These have been good years.

Slowly, I remove her hand from my cheek. I am confused, I'm exhausted.

'Your dad,' I say, eventually. 'Why did you need to lie about him?'

Tears fill Emma's eyes. Emily's.

'Oh, Leo,' she whispers. She presses a sleeve into her face. 'I just had to . . . I had to leave his death in my old life. I know that's impossible for you to understand, but I just couldn't bring myself to tell you Dad died of something I could have stopped. I'd already caused my mother's death, I just . . . couldn't go there.'

A tear slips down her cheek. John rearranges himself, grumbling again, opening up a space for Emma to sit on the sofa.

'But, Emma,' I say. 'Emma. Jeremy told me your dad died of alcoholism. How could you have stopped that?'

She just shakes her head. Another tear slides slowly down.

'I told you he died in Kinshasa, but he never made it. They sent another padre in his place – he'd been off work for months by then. He had a heart attack in the front room and died in the ambulance. His system was full of alcohol. I doubt he had any idea it was even happening.'

My heart is breaking.

'Emma . . .' I take her hand, because how could I not? 'Alcoholics die because nobody can stop them. It's the same with women and childbirth. Neither of those things are your fault. You couldn't have prevented them, no matter what you did.'

Tears seep from her eyes, until the first bird of the day starts singing outside.

'I know you'll need time to take this in,' she says, when she's regained composure. 'To figure out what you want.'

I nod, but the truth is that I have no idea what I need.

'I can sleep in the shed while you're doing that. It's me who's done this to us; you shouldn't have to sleep out here.'

'I'm fine,' I say, quickly. It's easier to play make-believe in a shed.

'Sure?'

I'm sure.

'Then take as much time as you need,' she says. 'But know that I love you. I always have.'

It feels like hours pass before she speaks again. Possibly, we both even drift off; the three of us on the sofa, as if nothing has happened. When I hear her voice it seems to come from far away.

'There's something else I need to tell you,' she's saying. 'Not about me,' she adds. 'It's about Janice. I think I've worked out where she is.'

I open my eyes. 'Really?'

Emma gets out a letter. She tells me Janice sent it her a couple of weeks ago: another thing I knew nothing about. If Emma and I were to try to salvage our marriage, this would go on for months. Years, maybe.

She hands me the letter.

Dear Emma,
I know this letter will come as a shock. But I had to write to you. You crop up in my thoughts often.

It's about that crab we spotted all those years ago. On Alnmouth beach remember. Of course you remember. I have watched your television series and know you've never stopped looking for it. Anyway, I think you should look on Coquet Island.

In Shakespeare, islands are like magic, and he knew what he was talking about.

Coquet Island is the only place on that coast that's completely out of bounds to human beings

& I paid a fisherman to take me out there once to look at the birds and although you're not allowed to land there I saw many things including, I'm sure of it, one of your crabs . . . I guess you only really get bird lovers going out there so nobody'd notice an unusual crab, they're all there for the puffins and roseate terns

I'm sorry I've kept this information from you for so long. I should have told you years ago. I mean it I am so sorry.

sorry again Emma
Janice

'She sounds drunk,' I surmise, tiredly. I'm not sure I have capacity to deal with Janice Rothschild right now.

'Yes – or on medication.'

'Maybe. But you think she's on Coquet Island?' I ask.

'No. I think she's in a shed.'

I rub my eyes. 'What?'

Emma tucks her hair behind her ear. It doesn't escape my notice that this is the first time in a year her hair's been long enough to do that.

'The day I decided to keep Charlie, I thought I was miscarrying.'

I search back through the memories I've had to store today. 'Yes,' I say. 'I remember.'

'Janice invited me to stay at their house. We went for a walk on the beach – far too big a walk, but, Christ, it was such a relief to know Charlie was going to be brought up by them, I just . . . Well, I just carried on walking. Eventually I think my body realised I wasn't going to stop, so it stopped me itself. I started bleeding, my back hurt, felt dizzy. I ended up in hospital.'

I remember her having back pain when she was pregnant with Ruby. She was petrified; she'd gone to the hospital before I'd even picked up her voicemail.

'But before that, it had started raining and we went and sat in this stone shed in the dunes. We had sandwiches and chocolate, and we watched a storm tear around the bay. It was lovely. Just me and this secret friend nobody knew I had, sitting among piles of sheep poo and cobwebs.'

She pauses, remembering. 'Janice felt it too. I know she did. When the storm cleared I felt so full of hope and relief and . . . I don't know. Fellowship, I think.'

'And . . . You think she's in that shed?'

Emma frowns, slightly embarrassed. 'Actually, I do.'

I wait for her to expand, but she doesn't.

'Really?'

'Yes. And here's why: in her letter, she talks about Coquet

Island and she keeps on saying she's sorry for not telling me. "I should have told you years ago," she says. It reads as if she's talking about the crabs, but I think she's actually apologising for not telling me the truth about the smothering.'

John pokes his head out from the duvet, suddenly, to look at Emma. After staring at her crossly, he stares at me, then withdraws again, muttering to himself. We're being too loud.

In spite of ourselves, we both smile. Emma strokes the mound of duvet he's huffing under.

'Janice is clearly out of it in this letter,' Emma says. 'Whether she's drunk, or on too much medication I don't know, but she's not right at all.'

I agree.

'I think she's up there. Alnmouth. With the island in sight, reminding her of what she's done.'

'But why would she be in a shed? Why would she not just stay at their house?'

'Because Jeremy would have found her straightaway. And she wanted time out.'

'I understand that. But why not a B&B, or a caravan or something – surely you can see Coquet Island from a whole bunch of places around there?'

She thinks about this, eventually pulling out her phone to study a map. 'I think you can probably see it anywhere between Alnmouth and Low Hauxley,' she says. 'So yes, she could be somewhere between those two points – I'd say it's an eight mile stretch, maybe ten. But something came to me earlier, when I was trying to sleep.'

I wait.

'I was thinking about this lovely feeling between us, when we were sitting in that shed, and I suddenly remembered. Proper lightbulb moment. She said, just as the rain was clearing up, "Wouldn't this be a perfect place to come and have a nice private breakdown? Just check out of life, sit and watch the sea, drink far too much wine?"'

'Really?'

'Yes. We were talking about how you could turn it into a little retreat, how you could kit it out. She said she was pretty sure it didn't belong to the National Trust, how she was going to track down the owner via the Land Registry. It's exactly what she was referring to in her diary entry.'

I look at her. 'I'm not convinced,' I admit. 'I hear what you're saying, but . . . well, it seems a little far-fetched. Apart from anything else, Janice doesn't strike me as the type to rough it. I don't know her personally, of course, but she seems very well groomed. Like she enjoys the finer things in life. Not cold stone sheds full of sheep shit.'

Emma gets up and sticks her head out of our own shed, as if listening. The wind has gone, now, the rain too. 'Can we go inside?' she asks. 'I don't like leaving Ruby on her own. I wouldn't be able to hear her if she woke.'

She is a good mother.

No matter what I might feel about her as a wife right now, she is a good mother, and she deserved to bring up Charlie.

Inside, Emma shows me her computer, where she's been looking at Alnmouth beach on satellite view. I see it straightaway, the hut; she's zoomed right in. A small pock in the dunes near the golf course, above the beach.

'The view of Coquet Island would be good from there,' she says. 'And she'd be able to walk to the shops easily. It's not as if she'd be completely roughing it.'

'But I thought Jeremy had already been looking up there? I thought he'd asked everywhere and nobody had seen her?'

After a moment, Emma sighs. 'Ah, you're right. There's a

million reasons why she's anywhere other than this stupid shed. Even if she'd actually bought it, kitted it out, she'd have done it with Jeremy. Not on her own, in secret. That would be too weird. Everyone in the village would have known about it.'

She looks down at the letter in her hands. 'But I just . . . I was there with her, that day, when all we had was hope. She said it was her private breakdown plan, and now she's disappeared somewhere to have a breakdown, and she's talking about Coquet Island. Surely that's got to count for something?'

I agree, not without reluctance, that it does.

I go to the fridge and get out some ham. Emma watches me, and I'm nearly laid out by sadness. I don't know if we'll ever joke about failed veganism again.

'But the thing is . . .' I open the packet. 'The thing I'm struggling with, is why you want to track her down in the first place. How can you find it in yourself to care about her, after what she did to you?'

'I don't care about her,' she says, quietly. 'Not really. Certainly not yet.'

I hover, not knowing what to say.

'I don't imagine I'll ever forgive her. I don't think anyone could. But this is about Charlie. He's terrified she'll take her own life, and he thinks it's his fault. If I can help him find her, I have to.'

'OK,' I say, eventually. 'Why don't you message Charlie, ask him to call you when he wakes up.'

So she does.

Emma. Emily. I take some more ham out of the packet, roll it up.

The clock ticks. I set the ham down. Emma gets a glass of water.

I put the ham back in the fridge and try to persuade John to get into his bed, just as Emma's phone rings. 'It's Charlie,' she whispers.

'Charlie?' she says, answering. 'I'm sorry, did my message wake you . . . ?'

She listens for a minute. Can't sleep, she mouths at me.

I get up and fill the kettle.

'Well, I know it sounds mad,' she begins. 'But . . .'

Fifteen minutes later, we stand at the doorway to our house.

Emma is wearing a waterproof and a beanie hat. She has tea, which I've made, and crisps; a couple of apples. It's quarter past four in the morning and she is about to drive to Highbury Fields, to pick up Charlie, and then she's going to drive six hours north to Alnmouth beach. Jeremy's already gone to work. He's on air at 6 a.m.

'What will you tell Ruby?' Emma asks. She tried to wake Ruby a few minutes ago, because she hadn't seen her last night. 'Hey,' she whispered, as Ruby half-woke. 'I just came to give you a quick kiss, because I'm off to—'

'Go away,' said Ruby's voice, in the darkness. 'You're squashing me.' So that was that.

'I'll work something out. But she'll be fine. She was having a brilliant time with Oskar and Mikkel yesterday evening. She'd no idea we thought you were missing.'

'I don't want her to feel like I've just abandoned—'

'She won't.' My voice is firm, because Emma needs it to be. 'Ruby knows you're her servant. She's very comfortable with it.'

Outside a bird is making tentative song. His call goes unanswered, but he tries again, and again.

'I can't ask you to forgive me,' Emma says, after pausing to listen to the bird. We're standing so close I can smell the warm tiredness of her skin. I close my eyes, imagining how it would feel to just lean my face into her hair, to slide my arms around her and pretend she is the Emma I know and trust.

'I can't ask you to forgive anything I've done,' she says, quietly. 'But I need to do this for him. I hope you can understand.'

And I can. I'd do anything for Ruby. We would all do anything for our children.

'I just need to ask you one thing,' I say.

'Of course.'

'And I beg you, Emma, please answer honestly.'

She stands on the garden path, framed by tangled creepers and trailing ivy.

'If Janice hadn't gone missing, if I hadn't dug up all those clues – would you have told me?'

Emma looks at me for a long time.

'No,' she admits, eventually. 'I don't think I would.'

'Right.'

She turns to go. 'I love you, Leo.'

My eyes well. I don't know if my grief is for Emma or for me. For Ruby, perhaps, or the chaotic, warm life the three of us have had together. I don't know anything, other than that it's only when something's damaged beyond repair that we realise how beautiful it was.

Chapter Sixty-One

EMMA

Charlie and I park up on the beach at lunchtime. Nearby a family is unpacking bodyboards from a car. The children are arguing and the parents aren't talking to each other, but somehow, everyone is OK. They're a family. They share a car, a house; probably only the most inconsequential of secrets.

I'm not sure I will still have a family when I get back to London, but I'm focused only on Charlie now. Yesterday he was wearing shorts; today he's wearing jeans. I want to know everything about him. Where he buys jeans – do his parents pay, or do they insist he earns his spending money? What is his summer job in Queens Park? How does he vote, where does he stand on Marmite? Did he shuffle round on his bum as a baby, like Ruby, or did he crawl?

When we stopped at service stations he bought exactly the snacks I'd expect an eighteen-year-old to buy. Large packets of sweets, greasy sausage rolls, crisps. He inhaled them, much in the manner John Keats inhales his bowl of dog food. I'm fascinated by this boy.

We took turns driving so the other could sleep, but all I could do was watch my grown-up son at the wheel of my car, an elbow resting on the door, taking measured swigs of an energy drink.

The idea of the shack seems like madness, now we're here. I felt such certainty about it last night, recalling the connection between me and Janice when we'd sat watching the storm. Hours later, sleepless and wired, I feel insane. This whole thing feels insane.

'Right,' Charlie says. 'Let's do this.' He gets out of my little car and stretches his long body, groaning with relief. I get out and look at the beach below us, the sheer scale of it. Pale gold sand and blue sea, like a child's drawing. Dunes doming and cupping the periphery, marram grass bent almost flat in the wind.

We haven't talked a great deal, even though we've been in a car together for several hours. Charlie's veered between conviction that his mum is going to be up here in the stone shed, and certainty that she won't. Apart from anything else, he said, his mum had never camped in his lifetime – not even for a night.

'She doesn't like roughing it?' I'd asked, tentatively.

'She just didn't feel safe. She was paranoid someone would come into our tent and steal me while she slept.'

That had made for an uncomfortable silence.

Every time I think about Janice Rothschild, something wrenches in my abdomen. Charlie didn't bring it up in the car, which was a relief, but it's there: malignant, appalling. I gave up my son because of her lies.

Charlie's zipping up a windbreaker, swapping his trainers for well-used walking boots.

I've always loved that brand of walking boot! I want to say, but I mustn't bombard him with similarities. I'm scared of anything that might make him think I'm desperate. But, even more than that, I'm scared this will be a waste of time, that we will find nothing but a dusty shed full of sheep shit and picnickers' litter.

I ask him how he's feeling.

He thinks about it. 'Anxious.'

'That we won't find her?'

There's a pause. 'No,' he says. 'Anxious that we will.'

It takes a few seconds for me to understand what he means.

'Oh, Charlie . . .'

'It's not just that she was buying paracetamol, it's her diaries. The recent ones. She sounds really bad.'

I am not equipped for this. I should have kept out of it; allowed Jeremy and Charlie to find Janice. Who was I to think I understood her? That I knew how her mind worked, just because we shared some sandwiches in a shed nearly twenty years ago?

'Look. Shall we go to your parents' house, before we go to the shed? Take five?'

Charlie shuts the boot of my car.

'No. I don't want to waste another minute. I want to find her, get her to see a doctor.'

I send up a silent prayer. Let Janice be safe. The woman who stole my son, let her be safe.

It isn't long before I see the shed. It's not exactly as I remembered, but that's the thing with memory: it makes up its own stories. They harden and calcify in just the same way as facts, and most of the time we have no idea which is which.

I remember the hut as much bigger, with a couple of windows and a crude chimney, and the remains of a wall circling it, where perhaps once sheep were overnighted.

Now there's a large bush sprouting into a hole that was once a window, and the door has been boarded over. There's the remnants of what's probably a local teenagers' bonfire outside, but it's the only sign of life. Nobody has been inside this building for a very long time.

We both stop to stare at it – this tiny, ridiculous shack we have driven for hours to search. Janice was never here. There's only the sea and the sky; the vast, knowing sky, with its circling marine birds and the secrets it never shares.

Charlie shoves his hands into his pockets and turns to look down at the waves as they fizz out across the sand.

Janice could be anywhere. Even if she's nearby, how would we actually go about finding her? Every new beach stretches right to the horizon here; you could go hours without seeing a soul. No wonder the Vikings landed on this part of the British coast. It might as well have been the moon.

I sit down in the crook of a sand dune, overcome by exhaustion. I haven't stopped since Jill semi-kidnapped me yesterday morning. I get out the miserable sandwich I bought somewhere near Newcastle and start eating.

I messaged Jill a couple of times, on the journey up here, but she hasn't replied.

I know a thing or two about long-term guilt. It burns you from the inside like swallowed acid; it reaches every corner of your thinking. I just hope she'll let me help dismantle these stories she's told herself for so long. God knows, I owe her.

Charlie sits down next to me after a while. Charlie, who's only here because of Jill.

I send her another message, while Charlie eats a pasty.

'I think we should walk into the village and get a pint,' I say, when we've finished our food. 'Have a think about where else we can look.'

Charlie stands up, dusting himself down. 'Mmm,' he says. 'Not sure it feels right to be in a pub when we could be looking for her.'

'Of course. I . . . Look, Charlie, I'm sorry I planted the idea of the shed. It seems absurd now.'

Charlie thinks for a moment, poking at a little shock of marram grass with his boot. 'The more I think about it, the more I agree with you, actually.' He points to the beach, just below where we're standing. 'It's always been here that we've had picnics. Always here that she used to spread out our towels and the windbreaker on beach days.'

'Really?'

'Yeah.' He stares down at the sand, remembering sun cream and bottled water, sandcastles and dinghies. 'This is her spot.'

I turn my back to the sea, to look at the shed again. Behind it, a golf course runs along the beach for a mile or so. I wonder if any of the regulars might have noticed a woman, walking – maybe sitting here in the evenings? There's a couple of golfers who are probably within shouting distance.

'Charlie,' I begin, and then I stop.

There is a strange synergy between me and Janice Rothschild, no matter how far we have circled from each other since Charlie was born. The day I bumped into her and Jeremy on this beach, four years ago, I felt her before I saw her.

And I feel her again now. She's here. Close by.

I turn around to look at Coquet Island. The lighthouse, long-abandoned, sits at the far end, blinking briefly in the sun. I follow back to the land, and scan slowly across the village of Alnmouth.

Where are you?

I search along the lane to the car park, across the golf course, to the coastal path above the exposed rocks.

Up to the horizon, back down to where the grass peters off into scrub and sand dunes. Then back to the coastal path above the rocks again.

‘Charlie,’ I say, carefully. ‘I really do think we should go to the village. Ask around again. I know your Dad told the shop to call him if Janice came back in, but she could have gone into a cafe, a pub, the deli – I think we need to ask all of them. And then I think we should go to your house, sit down and make a proper plan. We need to find her.’

It doesn’t take him long to give in. He’s exhausted.

We walk back to the village together, my son and I. As we turn up a lane to the High Street, I turn back once more to look, careful Charlie doesn’t see me.

There.

That’s where she is. I’m certain of it. But I don’t know if it’s safe to take Charlie there. I don’t know if we’ve arrived just a little too late.

Chapter Sixty-Two

EMMA

Charlie falls asleep within minutes of sitting on his parents' spotless cream sofa. I want to get him a proper pillow, a duvet, but I resist the urge. He's an adult, and he doesn't want to be mothered, least of all by me.

I leave him a note to say I've gone for another walk, and slip out of the door.

The wind has cleared and it's warm. There are more people on the beach now, some in the sea, which sparkles cheerfully all the way to the horizon. A child flies a kite, yelling at his dad, who is doing it all wrong.

The cabins I spotted earlier appear above the path, immaculate, recently painted. Adirondack chairs lined up outside in the sun, expensive-looking sun shades. They're exactly the sort of thing people pay vast sums of money to pretend to camp in: faux-rugged exteriors, interiors decked out with champagne glasses and luxury down-filled duvets.

Exactly the sort of place you'd go for a 'nice private breakdown' if you didn't really like roughing it, but you loved Alnmouth beach.

She's here. As soon as I spotted them, just a few hundred metres up from the sheep hut, I knew.

*

Two of the huts are closed up; tasteful blinds rolled down. One is occupied. Its Adirondack chair has been turned so it faces straight across the bay to Coquet Island.

As I approach the door, I see a dead crab on the picnic table. Its carapace is partly smashed, with a large section around the cervical groove missing. But my heart quickens, because the bristled chelae are intact. The signal-red spots along the remaining carapace, which is marked by four distinct spines.

This is it.

It's real. She found one.

I pause, outside the door. The crab shell looks polished; I suspect she's had it a long time. But even with the crab – my crab – there's nothing good about the feeling of this place. I used to sense Janice and her nervous energy, the times I followed her and Charlie round Islington, but I don't sense any energy at all now.

Gingerly, I knock on the door.

No answer.

I knock again. 'Janice?'

Nothing. I look out to sea, for a moment. If she is in here, and she's not alive, I'm not sure I'll cope.

I try the door, which is open.

She's propped up in bed, as if watching television, but her eyes are closed.

'Janice,' I say.

She opens her eyes, briefly, but then closes them. Then she opens them properly, and turns to me. 'Emily?' she says, slowly. 'Emma?'

'Janice,' I say, crossing to the bed. 'Are you OK?'

She closes her eyes again. 'Go away,' she says. 'Please.'

There are five packets of paracetamol on the trendy plywood bedside table. In my trance I find myself wondering if the owners could have imagined the table being used for this, when they kitted the cabin out. Five packets of paracetamol, and a packet of something else, something pharmaceutical, with Janice's details printed on a label on the side.

I pick one of the packets up. It's empty. I check the others. All empty.

'Janice,' I say. 'Janice, have you taken all of these pills?'

If she can hear me, she ignores me – this woman whose beautiful face, now puffy and pale, is known and loved by hundreds of thousands of people.

This woman who stole my son with her make-believe and her ability to convince. She ignores me.

'Janice,' I say, more loudly. 'Janice, have you taken all of these pills?'

'Not you too,' she says. 'Just go away. Please.'

Not me too?

I leave the hut, jabbing at my phone. I press 999, but the call won't connect. I have no signal.

Tears of panic are forming. 'Janice,' I call. 'I need to get you an ambulance.'

'No.'

'I have to go and find a signal. Please stay with me until then. Please.'

She mutters something else, which I'm sure is 'Not you too,' again, but I have no idea what she means. I leave the cabin, ready to run up the hill, but as I do I see someone running towards me.

Leo. It's Leo.

'What?' I stare at him, as he jogs down the final part of the hill. 'How are you . . . Why – I mean, what? How did you get here so soon?'

'I left at 7.15. Is she OK?'

'Yes, but—'

'Good. Right. You stay out here. There's an ambulance coming, but they'll need guiding. I think they'll have to drive across the golf course.'

'I – Leo, where's Ruby?'

He points to his car, parked haphazardly by a golf green. I must have walked past it. 'Fast asleep on the back seat,' he says. 'She doesn't know what's going on. I've been here less than ten minutes.'

I stand in the doorway, watching in confusion, amazement, as my husband goes back in and crouches down next to Janice.

'Janice,' he says, quietly. He touches her arm, and she opens an eye.

'I'm tired,' she says. 'Your wife was here. She's a lot louder than you.'

Her voice is laboured, but it's still the Janice I remember.

'She is,' Leo agrees. 'Now, let me help get you comfortable.' He moves her forward, gently, so he can stack another pillow underneath her.

I watch him, transfixed.

'There.' He pulls up a little stool and sits next to her. He takes her hand. 'There's help coming,' he tells her.

'I don't want help.'

'I understand. You can discuss that with the paramedics. But I had to call them.'

Leo watches Janice, as the minutes tick by. He leans close to her at one point, I think to check her breathing. 'It's OK,' he says again.

His voice is so gentle. I've never loved him so much.

As if hearing my thoughts, he looks up. 'Wait outside,' he says. 'So you can be seen. By the ambulance. By Ruby.'

*

Once Leo has shown the paramedics the pill packets, and told them what little he knows, he comes to join me outside.

The coastal grass sways on the breeze and the sea is sparkling, and the child with the kite has finally had success. It soars high over the beach, dipping and slicing through the warm air while the little boy screams with excitement.

Leo stands above me. 'Are you OK?' he asks.

I have no idea how I am. He sits down, and neither of us says a word.

Chapter Sixty-Three

LEO

Jeremy and Charlie are still at the hospital. We have no news yet, and a doctor friend has warned it could be two days before we know if Janice will survive.

Emma and I are sitting outside the Rothschilds' holiday house. The sky is darkening but the odd cloud glows pink near the horizon, and the temperature is still tolerable.

We can't see a great deal of sea from here, but the view from the room Ruby's staying in is outstanding. She'll be up at 5 a.m., wanting to go to the beach.

John is wandering around the garden, sniffing and peeing on things.

I had only an hour's sleep this morning before Ruby arrived in my bed at quarter to six, wanting pancakes. She remembered Emma coming in a few hours before. She didn't seem bothered to learn that Mummy had gone looking for crabs again.

We went downstairs and I started the pancake batter. Ruby changed her mind. 'I really want banana porridge,' she sighed, zooming her toy motorbike across the cluttered worktop.

Eventually, after she'd changed her mind twice more and had a minor tantrum, we settled for toast in front of *Sarah and Duck*. Emma would kill me if she caught me feeding Ruby breakfast in front of the telly. But it wasn't even 7 a.m., I'd been up nearly all night, and I didn't care.

I texted Kelvin and Sheila to say I was 'working from home' again.

Sheila called me straight back, in spite of the hour. 'What's the latest?'

I left Ruby and went into the kitchen to tell her.

'Oh, God,' Sheila said. 'This is awful, Leo. The whole thing. I must call Jeremy.'

'Do. He looked pretty bad last night. Although be warned, he's on air right now.'

'Do you think there's any likelihood Emma's hunch is correct?' Sheila asked. 'About this shed?'

'Not really. Nobody goes and spends two weeks in a shed when they've got a lovely house up the road. But I suppose nothing about the way Janice has conducted herself in the last few weeks has been predictable.'

Sheila didn't reply.

'Hello?'

'I'm thinking,' she said.

I perked up for a moment. Maybe Sheila could use her espionage capabilities again. Type Janice's name into some remote MI5 computer and have a satellite send us precise co-ordinates of her location.

I heard her scrabble around on the other end of the phone. 'Just looking on Google Maps,' she said. 'Tell me exactly where this hut is?'

I opened Maps myself and directed her to the little square that marked the spot.

'Yes,' she said, thoughtfully. 'Looks bloody unlikely to me.' Then: 'What about these glamping cabins?'

'What glamping cabins?'

Sheila sighed. 'The glamping cabins about three hundred metres from the hut Emma's gone to search.'

'I – what?'

'Leo, are you looking at Google Maps?'

'Yes! But – oh. Yes, I see them.'

I clicked on them, and my heart beat faster. 'These look promising.' I clicked through a load of photos, trying to see if they had a view of Coquet Island, but Sheila beat me to it.

'Coquet Island,' she said. 'Bingo. Right, let's find out if she's staying there.'

'Are you able to do that?' I asked, reverently. 'Do you still have access to surveillance systems, or something?'

After an abrupt laugh, Sheila picked up what sounded like a landline and called a number. I waited, almost excitedly, expecting her to ask to be put through to some field agent in a Northumberland bunker.

'Hello,' she said. 'Is that Alnmouth Glamping Cabins? Excellent. Now listen, I need to get hold of one of your guests, urgently. Her name is Janice Rothschild. Yes . . .'

A few seconds later, the call was done. 'Right,' Sheila said. 'That was the owner of these huts. She's in Sicily for the summer, but – yes, it says on her system that Janice is staying in hut number two. I suggest you call Emma. Get her over there as soon as she arrives in Alnmouth. She's what, four hours away?'

She paused. 'How was that for espionage?' She was polite enough not to laugh.

I stared at the cabins online, picturing Janice having a couple of drinks for Dutch courage before opening her pills. My stomach churned. Would she have chosen her outfit? Did she have a last meal? Did she know what she was going to do when she woke up that morning?

I pictured the sight of her, collapsed on the floor, and I

imagined Emma and Charlie walking into the hut, the sheer horror of finding her.

Then it was all very simple.

'Ruby,' I called. 'Ruby, find your shoes. We're going for a long drive in the car.'

I couldn't allow Emma to do it. I couldn't allow her to live another moment of this nightmare alone.

John wanders up to Emma and me, as we sit in silence. He wags his tail for a moment before heading off inside, in search of food.

I don't know if Emma's too tired to talk, or perhaps too nervous, but she sits perfectly still, arms wrapped tightly around her knees. She's wearing the beanie hat again.

I track a bird as it crosses the bay. Emma's taught me what these birds are before, but the name eludes me now. This drives her mad: she's always said I never listen to a word she says, but I do. Did. I thought about her words late at night when I was dropping off. When I sat at my desk, writing obituaries. I thought about her words when I was driving, walking, eating, and I did that because she was the only person who had ever made sense to me.

I prise her left hand from her and slide off her wedding ring. I put it in my pocket. Emma inspects her bare hand, silently, but doesn't look at me.

After a few moments I sense her body sag.

The bird cries, looping round above us. 'We're not married,' I remind her.

Emma shakes her head. 'No.'

I take her hand back. 'But what's clear to me is that we should be.'

She looks at me, sharply, then looks away.

'Emma?'

I watch her, patiently, until she turns to look at me again. In the fast-falling darkness her eyes are deep seas. Unknown oceans, but I can learn them again. They're the only ones I want to swim.

'I will trust you,' I tell her.

She hesitates. The bird loops over us again, wings still as it rides a current.

'I will trust you,' I repeat.

'But will you? Really?'

'Yes.'

'But – really?'

I nod.

'I know you, Leo,' Emma says.

'I also know me. Better than you might think.'

The bird disappears into the inky horizon, still calling.

'I want us to get married. Properly. With Ruby in a sweet little dress, stealing the show. We don't have to tell anyone, if you don't want to have to explain it. But I want us to be married.'

After a long pause, she drops down onto her elbows. I drop down onto mine.

'When Ruby and I were driving up here, I was trying to imagine shuttling her between two different houses for weekend custody. Us learning to become friends, trying to co-parent. One day meeting someone else. And it felt miserable. I don't want that, I want us. I've only ever wanted us.'

Emma nods, almost imperceptibly.

'Do you?' I ask, when she doesn't say anything. 'Do you want us?'

She switches round to face me, resting on one elbow. Then: 'Yes,' she says, quietly. 'More than anything.'

There's inches between our faces. I feel her breath, I see her hair, still tucked behind her ear.

Emma has endured more pain in her thirty-nine years than most people do in a lifetime. And yet she's still someone everyone's secretly in love with, someone everyone wants to talk to at a dinner party. She's still the funniest person I know, still the woman my boss would sack me for if she ever wanted a career change.

Yes, she's complicated; she retreats from time to time to a dark place. She has ever-worsening problems with hoarding, a compulsive need to check Ruby is breathing and many other things besides. But she's still Emma: vital, brilliant, infuriating Emma.

If she can hold on to herself after all she's suffered, I can too. I must.

And now it's just as it was the first time we were this close, in her friend's yurt in a field in Cornwall in the middle of the night, surrounded by specimen pots and hair straighteners and half-eaten snacks and marine biology journals.

We are inches apart, and I have never in my life wanted to kiss someone so much.

This time, I lean in first. I kiss her, and this is what comes next.

Epilogue

EMMA

Six months later

A dead flower hat jelly is an unremarkable sight on the beaches of the Northwest Pacific: a colourless mass of sand-pocked gel in among the cuttlefish bones and dead seaweed sprayed along the strandlines; something for a child to poke at with a spade.

But if you could find one of these jellies in the rayless waters of the sea bottom, you'd hardly believe your eyes. The pinstriped bell glows daffodil-gold and the tentacles, finely inked, are tipped with joyous pink. The jelly pulsates through those cold waters with otherworldly, bioluminescent beauty; a coruscating miracle.

I invite you to think about an event in your past you'd do anything to erase.

You're bound to have one, even if you're young. And if you're good at hiding it, it'll be there on the strandlines of your own story: sand-camouflaged, unremarkable; visible only to those who know what to look for.

I was good at hiding mine. Twenty years, I kept it there, in plain sight. Then along came my husband, and he poked at it with a stick; poked and prodded and jostled and pushed until, eventually, the abandoned, shameful mass of my past was carried back out to sea where it could unravel once again. It's alight in those deep waters, now. Alight, seen, impossible to hide.

But this is the thing: to Leo, my past really is as beautiful as that flower hat jelly. When he could see it clearly – once he'd recovered from the shock – he saw me clearly, too, for the first time, and he loved me even more.

The things we believe. The things we hide.

I'm not looking back anymore. I am here. All of me.

It is 6.45 a.m. and Leo is asleep. His face is folded into his pillow. He complains that he looks ancient these days, and because I promised myself never to lie to him again, I've had to agree: he needs at least three months in a spa. To me, though, he's perfect. Marrying him for the second time, nothing unsaid, was beautiful.

He is the love of my life.

Next door our daughter is asleep. She still has Duck in bed with her, but she no longer cuddles him all night: she's growing up so fast. I fear Duck's days are numbered, but these bittersweet transitions are precious to me – I saw nothing of Charlie's unfolding. I still don't know what toy he clutched when he slept, who his best friend was; how much pocket money he used to get or what he spent it on. There is still so much to learn about him, whereas with Ruby I get to witness it all in real time. This is a privilege; I will not allow myself to see it in any other way.

She is the love of my life.

Across the Atlantic, my son is at a Christmas party. I know this because he's sent me a text, which I've read at least thirty times since I woke up. A text! A drunken text!

Flying home tomorrow at 8am, he wrote. *At a party, have to get up at 4am for the airport, think I'm going to just drink on through. You're not allowed to give me sensible advice, by the way. Would be nice to have a walk on the Heath some time?*

Charlie will never call me Mum, but he's made an effort since he went back to Boston in September. Even with Janice still all over the place, he's chosen to stay in touch.

There won't be a time in my life where the loss of his childhood feels acceptable. I will never be at peace with the fact that I didn't get to cry at his portrayal of a penguin at the school nativity. But I have enough, now. Even if it never grows beyond an occasional walk, I will have had a portion of my life with Charlie in it. And a portion is good enough, for me, because I lived the alternative for nearly twenty years.

He, this young man, is the love of my life.

'Leo,' I whisper, because I can't wait any longer. 'Wake up! Kiss me!'

Dawn breaks from the east in amber shadows, as Leo begins to stir.

We burrow in towards each other, and I tell him about Charlie's message. 'Oh wow,' he says. 'How wonderful . . .' He's still waking.

I kiss him, again and again, my hand lying on the warm plane of his chest. I don't think I'll ever be able to convey to this man how much I love him, but I'm trying.

A few minutes later, we look at his phone to check Wikideaths, but nobody has died.

A few minutes after that, I break wind. 'Moped,' I say, and I shrug.

Leo laughs – even after all these years – he laughs, and says, 'You are disgusting, Emma.'

And this, now, is my life. My whole life, not my half-life. Emma and Leo. Leo and Emma.

We have been married for three weeks, together eleven years, and he knows every part of me.

Acknowledgements

And then there was a book!

This one didn't take a village, it took a small continent. I owe a huge debt of gratitude to a great many people.

First and foremost, my thanks to those who've spared their time and expertise:

Professor John Spicer, Professor Mark Bower, Tim Bullamore, Dr Natalie Smith, Hannah Parry-Wilson, Dr Karl Scheeres, Hannah Walker, Dr Mike Rayment, Betty Lou Layland, Andrew Brown and the obituaries team at the *Telegraph*, Nathan Morris, Melissa Kay, Stuart Gibbon, Dr Ray Leakey, Dr David Barnes, Kian Murphy, Rose Child, David Bonser, Richard Hines, Dr Matt Williams, Rosie Greenwood, Professor Carl Sayer, Sarah Denton, Rosie Mason, Max Fisher, Chippy Douglass, Sophie Kenny-Levick and Bill Markham.

And to those friends who have supplied everything from psychiatrist introductions to virtual tours of the BBC's New Broadcasting House:

Josie Lee, Kate Hannay, Natalie Barrass, Vikki Humphreys, Ed Harrison, Elin Somer, Claire Willers, Angela Waterstone, Emily Koch, Marc Butler, Alex Brown, Jack Bremer, Claudine Pavier, Michael Pagliero, James Pagliero, Jo Nadin and Dave Walters.

To my wonderful writer friends who've kindly provided feedback on drafts, or helped me brainstorm plotlines:

Emma Stonex, Emylia Hall, Kate Riordan, Rowan Coleman, Jane Green and Cally Taylor. Thanks also to George Pagliero, Caroline Walsh and Emma Holland.

To the many people I've spoken to informally at death cafes, charities, marine ecology events, obituary events, parties, even – so many hundreds of conversations have made this book possible. Thank you to you all.

Unending thanks to my miracle-worker publishers, Pan Macmillan (UK), Viking (USA) and the many others around the world who have published me in nearly thirty-five languages. Dream come true doesn't even begin to cover it.

My most grateful thanks to my brilliant UK editor, Sam Humphreys, who sent me back to this manuscript again and again. You were always right. Thank you for the many brainstorms – including that awful one when I was half dead with morning sickness – and your endless encouragement and kindness during a challenging writing experience.

To the amazing team at Pan Macmillan: Alice Gray, Charlotte Wright, Rosie Wilson, Ellie Bailey, Sian Chilvers, Holly Sheldrake and Becky Lloyd. Thanks, also, to my legendary US editor, Pam Dorman, for taking an unnecessarily dark story and pushing me to turn it into something people might actually want to read. You lifted this book in so many ways.

To Lizzy Kremer, my peerless agent, for the many reads and editorial suggestions, and for rescuing me more than once from writer's block and crippling self-doubt. Thank you for your belief in this book, your love of the characters, and for always wanting the very best for me – not to mention the book deals and years of skilful diplomacy. To Allison Hunter, my US agent, for the many plot brainstorms and reads, and for holding my hand through such difficult times – if a book deal of dreams wasn't enough, you've been an absolute rock to me. Thanks also to Maddalena Cavaciuti and Kay Begum.

To Alice Howe and her incredible translation rights team at David Higham Associates – I'm not sure I'll ever be able to thank you enough for what you've achieved on my behalf. Thank you for getting my words into the hands of readers even in the most far-flung corners of the earth.

To my writing partner, author Deborah O'Donaghue – Deb, I don't know where to begin. You must have spent weeks of your life reading and editing this book. So many of the breakthroughs I've had have been as a result of a Skype with you; so many good bits are yours. Thank you for your kindness and encouragement, your respectful questions and your inability to let me get away with *anything* that doesn't add up. You know how much of this book is down to you.

Sincere thanks to YOU, the reader of this book, for investing your hard-earned cash in Leo and Emma's story. Without you I would not be able to do what I do – I would not be able to do what I love. You have changed my life, and your messages over the last few years have been the highlight of my writing career. My sincerest gratitude to you all.

Thank you to Wendy, Clare and the many other amazing women who kept me sane and useful during the writing of this book. To my wonderful friends whose excitement about my career continues – genuinely – to be a huge joy in my life. Thank you to my dear family, Lyn, Brian and Caroline Walsh, who I've missed terribly in the madness of the pandemic; also Dave Mallows, and the Exton, Clyst St George, Exeter and London Paglieros, wonderful cheerleaders and in-laws.

Thank you to George, who took our children out time after time in the cruellest days of winter lockdown so I could meet my deadline, and who has always believed in this book – and me. We survived! (Just.) Thank you for never keeping secrets for me, and for being exactly who you always have been, right from the moment we met.

And thank you to my two children. To my little lockdown baby girl, the brightest light in a dark time, and my now big boy, who made me roar with laughter when I wondered if I'd ever smile again.

You three are the loves of my life.

Discover Rosie Walsh's previous novel
The Man Who Didn't Call

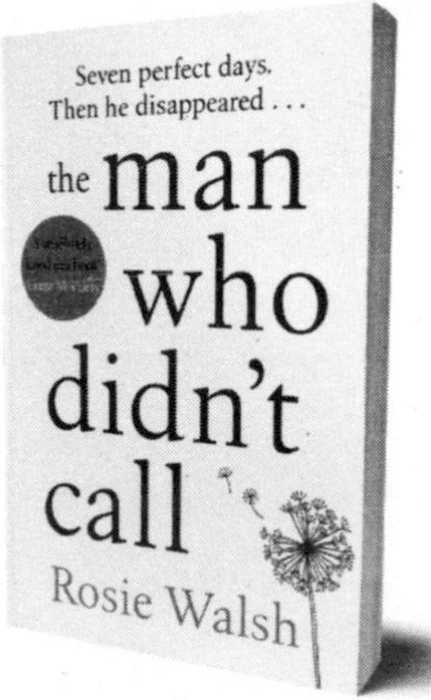

Over a million copies sold worldwide

Imagine you meet a man, spend seven glorious days together, and fall in love. And it's mutual: you've never been so certain of anything. So when he leaves for a long-booked holiday and promises to call from the airport, you have no cause to doubt him.

But he doesn't call.

Your friends tell you to forget him, but you know they're wrong: something must have happened; there must be a reason for his silence.

What do you do when you finally discover you're right? That there is a reason – and that reason is the one thing you share with each other?

The truth.

'I absolutely loved this book and didn't want it to end'
Liane Moriarty

'This book is the very definition of unputdownable'
Jill Mansell

'Wise, warm and beautifully written, with a fantastic twist'
Daily Mail